The

Uninvited Guest

Pam —
So great to
meet you!
Happy reading.
Debi
Aug '17

Debi Graham-Leard

Riverhaven Books

The Uninvited Guest is a work of fiction.
Any similarity regarding names, characters, or
incidents is entirely coincidental.

Published in the United States by Riverhaven Books,
Massachusetts.

ISBN 978-1-937588-50-2
Printed in the United States of America
by Country Press, Lakeville, Massachusetts

Edited by Riverhaven Books
Designed by Stephanie Lynn Blackman
Whitman, MA

Acknowledgements

My first novel exists with the encouragement and gentle critiques
from the following people:
my sister Jerri Burket;
Pam Loewy and Paula Norton
from the Plymouth Writers Group;
Ruth Weiner and Katherine Ventre
from the Stoughton Writers Group;
Professor Ann Sears from Wheaton College and
flute teacher Barbara Worthley for their musical advice;
Coletta Candini for her knowledge of flowers that flourish along
the coast of southeastern Massachusetts;
Det. Thomas Petersen for his expertise in
local police procedure;
Stephanie Blackman of Riverhaven Books
for leading me through the process of publication;
and my editor Ellen Goldsberry,
whose targeted suggestions added traction and depth to my story.
Additional thanks to my step-daughter Meagan Leard for her
modeling contribution to the cover photo,
taken by Robert Sinclaire.
And, of course, my deepest thanks to my husband Vinnie for his
never-ending support of my writing efforts.

Most favors are easy.
Others are weighted with unexpected consequences.

"What do you think about that, Amber?" Gwen asked as she settled the receiver into its wall cradle near the fridge, then squatted and hoisted her golden tabby into her arms. "Jack needs a favor."

Although Gwen had known Jack Miller for years, he'd never called her at home. His reason today was beyond unusual. It was curious. A favor for next weekend's Young Musicians' Competition, he'd said. Too complicated to discuss over the phone, he'd said. He'd asked – no, Jack had demanded – that Gwen rush to his office at the music shop *post haste*.

Stroking Amber's soft fur, Gwen peered through the bay window above the kitchen sink. Her wheelbarrow waited near the potting shed, overflowing with spent blossoms and errant weeds that thought they should live in her resurrected flower beds. When the house phone had rung, she'd just finished deadheading the coppery-colored Helenium and had been about to pinch back the black-eyed Susans.

Gwen wanted – no, she needed – everything to be perfect for the garden club's tour in two days. All summer she'd slaved to bring her property back to life. Now the floral colors exploded, the late-season perennials stood tall, the majestic grasses waved. In the patch of woods beyond her back gardens, the maple and beech trees swayed with the September breeze.

"I don't have time for Jack's nonsense," Gwen murmured into Amber's twitching ear.

But Gwen couldn't ignore the man either.

Although she'd sat in the competition audience as an

attentive music professor for nearly forty years, this time would be different. Gwen's most talented private student, high school senior Jenna Jenkins, had registered as a contestant. Gwen couldn't risk – wouldn't risk – any complications a week before the event. She'd never forgive herself if she ignored Jack's mysterious favor and jeopardized Jenna's chance to win the Baylies College scholarship.

"That settles it, Amber." Gwen squeezed the chubby cat and lowered her to the floor. "I've got to find out what Jack wants. The Olde Music Shop isn't far. I'll walk."

Gwen turned on the kitchen tap, grabbed a small brush, and scrubbed garden dirt from beneath her fingernails, wondering why she ever bothered to wear gloves.

***

Still spry at sixty-three, Gwen descended seven granite steps to her front walkway, crossed the cobblestones of Library Lane, and stepped into her favorite feature of Harbor Falls: the village green. Long ago she had decided that, on any given day, its meandering pathways beat out the concrete sidewalks rimming the perimeter.

Salty air drifted up from the waterfront and tickled her nose. She progressed at a steady pace through the small park, the hum of traffic reaching her ears long before she emerged onto North Street. It was clogged with vehicles.

Darting between a white service van and a bright red Corvette, she arrived safely on the opposite sidewalk and turned left, soon reaching the North Street Bridge. Halfway across, Gwen leaned on the fieldstone parapet to take in the pastoral scene.

On the far left bank a massive brick and stone structure pitched skyward. Originally a gristmill, the building had been converted into a music shop by the Olde family in the late 1800s to accommodate the musical needs of nearby Baylies College. Fastidiously maintained, it had long ago been added to

the Massachusetts Register of Historic Places. Although no
longer a working mill, tours of the original grindstones on the
lower level were often granted to school groups and visitors.

Below the bridge a creek flowed eastward, originating from
small inland lakes before winding through Gwen's modest
wooded acres on the other side. She followed a leaf on its
journey as it slipped beneath the bridge and merged into the
millpond. The lower branches of a graceful willow tree dipped
into the restless water that picked up speed, sluiced into the
mill race, and dropped onto the paddles of the antique
waterwheel, its ponderous rotation creating a deep rumble, both
soothing and unsettling.

Gwen had to force herself to stop dawdling. She moved off
the bridge and approached the music shop's entrance, peeking
through the large street-side windows as she passed. Three
young women, all wearing Baylies College tee-shirts, browsed
the sheet music kiosk. At the instrument counter, Alex
Fairfield, the shop's long-time and only employee,
demonstrated a French horn to an older couple and a young
man.

When Gwen pushed in the door, the bell jingled. Emily
Olde Miller, Jack's wife and the current owner of the landmark
building, emerged through a rear door, a huge cardboard carton
captured in her arms. Grime streaked Emily's toned muscles,
bared by rolled-up sleeves.

"Be right with you," she called without looking.

Gwen rushed over. "Let me give you a hand, Emily. You'll
throw out your back."

Before Gwen could grasp the other end of the unwieldy
box, Emily hoisted the shabby carton onto the back counter
with little effort, sending puffs of dust into the air.

"Thanks, Gwen. But moving boxes works as well as lifting
weights at the gym." A broad smile lit Emily's heart-shaped
face.

3

"The heaviest thing I lift these days is a shovelful of garden dirt. What's in the box?"

Emily's eyes widened with child-like glee. "I found it buried in a dark corner of the storage room. I think it's filled with old photographs of the Olde family. Get it?"

Gwen chuckled. "I got it. I've always loved the double meaning of your family name."

Emily tucked a strand of deep brunette hair behind her ear. "I'll sort through these later. Might frame and hang a few here in the shop. Our customers may enjoy seeing pictures from my family tree. But business first. What can I do for you today, Gwen?"

"Jack called and insisted I come over to talk with him." Gwen plucked a pale orange petal from the sleeve of her purple tee-shirt. "Do you know where he is?"

Glancing around the cavernous shop, Emily asked, "Did he say what he wants?"

"Something about a favor for the music competition."

"Hmmm," Emily murmured. "I wonder what that's all about." She tapped the top of the old box, raising more dust. "Come on. Let's go find him."

Gwen hustled to keep up with Emily's longer stride as they made their way down the well-worn floorboards, weaving around massive hand-hewn columns. They passed displays of new and used guitars, oboes, bassoons, tubas, and flutes. Just before they reached the corner office, the wooden door flew open, smacking the adjacent wall with a bang.

Jack Miller swore when his forehead met with the much shorter door jamb.

Emily's hand stretched forward. "Jack, are you all right?"

He swatted his wife away. "Oh, stop fussing, Emily."

She frowned, but said nothing, then turned and strode away.

Jack ducked before re-entering his office, barking at Gwen over his shoulder. "What took you so long?"

4

Gwen stared at his back. He should be more polite if he wanted a favor. What had enticed Emily to marry this man? Sure, he wasn't bad-looking. A strong jaw, a tall athletic frame, and a full head of black hair, worn long and captured in a short ponytail. But Jack usually wore a scowl – like the one he wore now – and prided himself on being cantankerous, his demeanor nothing like Emily's. Even if it was true that opposites attract, Gwen couldn't imagine sharing her life with a man like Jack.

She sat down on the hard-bottomed guest chair. "I came as soon as I could, Jack." Not exactly true, given her longer walk through the village green and her pause on the bridge, but Jack didn't need to know that. "I'm busy prepping my gardens for the tours this Saturday."

"This is more important than tending your flowers, Gwen." From a pile on his desk, Jack plucked a manila folder marked 'Competition' in bold letters and shook it at her.

"What's this favor you need, Jack?"

He gave her a stern gaze. "Don't be impatient. First, let me explain our situation."

Gwen nearly laughed out loud. He thought *she* was the impatient one? While she waited for him to explain his favor, she glanced around his office. She'd never been in there before, but it looked exactly as she'd expected. Papers neatly stacked on a mahogany desk, matching credenza and labeled file cabinets along the side wall.

When Gwen held the position as Professor of Music History and Jack worked in the Baylies business office, everyone on staff joked at the water cooler about his fastidious manner and lack of humor.

She crossed one leg over the other, flinching when she noticed her gardening sneakers. Holes at the little toe, an assortment of grass stains, dirt smudges. She tucked her feet beneath the chair.

Jack laced his fingers behind his head and leaned back until his chair squeaked. "Here's the thing, Gwen. One of our judges stepped down from the panel for medical reasons. Since our shop co-sponsors this event with Baylies, the committee asked us to contact judges from previous competitions, but none of them are available. The dean suggested a former professor who lives out of state."

Gwen scooted forward. "Who is it? Do I know him?"

"Let me finish." Jack snapped his seat upright. "The dean charged us with finding a place for this woman to sleep."

Gwen corrected her assumption. Not a man.

Jack kept talking. "We called every hotel and motel, plus the three B&Bs, *and* the homes that rent rooms. We even went back to the committee members, but none of them can take a guest."

"Interesting, Jack, but why are you telling me?"

He leaned across his desk, his expression grim. "We need her to stay with you."

Gwen shook her head. "No, no, no. I'm much too busy for a houseguest."

"But you're retired. You have plenty of time."

"You're dead wrong, Jack. I'm up to my dirty elbows getting ready for the garden tour. Next week, I'll be prepping Jenna for the competition."

The corners of his mouth turned down, giving him the pout of a petulant child. "This new judge insisted we provide restaurant vouchers, so you won't have to cook for her."

Gwen almost snorted. She barely cooked for herself since her husband Parker died a few years before. But she wasn't about to let Jack pressure her into hosting a woman she would basically ignore. Such bad manners.

A possible way out popped into Gwen's mind. "Don't you think it's inappropriate for me to host a judge when one of my private students is competing?"

Jack picked up a paperclip, twisting it out of shape. "The

dean suggested you. Your reputation in the Baylies community is flawless. He considers your integrity above reproach and trusts you won't influence this judge's opinion of Jenna's talent."

"Why can't this woman stay here with you and Emily?" Gwen swept her arm upward toward the family living quarters on the second floor of the old gristmill.

Jack lifted his hands in a gesture of defeat. "Emily said our extra bedroom is too shabby. You *have* to let her stay with you, Gwen. After all, you owe me."

She bolted upright, wincing when her exposed little toe connected with the leg of the chair. "What do you mean, I owe you?"

Jack's eyebrows scrunched together. "Jenna submitted her application three days past the deadline. I haven't mentioned her tardiness to the college committee, but I suppose I could..." His meaning was quite clear.

Unaware of Jenna's delay, Gwen's lip quivered. "You wouldn't do that!"

He snorted. "Why not? If you won't help me, why should I help Jenna?"

"You're not being fair."

"Fair or not, we need lodging for this judge."

When Jack's desk phone rang, he waved at it. "Emily will answer that."

Gwen refused to give up. "Where are the other two judges staying?"

"They live within driving distance and don't need lodging."

Gwen's resolve to argue disintegrated. What if Jack carried out his unspoken threat and removed Jenna from the list of competitors? The talented teenager would be heartbroken and Gwen would never forgive herself. Perhaps putting up with a houseguest was a small price to pay. Her right foot tapped a staccato beat on the floorboards.

7

"Oh, all right, Jack, your judge can stay in my guest room. But you tell her she won't be waited on hand and foot. I'm not a B&B."

He reached over and patted her hand. "Good. I'll let the dean know this is settled."

Withdrawing her hand, Gwen glared at him. "When's she coming?"

Jack glanced at his watch. "She's probably with the dean now."

Gwen jumped to her feet. "What? She's here *now*?"

"It couldn't be helped. The committee was grateful this woman agreed to fill in, so no one argued when she said she'd drive down a few days early."

Gwen began to pace the limited space of Jack's office, her voice rising several decibels. "A few *days* early? The competition is more than a week away!"

A knock sounded at the door. Without waiting, Emily entered and handed a pink slip of paper to Jack. "The dean left this message for you." She glanced at Gwen. "You're still here?"

Before Gwen could respond, Jack said, "Thank you, Emily," in a dismissive tone.

Emily shot Gwen a look as if to say, *Well, isn't he high and mighty?*

As the door closed behind Emily, Jack scanned the note.

"The former professor requested a tour of the campus before lunching with the dean. You won't see her for a few more hours."

Moving swiftly to his desk, Gwen slapped her hands on its gleaming surface, making his papers flutter. "You were so sure I'd agree to this?"

Jack raised one eyebrow. "You did, didn't you?"

Gwen's blood boiled, but she could fathom no way out of Jack's manipulation without risking Jenna's scholarship

8

dreams. She yanked open his office door and glanced back at him over her shoulder. "I'd better not regret this, Jack."

As she passed the instrument counter, Alex waved her over and tilted his blonde head to one side. "What's wrong, Gwen? You look upset."

During Gwen's decades of living in Harbor Falls after graduating from college, she couldn't remember a time when Alex hadn't worked in the music shop. He knew every feature of every instrument. She'd always considered this gentleman her friend so didn't balk at his question.

"Jack has outdone himself this time," she answered.

"What did he do?" Alex placed his age-spotted hand on her arm, his manner concerned.

Gwen inhaled a deep breath and let it out. "Oh, he's tricked me into hosting the woman hired to replace a judge for the competition. I don't think talking about it will help."

"You know what *will* help, Gwen? It's been a while since you and I dueted. You've told me more than once that playing your flute makes you forget all your troubles. Why don't I drop over this afternoon?"

She couldn't help but smile at him. "You're right, Alex. I'll need a break from my gardening by then."

He glanced up at the shop's antique clock. "How's three? There's usually a lull in customers about then. Jack and Emily can spare me for a half hour or so."

"I'll see you then. And thanks."

When the shop door closed behind her, the brass bell jangled wildly, but she barely heard its tinkle. Gulping a lungful of salty air, Gwen realized Jack hadn't mentioned the judge's name.

Who was this judge, anyway? Many professors had come and gone during Gwen's tenure. Had Gwen worked with this woman? Was she someone Gwen had liked or, worse, hadn't cared for? Several smug faces came to mind. She half-turned to go back inside to ask, then stopped. She'd had quite enough of Jack for one day. Stretching to her full five-feet-three-inches, Gwen's fingers barely reached the lower edge of the shop's hand-carved sign. She smacked it as hard as she could and stomped away as the antique placard screeched behind her.

Chapter Two

Storming down the sidewalk, Gwen tossed a dirty look at a trio of seagulls that had drifted up from the harbor and circled lazily above, screeching their plaintiff cry. She silently dared one of them to deposit a gloppy gift on her head.

She practically ran across the North Street Bridge, without stopping to admire the view. When she dashed back across the street, a motorist honked his horn and veered. Her heart raced as she slipped into the village green and ducked into the gazebo near the entrance. She collapsed onto the bench, her lungs heaving, her fingers absently stroking the rock-hard red and yellow berries of bittersweet that covered the latticework.

Gwen had never liked being pressured. Parker had often teasingly called her stubborn, to which she'd always retorted, *'I simply have a mind of my own.'*

If Jack had been more pleasant and explained his problem, she might have offered her guest room, despite her busy schedule. But to blackmail her with Jenna's late registration was unfair, not to mention outrageous and unforgivable.

Additional unkind words tumbled in her head.

Come to think of it, why had the new dean nominated Gwen as hostess? Had Jack planted the seed, knowing he had the ammunition to force her cooperation?

Concerns raced through her mind. Would she and this woman be compatible? Living under the same roof could be awkward at best, hellish at worst. For Jenna's sake, Gwen would have to find a way to endure a stranger in her home for the coming nine days. Thankfully they wouldn't be sharing meals, allowing Gwen some semblance of privacy. And when this woman drove off after the competition, Gwen could resume her delicately reinvented life of widowhood.

Rising to her feet, she drifted from the deceptive peace of

the gazebo and stepped onto the footpath that curved toward her home on the northwest corner of the village green.

"Is that you, Gwen dear?"

Gwen looked up seconds before bumping into Myrtle Mueller. The woman's helmet of mousy brown hair appeared immobile, her generous proportions squeezed into a dated tweed suit. During Gwen's years of membership in the garden club, she'd never warmed up to Myrtle.

"Hello, Myrtle. How're you?" Gwen's voice carried no enthusiasm.

Behind Myrtle, three garden club members up-ended autumn flowers from containers labeled with the Jenkins Nursery logo. Each season, Hal Jenkins – Jenna's grandfather – donated annual flowers for garden club members to plant in the antique horse trough commandeered years before. If Gwen hadn't been busy prepping her own gardens for the tour, she'd be digging in the dirt beside them.

"Fine, just fine, thank you, dear," Myrtle chirped in her trilling voice. "My family is so excited about the music competition. If they engage competent judges this year, we're certain our Herbert will win." Myrtle's nose inched higher, her jowls jiggling at the effort.

Herbert, Myrtle's tuba-playing grandson, had competed each year since middle school, never placing in the top three. As a high school senior, this was his last chance.

Drawing on deep-seated manners, Gwen murmured, "Best of luck to your grandson."

Myrtle clasped her pudgy hands across her heavy bosom and babbled on. "I understand one of your little flute students is competing."

Gwen stiffened. "That's right."

Myrtle sniffed, as if any student of Gwen's was no match for Herbert. "Well, dear, it's been nice chatting with you." Myrtle turned her back, waving a white-gloved hand at a pesky sheep-fly trying to land, then looked down her nose at the gardeners tamping soil around maroon and bright yellow mums, oblivious to their expressions of exasperation.

Why did Myrtle bother signing up for the planting committee? She never got her hands dirty.

One of the other three women called over, "Gwen, don't forget the meeting this afternoon."

Betty Owens – an enthusiastic member of the garden club – and her husband Bob owned the bed and breakfast at the top of Harbor Hill. Gwen could practically wave to them across the expanse of the village green.

"I'll be there," Gwen shouted back. "Sorry I can't stay and help. I'm expecting a guest."

"Not a problem, we're almost done. See you later."

Warm friends like Betty made up for irritating people like Myrtle.

A minute later, Gwen stepped from the village green, crossed the cobblestones of Library Lane, and stood on her front walkway. She glanced up at the sturdy building. On a normal day, she'd marvel at the word '*LIBRARY*' carved into the brownstone blocks above the arched entrance. On a normal day, she'd glance left at the second floor gable, where the date '*1887*' indented the window lintel. On a normal day, Gwen would savor her recurring giddiness that Baylies had sold the village library – abandoned for quite a while after the new library was built – to her and Parker ten years before.

But not today. Angered by Jack's trickery, irritated by Myrtle's snippiness, and now saddled with an uninvited guest, Gwen stomped up the granite steps and entered her home through the antique oak doors.

In the foyer, she stopped at a narrow table and picked up her favorite photograph of Parker, taken during a summer stroll along a beach in nearby Duxbury. His pants were rolled up to his knees, his sneakers dangled from his long fingers, and his grin was broad as he waved back at the camera. Gwen touched his image, losing herself in the twinkle of his hazel eyes, almost smelling the spicy scent of his aftershave, missing the press of his flesh against hers. "I miss you, Parker."

This wasn't the first time Gwen had spoken to her husband's likeness. They'd shared nearly thirty-seven years of marriage before his death the year before last. The deep cracks in Gwen's heart were healing, but her profound sense of loss lingered. When she retired from Baylies this past spring, she'd vowed to resurrect their beloved gardens, neglected since Parker's passing. The never-ending chores during the summer months had kept Gwen's loneliness at bay.

She returned Parker's photo to its place of honor and stepped into the openness of the first floor, admiring every nook and cranny. Parker's innate sense of space was the reason he'd become an architect. His open floor plan provided a view into all four corners of her home, broken only by the wide swooping staircase and the double-sided fireplace.

Gwen lived here alone now, with only her cat for company, custodian of their memories.

She shook her head to break the spell of regret. Time to prepare for a guest, uninvited or not. From the dining room to her right, she mounted the massive split staircase and climbed to the second floor. An open balcony – Parker's tribute to traditional libraries – rimmed the mezzanine.

In the front guest room, she changed the sheets on the queen bed, then placed new soaps and fresh towels in the adjoining bathroom. The suite was ready, even if Gwen was not.

When a cold nose touched her ankle, she glanced down into Amber's green eyes. Scooping the cat into her arms, Gwen buried her face in the soft fur and whispered, "A lady will be staying with us. I hope she doesn't upset you."

Jack hadn't mentioned if the judge was allergic to cats.

With the open floor plan, Amber had the run of the indoor spaces, so there was no getting away from the cat dander.

Standing at the upstairs balcony railing, Gwen looked across to the sitting room along the back wall, another of her favorite spaces. After Parker died, Gwen's sister suggested moving into a fifty-five and over condo complex outside of town, but Gwen had resisted. She'd feel lost living anywhere else. This old library was Gwen's last connection to Parker. Besides, most of those communities didn't allow animals, and Gwen would never abandon Amber.

Gwen bolted upright. How could she have forgotten? Her sister was due to arrive next Thursday for the weekend music competition. Damn. Gwen lowered Amber to the floor and patted her pants pocket for her cell phone. It wasn't there. She strode along the balcony to her bedroom in the gable, picked up the landline and dialed a Berkshire number.

"Tess, it's me. About your visit, I'm afraid I've gotten myself into a jam."

"What have you done this time?" her sister teased.

"I haven't *done* anything."

"Oh, stop being so sensitive. Whatever it is, we'll handle it. Before you tell me what's going on, thanks for asking me to be Jenna's accompanist. I still can't believe you're not doing it yourself. You play while you're teaching Jenna, don't you?"

"Sure I do, but I'd be way too nervous in front of a crowd. Besides, you're the one with competition experience, so who else would I ask?"

"Can't answer that one. But it gives me a good excuse to visit. What's this jam you're in?"

"Not a what. A who." Gwen explained her predicament of hosting a replacement judge who would be occupying the guest room beginning that very afternoon.

Tess snickered. "Geez, Gwen, how'd you let this fellow Jack talk you into hosting?"

"He claims Jenna registered late. He hasn't told the college committee, *yet*. If that's not a threat, I don't know what is. I can't risk Jenna's chance to compete, and I won't upset her by asking why she submitted her application past the deadline. The competition is too close."

"I agree," Tess said.

"You do realize," Gwen warned, "you'll be sharing my bed until the judge leaves?"

"Not a problem, little sister. It'll be like we're kids again. And I promise I won't kick you, too hard." Tess's laughter bubbled through the receiver.

Hanging up a few minutes later, Gwen realized Tess didn't seem concerned about the imposition of a stranger. Maybe having a guest wouldn't be so bad after all.

On a whim, Gwen went downstairs, grabbed her clippers from the wicker basket beside the French door, and headed outside to harvest fresh flowers for a guest room bouquet. If she was stuck with hosting duties, she may as well be gracious about it. She drifted through her flower beds, clipping golden heads of Patrinia, purple spikes of Russian sage, and a few stalks of coppery-colored Helenium.

At the kitchen sink, she arranged the blossoms in a woven basket, attached ribbons of sage green and deep pink to match the guest room décor, and carried the colorful array upstairs, placing it on the dresser to reflect itself in the mirror.

***

The hands on the clock dragged as Gwen waited for the judge's arrival. Not one to waste time, she returned to her flower beds, removed spent blooms, yanked weeds, and scattered fragrant cedar mulch. Bringing the gardens back to life after two years of neglect had taken more effort than she'd estimated. Of course, without Parker working beside her, every chore took more than twice as long. For all of May, June, July, and August, she'd planted, fertilized, mowed, weeded, trimmed, and mulched. Each day the flowers and bushes rewarded her with new sprigs of emerging buds, easing Gwen's ache for Parker.

Mother Nature, the best grief counselor.

The rumble of an engine echoed from the western side of the library. No doubt the judge, Gwen grumbled. *This should be interesting.* She stepped from a patch of Shasta daisies, crossed the back lawn, and bypassed the small-scale fish pond, stopping at the top of the driveway.

A sleek black sedan with Vermont plates came to a stop. The driver's door on the other side flew open and a tall woman emerged. She rested her forearms on the car's shiny rooftop and gazed across at Gwen.

The eyes were hidden behind huge sunglasses. But the smirk was all too familiar.

Gwen's mouth gaped open.

It couldn't be her. Please no. Anyone but her.

Chapter Three

Gwen blinked several times. Was she hallucinating? *This* woman was the dean's judge?

Henrietta Wickham, who hated Gwen more than anyone, seemed to dare a reaction.

It was all Gwen could do to remain calm. Twelve – or was it thirteen? – years ago, vengeful Henrietta resigned her professorship at Baylies College and left Harbor Falls without explanation. Flooded with relief that the woman's verbal torment was a thing of the past, Gwen had not cared about Henrietta's reason for leaving.

And now mean, nasty Henrietta was not only back in town, she'd be sleeping under Gwen's roof. This was unacceptable. This would be intolerable. There had to be a way out of Jack's ridiculous arrangement without endangering Jenna's participation in the music competition.

Henrietta glared at Gwen for a long minute, like a jungle cat sizing up its prey.

Regaining her composure, Gwen spoke. "So it's you."

Removing the sunglasses to reveal a spiteful gleam in her eye, Henrietta wiggled one red-taloned fingernail up and down Gwen's body. "You're a mess, Gwen. I never understood what Parker saw in you. Did you forget I was coming?"

"Forget you were coming? Jack only asked me a few hours ago to host a replacement judge. I had no idea it was you!"

"He didn't tell you?" Henrietta, as haughty as ever, asked in an oh-so-innocent tone.

"Jack knew it was you?" Gwen's head was about to explode.

"Of course he did." A wicked smile widened Henrietta's bright red lips. "I'm quite sure he and the dean spoke several times while they finalized my contract and lodging."

Gwen considered strangling Jack. A few hours ago, he'd intentionally neglected informing her of the judge's identity, rightly guessing Gwen wouldn't agree to his hosting plan if she knew the woman was Henrietta. He'd been well aware of Henrietta's one-sided animosity back in the day. All he'd wanted was a bed for the dean's judge. After all, Baylies College was the music shop's most valuable customer, and the dean controlled the purse strings. Jack was nothing if not a good businessman.

Gwen mentally kicked herself. Though would knowing the judge was Henrietta have made any difference? Jack could have still threatened Jenna. Heat worked its way up Gwen's neck and warmed her cheeks.

Fuming, she studied Henrietta. The woman looked only slightly different than before her unexplained exodus. She'd maintained her slim figure but, beneath the straw hat, her mane of thick black hair was sprinkled with grey streaks as it cascaded past her shoulders. Given Henrietta's vanity, Gwen was surprised the woman didn't have it colored.

No one had ever called Henrietta pretty. With her long face, square chin, and Roman nose, she'd be considered handsome at best. It was her flair with makeup and knack with flattering clothing that created her distinctive style, and no doubt her excess of self-importance.

Henrietta strutted around the front of the sedan, coming into full view on designer sling-backs with four inch heels. She wore black slacks, a flattering turquoise silk blouse – cut to show off her ample bosom – a wide black belt cinching her still-narrow waist, plus a necklace and earrings of pale blue stones that appeared to be Larimar.

Henrietta threw open the passenger door, making Gwen jump back to avoid being hit.

"You never did say why you're so dirty." Henrietta leaned into the passenger seat.

19

Gwen clenched her teeth. "Just working in my gardens." She longed to toss this woman off her property. But Gwen needed to be cautious until she located alternate lodging.

"Aren't you a little old for digging in the dirt?" Henrietta spoke over her shoulder in a voice muffled by the car's interior. "Why don't you just hire a gardener?"

Gwen squared her shoulders, resolving to endure Henrietta's snide remarks for Jenna's sake. "Plunging your hands into the earth is invigorating. You should try it sometime."

Henrietta wriggled out butt-first, emerging with a snakeskin patterned tote and a huge black purse. "You'd never catch me doing anything so menial. Digging in the dirt indeed." She waggled the same long red fingernail toward Gwen's head. "You've got something stuck in your hair. And your pants are filthy. Same old Gwen," Henrietta snickered.

Gwen's plan to be polite blew out on the September breeze. "Same old Henrietta," she snapped back.

Henrietta posed with one hip extended, as though someone might be watching her. "Imagine my surprise when the dean told me I'd be staying in the old village library. I had no idea Parker bought this place."

Gwen's jaw muscles tightened. "You're staying here for the sake of the competition. Not because we're old gal pals."

"I can't argue with you there, Gwen. You're the last person I'd consider a friend. Like I said, I never understood what Parker saw in you."

Henrietta gazed off into the distance. "He and I made such a handsome couple. With my encouragement, he could have become much more than a local architect. We could have gone places, Parker and me."

"Now don't you start," Gwen chided. "Parker told me during that dinner dance that the two of you were not a couple. Why can't you grasp the concept?"

Parker's actual words had been much harsher. He'd said Henrietta was pushy and possessive, not at all tempting in the romance department.

"Well, we could have been a couple if you hadn't come to town," she snapped.

For Jenna's sake, Gwen swallowed a snide retort.

Striding to the rear of the sedan, Henrietta popped the trunk as she focused somewhere above Gwen's head. "I hope you removed the mold and mildew from this old building. I've developed terrible allergies." Henrietta's nose wrinkled in confirmation as she yanked out a larger matching suitcase and balanced it on the rim of the trunk.

Ignoring Henrietta's insinuation of poor air quality, Gwen stepped forward. "I have gardening to do. Let's take your things inside."

Henrietta winked. "Why don't you ask Parker to come out and carry my bags?"

Gwen stumbled backwards, her arms flailing. She bumped into the deck steps, plopping down with a thud, staring up at Henrietta, who stood with hands on hips, smirk on face.

How could Henrietta not know? Surely the woman had kept up with the local news after she moved to Vermont. The article about Parker's accident, accolades about his architectural cleverness and his community activism had been well documented in the Harbor Falls Gazette.

The reminder of Parker's last day made Gwen dizzy. She dropped her head into her hands, willing herself not to cry in front of Henrietta.

"What's wrong, Gwen? Did Parker wise up and divorce you?" Henrietta threw her head back and laughed. The sound bounced off the brownstone and brick of the old library. "I told Parker repeatedly to dump you and marry me."

Gwen struggled to her feet on shaky legs. "You...you don't know?"

Henrietta lifted one eyebrow. "Know what?"

"Parker..." Gwen forced the word past her lips, "died."

Henrietta's dark eyes flashed. The unwieldy suitcase clattered back into the trunk. "That can't be true! Why would you tell me such a lie?"

It took all Gwen's strength to respond. "Because it's true."

Henrietta sagged like a ragdoll against the car's bumper. "When? Where? How?"

Gwen found Henrietta's ignorance difficult to comprehend but managed to answer the woman's questions. "More than two years ago. On the golf course. He was struck by lightning."

Gwen could not stop the memory of that mind-blowing day from surging forward. She'd kissed Parker goodbye before he drove off to his weekly golf game, like she had on so many previous Saturdays. A few hours later, the phone rang. Despite the panic in the man's voice, Gwen recognized the Irish brogue of Ernie Maguire, Parker's best friend, attorney, and golfing buddy. Ernie stumbled over his words. A freak thunderstorm. Their run to the club house. Parker lagging behind. The bolt of lightning. The call to 911. The rush to the hospital.

Gwen had driven like a mad woman to the emergency room. All through the night and into the next day, she and Ernie sat by Parker's hospital bed, holding his hands and whispering to his unconscious body. The following afternoon, Parker's heart stopped, and he abandoned Gwen without his knowledge.

Gwen hadn't been prepared for Parker to leave her so soon. Despite their discussions about which of them would be left behind, the reality of his death hit her hard. For two years, she struggled with her grief until her resurrection of their beloved gardens pulled her back into life. "You stole Parker from me!" Henrietta's shouted accusation jerked Gwen back to the present. "And now he's gone. I can never steal him back. I'll never forgive you, Gwen. Never."

22

Gwen said nothing. What could she possibly say to defuse Henrietta's animosity?

In the next instant, Henrietta surged to her feet, her voice rising in volume. "I can't believe this. Why didn't the dean tell me?"

To Gwen, the question made no sense. "Why would he, Henrietta?"

"Well, when he called about the lodging problem, I told him I was sure I could stay with my old colleague Gwen Andrews." Henrietta's eyes widened when she realized she'd just admitted her part in this absurd housing arrangement.

As the pieces fell into place, Gwen could barely contain her rage. "You invited yourself into my home because you wanted another crack at Parker?"

Before Henrietta could utter a word, a quavering female voice called out, "Gwen, dear, are you all right over there?" Through a grove of bamboo lining the far side of the driveway, a pair of oversized spectacles enlarged the eyes of an elderly woman.

Gwen cupped her hands around her mouth. "Mrs. Martin, sorry we disturbed you. Everything's fine. My guest just had a bit of a shock. No need to worry."

The octogenarian clucked her tongue as she inspected both Gwen and Henrietta. "Well, all right, dear, if you say so. You let me know if there's anything I can do." The bamboo slid back into place and the sound of the old lady's lightweight footsteps faded.

Henrietta pushed herself off the sedan's bumper. "Who was that busybody?"

"Mrs. Martin. She's my neighbor."

Henrietta closed her eyes, her shaking head falling forward. "I shouldn't have come."

Gwen didn't know what she'd expected Henrietta to say, but it wasn't that. Was the woman planning to hop in her car and drive back to Vermont? If she didn't stick around to judge the competition, the committee would be short one judge, again. What would they do if they didn't have the required three?

"But the competition…" Gwen's voice trailed off.

Henrietta's head bobbed up and down, speechless for perhaps the first time in her life. No quick comeback. No snide remark.

Unwilling to risk Jenna's shot at the scholarship, Gwen needed to move Henrietta inside, and quickly. Not only had Gwen been forced to give up her guest room, but now she had to play nice – or at least as nice as she could manage – to keep Henrietta in town.

Gwen picked up the tote bag from the driveway and repeated, "Let's take your things inside."

As Henrietta hauled the larger piece of luggage from the trunk, Gwen noticed a stuffed black cat sneering out from the sedan's back window. The perfect mascot.

Henrietta hefted the bulging suitcase and followed Gwen up the steps. Crossing the long expanse of deck, they entered through the French door and stopped in the open space between the kitchen and the music studio. Henrietta scanned the layout, her gaze settling on the staircase. Her lips moved, appearing to count the steps to the second level.

"Your guest room is up there?" Henrietta's tone was incredulous.

Gwen hadn't anticipated resistance. "It's an easy climb."

"We'll see." Henrietta grabbed the smaller tote.

Gwen's jaw worked as she struggled with the heavier piece. "After you."

Clinging to the wooden banister, Henrietta's knuckles turned whiter with each step.

"Turn left," Gwen instructed when they reached the midway split and again on the upper landing. Henrietta avoided the balcony railing, staying close to the front window wall until she entered the guest room.

Hefting the cumbersome suitcase onto a cedar chest, Gwen startled the sleeping Amber, who hopped off the queen-sized bed and bolted out the door.

After she dropped her tote bag onto the embroidered coverlet, Henrietta glanced beyond the curtains billowing in the September breeze. "Nice view. Parker designed an interesting layout."

Before Gwen could take any credit, Henrietta sneezed.

Once, twice, three times. She pointed at the dresser, where Gwen's fresh flowers nodded brightly in the wicker basket.

"Get those damned weeds out of here!"

Snatching up her floral arrangement, Gwen raced from the room, down the stairway to the halfway point, and up the other side into the sitting room. She placed the basket on a table near her reading chair snugged against the balcony railing. She'd be damned if her beautiful flowers would go unappreciated.

When Gwen re-entered the guest room, she found Henrietta slumped on the bed, wiping at mascara streaking down her cheeks, her eyes red and swollen. Was this the result of her allergies, or was Henrietta having a delayed reaction to Parker's death? Gwen almost felt sorry for the woman. Almost.

Gwen tapped the dresser top. "I emptied these drawers for the judge's, uh, your stay. If you need to hang anything, use the wardrobe at the top of the stairs." Gwen retrieved a key from her pants pocket and tossed it onto the comforter. "This is for the front door, although I rarely lock it."

Gwen's eye caught the time on the bedside clock. Five before one. She looked down at her soiled gardening clothes. "I have to go. Garden club meeting."

Henrietta reached sideways and snapped open the suitcase latch. "Don't let me stop you. I don't need a baby-sitter, and I don't plan to steal any of your pitiful belongings."

25

Biting her tongue, Gwen headed for the guest room door, then turned around, forming her question on the fly. "I'm curious. Why are you here more than a week ahead of the competition?"

Henrietta's eyes bored into Gwen's. "A bold question for a little mouse like you. As a reward, I'll tell you. The invitation to return to Harbor Falls gives me the opportunity to clear my conscience and set a few things straight."

What did Henrietta mean, clear her conscience? Everyone knew the woman never had one. And what things did she have to set straight?

And Gwen couldn't forget Henrietta's third reason for driving back to her old home town and arranging to stay here. She'd planned one last try at snagging Parker.

Chapter Four

Five minutes late and nearly breathless, Gwen snuck into the historic schoolhouse on South Street. When the antique door hinges squeaked, the sound reverberated throughout the cramped quarters of the old classroom. Everyone swiveled in their chairs to gawk at the late-comer.

Claudia Smith, this year's garden club president, stood at the podium. Her dark eyes blended artfully with black hair swaying in a graceful pageboy style. Not unlike Cleopatra, but without all the bling. She lifted her head and smiled in Gwen's direction.

Rapping her gavel, Claudia's crisp voice filled the small space. "Before we begin our review of Saturday's tours, let's thank Otis Bascom from Coastline Tours for donating and driving one of his buses. It will eliminate the parking problems we experienced last year."

She motioned to a uniformed older man on the side aisle. "Otis, please stand and take a bow."

He stood up, his face alight with his practiced tour guide smile. "My pleasure."

When the clapping died down, Claudia waved a brochure in the air. "Does everyone have the printed schedule?" She waited as paper rustled and voices murmured.

"At noon on Saturday, ticket holders will park in our back lot and board Otis's bus. We've allowed thirty minutes for each garden, plus travel from one location to the next. The final stop will be around four o'clock at Gwen Andrews's gardens on the village green. She has also offered a bonus tour of the old village library and will host our garden party in her back yard. When the festivities end, everyone will re-board the bus for the return trip here to their cars."

Claudia ran her finger down her notes. "Are there any questions or comments?"

Betty and Bob Owens, owners of the Harbor Falls B&B, raised their hands. "Bob and I would like to make a suggestion."

"What do you have in mind?" Claudia asked.

Betty's voice rang out. "We can follow Mr. Bascom's bus in our oversized van. As each tour ends, the garden owners can climb aboard to see the rest of the properties and attend the garden party at the end. Then we'll drive you back home afterwards."

"That's very generous of you." Claudia's gaze slid from one face to the next, finding a sea of nodding heads. "Can I see a show of hands to make this official?"

All hands flew into the air.

Myrtle Mueller stood up, her face a study in smugness. "I don't know why we're having a garden party in Gwen's back yard. Eating food outdoors is messy."

Claudia kept her expression neutral. "I'm sorry, Myrtle. It's too late to change our program. Perhaps you should have signed up for the planning committee."

Myrtle tossed a backwards glance at Gwen, huffed, and plopped back down.

Claudia raised the gavel. "The weather forecast sounds promising. Good luck on Saturday. If there's nothing else, this meeting is adjourned." The bang of the gavel reverberated.

As the members left the schoolhouse, many chatted with Gwen, welcoming her after her two-year absence. It warmed her heart to be back in the thick of a community activity. Myrtle averted her eyes as she walked out. *Well, I can't expect everyone to like me,* Gwen conceded.

Coming out behind Myrtle, Claudia locked the schoolhouse door. "Can you believe Myrtle?"

"She's a character, all right. Let me walk you to your car."

"I thought you were gonna miss our meeting, Gwen."

"Sorry I snuck in late. If not for those squeaky hinges..."

The corners of Claudia's lips curled into a smile. "Well, I'm glad you made it. You've notched up the excitement by offering a house tour. I'm sure it increased ticket sales."

Gwen chuckled. "Showing the old village library to the community was way overdue."

"Good one, Gwen." Claudia had not missed the *late book* pun.

A familiar sadness draped over Gwen. "Parker and I should have shared our conversion with the town years ago." She hesitated as a lump formed in her throat. She still found it difficult to refer to Parker in the past tense. "I thought we had at least another twenty years together."

Claudia placed a gentle hand on Gwen's arm. "I can't imagine living without Pete. You seem to have found some peace."

"Mother Nature gets all the credit, Claudia. Bringing our gardens back to life over the summer reminded me of all the good times with Parker. I'm ashamed I ignored them so long."

"No one faults you for mourning your husband, Gwen. And I hope the club didn't overstep with the garden party."

They made their way along the fieldstone walkway. "Not at all. The members will prepare the food in my kitchen. And I've certainly got the outdoor space for a large gathering."

As they approached a dark blue SUV, Claudia pointed her key fob at the car door until the lock clicked open, then turned to Gwen. "If you don't mind me asking, why were you late for the meeting? You always used to be an early-bird."

"Are you familiar with the Young Musicians Competition?"

"Sure am. Years ago, when I was secretary to old Dean James; I helped organize the competition details for the college committee. I even signed up to usher next weekend."

Gwen quickened her pace to keep up with Claudia. "You may not know, but the committee hired a last-minute replacement judge. Jack Miller at the music shop asked me to host her." She decided not to share Jack's maneuvering. "I was preparing my guest room and lost track of time."

Claudia opened her car door. "I heard one of the judges withdrew because of medical problems. I didn't know they'd found a substitute. What's her name?"

"Henrietta Wickham."

Claudia reached out and grasped the car door frame. "Henrietta Wickham? Are you sure?"

"I'm sure. She pulled into my driveway about an hour ago."

"She's back in Harbor Falls?" Claudia's voice was nearly a whisper, her eyes wide.

Claudia's spooked reaction surprised Gwen. She'd been so distracted by her own outrage, she hadn't considered there might be others less than thrilled about Henrietta's return.

"Everyone knows about the verbal abuse Henrietta heaped on me. What happened between the two of you?"

Claudia took a breath, her eyes closing for a second before popping open to stare at Gwen. "I can't believe Jack is involved in that woman coming back to town."

Gwen's question remained unanswered. However, despite her own red-hot anger at Jack, she didn't want to misrepresent his involvement in Henrietta's return. "Daniel Chartley, the new dean, suggested Henrietta." Many people connected to Baylies still referred to Daniel as the 'new' dean, regardless that he'd been in the position for more than a dozen years.

"Well, it doesn't matter who invited her, does it? She's here." Claudia's head snapped up. "And a week ahead of the competition. You know she's up to something."

Gwen couldn't argue with Claudia's assumption. "Henrietta told me she wants to clear her conscience and set a few things straight, whatever that means. I'm not sure I want to know."

Making a show of checking her watch, Claudia said, "Listen, I've gotta run. Will that woman be at your place when I bring Kenneth for his lesson tomorrow afternoon?"

"I've no idea." An image of Claudia's lanky pre-teen son came into focus. The boy had been struggling with his flute lessons all summer.

Claudia dropped into the driver's seat and tossed her garden club folders onto the passenger's side. "Be careful while Henrietta's living with you, Gwen. She's a wicked woman." Claudia started the engine and drove off, her tires throwing up tiny pebbles.

***

Instead of heading straight home, Gwen had continued up the sidewalk to the music shop and now stood in front of Jack's desk, her question hanging in the air.

He rolled his eyes. "Of course I'd heard about your tug of war with Henrietta over Parker. Everyone at Baylies knew about it. But you won, Gwen. The man married you."

"Then you also know she never stopped harassing me until the day she left Harbor Falls. So why did you force her on me, Jack? Do you dislike me? Have I offended you somehow?"

"Calm down, Gwen. She won't be here long. We can certainly tolerate the woman for a week. When she drives off, she won't bother us anymore."

"What do you mean 'we' and 'us', Jack? I'm the one doing all the heavy lifting here."

He slammed his hand on the surface of his desk. "I don't want Henrietta here any more than you do. But the committee refused to cancel her contract. They need three judges for the competition. You know that, so we're stuck with her. Besides, we couldn't find any other place for her to stay."

So Jack also resented Henrietta's return. What was his story? Did Gwen give a damn? She glared at him. "You could have searched harder."

He grimaced, shaking his head. "We ran out of time. You were the only person I could think of who has an empty guest room."

She narrowed her eyes. "Or was I the only person you could blackmail?"

His face reddened as he tapped the tip of his A.T. Cross pen against the desk blotter, leaving a trail of black dots. "Now, Gwen, let's not lower ourselves to accusations."

"Can't you help me out of this?" Gwen hated the whine in her voice. "Henrietta hasn't changed, Jack. She still hates me."

He reached for a stack of papers. "Sorry, there's nothing I can do." His gaze lowered to the documents. "If you'll excuse me, I have invoices to review."

Outraged, Gwen bolted from his office and headed for the exit. If there was a vacant bed anywhere in Harbor Falls, she'd have to find it herself.

When she reached for the doorknob, Emily rushed in from outside, hopping sideways to avoid a collision. "I didn't see you coming out, Gwen. Sorry."

Gwen shuffled backwards, waving Emily in.

When they stood side by side, Emily asked, "Why are you here again, Gwen?"

"I needed to have a little chat with Jack." Gwen placed her hand on Emily's arm. "Tell me something. Why did you tell Jack the new judge couldn't stay with you? Surely your extra bedroom can't be that bad."

"What on earth are you talking about, Gwen? Jack never asked me anything of the sort."

Gwen tilted her head, studying Emily, who appeared to be telling the truth. Why had Jack fibbed about that detail? He did say he didn't want Henrietta back in town. Even tried to cancel the woman's judging contract. But why keep it from Emily?

"Did he tell you he blackmailed me to host Henrietta?" Gwen asked.

32

Emily plopped onto the cushioned bench seat beneath the north-facing window, dropped her head into her hands, and spoke between her fingers. "Did you say Henrietta?"

"Yes, Henrietta Wickham. I assumed you knew, Emily. You handed that phone message to Jack earlier this morning."

"Yes, but the dean didn't mention the judge's name. Neither did Jack. He told me he'd found a replacement judge, but he didn't even tell me if it was a man or a woman."

Emily rose in slow motion then stomped to the back counter where the old sepia photos had been arranged into neat stacks. She kicked the now-empty box at her feet and sent it skittering across the wide boards. One arm stretched over and swept every picture into the air. For a brief moment, they hung, suspended, before falling out of sight behind the counter.

Horrified at Emily's display of temper, Gwen was relieved no customers had witnessed the outburst. Was Emily upset with Jack for keeping her in the dark about Henrietta's hiring, or was she upset with Henrietta herself?

Once more, Gwen scolded herself for assuming she was the only one in town with a less-than-pleasant history with Henrietta. Jumping up from the window seat, she rushed to Emily's side and laid a hand on her back. "How can I help?"

"Thanks for asking, Gwen, but there's nothing. Jack makes me so mad sometimes. I made a mistake asking him to leave his office job at Baylies to be my business manager after my father passed away and I inherited the shop."

Emily tapped the now-empty counter top. "But I need to calm down before I confront Jack about his poor handling of this situation. If he wasn't my husband, I'd probably fire him. Tell you what, Gwen. I'm aware of the nasty way Henrietta treated you, but I never heard the story behind it. Why don't you tell me now while I cool off?"

Chapter Five

Gwen paused. If she recounted her dealings with Henrietta, Emily might sympathize and offer her extra bedroom. Gwen wiggled to find a comfortable spot on the bench.

"Well, I met Henrietta the same evening as my future husband Parker. That was back in the early '70s, when I first arrived in Harbor Falls."

"Haven't you lived here your whole life?" Emily asked.

Gwen shook her head. "No. I was born and raised in the Berkshires. My sister still lives there with her husband. I moved here after college to accept the position of Associate Professor of Music History at Baylies. I have to tell you, Emily, I instantly fell in love with your town."

"Most people do," Emily commented. "But I figured out why I have a misconception of how long you've lived here. I wasn't born until 1975, so I've known you my entire life."

Gwen grinned. "That explains it. I remember you as a toddler when your father brought you here to the shop and I happened to stop by. And here we sit nearly forty years later."

Emily's face fell. "I miss my dad. Everything worked so smoothly when he was in charge."

"Oh, I don't know, Emily, you seem to be handling the business. Except for this situation with Jack, things are good, aren't they? Business is good, yes?"

"Good enough to keep the doors open."

At that moment, the bell above the door jingled, announcing the arrival of a gaggle of coeds. Without noticing Emily and Gwen on the bench, the girls headed for the instrument section.

"Alex will take care of them," Emily said, making no effort to get up. "But I keep interrupting your story, Gwen. Please go on." Emily eased into the bench cushions.

"Well, okay, if you want to hear it. The evening after I arrived, the college sponsored a dinner dance to introduce new hires to other staff members and some of the local citizens. In the buffet line, I tipped my plate and splashed tomato sauce onto the jacket sleeve of the man behind me. I was so embarrassed, Emily."

Gwen stopped talking and covered her face with her hand, the memory still so vivid. "I grabbed some napkins and wiped at the sauce, but all I did was grind it into the tweed fabric. And then he laughed."

Emily sat forward. "He laughed? What did you do?"

"I looked up and found amused hazel eyes set in a rugged face. He took my breath away."

"Your Parker was a good-looking man. But you didn't know his name yet?"

"Not yet. A tall woman with wild black hair stepped around him, eyed the stain, and glowered at me. She said, 'What a mess. Let's get that jacket off.' She folded it inside-out and tossed it over the sleeve of her beaded black suit. The man rolled his eyes, extended his hand to me, and said, 'My name is Parker Andrews. I've lived in Harbor Falls all my life, so if you have any questions about this town, ask away.' He grinned and thumbed toward the black-haired woman. 'This is Henrietta Wickham, an associate professor at Baylies."

"Aha," Emily squealed. "Your first encounter with Henrietta. What happened next?"

"Well, he tugged the soiled napkins out of my hand and tossed them into a trash can. 'Come and sit with me. We'll chat.' He gazed around the crowded event hall and pointed. 'There's an empty table over there.'

"By that time, I wasn't so embarrassed, so I followed him across the dance floor, my plate of food grasped securely in both hands." Gwen paused and demonstrated. "Henrietta took the chair on his other side. As we ate, she tried to monopolize

Parker's attention, but he always turned to include me. I have to tell you, Emily, I was very flattered. He asked about my hometown in the Berkshires and my student days at college. His local anecdotes made me laugh. And then he pushed his empty plate aside, stood up, and extended his hand asking, 'Would you like to dance, Gwen?'

"Well, of course, I was dying to dance with this handsome guy, and I didn't want to be impolite, so I ignored the daggers Henrietta was tossing my way and followed Parker onto the dance floor. We gyrated to the Lovin' Spoonful's 'Do You Believe in Magic'. When the song ended, he asked, 'Wanna stay up for the next one?' The Beatles began to croon 'Yesterday' and he pulled me closer. He was several inches taller, but my body clicked into his like a piece from a jigsaw puzzle. I glanced back at our table, and I couldn't ignore Henrietta's hostile glare, so I said, 'Your companion doesn't look very happy'.

"Parker bent down until his lips were close enough to my ear so I could hear over the music. 'Henrietta and I are not a couple, but nothing I say discourages her. She follows me everywhere.' When he pushed me to arm's length for a twirl, he said, 'You smell like fresh baked cookies. I like it.'"

"Wow, that's romantic, Gwen," Emily commented. "Jack's courtship was nothing like that."

Even now, Gwen could summon the sensation of Parker's warm breath tickling her ear. And she still wore that same vanilla scent.

Gwen must have zoned out because she snapped out of her stupor when she felt a tug on her sleeve.

Emily stared at her. "You can't stop now, Gwen. There must be more."

"Oh, there is, Emily. Give me a second." She got to her feet and stretched her arms high, weaving back and forth before sitting back down.

"The morning after the tomato sauce incident and the dancing, Parker called and asked if I liked books. When I confessed I was a bibliophile, he described the village library and invited me to meet him there during his lunch break. I wasn't scheduled to start teaching until the following week, so I went."

"Oh, my gosh, Gwen! You had no idea the two of you would live there years later?"

"Not a clue, Emily," Gwen said, feeling a happy smile on her face. "Anyway, we poked around the shelves until it was time for him to head back to the local architectural firm where he was an apprentice. Well, that Friday evening, we explored the shops down on the waterfront, and on Saturday he drove me up the coast for a delicious clam and scallop dinner. I have to tell you, none of my college boyfriends wined and dined me like Parker did, and I enjoyed his attentions."

Gwen stopped talking and took a deep breath. "The following week, everything changed. When I left my classroom after my first day of teaching music history, Henrietta blocked the door to the hallway and wouldn't let me pass. She said, 'Parker is mine, honey. You stay away, or I'll make your life miserable.'"

Emily raised an eyebrow. "I guess I shouldn't be surprised."

"Well, I sure was at the time, Emily. I wanted no part in a love triangle, so I sprinted to my car and drove to Parker's office. My heart did a little dance when he strode into reception. I didn't waste any time with a greeting. 'Henrietta Wickham claims you're her property, Parker.'

"He reached for my hand and led me to a seating area beneath an arched window. His hazel eyes searched my face, and I could see him thinking about what to say. He finally said, 'Like I told you at the dance last week, Gwen, Henrietta and I are not a couple, no matter how much she thinks it's going to

37

happen. I've told her repeatedly I'm not interested. She doesn't hear me. She says I'm wrong and I just don't know it.'

"I said, "I'm telling you, Parker, she's convinced herself you belong to her.'

'Well, she's delusional, not to mention pushy. She's not the least bit tempting in the romance department." He brushed a lock of hair from my cheek and let his fingertips linger on my skin. "I want a gentler soul. Someone like you, Gwen.'

"Naturally, I was flattered, and I had to fight to keep my wits. Parker didn't understand the concept of a woman scorned."

"Most men don't, Gwen."

"He must have noticed my hesitation, because Parker said, 'Don't worry. She'll find another man to boss around.'

"I said the only thing that came to mind, Emily. 'I hope you're right, Parker.'

"Well, we dated through the fall and winter months and got married the following spring. You can probably guess we didn't invite Henrietta, but she crashed our reception, dressed in a black ball gown and black feathered hat with matching organza veil. She made a grand entrance, shouting she had come for Parker's funeral."

Emily roared. "I can picture that scene, Gwen, but you must have been horrified."

"I was, but Parker grasped her elbow and steered her through the doors of the function room. My sister Tess, and my friend Liz, my matrons-of-honor, walked with me as we followed Parker and Henrietta to the parking lot. After forcing her into her car, he stood with his arms crossed until she disappeared. He smiled at me and escorted us back to the reception. Our guests were chattering about the incident, so Parker shouted out a joke about being stalked. Everyone laughed. To me, he whispered, *'She's gone,'* and led me to the dance floor."

"I can guess the next line, Gwen," Emily offered. "Henrietta was *not* gone."

"Right you are, Emily. Her anger and jealousy twisted into evil revenge. From the wedding day forward, whenever she and I crossed paths, she let loose a torrent of insults, and she usually didn't care who was listening. Nothing I did, nothing I said, nothing I wore was ever good enough for Henrietta."

Emily reached for Gwen's hand. "It's unfortunate you both worked at Baylies. It must have been nearly impossible to avoid her."

"I tried, Emily. I tried. Whenever she caught up with me, I turned and walked away."

"Did you ever tell Parker?" Emily asked.

Gwen nodded and shifted her position. "For the first few months of our marriage, Henrietta's tongue lashing was a topic at our dinner table. After a while, I figured I was beginning to sound like a whiny wife, so I stopped mentioning her. I always hoped she'd give up, but she never did."

"Didn't she ever get in trouble for it?"

"Unfortunately, no. She was clever enough to mind her manners in the presence of the dean and other college officials, so they never witnessed her unprofessional conduct, and she was never reprimanded."

"Did any of your colleagues try to stop her?"

"A few tried. In fact, anyone who made the attempt only turned Henrietta against them, too. Everyone eventually gave up. I developed what I considered a thicker skin and prepared myself for Henrietta's abuse whenever I saw her strutting my way. I suffered her hateful words year after year until she left town. As you know, Henrietta abandoned her professorship and left Harbor Falls without a backward glance. I never heard the reason. Not that I cared. I was just glad she was gone."

Gwen glanced sideways at Emily. "Do you know why?"

Emily shrugged and got to her feet. "That was a fascinating

39

story, Gwen. Thanks for sharing it with me. I've calmed down now, and I'm ready to face Jack as a sane woman. You said earlier that he blackmailed you to host Henrietta?"

"That's exactly what he did," Gwen confirmed. "He threatened to remove my student Jenna Jenkins from the list of competitors if I didn't let Henrietta sleep in my guest room."

"I'm sorry he put you in such an awkward position," Emily said, not sounding sorry at all. "But just so you know, if Jack *had* asked me about hosting her, I would have refused."

Gwen's hopes were dashed. Her recounting of her sordid history with Henrietta apparently hadn't moved Emily to offer her extra bedroom above the shop.

"But why?" Gwen asked.

"I have my reasons." Emily reached over and grasped Gwen's shoulder.

Gwen flinched at the strength of Emily's fingers. "I don't understand. You own this shop, and Jack was involved in hiring Henrietta for the competition. He saddled me with the woman, and now you're not willing to step in?"

Emily stood tall. "Jack has a lot of explaining to do." Without another word, she strode to the southern end of the shop. Seconds later, Jack's office door slammed shut.

For a moment, Gwen put aside her own distress about Henrietta's invasion. Everyone she'd spoken to during the past few hours had reacted to the woman's return in a negative way.

There was Jack's attempt to cancel Henrietta's contract. Then Claudia's alarm when she learned Henrietta was back in town. And now Emily's refusal to let Henrietta step foot in their living quarters above the music shop.

What had Henrietta done to Jack, Claudia, and Emily?

Chapter Six

Within minutes of walking in her front door, Gwen pulled out her cell phone, dialing as she retreated to the back deck for privacy. Henrietta might or might not be upstairs, but Gwen didn't want to risk the woman eavesdropping.

"Tess, it's me again."

"Wow, twice in one day. How lucky can I get?"

Despite Gwen's sour mood, she softened at her sister's teasing. "I don't know if you'll consider this lucky. Do you remember Henrietta Wickham?"

Tess whistled. "Now there's a name from the past. Didn't she leave town years ago? Why bring up her name now?"

"Because she's the replacement judge."

"Henrietta is the woman staying in your guest room? That's terrible. Can you get rid of her?"

"I want to, but I don't know how quickly that's going to happen. I confronted Jack about his underhanded tactics, but he's not willing to help me find her another bed."

Tess didn't speak for a few beats. "Does she still hate you for stealing her man?"

Gwen walked to the deck rail. "I did *not* steal Parker!" When she banged her fist, it slid sideways onto a rough patch of wood. "Damn."

"What happened, Gwen?"

"Oh, just me losing my temper." She sucked on the blood oozing from the side of her hand.

"That's not like you, sis. Sorry I brought it up. I was only joking."

"Not funny, Tess. Henrietta hasn't mellowed."

Tess's voice took on an edge. "She's ridiculing you like before?"

"The second she got out of her car."

"What are you going to do, sis?"

"No idea. I can't make any wrong moves and risk Jenna's performance."

"I'm not surprised. You've become fond of that girl over the summer."

"You're right. She's a sweetie. I can't wait for you to meet her."

"Me, too. Listen, I'll call you from the road next Thursday and let you know what time my GPS says I'll get there." Tess hesitated. "Sorry, Gwen. Nathan just brought in what I think is our last basket of garden tomatoes. We're making sauce. I'll bring a few jars with me. Gotta go. Good luck getting rid of Henrietta. Call me if you need a sounding board."

Gwen hung up and leaned against the deck rail, inspecting her hand as she pondered her next move. Until she could find another hostess, she was stuck with Henrietta. Her resolve hardening, Gwen vowed she wouldn't endure Henrietta's proximity, or her wicked tongue, for one second longer than necessary. Why would Jack care where Henrietta slept as long as she remained in Harbor Falls to judge the competition?

A basic strategy began to take shape. First thing on Monday, after a day of rest to recuperate from the garden and house tours, Gwen would begin her search. Given Claudia's negative reaction, asking her to provide a bed for Henrietta was definitely not an option. There must be someone who hadn't known Henrietta before she left town and would be delighted to host a former Baylies professor. Gwen would start with the relatively new professors at Baylies.

Relieved she had a plan, Gwen swept her gaze across the gardens, viewing the various details from the tour group's point of view. Parker's wooden structures stood as strong as ever. At the top of the driveway, his 24-foot-long arbor, its top obscured by trailing vines of Virginia creeper, bordered the property line to the west. A second smaller arbor beside the potting shed provided shelter from a rain shower. A trellis, covered with a vigorous clematis vine, led off the lower deck onto the back lawn. An archway beside the huge field rock straddled the pathway into the wooded acres. Three tall posts supported old-fashioned carriage lamps with battery-operated candles timed to flick on at dusk.

Gwen's choices of flowering bushes, grasses of all textures and heights, hardy perennials, and colorful annuals softened the rough lumber, creating a fairytale setting.

Parker's favorite saying: he built the hardware and Gwen installed the software.

What she wouldn't give to hear him teasing her now.

She made a mental note to mention tour day to Henrietta, hoping the woman would have no interest and would leave for the day. Or would she stick around and embarrass Gwen in front of friends and strangers just for old time's sake?

Spotting newly-sprouted weeds in the closest flower bed, Gwen reached inside the French door and grabbed her garden gloves and clippers. A few minutes later, as she yanked a clump of crab grass from a bed of bright salmon impatiens, she heard the French door open and close. Without turning around, she listened as Henrietta's shoes clicked along the deck.

A minute later, a car door slammed and the black sedan started up. Gwen didn't know where Henrietta was off to, and she didn't much care. Hopefully the woman would stay away for most of the day, maybe visit The Olde Music Shop and grate on Jack's nerves.

When Gwen's cell phone vibrated, she removed one glove and slid the instrument from her jeans pocket, wincing at the caller ID. "Hi, Liz. I'm sorry. I should have called you."

With the upheaval of the past few hours, Gwen hadn't thought to warn her best friend that Henrietta was back in town.

Liz chuckled. "I guess my ESP is working. What's up?"

Nearly four decades ago, during Gwen's first few days in Harbor Falls, she walked into Liz's *Fiction 'n Fables Bookstop* down near the harbor. After a signing event for a mystery author, Liz approached Gwen and their friendship was born. Over the decades, they'd kept each other balanced through life's joys and sorrows: both of their weddings, the birth of Liz's two children, and Parker's death.

Gwen strolled to the side yard and eased onto a concrete garden bench tucked beneath a sugar maple, the edges of its leaves hinting at the color change to come. "I've got some news, Liz."

"I'm listening."

Before Gwen could warn Liz about Henrietta, a commotion erupted on the other end of the line. A door slammed. Gwen couldn't understand the words shouted by a muffled voice.

"Oh, my God!" Liz hissed into the phone. "Henrietta Wickham just stormed into the shop. I gotta go."

Gwen could only imagine the uproar. Many years ago, she'd walked into the bookstore to find the two of them yelling at each other. After Henrietta stomped out, Liz explained they'd been arch enemies since their days at Harbor Falls High. If Liz said white, Henrietta said black. If Liz said up, Henrietta said down.

Gwen considered rushing down to Liz's side. But, no, that wouldn't be necessary. Liz could give as good as she got.

Chapter Seven

At three o'clock, Alex stood beside Gwen in her music studio, twisting the sections of his flute into alignment with a final flourish.

They rifled through their cache of sheet music and chose No. 2 in C Minor from J.S. Bach's *Inventions* for two flutes. For several enthralling minutes, they chased each other up and down the musical scale.

"Oh, Alex, that was wonderful," Gwen said, dropping onto the piano bench. "You were right. It's been too long since we've dueted."

He slanted his head and tapped his temple as if he were doffing a hat. "I knew this would cheer you up."

When someone started clapping, Gwen jerked and nearly slid off the bench. She flipped around to see Henrietta leaning against the kitchen island, her ankles crossed, her hands still moving. She wore beige slacks, beige flats, and a salmon colored blouse. A leaf-patterned cardigan hung artfully around her shoulders without covering a bold gold necklace. Matching earrings reflected the light. Such a clothes horse, Gwen mused, not bothering to look down at her own outfit, unchanged since she came in from gardening when Alex arrived.

Henrietta didn't acknowledge Gwen. Instead, she said, "Alex, I had no idea you were so adept on your flute. Such panache, such flair."

"There are probably lots of things you don't know about me, Henrietta."

Although Alex's tone was neutral, Gwen sensed an unease beneath his words.

Raising one perfectly plucked eyebrow, Henrietta said, "Why, you play better than Gwen."

Though stung by the insult, Gwen was not surprised. What *did* surprise her was Henrietta's manner. Where was the woman devastated by the news of Parker's death just a few hours ago? Gwen had never seen anyone recover so quickly. Henrietta appeared confident and grounded. Or was she simply putting on a brave face?

"Oh, I don't think that's an accurate statement," Alex said, his voice unemotional. "My sensibilities and my ears tell me that Gwen and I are equally matched."

Henrietta blew air out her nose like a winded horse. "Well, you're entitled to your opinion, as am I. Will you play another duet?" Assuming they'd do her bidding, Henrietta strutted to a nearby wing chair, sat down, and perched two fingers against her chin.

Gwen bristled under Henrietta's presumption but turned to Alex. "Do you have time?"

He sent a sidelong glance at Henrietta. Gwen wasn't sure how to read his reaction. Did he resent Henrietta for interrupting their private duet time, or did he just dislike the woman on general principles like most people in town?

In answer, Alex flipped to the next piece of music, No. 3 in A Minor, another of the Bach *Inventions*. "I'm willing if you are, Gwen."

As she and Alex intertwined their notes, Gwen glanced at Henrietta and found her eyes closed and a half-smile on her lips, her foot tapping in time to the music.

When they lowered their flutes, Henrietta simply said, "Splendid, Alex."

The chime of the doorbell filled the awkward silence. Gwen laid down her flute, circumvented the staircase, and opened the front door. "Hello, you two. What a nice surprise. Come in, come in."

"Hi, Mrs. Andrews," Jenna Jenkins chirped, stepping inside. "Bet you didn't expect us!"

46

Gwen's smile widened. "No, I didn't."

Jenna was the reincarnation of her mother Elizabeth, one of Gwen's most gifted music students at Baylies nearly two decades before. The same silky blonde hair. The same blue eyes. The same petite body.

Within days of graduation, Elizabeth and Jenna's father Matthew had been killed in a car crash. At the double funeral, preschooler Jenna had clung to her grandfather's pants leg, bringing tears to everyone's eyes.

And now here stood high school senior Jenna, her face beaming, her spirits high.

Behind Jenna, her grandfather, Hal Jenkins, his slim frame muscled from laboring at his plant nursery and garden center south of town, ran his weathered hand through his salt and pepper hair. His resemblance to actor Hal Holbrook always made Gwen's heart do a little dance.

"I can't find my cell phone, Gwen. Thought maybe it fell from my pocket."

Since May, when he'd hired Gwen to prepare his granddaughter for the competition, he'd driven Jenna to town every Saturday afternoon. He always stayed and listened, ready with a compliment for Jenna's delicate technique on her flute.

Gwen now considered him a friend.

When the light streaming through the stained glass of the foyer danced in Hal's blue eyes, Gwen blinked. "Uh, sure, let's go take a look. Do you know Alex from the music shop? We've been dueting." She paused when she remembered Henrietta. "Oh, and I have a house guest."

Jenna bounced around the staircase, with Gwen and Hal close behind. When they reached the studio, he called out, "Sorry for interrupting."

Alex disassembled his flute and dried the inside before packing it away. "Don't apologize, Mr. Jenkins. I've got to get back before the afternoon rush." He touched Gwen's arm. "Let me know when you need another session." He winked at her and tucked his flute case under his arm. "If you don't mind, I'll circle through your patch of woods to the new library, then backtrack to the music shop."

"Of course, Alex. That's a very pleasant stroll. Be my guest."

After Alex closed the French door behind him, Henrietta made her way toward Hal and thrust out her hand. "Mr. Jenkins, I'm Henrietta Wickham. Years ago I was a music professor at Baylies. Your daughter Elizabeth was a great musical talent."

Conflicting emotions flitted across Hal's face. Gwen speculated it was a mixture of pride that someone remembered his deceased daughter and curiosity about Henrietta's reason for dredging it up. "I'm...I'm sorry, Ms. Wickham. I don't think we ever met. Which course did you teach?"

"Performance Theory. And please call me Henrietta. Elizabeth was one of my brightest students. Her command of the flute was truly enchanting."

"I agree with you." Hal's expression remained baffled as he placed his arm across Jenna's shoulders. "I'm proud to say my granddaughter inherited her mother's talent."

Henrietta turned a megawatt smile on Jenna. "I noticed your name on the contestants' list for next Saturday, so I shouldn't befriend you before the competition. But if you ever need musical advice in the future, Jenna, I'll be glad to share my expertise."

Jenna appeared awestruck. "Thank you, Ms. Wickham."

Stunned, Gwen glimpsed another side of Henrietta. The professor adored by her students. A kinder Henrietta never offered to Gwen, or most other adults either.

However, if Jenna needed musical advice, Gwen would damn well be the one to dispense it.

Henrietta refocused on Hal. "I was devastated when I heard

about Elizabeth and Matthew's accident. Unfortunately, I was in the process of moving to Vermont and couldn't attend their funerals. I'm years too late, but please accept my sincere condolences."

Hal glanced down at Jenna, who didn't appear upset by the reminder that her mother and father had died when she was a toddler.

Henrietta didn't give Hal a chance to respond. "If you could find some time for me while I'm back in town, I'd like to talk to you about Elizabeth."

He stiffened. "You would?"

"Well, yes. As I mentioned before, I cannot fraternize with Jenna before the competition." She reached over and smoothed Jenna's blonde hair. "But I thought you and I could have a private chat. Perhaps I can provide us both with a modicum of closure."

Hal stared at Henrietta, his confusion obvious. Jenna wandered away. Gwen stayed put.

Reaching into her purse, Henrietta brought out her phone and raced through her calendar. "How's Monday morning?"

After a slight hesitation, Hal nodded. "Fine. I'm usually at Sugar 'n Spice with my crew around seven. Why don't you meet me there?" He waved his hand toward the popular cafe on the southern edge of the village green.

"Oh, no, no. Sweets do such a number on my girlish figure." Henrietta placed one hand on her slim hip and tossed him a winning smile.

Gwen nearly threw up at Henrietta's bold flirtation. Hal appeared immune.

Wait a minute. Gwen mentally back tracked. Could Hal, or even Elizabeth, be one of the reasons Henrietta accepted the judging seat and returned to Harbor Falls? Which of her reasons for coming back would apply? To clear her conscience? Or to set a few things straight?

Concerned Henrietta would run rampant over the unsuspecting Hal, Gwen stepped forward. "Why don't you two meet right here?"

Henrietta's head whipped around, daggers flying from her slitted eyes. She couldn't refuse Gwen's offer without seeming manipulative.

Hal turned to Gwen. "That's generous. Are you sure?"

"Of course." Gwen tossed her own smile his way. "If you're coming into town anyway, and Henrietta is staying here, my home is the most logical location for your little chat." *Besides, I don't think I can find her another bed by Monday morning.*

Hal nodded. "Sounds good to me."

For a few seconds, Henrietta seethed, then relented. "All right, I'll see you here on Monday morning around eight." Turning her back to Hal, Henrietta scowled at Gwen. "I'm leaving for the rest of the day. Don't wait up." She smiled, gave a finger wave to Jenna, and rushed out the French door, her heels clicking as she crossed the deck.

Gwen had no intention of waiting up. Nonetheless she felt pleased with her bold new self where Henrietta was concerned. By forcing their meeting here, Gwen would be nearby if disaster struck.

She turned to Hal. "Let's see if we can find your missing phone."

He strolled to the wing chair Henrietta had abandoned and shoved his hand between the tapestry cushions. Within seconds, he yanked his phone free and held it up for Gwen's inspection. "If I used this thing more often, I'd have missed it days ago."

Jenna giggled. "Granddad, you're so helpless."

Gwen envied their close relationship. In the third year of her marriage to Parker, she'd miscarried. A little girl. The doctors advised she was unlikely to become pregnant again.

And she hadn't. A fleeting thought niggled. Had Gwen opened her home studio for private lessons to fill that void? Was her childless status the reason she guarded a soft spot in her heart for Jenna? A surrogate grandmother of sorts?

Reaching over she re-positioned an errant strand of blonde hair behind Jenna's ear. "I have a question for you both. Since my garden tour is Saturday afternoon, can I reschedule your lesson to ten that morning?"

Seeing Jenna's nod, Hal said, "Fine with us."

Jenna moved closer to Gwen. "Can I play with your cat?"

"Of course. Amber has a wicker basket full of toys in the sitting room on the second floor."

Within seconds, Jenna ran up the stairs with Amber in her arms, leaving Gwen and Hal alone for the first time.

"Henrietta was quite a surprise," he commented. "I can't imagine what she wants to tell me about Elizabeth. Or why she thinks she can provide closure."

"I'm the last person who can explain Henrietta. I hope she doesn't cause you any distress."

"I don't know. She sounded genuinely fond of Elizabeth. Why would she want to upset me?"

Inwardly, Gwen cringed. "The Henrietta you witnessed is the polar opposite of the Henrietta I used to know." Gwen managed a half-laugh.

His eyebrows shot up, but he made no comment as he ran his fingers along the smooth surface of the piano. "I think of Elizabeth every time I look into Jenna's face. She's the spitting image of her mother at the same age."

"And she has Elizabeth's calm disposition and generosity, too." Gwen eased down onto the piano bench. "I remember one of my sophomores telling me Elizabeth shared association tricks for remembering the composers we studied."

"That sounds like my Elizabeth. She wasn't her usual easygoing self the day of her accident."

51

Gwen sensed he wanted to talk and met his gaze, seeing both inner strength and vulnerability in his blue eyes. She could relate to his pain.

"I'm a good listener, Hal."

Chapter Eight

Until this moment, Gwen's relationship with Hal had been based solely on her status as a longtime customer at his garden center and now her role as Jenna's music tutor. Was it appropriate for her to become his sounding board? She glanced over to find he wasn't looking at her and studied his face for a moment. She recognized the ache of losing a loved one.

Hal sat down on the wide windowsill and crossed his arms before lifting his eyes to hers. "Are you sure you want to hear my story?"

"I wouldn't have offered if I didn't. Maybe I can help you make sense of what happened. Maybe not."

Laughter drifted down through the balcony opening, indicating that Jenna was preoccupied with Amber and not paying any attention to the adult conversation. Gwen relaxed.

"Well, all right then," Hal said. "Let me give some background first. My dear wife Claire – God rest her soul – fell ill and died the spring before Elizabeth began college classes at Baylics." He retrieved his wallet and removed a photo with worn edges, extending it to Gwen.

She studied the picture and remembered this curly-haired woman with an easy smile and helpful manner at Hal's garden center. With the seasonal employees coming and going over the years, Gwen hadn't noticed when this woman disappeared, and, until this second, hadn't realized she'd been the wife of the owner.

Returning the photo to his open palm, Gwen respected his safeguarding of a treasured photograph, so similar to her own. "I'm sorry to hear about your wife's passing. How did Elizabeth handle it?"

Tucking his wallet away, Hal resumed his resting spot on

the windowsill. "Not well, I'm afraid. In August, she came to me in tears. She was pregnant. Her boyfriend Matthew offered to marry her, but she refused. Said having a child was not a good reason to get married. She wanted to know him better before agreeing to what she considered a life-long commitment."

"Very pragmatic. What advice did you give her?"

"Well, after I got over the shock, I told her I'd support whatever decision she made. She continued to live with me, commuted to college, and gave birth to Jenna that spring."

A crooked grin momentarily brightened Hal's somber face. "I fell in love with Jenna the instant she smiled at me from her hospital crib. Owning my own business gave me the flexibility to take care of her while Elizabeth attended classes. Jenna went with me everywhere. Into the greenhouses, out in the fields, on buying trips."

Gwen remembered the little towheaded girl who ran around the display benches at the Jenkins Garden Center, charming everyone who stopped by to peruse the plant offerings.

"Growing up at your nursery must have been quite an adventure."

"That girl is the center of my life." His smiled a crooked grin. "Anyway, Matthew and Elizabeth dated all through college. He came out to the house as often as he could. Nice kid. I liked Matthew. He was a good father and Jenna adored him. In the spring of their senior year, he and Elizabeth announced they'd get married after graduation."

Hal shifted his weight and looked down at his shoes.

Gwen noticed. "If you don't want to say anymore, I understand."

"It's not that. I've never spoken to anyone about that day. I was an only child. Claire was gone. My best friend had moved overseas the previous winter. I didn't want to burden my foreman or crew."

The pain in his eyes clutched at Gwen's heart. When Parker died, she'd had her sister and a circle of close friends to lean on. Would she have survived without them? A flood of empathy for Hal nearly overwhelmed her.

His voice snapped her to attention.

"The afternoon of Elizabeth's accident," he went on, "I was sitting on my front porch waiting for Jenna to wake up from her nap. Elizabeth barreled into the far end of my lane and stirred up a cloud of dust."

"She was usually a more cautious driver?"

He nodded and crossed his arms. "I'd never seen her drive so recklessly. Matthew's car pulled up seconds later. Elizabeth flew at him, pounded him with her fists, screamed at him." Hal's voice quavered. "I headed down the lane, but I was too far away to understand her words. Neither one of them heard me calling their names. Elizabeth jumped back into her car, and Matthew hopped into the passenger seat. She zigzagged across the field and onto the road."

Hal lifted his head, his focus somewhere beyond Gwen's shoulder. "When I returned to the house, Jenna was still asleep, so I waited on the porch for Elizabeth and Matthew to come back. An hour later, a state patrolman drove up and told me Elizabeth had crashed into a telephone pole out on Route 3. She and Matthew died instantly. I never found out why she was so mad at him."

He turned and faced out the studio window, shoving his hands into his pants pockets. He stood for a moment, gazing above the trees into the afternoon sky.

Gwen spoke to his back. "I'm sorry, Hal."

He turned and sat next to her on the piano bench. "I've always wondered if I'd moved a little quicker, if I would have reached them in time to stop Elizabeth from driving off."

Gwen laid her hand on his knee. "I've had the same thoughts about Parker. If I'd asked him to skip his golf game and work with me in the gardens that day…" She lifted her eyes, startled by the intensity of Hal's gaze so close to her face.

"I guess we'll never know if we could have changed the outcomes, Gwen."

They both sat quietly until Gwen spoke. "How did Jenna react to her parents' deaths?"

Hal managed a half-smile. "She was very brave. For the first few months, she crawled into my lap all the time and we cried together. One day, she begged me for a kitten, and we adopted a rescue from the local shelter. Jenna carried Snowball everywhere, always whispering into the cat's ear. We lost her this spring at the respectable age of twelve."

Gwen raised her eyes to the playful noises tumbling down through the balcony opening and grinned at Hal. "If I'm not being too nosey, how did you end up with custody?"

His shoulders relaxed. "I don't mind telling you. Matthew's parents lived in Michigan. They didn't want to uproot their granddaughter from the only home she'd ever known. We were hoping they'd join us for the competition, but Matthew's dad developed a heart condition and doesn't fly now."

Jenna bounded down the staircase with Amber in her arms, stopping at the mid-way split to smile at them.

Hal's face lit up. "We should be going."

"But we just got here." Jenna came down the remaining steps and released Amber, who bounded toward her food and water bowls at the end of the kitchen island.

Gwen stood up. "Why don't you both have a snack before you go? I have almond poppy cookies from the Sugar 'n Spice." She headed for the kitchen before they could protest.

"How can we refuse?" Hal pushed off the piano bench.

Jenna stood on her tiptoes and kissed his cheek. "Thank you, Granddad."

As they munched on the cookies and drank iced tea, Hal said, "I'm curious why Henrietta is staying with you."

Gwen chose her explanation carefully. "She lives in Vermont, so when the dean suggested her as a replacement judge, she needed a place to sleep." Gwen left out their checkered past, Jenna's late registration, and Jack's blackmail.

The conversation of the threesome shifted to the competition, and Jenna's youthful excitement bubbled like a water fountain. "Do you think I have a chance of winning?"

"You know I do." Gwen twirled the ice in her glass. "And I'm not saying that because I've been coaching you. Any judge will recognize your talent."

Jenna's mouth turned down. "But we don't know how good the others are."

"That's true. All you need to do is perform with the skill and emotion you've shown me all summer. I'm sure you'll wow the judges."

Hal glanced at his watch. "Looks like we've taken up the rest of your afternoon, Gwen. Would you like to join us for dinner? Jenna and I are trying out that new place on the harbor."

Startled by his unexpected invitation, Gwen scrambled for words. "Uh, thanks, but I need to finish a few garden chores while there's enough daylight to see what I'm doing."

He frowned and took a step toward the front door. "Maybe another time then. We'll see you Saturday morning."

Hal's grey Volvo zipped around the village green and disappeared down Harbor Hill toward *The Wharf Restaurant.*

Gwen retreated inside, wondering why in the world she'd balked at his invitation. The few garden chores she had on her list could have waited until the next day. Damn, she should have gone. Nothing wrong with enjoying a nice meal with Hal and Jenna.

Leaning against the oak doors, she gave her reaction some more thought. Was she afraid that Hal would pull her into his personal life? She liked Hal, she really did – as a friend. Gwen wasn't ready to file away her treasured memories of Parker and move on with another man. And she didn't want to give Hal the impression that she was.

She considered his invitation. Was he over-reacting to their discussion about Elizabeth's accident? Was he simply being polite? Or was he developing feelings for Gwen beyond friendship? What if she was reading him all wrong? What if he meant nothing by his dinner invitation?

Best to keep her distance and not provide him the opportunity to express his intentions – whatever they were.

Chapter Nine

On Friday morning, Gwen was sliding oatmeal bread into the
toaster oven when she heard a noise on the staircase. She
turned around and watched Henrietta's slow and tentative
descent. She idly speculated about the woman's malady. Weak
leg muscles? Inner ear problem that affected her balance?

How soon could she find another household willing to host
Henrietta? Until then, Gwen had to remain civil. She called
over, "Did you sleep well?"

Henrietta responded with a poisonous glare. "Do I look like
I slept well?"

Dark shadows and reddish splotches marred her skin.
Henrietta did indeed look like hell.

She wandered over to the island and sat on a stool, peering
at Gwen beneath half-closed lids. "Your guest room door won't
close, and your damn cat kept sneaking in and jumping up on
my bed. I kicked her off every half hour. I hardly slept a wink."

Gwen's breath caught. After a quick survey, she spotted
Amber poised inside the French door, yipping at the chickadees
fluttering around the bird feeder just off the deck. The cat
didn't appear injured by her nighttime maneuvers with
Henrietta. Gwen swallowed her irritation. Jenna's musical
future rested on Henrietta staying in town. "I'll see if I can fix
the door latch."

"Well, it's a good thing I'm not allergic to cats or we'd
really have a problem."

"Yes, we're very lucky."

Henrietta didn't react to Gwen's sarcasm.

"The guest bed is Amber's favorite napping spot. I'm afraid
she considers *you* the intruder."

A loud snort was Henrietta's only reaction.

Now was as good a time as any for the warning. "Henrietta, I'm the final stop for the garden club's tour tomorrow afternoon. I'll also be showing the library and hosting the season's-end garden party." She could only hope Henrietta would make herself scarce.

A smirk replaced Henrietta's frown. "A garden tour *and* a house showing? How mundane. Will my belongings be safe?"

The toaster oven dinged and Gwen turned to remove her oatmeal slices. Henrietta apparently wouldn't be sticking around. Masking her relief, Gwen opened a cabinet door, all the while speaking over her shoulder. "The wardrobe at the top of the stairs has a key."

Her bad mood still intact, Henrietta snapped, "Is that the best you can do?"

Squeezing golden honey from a little bear onto her toast, Gwen fantasized about Henrietta hauling her snakeskin luggage to her black sedan and driving off to another household. Finding a new hostess couldn't happen soon enough.

The musical strains of *I Am Woman, Hear Me Roar* drifted through the balcony opening, and Henrietta waved her hand toward the upstairs guest room. "My cell phone." After pausing on the bottom landing, she pulled herself up each step as if she were climbing a mountain.

Henrietta surely wouldn't complain if Gwen found someone with an extra first floor room.

As Gwen swallowed the last bite of her toast, her own cell phone vibrated on the island counter top. She grabbed it and glanced at the caller ID before speaking. "Mornin', Liz."

"Sorry I didn't call you back sooner. I've been out straight." Liz hesitated. "Can you believe Henrietta Wickham strutted into my store yesterday?"

Glancing up the staircase, Gwen exited through the French door to the upper deck. No sense in Henrietta eavesdropping on their conversation.

"You hung up before I had a chance to tell you she's back in town."

"You knew?" Liz barked into Gwen's ear. "What's that woman doing in Harbor Falls after all these years?"

Gwen flinched. "Henrietta didn't tell you?"

"Nope. Too busy looking down her nose, insulting my displays, my book offerings, even my view of the harbor." Liz's voice held more than a little irritation. "So tell me why she's here."

For the third time, Gwen explained the replacement judge, Jack's threat to disqualify Jenna unless Gwen agreed to host the woman, and her own surprise when Henrietta showed up.

The bang of Liz's fist traveled through the cell phone. "Damn it all! When did she arrive?"

"Yesterday afternoon. She accidentally admitted she suggested staying with me."

"You're kidding."

"Nope. She's as bold as ever, Liz. But listen to this. She wasn't aware of Parker's passing. After I told her about his accident, she mumbled that coming back to Harbor Falls was a mistake. So I moved her into the guest room before she could drive back to Vermont."

"Why didn't you just let her leave?" Liz's tone bordered on incredulous.

"I couldn't do that. She has to fill the judging panel. Jack said that without three judges, the committee might cancel the competition. I can't risk it, for Jenna or the other kids."

"So you have to play nice to keep her in town?"

"That's it in a nutshell. For the moment, at least. But Liz, she's up to something. Jenna and her grandfather stopped over yesterday. Henrietta requested a private chat with him about his daughter Elizabeth."

"Jenna's mother? How nasty of Henrietta to remind him of that poor girl's death."

61

"My reaction, too. Hal's curious, so he agreed to meet with her on Monday."

"Interesting. I've never met Hal. Will he tell you what she says?"

"I guess that depends on what she says."

"Do you need my help with Henrietta?"

"Thanks. I'll survive. As soon as my tours are over, I'll start searching for someone willing to take her off my hands." Gwen paused. "Don't you have a spare bed, Liz?"

"Very funny," Liz snorted. In the background, a printer rumbled. "Sorry, Gwen. I've got a stack of paperwork that needs attention. See you tomorrow for your tour. Bye." The line clicked.

For years, Liz had never missed a local garden tour. Although she admitted her thumb was black rather than green, she admired the floral beauty in gardens that others created.

Gwen went inside, grabbed the fish food and headed out to the small pond. She popped the lid off the tin, shook out the flakes, and watched her five koi drift to the surface to snatch breakfast with their pouty lips.

The moment Gwen snapped the lid shut, she heard a car door slam and turned. A lanky man ambled across the lawn in her direction.

"I apologize for not stoppin' by more often, Gwen, darlin'."

She stretched up and threw her arms around the man's wrinkled neck, planting a loud, sloppy kiss on his clean-shaven cheek. "Ernie Maguire! You old coot."

Parker's attorney and best friend, and the man who had sat vigil with Gwen over Parker's unconscious body, Ernie extended a roundish bundle encased with aluminum foil. "My Fiona baked this for you."

Gwen hadn't realized how much she'd missed Ernie's Irish brogue, undiluted after decades of living in the States. She took the warm package from his large speckled hand, unwrapped

62

one corner and sniffed. "Is this her Irish soda bread? Smells yummy." At his nod, she re-wrapped the foil. "Tell Fiona thanks. I'll fix us a nice cup of tea and we'll have a slice."

"That'll be grand." He surveyed Gwen's riot of flowers. "You've been busy, my girl."

She basked in his unspoken praise. "I worked all summer to get our gardens into shape for Saturday's garden tour. I'm ashamed to admit I let them run wild after Parker died."

He grinned down at her. "I can't believe you did this by yourself. The lawn looks spotless. And your flowers are stunning." He shifted his weight. "I'm too late to help you with the gardening. Is there anything else I can do?"

Gwen raised her hand to block the morning sun. "I do have one problem."

His keen eyes swept over the exterior of the old library. During Parker's ambitious conversion project, Ernie had offered not only design suggestions but sweat equity as well. "Has something happened to this old building?" His bushy eyebrows shot up.

Ignoring Gwen's shouts that nothing had shifted, Ernie headed around the corner to the side yard and disappeared from her sight. She moved onto the upper deck, knowing he'd circle around and rejoin her from the driveway.

Five minutes later, he reappeared, rushed past her, and went in through the French door without comment.

There was little Gwen could do to stop his frantic inspection. She followed him inside and placed the bundle of soda bread on the kitchen counter, then put on the kettle to boil. Out came her cutting board, a serrated knife, and her cast iron teapot.

Moving like a small tornado, Ernie checked the walls for bulging, the mantels for drying wood, and the mortar between the chimney bricks for cracking. He grasped the bookcases in the music studio to test their stability. He examined each window pane, every floorboard. When he finally sat down at the kitchen island, he wore an expression of confusion. "I haven't found anything amiss either outside or on the first floor. Is yer problem upstairs?"

The bang of the guest room door reverberated and heels clicked on the upstairs floor planks. Gwen nearly laughed out loud that Ernie had identified her problem without even knowing it.

"You've hit the nail on the head, Ernie."

A buzz of panic tickled Gwen's neck as Henrietta made her methodical descent, staring at her feet as she moved slowly from one stair tread to the next, clinging to the banister until she reached the halfway split.

Looking up, Henrietta spotted Gwen near the stove. "Not that it's any of your business, but I'm spending time with my uncle today. No idea when I'll be back."

Ernie swiveled and turned toward the voice. "Henrietta Wickham? What in the name of all that's holy are you doin' here?"

Chapter Ten

Ernie's outburst at the sight of Henrietta surprised Gwen. Those two hadn't traveled in the same circles, or so she had assumed.

Henrietta took her sweet time strutting down the remaining steps, her haughty glare never leaving Ernie's face. "I'll have you know I was invited back to judge the music competition."

His posture went rigid. "That might explain why you're in Harbor Falls. It doesn't explain what you're doin' in Gwen's home."

"Not that it's any of your business," Henrietta said, repeating her seemingly favorite phrase and dropping her purse onto the dining room table, "but when those idiots at the music shop couldn't find suitable lodging, I suggested staying with my old colleague Gwen." Henrietta tossed a wicked smile in Gwen's direction, insinuating this was their private joke.

Ernie glowered. "Why in blazes would you propose such a foolish idea?"

The answer flew from Gwen's mouth unbidden. "She thought Parker still lived here."

"You didn't know?" Ernie asked, his expression incredulous.

The cocky grin slid from Henrietta's face. "No, I didn't."

"Don't they deliver the *Harbor Falls Gazette* to Vermont?" Ernie's tone dripped sarcasm.

"They do. I don't subscribe. What happens here means nothing to me now."

"I don't believe you." Ernie shook his shaggy head. "After all the years you chased after Parker, there's no way you stopped carin' just like that."

"What good did my caring do me, Ernie? I tried over and

over to convince Parker I was the better woman for him. He wouldn't listen to reason. He made the biggest mistake of his life when he married *her*." Henrietta's long-taloned finger, re-polished the same bright pink as her silk blouse, swung in an arch and pointed at Gwen.

Gwen gripped the edge of the counter. It wasn't true. Parker had not made a mistake. He rejected Henrietta decades ago. Henrietta still could not grasp the concept that Parker would never have been hers.

The water kettle behind Gwen whistled, giving her an excuse to avoid a confrontation. How many times had she avoided Henrietta in the past? Some things never changed.

Henrietta's strident voice cut the air. "Don't you have something to say, Gwen? I always told Parker you were such a wimp."

"Henrietta!" Ernie roared. "Leave Gwen alone. You'll make me forget my manners."

"Your manners!" Henrietta spat back. "Don't you pretend you're a gentleman."

With each volley, Ernie moved closer to Henrietta. Now only a few feet away, he slammed his fist onto the dining room table, rattling Gwen's porcelain vase of dried flowers. "And don't *you* pretend you're a lady. How many times did I toss your skinny arse out of Parker's office?"

Gwen's head snapped up. What was Ernie talking about? Parker had never mentioned Henrietta stopping by his office. A chill settled. Gwen's hand trembled as she poured the boiling water into the teapot. The scalding liquid hit the wide rim and splashed back. Gwen dropped the kettle and rushed to the sink to run cold water over her reddening skin.

Ernie and Henrietta didn't notice.

Henrietta's arrogant voice lashed out. "Parker only *pretended* he wanted me gone when you stopped by. Think about it, Ernie. You're the only one who ever threw my *'arse'* as you say – skinny or otherwise – out his door. Parker never lifted a finger." She sighed dramatically. "He and I always had such a delightful time together. It's a shame I moved to care for my parents."

Trying to pretend Henrietta's little drama had no effect, Gwen whipped open a drawer and rummaged around for burn salve and gauze, then applied the first aid to her hand.

Wait a minute. What did Henrietta say about the reason she moved to Vermont? To take care of her parents? Gwen remembered donating to an office collection for funeral flowers a few years before Henrietta left town. The woman either lied about their earlier passing, or just now lied about the reason she moved to Vermont. Which version was true?

This scene could have been written for a daytime soap opera, but Gwen wasn't entertained.

She poured the remaining hot water into the teapot and left it to steep. If she let Ernie and Henrietta rant without interruption, there was no telling what other sordid details might come out. Maybe Gwen would even hear the real reason Henrietta high-tailed it out of Harbor Falls. Picking up the serrated knife, Gwen resisted the temptation to fling it at Henrietta and began slicing the soda bread instead.

"Give me a break," Ernie went on. "Parker put up with your pitiful little visits because he felt sorry for you, that's all."

Henrietta stomped her foot. "That's a bunch of hogwash and you know it. Parker found me utterly fascinating."

His expression grim, Ernie took the last few steps and stood within inches of Henrietta. Equal in height, she didn't flinch. They stood eye to eye for several seconds until he spoke in a voice low and ominous. "You should leave. I'm sure your uncle is wondering where you are."

Reaching sideways, Henrietta snatched her purse and bolted for the foyer. She slammed the front door behind her, its echo reverberating throughout the old library.

Ernie's keen eyes focused on Gwen's bandaged hand. "What happened?"

"I spilled boiling water and burned myself."

"Just now? And I didn't notice?"

"You were busy arguing with Henrietta."

"Sorry about that, Gwen. That woman always knew how to push my buttons." He lifted her forearm, inspecting her hand without disturbing her first aid attempts. "Should I take you to the emergency room?"

"No, no. It's not that bad. It'll heal." She pulled from his well-meaning grasp. "Is it true? What Henrietta said?"

"She said a lot of things."

"Don't play games with me, Ernie. Did she visit Parker's office?"

Ernie's face blanched. "He never told you?"

So it was true. A lump caught in Gwen's throat. Henrietta had never given up trying to sink her hooks into Parker. How naïve and stupid Gwen had been.

Without waiting for an answer, Ernie pulled her to his chest, resting his chin on the top of her head, patting her back in a brotherly fashion. "He had no romantic interest in Henrietta and never cheated on you with her."

Gwen shoved him back. "What are you saying? That he cheated on me with women *other* than Henrietta?" Tears of sadness and anger threatened to spill. Gwen forced them back. She had never suspected Parker of being unfaithful. Had her instinct been right or wrong?

The surprise on Ernie's face was tinged with hurt. "Now don't you twist my words. Parker had his faults, like we all do. Bein' unfaithful to you was never one of 'em. Gwen, darlin'. Your marriage with Parker was a good one. The man loved you."

Could Gwen believe Ernie's claim that Parker had been too polite to kick Henrietta out? That he'd simply played along with her little game? That nothing else had happened between them?

Ernie let his arms drop away, strode to the kitchen sink, and began to wash his hands.

Gwen spoke to his back. "How long did this go on? How many weeks, months, or even years did Henrietta chase after Parker?"

Ernie grabbed the towel from the bar at the end of the island, facing Gwen as he dried his hands. His expression was a perfect poker face, no doubt honed from years of practicing law. "You must let this go, Gwen."

Could she do that? Let it go? Was Gwen a fool to believe Parker had loved only her?

Something was still off. There was more to this story. What was Ernie not saying?

"Tell me, Ernie, if nothing was going on, how come you and Parker never mentioned her?"

When Ernie threw the towel at the sink, it landed instead in the bay window and knocked over the pot of fresh mint, spilling dirt everywhere. Gwen flinched. She'd clean it up later.

"You win, Gwen. Parker made me promise not to mention Henrietta when you were around." He lifted his face to the balcony and made the sign of the cross. "Sorry, old buddy." Ernie lowered his gaze. "After your wedding, you told Parker almost every day about Henrietta's snippy remarks. Well, about the time she began to drop by his office, you stopped complaining. Parker thought she wasn't harassing you because he tolerated her visits."

Under other circumstances, Gwen would have found the irony laughable. Parker had kept Henrietta's visits a secret because he thought he was protecting Gwen. And she hadn't told Parker about Henrietta's continued harassment because she didn't want him to think of her as a complainer or a feeble female, a woman who couldn't handle her own problems. If only they'd been more honest with each other, Parker would have sent Henrietta packing next time she darkened his office door. Would Henrietta have given up her harassment? Would Gwen's life have been any different?

She reached over and tucked the slices of soda bread into the foil wrapping, then lifted the steaming teapot from the bamboo tray, carried it to the sink, and dumped its contents.

Ernie's face fell. "What are you doin'?"

"I've lost my appetite."

He cupped her shoulder. "Don't be mad at me. And certainly not Parker. Blame Henrietta." His unruly eyebrows drew close together, nearly touching.

Gwen's shoulders slumped, her energy gone. "I just wish someone had told me back then."

Ernie's face took on the expression of a chastised child. "Do you want me to get rid of her?"

"No need." Gwen didn't dare share her plan to re-locate Henrietta. Ernie might take control, probably with disastrous results.

Now Gwen was keeping a secret. How easy it had been.

Chapter Eleven

Gwen leaned on the counter, her head bowed. "I don't want to talk about this anymore."

Ernie took a step toward her, then seemed to change his mind. "You call if you need my help with Henrietta, or anything else for that matter. I mean it."

After he left, Gwen escaped to her gardens. She barely noticed butterflies sucking nectar from the bee balm's spiky pink heads or the cloud-shadows flickering across the lawn.

Why was she surprised that Henrietta pursued Parker until the day she left town? Could Parker have been involved in Henrietta's unexplained exodus?

Gwen considered her illusion of a perfect marriage. Had Parker kept other secrets? Would another one slap her in the face when she least expected it?

She had to calm down. Losing control of her emotions now would not change the past, and it would make the present that much more difficult.

Working in her flower beds was always therapeutic. Gwen retrieved her wheelbarrow and assorted gardening tools from the potting shed and went to work, waiting for Mother Nature to work her magic. Several hours later, Gwen admired the ever increasing neatness of her plantings and glanced at her watch. Lunchtime had come and gone. No matter, she still had no appetite. A change of scene, though, might just do the trick.

Before she headed into the wooded acres beyond the back yard, Gwen ducked into the potting shed and grabbed a trash bag and extra pair of clippers: the first for removing litter she usually found out there; the other to snip small branches that snagged her hair or clothes as she passed. She skirted the huge field boulder and stepped onto the pathway, instantly surrounded by the rustling leaves of sugar maples, beech trees, and white birches. Her footfalls disturbed leafy castoffs, releasing the sweet aroma of woodsy decay. Gwen breathed deeply, filling her lungs and her spirit with the earthy scent.

About fifty yards in, Gwen approached one of two footbridges Parker had built to span the wide creek. Over the centuries, the water action had carved a gorge twenty feet deep. The sound of water tumbling over rocks delivered the anticipated soothing effect on Gwen's frayed nerves.

She stepped onto the bridge boards, intending to watch the water's journey as it meandered toward the North Street Bridge and the waterwheel of the old gristmill. When she rested her elbows on the footbridge railing, it wiggled, throwing off her balance. She teetered, flashing on an image of taking a nose dive onto the rocks below.

Without thinking, Gwen instinctively flung her upper body backwards. The trash bag flew from her hand and sailed off on the breeze. She lost her grip on the clippers and they nicked her right calf before continuing their flight into the gorge. When she landed hard on her fanny, what had felt like slow-motion sped up to real time. Her lower legs dangled over the edge of the footbridge, her toes pointing down. Dampness from the platform boards seeped into the fabric of her khaki cut-offs. Blood trickled from the gash in her calf.

Gwen's pulse quickened. If she hadn't reacted fast enough, would she be lying at the bottom of the gorge? With broken bones? Or unconscious? Or worse? Who would come looking for her?

Gwen waited until her adrenaline subsided then struggled to her feet. She stepped to the railing and examined the framework. The nails had backed out, leaving a wide gap between the supports. No wonder it had given way under her weight. The footbridge was ten years old. No surprise that some of the lumber had softened with age.

She tested the platform, deeming it safe to cross. Then the local kids who hung out in these woods came to mind. The kids who left empty soda cans and candy wrappers in their wake. She couldn't risk one of those youngsters tumbling through the railing into the gorge. Maybe she should buy some "no trespassing" signs.

Had Alex noticed the condition of this lumber when he took this path through her woods after their duet? She'd have to ask him. And she'd have to come back out here with a hammer and bang those struts back together. Her amateur repair would be a temporary fix until a handyman replaced the timbers. If Parker were still alive, he'd have those railings restored in a few hours.

Worried about the condition of the second footbridge higher on the ridge, Gwen continued along the path at a brisk pace, pausing for a moment at the northern edge of her property. Through the trees she could see the modern new library. At first she was surprised that there were no cars in the parking lot, then she realized it was after two on a Friday. Budget cuts had decreased their hours, so the modern building stood in eerie silence. It occurred to Gwen that if the town officials hadn't built this new library, the village library wouldn't have been abandoned. She and Parker wouldn't have bought it and enjoyed the thrill of living there. Life was simply a game of dominos.

She moved along the path as it curved to the left and delivered her a few minutes later to Parker's second bridge. She grasped both railings, relieved they didn't wiggle. No immediate danger there. Still, to be on the safe side, she'd have this lumber replaced as well.

Completing the loop, Gwen re-entered her backyard and headed inside. In the half-bath, she found a canister of bandages, cleaned the blood from her calf, and applied first aid ointment. Tending to yet another injury was getting tiresome.

Then she descended the steps to the basement, not stopping until she reached the far corner. Switching on the overhead fluorescents in Parker's woodworking shop, she felt a chill. She hadn't ventured past her laundry area into Parker's man cave since he'd died.

As she approached the pegboard of hand tools, she drew in a sharp breath. A birdhouse-in-progress sat atop Parker's workbench. Gwen dropped onto his tall stool, her hand flying to her chest. She pictured him measuring and sawing the lumber, tapping in the nails, painting the colors. Parker had created at least half a dozen of them, each one kept a surprise from Gwen until the final twig perch was attached. His unique birdhouses were scattered around the gardens for a whimsical effect. This one would remain forever unfinished.

Saddened that this birdhouse would never join the others, Gwen struggled to regain her equilibrium as she scanned Parker's menagerie of power tools. Table saw. Drill press. Belt sander. And a few other electrical monsters that escaped her identification.

She had no doubt that Parker would agree another clever carpenter should be using these tools. The longer they lingered in the basement, the sooner they'd become useless. She plucked the blue-handled hammer from its hook, making a mental note to locate used tool dealers.

Upstairs, Gwen made her way toward the French door and noticed Amber napping on a wing chair in the music studio. She paused and called over. "You're staying off the guest bed, I see."

Amber lifted her face and, for a split second, Gwen swore she glimpsed a Cheshire-cat grin.

Hammer in hand, Gwen had no sooner grasped the handle of the French door to head out to the footbridge when the front doorbell chimed. She placed the tool atop her gardening gloves in a wicker basket and hurried to the foyer. She glanced at her watch, taken aback that this would be her Friday afternoon student. Where had the time gone?

Standing on the top step, Claudia blinked rapidly. Her preteen son Kenneth stood one step down, making the tops of their heads the same height. "Is Henrietta here?"

Gwen had been outside for much of the day. She hadn't heard or seen Henrietta since the blowup with Ernie that morning. "I don't think so," she said to Claudia.

Frowning, Claudia turned to her son. "I'll be back after your lesson."

Gwen's head jerked in surprise. This was the first time Claudia hadn't stayed.

If only Claudia would confide in Gwen about her history with Henrietta, the two of them could be partners in misery. However, with Kenneth standing right there, Gwen opted not to ask the question. There would be ample opportunities to approach the subject later.

Kenneth's face frowned. "You're not staying, mom?" He'd soon enter the teenage years when he'd have no desire to spend time with his mother. For now, they were still close.

"Uh, no. I...I've got errands to run." Claudia moved around him and down Gwen's front steps. Moments later, she zoomed off in her SUV.

Gwen headed inside with Kenneth. He ambled toward the music studio on legs that grew longer each week. Not a word was said about his mother's unusual behavior. He repositioned the music stand to a much higher height and unpacked his flute.

Kenneth's playing affected Gwen like chalk screeching across a blackboard. Halfway through his first piece, she reached over and lowered his flute. "If you could choose another instrument, what would it be?"

He studied her through wire rim glasses, his deep brown eyes wide. "I wanna play the cymbals like my friend Todd. He only has to smack 'em together at the right time!"

75

Gwen smothered a laugh. "You've given this some thought."

"Yeah, for a while now." Kenneth nudged his dark hair off his forehead, a useless gesture.

Gwen had grown quite fond of this boy, despite his lack of musical talent. "I can talk to your mom about switching instruments if you want."

His eyes lit up. "Would you? That'd be great, Mrs. Andrews!"

Instead of making Kenneth suffer through his flute lesson, Gwen invited him to tell her about school and sports. He became quite talkative. At the half hour mark, the front doorbell chimed.

Again refusing to enter, Claudia remained on the top step. "Is Kenneth ready?"

When he appeared behind Gwen with flute case in hand, she moved aside. "Let's go, son," Claudia said.

Kenneth glanced back at Gwen, his expression dejected. So much for discussing his instrument switch with his mother.

Claudia paused before dropping into the driver's seat and gazed up at Gwen. "I'll see you around four tomorrow with the tour group."

As the SUV zoomed off, Gwen's curiosity about Claudia's history with Henrietta was heightened even further.

Gwen retrieved the blue-handled hammer from the wicker basket and exited to the rear deck, only then realizing it was too late to be wandering around in the woods where it would be much darker beneath the trees. She'd have to take care of that repair first thing in the morning.

Daylight morphed into dusk, the floral colors fading with each second that passed. Gwen's critical eye surveyed her property. With her final afternoon efforts, on top of her sweat and tears for the past few months, her gardens appeared more than ready for tomorrow's tour.

Retreating inside, Gwen was suddenly ravenous. She opened the fridge door, surveyed the paltry contents, and slammed it shut. The cupboard offered canned soup, chili with beans, and ravioli. She needed to pay more attention to her diet. Gwen grabbed chicken and rice soup and heated it in the microwave. Along with a piece of buttered bread, the meal sufficed.

When she climbed the staircase to the second floor sitting room, Amber followed on her heels and hopped onto a window seat. The cat yipped at the birds winging their way from the feeders to their woodland perches for the night.

Gwen eased into her overstuffed reading chair snugged against the balcony, toed off her sneakers, and curled her feet beneath her. On the side table, two paperbacks awaited her attention. The first was the latest Carolyn G. Hart mystery in the *Death on Demand* series, which Gwen hadn't yet begun. The other was a torrid romance from a first-time author, the pages already dog-eared. Gwen picked up the latter. When she found herself re-reading page fifty-seven for the third time, she inserted the tasseled bookmark and returned it to the table.

Restless, she un-tucked herself from the chair and walked to the bank of windows. As darkness descended, the landscape lights blinked on one at a time.

Gwen's eye caught a movement at the edge of the woods. Someone was walking in the shadows. With the waning light, Gwen couldn't tell if it was a man or a woman.

She wasn't concerned. Visitors to Harbor Falls had often meandered onto the grounds, thinking the village library was public property. All Gwen had to do was go outside and tell the person that the building was now a private home. She slipped her feet into her sneakers and hurried downstairs.

By the time Gwen flipped on the flood light and exited to the rear deck, the visitor had vanished.

Chapter Twelve

In the morning, before heading downstairs, Gwen walked to the sitting room and peered out the windows, hoping last night's wanderer hadn't strayed into the woods or anywhere near the footbridge with the wobbly railing. It was odd that he, or she, had stayed in the shadows. A casual visitor would meander freely through what they believed to be a public garden. Was Gwen fabricating menace where it didn't exist?

Dismissing her highly active imagination, Gwen descended the stairs. Her hopes for a solitary breakfast evaporated at the sight of Henrietta standing at the kitchen sink, gazing out the bay window. The bright gold of her blouse, although a perfect color for the cheerful sunflowers nodding in a vase on the bay window, was not the most flattering color against Henrietta's pink skin tone.

And why wasn't the woman sleeping late? She'd snuck in well past midnight, when the snick of the front door latch woke Gwen from a light slumber.

Henrietta whipped around, deep brown liquid flying from her mug, splattering the cabinets, the countertop, the tiled floor. "You startled me!" she shouted, glaring at Gwen before grabbing a handful of paper towels and gesturing toward the coffee maker. "I couldn't wait for you any longer, so I brewed a pot."

Gwen ignored the dig. It was barely seven o'clock. She poured herself a cup of Henrietta's coffee and risked a sip. The dark goo approached espresso. She lowered her mug to the counter, unsure if she'd survive another swallow. "You came in late last night, Henrietta. I didn't think you'd be up this early."

After tossing the coffee-soaked towels into the trash can, Henrietta focused on Gwen. "You were still awake? I thought you went to bed with the sunset."

How many more digs had Henrietta stowed in her repertoire? Still, this latest zing didn't carry much of a punch. With Parker no longer an issue, was Henrietta's anger fading?

Gwen opted to remain polite. "Did you have a nice visit with your uncle yesterday?"

Henrietta poured a replacement cup of the lethal brew. "Uncle John invited some relatives for a gathering."

Gwen's spirits lifted. Maybe one of them would invite Henrietta into their home for the rest of the week. "Seeing any of them again?"

The hint of a smile twisted Henrietta's lips. "I'll be with my cousin Mary today."

Tamping down a whoop of joy that Cousin Mary was taking Henrietta away on tour day, Gwen crossed her fingers that the idea of hosting Henrietta would occur to Mary.

The lyrics of *I Am Woman* blasted the air. Henrietta reached over to a stool and pulled her cell phone from her purse, glancing at the caller ID before answering.

Gwen measured oatmeal and dried cranberries into a bowl, then added filtered water before sliding it into the microwave. Although the glass tray clattered as it rotated for two minutes, she could still clearly hear Henrietta's side of the exchange.

The woman's strident voice became more clipped as the conversation progressed. "I don't know why that's necessary." A pause. "I'm leaving for the day." Another pause. "I'll let you know later." Henrietta snapped the phone closed.

Was that cryptic call about the competition? Gwen was curious. "Is there a problem?"

Henrietta raised one perfectly-shaped eyebrow. "You listened to my conversation?"

"You were standing right next to me. How could I have missed it?"

"If you must know, I'm second-guessing the wisdom of returning to Harbor Falls."

Gwen panicked. "But you're judging the competition next weekend."

"Don't get bent out of shape, Gwen. I have no intention of leaving before I fulfill my contract. Besides, didn't I tell you I need to ease my conscience and set a few things straight?"

"You did say that. But you didn't explain what you mean."

Henrietta hesitated. "I'll tell you this one thing. That was one of the more irritating people on my list."

"Your list?"

"Yes, my list. Don't poke your nose into my private business."

Henrietta's flip-flopping between sharing information and then holding back was giving Gwen a headache. Just when she expected Henrietta to transform into a tolerable guest, the woman resumed her arrogant attitude.

Putting a hold on her raging curiosity about the list, Gwen withdrew a writing tablet and pencil from an island drawer and jotted down her house and cell numbers. "We should exchange phone numbers while you're in town."

When Henrietta slid her hand into the pocket of her navy slacks, Gwen expected her to pull out a personal card with the requested numbers. Instead, Henrietta's fingers gripped a tissue, blotted her nose, and tucked the used tissue back into her pocket. "Don't bother. I'll have no need to call you. What time is your little tour this afternoon?"

Gwen clenched her jaw muscles. "Around four."

Henrietta harrumphed. "In that case, I'll be back before the riffraff starts wandering around this old place. I'll be changing my outfit before I drive into Boston tonight." She glanced at her designer watch, the face glittering with what appeared to be diamond chips. "Right now, I'm driving to the harbor to meet my cousin for breakfast."

"Why don't you walk? The morning air is refreshing and the harbor's not far."

"And get all sweaty?" Henrietta snorted. "Besides, I have to stop at the pharmacy and refill a prescription." She hefted her purse to her shoulder and disappeared through the French door.

Did the woman ever tire of her own prickliness? And what was that about a prescription? Maybe something for her allergies?

With a shake of her head, Gwen pushed aside her fruitless analysis of Henrietta and became a whirling dervish. With dust cloth and furniture polish in hand, Gwen made the rounds, both upstairs and down, making sure every surface gleamed. She hauled out the vacuum cleaner to suck up Amber's daily cat hair contribution from the hardwood floors and area rugs.

Amber herself, not a fan of loud noises, escaped to the basement, biding her time until her mistress returned the evil machine to its lair.

What Gwen wouldn't give to have the option of hiding until Henrietta left town.

Chapter Thirteen

Within seconds of Gwen storing the vacuum, Hal and Jenna arrived for the rescheduled lesson. Hal settled into his usual wing chair at the fireplace and listened as Gwen and Jenna worked on various sections of the four competition arrangements.

When the hour was up, Gwen smiled at Jenna. "The judges are going to love you."

A pale pink glow suffused the girl's youthful skin as a worried expression settled on her face. "I don't know, Mrs. Andrews. I'm getting a little nervous."

"Nervous is good, Jenna." Gwen opened her lesson planner and ran her finger down the page. "My sister Tess is driving over on Thursday. She's looking forward to accompanying you on the piano for the competition."

Jenna collected her sheet music. "I can't wait to meet her."

Gwen smiled at the teenager. "And don't forget our extra rehearsal this Friday."

"That's right." Hal's blue eyes studied Gwen's face before turning to Jenna. "You'll need a note for your teachers so they'll excuse you for the day."

Holding her pencil aloft, Gwen said, "I have a request, but only if it's okay with you, Hal."

"What's that?" he asked.

"I have no doubt that Jenna practices at home every day after school." Gwen winked at Jenna. "But next week, I'd like her to practice here with me instead."

"I'm okay with that," Hal said, his head turning toward Jenna. "Do you have the same last class every day? I can pick you up."

Jenna shook her blonde head while she packed away her flute. "No need, Granddad. The high school isn't far. I'll walk."

She turned admiring eyes to Gwen. "I should be here around four."

Though Hal didn't look comfortable with Jenna's plan to walk, he said nothing. "Then I'll drive into town at five and pick you up."

He refocused on Gwen. "We'd better go. Have fun with your tours this afternoon."

Jenna headed out. When Hal passed Gwen, he bent down and kissed her cheek.

If the man had slapped her, Gwen couldn't have been more surprised. Before she could react, the front door closed behind grandfather and granddaughter. First, Hal's invitation to dinner the other night, and now a kiss on her cheek. Both seemingly innocent enough. Or were they?

Gwen chided herself to stop reading romance novels and stick to mysteries.

***

The moment Gwen finished her lunch, the house phone rang.

"Gwen?" asked a female voice.

"Yes. Who is this?"

The woman laughed. "It's Emily, silly."

"You know, Emily, I don't believe we've ever spoken on the phone. It changes people's voices. Sorry, I didn't recognize you."

"No need to apologize." Emily cleared her throat. "I called to ask if you're surviving Henrietta's visit. Jack told me the whole story. He was worried Henrietta would drive back to Vermont and leave the competition one judge short. You know, the dean was counting on Jack to handle the lodging arrangements. Thank God you stepped up and donated your guestroom."

Stepped up? Donated my guestroom? That was some story Jack had fed to his wife. He'd convinced Emily that Gwen volunteered to host Henrietta. "That doesn't explain why you and Jack aren't willing to take Henrietta off my hands."

Emily didn't respond. The silence hung between them, and Gwen finally glanced at her watch. The garden club members would arrive any minute to prepare the party food. "Emily, I've gotta go. Garden tour today, you know."

"Oh, that's right, Gwen. Sorry I can't come. Saturdays are too busy at the store. Will Henrietta be there?"

Why did Emily care? "I doubt it. She's off somewhere with her cousin until later this afternoon. Listen, I have to go."

"Oh, all right. Bye."

Gwen tried to wrap her mind around a second awkward conversation with Emily in so many days. After being so upset with Jack the day Henrietta arrived, Emily was now defending his underhanded manipulation. Those two were quite the pair.

A few seconds later, Gwen heard car doors slam in her driveway, followed by footsteps along her rear deck. She rushed to the French door and held it open while six chattering women, arms laden with grocery bags, traipsed into her kitchen. Covering every surface with ingredients, they proceeded to make fillings for finger sandwiches, salads, and desserts.

Gwen's offer to help was soundly rejected, so she went outside. Splendid day for a garden tour. The blue September sky offered plentiful sunshine. The slanted rays backlit the translucent flower petals, emphasizing their delicate beauty. The windows of the old library reflected Gwen's floral panoramas like a series of Thomas Kinkade paintings. Picture perfect.

Gwen wandered the gardens, pinching off crimson coneflowers that had drooped during the night. She yanked newly-sprouted black mustard weed and witch grass. When she smoothed the cedar mulch over the disturbed soil, its pungent tang filled the air. Aromatherapy at its best.

The stark difference between the shambles she'd finally noticed at the beginning of the summer and these stunning gardens was mind-boggling. Her benign neglect during the two summers since Parker's death had invited chaos. Rampant vines had twined around his wooden structures. Stinging nettles choked the flower beds. Beastly dandelions confiscated the once-verdant lawn. Gwen's pride had surfaced and she'd vowed to bring the gardens back to their former glory. Signing up for the September tour had provided the extra incentive she'd needed to keep at it, despite her daily exhaustion.

Now, as Gwen rounded the corner to the front yard, the chime of the floor clock in the foyer struck four times and floated to her ears through the open door. Again, the time had gotten away from her. The tour bus would be pulling up any minute.

She rushed inside to the smell of baking brownies, which masked any lingering odor of Henrietta's potent morning coffee. Gwen topped off her oil diffusers and flipped the sticks, adding a subtle spiciness to the mix.

She scooted upstairs and changed into the tour day outfit of beige khakis and a pale green tee-shirt emblazoned with a print of Picasso's *Flowers in Hand*. After adding a pair of floral earrings, she slipped her feet into her most comfortable pair of canvas shoes and caught a glimpse of herself in the mirror behind her bedroom door. Not bad for sixty-three. She touched her cheek where Hal had kissed her that morning and wondered again what, if anything, he'd meant by his gesture.

She circled the second floor, making sure everything was still tidy. Peeking into the guest room, she spotted a hand-painted silk blouse in bold colors and translucent black harem pants arranged on the bed. Spiked black heels rested on the tapestry area rug. Jewelry of bright beads interspersed with silver glittered on the bedside table.

Gwen glanced at her watch. Ten minutes past four.

Henrietta should have come and gone by now. She'd been adamant about avoiding the *riffraff* of the tour group. Gwen could only hope Henrietta would be so rushed when she returned to change her clothes that she wouldn't have a chance to make a scene and embarrass Gwen.

Out the guest room window, Gwen caught sight of Liz's husband, Tony, crossing the village green and hurried downstairs to greet him. He met her on the front sidewalk, snappy in black slacks and a red golf shirt. The sun glinted off silver streaks surfacing in his pale blonde hair. "Hi, Gwen! Where do you want your bartender?"

"You're early." Gwen hugged him, inhaling his musky cologne. "Thanks for helping out."

He squeezed her tight before letting go. "My pleasure."

"Would you mind putting ice in the coolers and carrying the beverages to the arbor? Just ask any of the ladies in my kitchen. They'll point you in the right direction."

"Sure thing." Tony sauntered up the granite steps to the front door.

Seconds later, whoops of laughter emanated from inside. Tony flirted with every woman, regardless of age or availability.

Gwen turned at the sound of Mr. Bascom's bus pulling to a stop at the front curb. Claudia stepped off first, followed by twenty-five or so chattering women and a handful of men. Betty and Bob's van parked behind, delivering the seven garden owners and a few spouses from the previous properties.

Claudia hurried to Gwen's side, speaking in low tones. "Is Henrietta here?"

"No. Off somewhere with a cousin." Gwen opted not to mention that Henrietta was due back any minute for a change of outfit.

"Good," Claudia commented with a bob of her head. "I'd hate for her to embarrass you."

Gwen knew that couldn't be the real reason. But now was not the time to pursue it.

"Today's weather is perfect," Claudia continued. "The forecasters were dead on."

Claudia patted Gwen's arm and moved away to organize the tour group on the front sidewalk. Gwen used the time to find Betty Owens. "I need a favor, if you don't mind."

"Sure, Gwen. What is it?"

"When I bring the group inside for the house showing, would you follow behind them? Not that I expect any sticky fingers, but these days, a person can't be too careful."

Betty patted Gwen's arm. "Not a problem. I'll keep my eye on everyone."

Gwen relaxed. "Thanks."

The last thing Gwen needed was for Henrietta's precious possessions to go missing.

Chapter Fourteen

Linking her arm with Gwen's, Claudia pulled them both up the seven granite steps, artfully decorated with orange pumpkins and purple cabbages. Each of the wrought iron flower boxes beneath the front windows were planted with trailing red geraniums. The combination provided a cheerful tableau.

Claudia clapped her hands. "Welcome to the final stop on our September Garden Tour. This is Gwen Andrews, the owner of the old village library."

Stepping forward, Gwen scanned the crowd. She recognized neighbors, colleagues from Baylies, and club members. There were a few strangers, and some faces were hidden from her scrutiny. At the back of the crowd, Liz's fiery red hair popped up next to Hal's salt and pepper crop. Why hadn't he mentioned this morning that he'd be on the tour?

Pushing her curiosity aside, Gwen raised her voice. "Good afternoon, everyone. Let's begin the garden tour on the west side and work our way around." She lifted her hand in a "follow me" motion, identifying an American smoke tree and Chinese dogwood as they made their way through the front yard. Rose of Sharon bloomed between the tall windows on the side.

After dodging between the cars of the food committee parked in the driveway, Gwen stopped beneath a grove of spiraling green spikes. "We planted this bamboo as a boundary marker when we moved in ten years ago."

An elderly man with a few wisps of hair around his ears tapped her shoulder. "I've heard bamboo can be invasive."

Like some houseguests, Gwen thought.

"That's true," she commented. "I break off new shoots when they jump over the barrier."

At the wrought iron fence along the front sidewalk, Gwen

reached into a cluster of pink and red roses, holding up several bright scarlet spheres. "These rosehips make a healthy tea."

Tucking the fruit into her pocket for a later cup, Gwen stole a glance along the cobblestoned street of Library Lane. No black sedan. No Henrietta. Where was the woman?

On the eastern side of the library, Gwen stopped beside four raised beds – a five-sided star, a square, a circle, and a rectangle – planted with black-eyed Susans, deep red dahlias, purple asters, and Nippon daisies. Bees swarmed from one flower to the next. "My husband Parker built these whimsical beds as a joke."

Gwen approached the center of the sunny lawn and paused near three maple trees. Pots of bright orange and white mums peeked out from the sweet woodruff groundcover. Along North Street, seven majestic white birch trees, each hung with a basket of burgundy and yellow mums, marked the property line.

It wasn't until she turned the group to walk along the tree line toward the backyard that she realized she'd forgotten all about her repair. She positioned herself between the ticket holders and the path that led to the unstable footbridge to discourage any adventurous types.

When a commotion erupted behind the group, Gwen glanced back to see Hal berating a man with a pair of scissors in one hand and perennial clippings in the other. When Hal's glance found Gwen, she gave him the universal okay sign with thumb and forefinger, along with a smile.

The plant-stealing man fled, a short woman trailing behind him, her head down, her tiny steps working to keep up. In the wake of their hasty retreat, Gwen once again surveyed the parking spots around the village green. Still no black sedan. Still no Henrietta.

Damn that woman for distracting me on tour day.

Chapter Fifteen

When everyone arrived in Gwen's backyard, she called out, "This is the last section of my garden tour. Please explore all these flower beds. Every plant is labeled. I'll wander among you and answer your questions."

As the crowd dispersed in different directions, Gwen looked around until she spotted Hal. She wandered toward him, smiling. "Why didn't you tell me you'd be on the garden tour?"

"Guess I should have mentioned that I take this tour every year. I like to see what plants succeed in the local gardens. It helps me plan which species to offer in my store." He tucked a notebook and pencil into his pocket.

"You made notes about my plants?"

"Of course. I've only seen your gardens from the music studio window on Saturdays." He paused and glanced around. "I have to congratulate you, Gwen. Your grasses, perennials, and annuals are all thriving. I like the whimsy of the birdbaths and birdhouses. And where did you find those unusual tree roots?"

"Parker and I used to hunt for them at construction sites."

The memory of those happy jaunts with Parker made Gwen feel guilty about enjoying this time with Hal. She shook her head. Nothing wrong with talking to people.

She guided Hal to the beds fronting the potting shed at the edge of the woods, where copper-colored Helenium, the flower that most likely made Henrietta sneeze, bobbed in the afternoon breeze. Beside her small fish pond near the lower deck, Hal said, "These ferns and hostas are perfect for this shady area." He pulled out his notebook and jotted down the botanical details from Gwen's detailed labels. She noticed the tour group no longer wandered the flower beds but stood talking in small groups.

"Excuse me, Hal. Time for the house tour." Gwen walked across the lower deck, onto the upper deck, clapped her hands, and waited for the faces to turn in her direction. "It's time to walk you through the converted library. I'll take the first twenty and be back for the second group in about fifteen minutes."

Careful not to knock over the pots of purple verbena flanking the French door, Gwen counted heads as each person moved inside. Claudia led the way at number one, whispering as she passed, "Nice job. Your gardens are spectacular."

Gwen kept counting until she reached Hal at number nineteen. He only smiled at her. Number twenty was Liz. She pointed at Hal's back and winked. "He's a sweet man."

It didn't take long for Gwen to recognize what her old friend was up to. Over the summer, Liz had turned matchmaker, undaunted that Gwen refused every blind date. If nothing else, the men Liz presented provided Gwen with a source of amusement. And now Liz seemed to view Hal as her next project.

Following Liz inside, Gwen returned to tour guide mode and made her way to the front of the group. She stopped in front of a trio of potted weeping fig trees that filled the space between the staircase above and the chimney wall to her right. She cocked her head, straining to hear noises upstairs. Henrietta could have snuck in the front door while Gwen was giving the garden tour. Hearing nothing, she assumed the woman had come and gone.

"Welcome to the old village library. Ten years ago, my late husband and I bought this abandoned building from Baylies College and converted it into our home. Parker was a talented architect and designed the living spaces I'm about to show you."

A willowy brunette wearing an *I Visited Harbor Falls* tee-shirt raised her hand.

Gwen nodded in the young woman's direction. "You have a question?"

The brunette's face melted into a wistful look. "I just wanted to tell everyone that my mother brought me to the children's stacks every week when I was a kid. Being here takes me back."

Gwen smiled at her. "I'm sure a lot of residents have similar memories. When I first moved to Harbor Falls and met my future husband, this is where Parker brought me for our first date."

The women smiled. The men looked down at their shoes.

It took Gwen a second to remember where she'd left off. "Okay, let's move on. Parker designed the open floorplan around this staircase," she waved behind her, "and the original double-sided fireplace." She indicated the brick chimney to her left. "What I want to highlight is Parker's mezzanine honoring the traditional library." She pointed up. All eyes followed her finger and the group gasped at the balcony above their heads. "The opening measures twenty feet wide by fifteen feet deep. The staircase splits front-to-back at the halfway point. Steel girders support the weight of the upstairs. The chimney is exposed until it exits through the cathedral roof." Shadows played within the dark exposed beams of the slanted roofline high above their heads.

"How positively gothic," one man said, his eyes widening. The rest of the group appeared mesmerized. Warmth spread through Gwen's mid-section, her pride in Parker's architectural cleverness nearly overwhelming. How fortunate she was to live in such a special space.

After a minute, the group moved as one into the music studio where a dainty woman stroked Gwen's Steinway. "What a beautiful piano."

Gwen smiled and pressed several keys, sending a melodic chord of notes into the air. "On the day we moved in, my husband surprised me with this antique baby grand to replace my old upright. He said it was more appropriate for this space, and made this an authentic music studio."

"Have you played your entire life?" she added.

"Our mother signed us up for lessons when I was eight, but my older sister Tess is the real pianist in the family. She used to win competitions in college. I still play for the purpose of teaching, but I prefer my flute."

"So you give lessons?"

"I do," Gwen answered, pleased with the question. "Mostly to the younger folks in the area, but I wouldn't turn away a budding musician of any age."

With a wistful expression, the woman smiled and melted into the crowd.

Returning her thoughts to the tour, Gwen waved toward the rear and side walls of the studio. "We preserved the character of the village library by salvaging these floor-to-ceiling bookcases." The shelves, tucked between the tall mullioned windows, were filled with music books and novels bookended with busts of composers and cat statues.

She moved around the Steinway until she stood between the wing chairs flanking the fireplace. In the firebox, a bevy of battery candles flickered between clouds of dried flowers. "This is the double-sided fireplace we retained from the original library. Come and see the other side in the living room." The group followed her around the far end of the chimney wall.

What would Parker have thought about this house tour? Would he have enjoyed showing off his creative talents or considered these people an intrusion? They had never discussed the possibility of offering a tour, so Gwen had no idea.

She pushed her concern aside and stopped at the living room hearth where the glow of the candles softened the fire-blackened bricks inside. She waited for the men and women to arrange themselves among the leather sofa and loveseat, the coffee table and Parker's recliner.

"So here we have the other side of the double-sided fireplace. It's cozy on a chilly winter night when the snow is falling and the wind is howling."

A pony-tailed man raised his hand. "How'd you install the flat TV above the mantel?"

Gwen grinned at the memory of Parker's curses as he struggled with the project. "My husband snaked the wires between the firebox and the bricks, then down into the basement before connecting to the cable service."

The man stroked his bearded chin, his face animated with the same do-it-yourself gleam Gwen had seen in Parker's eyes so many times.

Claudia pointed toward the end wall. "Gwen, what's that painting?"

Gwen turned. "Oh, that's a reproduction of Renoir's *Two Girls Drawing*. It made me think of me and my sister when we were children. Without the hats, of course." The comment brought a chuckle from the women.

Before taking them into the dining room, Gwen suggested they peek through the front windows for a view of the village green. As she led them past the foyer entrance, she noticed a kaleidoscope of colors dancing on the tiled floor, the result of the late afternoon sun slipping through the stained-glass windows of the western panels.

Parker's photograph on the slender table seemed to be watching her. No, that couldn't be. It must be a trick of the shimmering light. She'd read of paintings that followed a person's movement across a room, though she'd never seen one up close. She stared at Parker's face, waiting for the sensation to repeat. Nothing. Parker was frozen in time during that beach walk.

"Are you all right, Gwen?"

Liz's voice startled her. "Oh, sorry. Yes, I'm fine. Let's keep moving." Gwen forced herself to enter the dining room area where she pointed to the wide floorboards.

"Parker had to sand these wide planks several times until they reached an even walking surface." The few men snorted, including Hal, apparently familiar with warped lumber.

At the far end of the dining room table, she stroked its polished surface. "These burl maple pieces were crafted for my great grandmother the same year this library was built, in 1887. The hutch," she indicated the huge piece centered between the two front windows, "holds my good china and crystal. They don't make furniture like that nowadays."

Several women peered through the glass panels. Gwen overheard snatches of their conversations. "That would never fit in my tiny house," and, "How beautiful."

While Gwen waited for everyone to finish their explorations, her mind wandered back to Parker's photograph in the foyer. The sensation that he'd been watching her remained, and she shivered. She'd have to research the phenomenon. Maybe that would ease her mind.

She glanced over toward the kitchen where the club women were plating the party food. "Let's head upstairs now." She mounted the staircase directly from the dining room.

She walked up backwards to maintain eye contact, climbed to the half-way split, and blocked the steps leading right. The group ascended two and three abreast, their hands running along the smooth maple banister. Once they reached the upper landing, several of them leaned over the balcony, peering down into the first floor below. Though no one had ever fallen, the sight made Gwen's heartrate jump.

"There's a breath-taking view of the harbor from these windows," she called over their heads. The balcony-leaners migrated away from the railing, easing her tension.

95

At the door of the guest suite, Gwen stopped. "Someone is staying here this week. If you'll walk through the guest bathroom and out the opposite door, you'll find yourselves in the sitting room along the back of the library."

When she walked into the room, Gwen was surprised to see Henrietta's outfit still lying on the comforter. She tossed a quick glance at the bedside clock. Ten past five. The woman was more than an hour late. Any number of reasons would explain. Henrietta might be enjoying her time with her cousin and simply running late. Or perhaps she'd driven to Boston in the clothes she was wearing. Or skipped the show entirely.

Standing beside the bed, Gwen guarded Henrietta's outfit like a sentinel. When Liz passed through, she smirked at the outfit then gave Gwen a lop-sided evil eye.

Coming in last, Betty Owens whispered, "So far, so good, Gwen. No sticky fingers."

"Thanks, Betty," Gwen murmured.

Gwen glanced at Henrietta's ensemble once more before following Betty through the guest bathroom and into the elongated sitting room, its windows running the length of the back wall. Liz stroked the upholstery of Gwen's reading chair near the chimney. Several of the women sat on the wide sill cushions; one man had eased into a rocking chair. The others wandered among the multiple seating areas. Hal stood at the windows, gazing down at the decks, the fish pond, and the rear gardens.

Gwen hated to disturb their respite. However, the other half were waiting for their tour. She called the group to follow her through her personal bathroom and into her own bedroom in the deeper front gable. A subtle floral print papered her walls. The angled ceiling soared upwards along the sloping roofline. A fan whirled high above. While they moved through and out, Gwen eased to the window at the head of her king-sized bed and glanced around Library Lane.

No black sedan. No Henrietta. *Forget about her. She'll return when she'd good and ready.*

At the top of the staircase, Gwen paused. "This concludes the tour of the old village library. Please hold onto the handrail as you go down, and go out to the backyard. The garden party will begin after I bring out the second group."

She jumped when arms wrapped around her from behind. Liz laughed. "Congrats, Gwen! You're the best tour guide!"

Hal came up beside them. "She's right, Gwen. I've never seen your entire home. Very impressive."

Liz reached over and grabbed Hal's hand. "Come on, Hal. Let's get in line."

Gwen stared after her oldest friend and her newest. How long would it take Liz to begin her match-making efforts?

Being tired and hungry, the second half of the tour group had fewer questions. Gwen hustled them through the house and out to the backyard in record time.

In the kitchen, Gwen hefted the last tray and carried it to the buffet tables arranged on the lower deck. She snagged a chicken salad sandwich, one creamy pesto pinwheel, and a skewer of grape tomatoes alternated with chunks of mozzarella.

Wiping her fingers with a colorful paper napkin, she heard the rumble of thunder. A moment later, she blamed the noise on a delivery truck bouncing along North Street on the far side of the village green.

Liz popped up at Gwen's elbow, sans Hal, and pointed at Tony, who was smiling widely to a bottle blonde as he served her lemonade. "My husband makes one good-lookin' bartender, don't ya think?" Winking at Gwen, Liz strolled toward the arbor.

How did Liz and Tony manage to stay together? He flirted with every woman he met, and Liz sidled up to men she didn't know without a second thought. They must have agreed on an invisible line that neither of them would cross.

"Your gardens are delightful, Gwen."

Gwen turned to see Betty Owens, her smile wide. "We were thrilled to see what you and Parker did with the old library. Are you joining Bob and me for the reverse tour tomorrow? We're leaving from our B&B at ten."

After Gwen's constant labor, she looked forward to viewing the gardens others had created. "I'm planning to, Betty."

A rising breeze flipped several napkins from the buffet table, danced them across the deck and out onto the lawn. The afternoon sun no longer cast shadows in the flower beds.

Overhead, ominous clouds approached from the west.

Damn! It's not supposed to rain until tomorrow.

Chapter Sixteen

A tug on Gwen's sleeve made her forget about the darkening sky. She turned to see the smiling face of Rachel Cooper, a former colleague from the Baylies' business offices. Before Gwen could offer a greeting, Rachel smothered her in a bear hug.

Gwen stepped away to catch her breath. "Rachel, how come I didn't see you before now?"

"Simple. You were busy with your other guests."

"It's so good to see you!"

Rachel pushed Gwen to arm's length. "Is it true Henrietta's staying with you?"

"I'm afraid so." Gwen paused. "I didn't realize you knew her."

"I didn't. She never paid much attention to a lowly file clerk like me. Whenever she came into the offices, she gave someone a hard time about something." Rachel rolled her eyes. "The stories people used to tell!"

Of course, Gwen knew all about those stories; she had lived them. Henrietta's return, however brief, had resurrected the agony of the *good old days*.

"I've been wondering about the real reason she moved to Vermont," Gwen murmured. She wasn't buying Henrietta's claim that she relocated to take care of her parents.

Rachel said, "Hey! I just remembered something. The day before she left, I overheard her arguing with someone."

Gwen's ears perked up. Her tongue seemed tied in knots. "You did? Who was it?"

Rachel eyed several people standing nearby and leaned closer to Gwen's ear. "I didn't know the man's voice. But I recognized Henrietta's haughty way of talking."

"Why haven't I heard about this before?"

"Well," Rachel stumbled, "because I never told anyone. She left the next day and I forgot all about her. It only occurred to me just now because she's staying here."

"She's only sleeping in my guest room until I can find other accommodations," Gwen countered. "How about you, Rachel? Would you like to host a former Baylies professor?"

Before Rachel could commit one way or the other, the sky darkened and heavy, cold raindrops pummeled their heads.

Mr. Bascom yelled, "To the bus, folks!" and began his sprint around the corner of the library toward the front curb. Covering their heads with napkins and paper plates, the men and women followed him helter-skelter.

"Holy Mackerel!" Rachel yelled above the ruckus. "Guess I'd better go! Let's do lunch next week." She lumbered toward the end of the deck, holding her purse above her head in a useless attempt to divert the downpour. At the bottom of the steps, she put pinkie and thumb against her head, mouthing, "Call me," and vanished from Gwen's sight.

The crowd disappeared in an instant. She dashed under the awning on the deck, undecided if she was sad or glad to be alone.

Pounding footsteps announced someone running her way. Hal hopped up the deck steps from the driveway and ran toward her. She stretched out her hand to prevent him from knocking her over. "I thought everyone headed for the bus?"

"It'll take more than a little rain to chase me away, Gwen."

He gazed up into the roiling black clouds. "Is it okay if I hang here until the storm plays out?" When she nodded her assent, he moved to the far end of the awning.

Tony and Liz bounded up from the lower deck, their hair dripping. "Hey, Gwen. We decided to stay, if that's okay." They shook their heads, flinging water droplets like a pair of dogs.

"Glad to have you," Gwen said. "Hal's here, too." She pointed toward him and he waved.

Behind Gwen, the French door opened. "I have to say, Gwen, that was one clever way to end tour day."

Gwen turned toward the voice. "Claudia, you didn't leave with the rest?"

Claudia stretched her hand out, letting the rain dampen her palm. "I sent the food committee home. Thought I'd stay and help tidy up your kitchen."

"You didn't have to do that, but thanks." Gwen paused. "Actually, this is perfect. There's something I need to discuss with you." Gwen glanced over at Hal, Liz, and Tony, all chattering like squirrels at the far end of the deck. *They'll never miss me.*

Removing a napkin from her pants pocket, Claudia wiped the dampness from her hands. "Gosh, I don't know, Gwen. The last time we had a chat, you told me Henrietta was in town. I guess nothing can be worse than that."

Henrietta again. Gwen rolled her eyes and followed Claudia into the kitchen.

Claudia leaned against the island. "I'm relieved she didn't disrupt your tours."

"I'm curious, Claudia. Why did you panic when I told you she was here to judge the competition?"

"You of all people know how unpleasant she is."

"She was nasty to me because I married Parker. I didn't know you two had issues."

Claudia snorted. "She had issues with everyone. I was relieved when she high-tailed it out of town. And good riddance to her. I just wish she hadn't come back."

"What happened between you and her?"

"Can we not talk about Henrietta?"

Gwen transferred containers and serving platters to the sink and began to wash them.

Claudia slid three serving spoons into the sudsy water. "I hope you have something to discuss besides your house guest."

"I do. It's Kenneth's flute lessons."

Claudia groaned. "I know he's struggling. I've been hoping he'd improve."

Gwen rested her dripping hands on the edge of the sink. "I'm afraid the flute isn't his instrument. He told me he'd rather play the cymbals."

A half-smile curved Claudia's lips. "Cymbals, huh?"

"That's what he said." Gwen rinsed a plastic bowl and handed it over. "He can probably stay in the school band. I can check if you want."

The pile of the clean containers grew as Claudia mulled it over. "Oh, all right. I've always known Kenneth doesn't have a musical bone in his body. Let me know what you find out." Claudia's expression softened. "You know, Gwen, when I was a girl, I wanted to play the flute. My parents couldn't afford the instrument or the lessons. I guess I was hoping to live my dream through Kenneth."

They worked in silence until Claudia spoke again. "Is my son the first student you've lost?"

"I hadn't thought about it like that. But here's an idea. Why don't you take over Kenneth's lesson? It would be a shame to bury his flute on a closet shelf."

Claudia's eyes widened. "You don't think I'm too old?"

"Well, if you wanted to learn when you were a girl, why not give it a try now?"

A crooked grin brightened Claudia's previously sullen face. "I like it. When I bring Kenneth for his lesson next Friday, we'll spring our plan on him."

Gwen grabbed a towel, dried her hands, and hugged Claudia. "He'll be thrilled."

Claudia glanced up at the kitchen clock. "Listen, I need to get home. It's been a long day."

"Thanks for everything, Claudia. You did a great job organizing the tours." Gwen peered out the bay window to see the deluge had slowed to a light rain. "Is your car parked at the schoolhouse?" When Claudia nodded, Gwen said, "Let me walk you over there." She grabbed an umbrella from a stand in the foyer. Outside, the wind had lost its punch, allowing the drizzle to fall straight down. They entered the village green and walked the diagonal pathway to South Street and the old schoolhouse.

When they reached the back parking lot, Gwen said, "Thanks for your help to clean up my kitchen. When I return those containers to the club members, I'll ask if anyone wants to take Henrietta off my hands."

Claudia snorted. "You might get lucky if one of them didn't know the woman." And with that she belted herself into her SUV and drove off.

Gwen stared after the departing taillights. That same undertone of animosity had underscored Claudia's parting comment. Perhaps after the competition, once Henrietta was gone, Claudia would be willing to share their history.

Hugging herself against the rain-cooled evening air, Gwen wandered home via the sidewalk edging the perimeter of the village green as a change of pace. She passed the *Sugar 'n Spice Bakery*, its interior dark on a Saturday evening. The windows of the private homes were lit from inside, throwing a gentle light out onto Library Lane. As she approached Mrs. Martin's house, Gwen stopped abruptly.

Parked on the glistening cobblestones stood a black sedan with Vermont plates and a stuffed black cat glaring out the back window. Henrietta's car. Gwen quickened her pace until she reached her own front steps.

She dropped the dripping umbrella into the foyer stand and hustled upstairs, delaying her return to her three guests laughing beneath the awning out back. Placing her ear against

103

the guest room door, Gwen heard no movement and nudged open the unlatched door. She switched on the overheard light and saw Henrietta's outfit, still waiting, untouched. No telltale noises from the bathroom. Peeking in, Gwen found it empty as well.

What in the world was going on? Henrietta's car was parked down the street. So she had returned from her day with Cousin Mary. She hadn't changed into her evening clothes. Of course, she could have decided not to bother. But why hadn't she driven her car to Boston? What an odd set of circumstances. There could be other explanations, of course. Gwen shook her head.

None of my business how Henrietta lives her life.

Before Gwen headed downstairs, she grabbed two sweaters from her bedroom, slipping her arms into one. The storm had cooled the air. Liz would appreciate an extra layer.

Returning to the kitchen, Gwen decided to whip up hot chocolate as a treat. She mixed cocoa, almond milk, raw sugar, and vanilla with a pinch of salt, stirring the concoction to a silky-smooth texture. She ladled the mixture into four mugs on a tray, tossed the extra sweater over her arm, and nudged the French door open with her hip.

Hal jumped up and took the tray from her. "This smells great. Where have you been?"

His question touched her. No one had cared where she was since Parker died. "I haven't been gone that long."

Hal placed the tray on a deck table and passed the hot chocolate around. Gwen handed the extra sweater to Liz before accepting the last mug. Gwen's next words surprised even her. "Have any of you seen Henrietta?"

Tony looked up. "Why are you asking?"

"I just found her car parked up the street. She told me she'd be driving to Boston tonight."

Liz snorted. "Why do you care?"

"Well, her fancy clothes are still laid out."

"So what?" Liz said. "Here's your answer. She didn't change and someone picked her up."

Gwen shook her head. "Henrietta is too much of a clothes horse to plan an outfit and not wear it." Beneath the warmth of her sweater, Gwen's hairs stood on end.

Hal lowered his mug. "Are you sure it's her car?"

"Positive."

"I need to stretch my legs. Why don't we have a look?" Hal headed toward the deck stairs and Gwen followed.

When they reached the sidewalk, she pointed toward the black sedan, glittering with speckles of rain, hunkered down like a sleeping beast in front of Mrs. Martin's house. As they got closer, the Vermont license plate came into focus. Gwen pointed at the back window. "See the stuffed black cat? I noticed it when Henrietta arrived on Thursday." The stuffed animal glared back. Too bad the little critter couldn't talk. "This is definitely Henrietta's car. So where is she?"

Hal shook his head. "No idea." He squatted down and touched the pavement beneath. "These cobblestones are dry. She parked here before the storm hit. That was more than an hour ago. She must be around here someplace. Why don't we head back?"

Gwen fell into step beside Hal. When they approached the deck, Tony looked over. "Was it Henrietta's car?"

"Yep," Gwen answered.

"I'll ask again," Liz said, "why do you care?"

"I'm not sure. Something about this situation doesn't sit right with me."

"I bet she's hiding in your guest room closet, eating Godiva chocolates she doesn't want to share." Liz cackled at her own humor.

Gwen reached for the handle of the French door. "I'm going to check again."

105

"Hang on." Liz pushed herself from the deck chair. "I'll go with you."

Although Gwen was surprised by Liz's offer, she was relieved to have a second pair of eyes for the search. They explored the kitchen, the half bath, the dining room, living room, and music studio, all the time calling for Henrietta.

Upstairs, Gwen knocked on the guest room door before peeking inside. The outfit lay undisturbed, the shoes were in the same spot, the jewelry was untouched.

Gwen and Liz opened the closet door, checked behind the bathtub curtain, and walked through the sitting room and Gwen's gable suite. They climbed the ladder into the third floor storage loft. No sign of Henrietta.

Liz placed her hand on Gwen's arm. "Let's re-join the boys." Liz flew down the stairs, the hem of her long skirt billowing from the updraft, her leather sandals slapping the stair treads. When they returned to the rear deck, Hal stepped forward. "Did you find her?"

Gwen shook her head. "She's not inside."

"Are you seriously worried about her?" Tony asked.

Gwen could understand their lack of concern. There was no love lost between Liz and Henrietta. Tony probably didn't know her at all, and Hal had only met her a few days ago. Still, Gwen expected some grain of curiosity. "Don't any of you think it odd her car is parked on the street but she's not here?"

"I know," Liz suggested. "Dial her cell phone and ask her where she is."

Gwen huffed. "She wouldn't give me her number."

"Maybe she took a stroll down to the harbor," Tony suggested.

Gwen shook her head. "Not Henrietta. She'd never walk in the rain. Plus she had plans for the evening."

"If you want to check around out here, I'll help you," Hal offered, downing the last of his now-tepid chocolate.

106

"Great idea. Let's all go." When Gwen linked arms with Liz, Liz pulled away, gesturing at her clothing and shoes. "Hold on there, girlfriend. I'm not traipsing around your property. Everything's soaking wet."

"Are you sure a search is necessary?" Tony didn't budge from his chair.

Gwen stretched to her full height. "Regardless of Henrietta's uninvited status, I'll sleep better tonight if I have a look around." She recounted Henrietta's fear of the stairs and the avoidance of the balcony railing. "This morning she mentioned refilling a prescription. I don't know the medical reason. Maybe she's passed out somewhere and doesn't hear me calling."

"You make a good point, Gwen," Hal said, moving closer. "Let's go."

Chapter Seventeen

Gwen and Hal stood together on the lower deck, gazing into the backyard.

"Where do we start?" he asked.

"This way." She stepped through the trellis, fragrant with the tiny white flowers of sweet autumn clematis. The second her foot touched the grass, the landscape lights blinked on and startled her.

Hal bumped into her from behind. "Why'd you stop?"

She moved sideways so he could stand next to her and pointed at the soft glow illuminating the flower beds and pathways. The raindrops glittered like diamonds on every surface.

His gaze wandered the area. "Nice."

"Thanks. Parker and I always called it our own little Disney World."

Ignoring the party debris as they searched for Henrietta, they checked behind the arbor, finding bamboo had sprouted, leaving no room for someone to hide. They peered into the small fish pond, thinking Henrietta could have stumbled in and knocked herself out. An image of Henrietta's feet sticking skyward like the Wicked Witch of the West popped into Gwen's head. She chided herself. Joking was fine if the woman was sitting in a Boston theater. What if she was in real trouble?

Out in the expansive side lawn, Gwen and Hal drifted back and forth in methodical sweeps, calling out Henrietta's name at each bush and tree trunk. Hal checked the thick perennials in the raised geometric beds. Gwen followed the stepping stone path, peering into the heavy bed of pachysandra snugged up against the eastern wall of the old library.

Hal came up beside her. "Do you think she might have walked into your woods?"

"I doubt it." Gwen stopped short of a snicker. "But if you're willing to humor me, let's take a look out there."

Hal's shook his head. "I'm not humoring you. If you're this concerned about your guest, I'd be a fool not to help."

Gwen considered Henrietta more an intruder than a guest, though she didn't say so to Hal. "Hang on a second." She entered the potting shed, emerging seconds later with two flashlights. She uncapped both and inserted fresh batteries into each.

"Which way?" Hal asked.

She led him behind the huge field boulder and onto the path. Beneath the starless evening sky, the woods loomed dismal and dreary. The waning moon peeked through the retreating clouds, providing little light. They picked their way along the leaf-strewn trail, their beams illuminating limited details in the deepening shadows. As they approached the first footbridge higher on the ridge, the roar of water reached their ears. The normally gentle creek had swollen to a raging torrent. Gwen cupped her hands and shouted Henrietta's name. No reply.

Stepping off the other side of the bridge platform, Gwen flinched when a shower of raindrops cascaded from the leaves above. She lurched sideways and, before she knew what had happened, was looking up at Hal from the soggy ground. He roared with laughter.

"Hey, this isn't funny."

He extended his hand and pulled her to her feet. "Sorry. I couldn't help myself."

His apology did nothing to ease Gwen's embarrassment. She forged up the path, leaving him to stare after her. At her northern property line, she peered into the parking lot of the new library. No cars. No people. No Henrietta. The path curved back on itself as it meandered down the gently-sloping hill. When her flashlight beam found the lower footbridge near

109

North Street, she rushed forward. Splintered railings pointed into the gorge at awkward angles. Had Henrietta fallen in? Gwen gasped and aimed her beam into the gorge, straining to see – well, Henrietta. There was no sign of a body. Nothing except the raging water rushing toward the North Street Bridge.

Hal caught up with her, breathing hard. "I'm sorry I laughed at you, Gwen."

When she said nothing, he peered over her shoulder, then reached out to finger the damaged wood. "What do you think happened here?"

Good question. Should she tell Hal she'd discovered the loose struts yesterday and didn't hammer them back together?

Before she could make up her mind, Hal called out, "Hey! Look at this." From the other end of the footbridge he pointed at a huge branch stretching down the steep bank, its ends newly split. "This must have blown down during the storm and broken your railing."

Gwen hoped Hal was right. Her fear that Henrietta had fallen through the railing was sheer speculation, and not even logical. Walking in these soggy woods was the last thing Henrietta would do. Gwen doubted the woman even owned a pair of sneakers. And Hal's big branch theory made sense. Then Gwen zeroed in on another concern. What about the local kids who sometimes ventured through here? Gwen glanced around the area.

"What are you looking for now?"

"Candy wrappers. Soda cans."

"Why?"

"Oh, I'm letting my imagination run away with me. Youngsters sometimes walk my woods. What if one of them leaned on the railing?" Gwen visually scoured the area. No debris in sight.

Hal reached over and squeezed her shoulder. "I think you're worrying about nothing."

110

Gwen mentally conceded he was probably right.

They squished their way along the muddy path and wet leaves until they re-emerged in Gwen's backyard. She returned the flashlights to the shed then mounted the deck.

Tony turned his head and called, "Any sign of her?"

"No," Gwen murmured. "We even searched the woods."

"Found a tree branch that crashed through a railing," Hal said. "Nothing else."

Gwen let Hal's assumption slide by without argument.

Liz draped her arm around Gwen's waist, then screeched and jumped back. "Ew!"

Reaching around, Gwen's fingers touched slimy oak and maple leaves on her khakis. "Oh, that. I slipped in the woods."

Liz tossed a questioning glance in Hal's direction but didn't pursue it. "Here's what you do, Gwen. Forget about Henrietta. If she's not back by morning, call the police."

"Should I call them now?"

Hal shook his head. "I wouldn't bother. Doesn't a person have to be missing twenty-four hours before the police will do anything?"

"You're right. I should have thought of that." She'd read enough mysteries and watched enough reruns of *Law and Order* to know about the twenty-four hour rule.

Tony stood up. "We're heading home."

"Thanks again for being my bartender, Tony. You charmed all the ladies, as usual."

"My pleasure." He hugged Gwen and winked at Liz. "I'll give you a lift to your car."

"Oh, that's right. I forgot we didn't drive together." Liz grasped Gwen's hand. "Remember what I said. Forget about Henrietta. When she shows up and starts insulting you again, you'll be sorry you worked yourself into a tizzy. Can't wait to hear her sorry excuse tomorrow when I come over for our Sunday morning coffee and girl talk."

111

Tony and Liz descended the deck steps onto the driveway. The sounds of their shoes slapping on the wet blacktop faded as the distance increased.

Hal moved to Gwen's side. "Let me help you pick up."

"Thanks," she said, only mildly surprised at his offer.

A few minutes later, they tossed three bags of used napkins, squashed paper cups, soiled paper plates, and dirty plastic utensils into Gwen's trash barrels. When she turned to thank Hal again, she bumped into his chest.

He leaned down and whispered, "Thanks for letting me stay this evening." When he pulled away, his lips brushed her cheek. Gwen had been wrong about him. Hal definitely wanted something more than her friendship.

"You're welcome." She struggled to keep her tone light. "That storm certainly flipped tour day upside down." She retrieved a stray fork, avoiding Hal's eyes. "Thanks for helping me search for Henrietta. And for cleaning up."

"Uh, sure. My pleasure." Hal backed up a few steps, running his hand through his salt 'n pepper hair. "Guess I'll see you Monday afternoon when I pick up Jenna." He turned and walked down the driveway without looking back.

Gwen gazed after Hal until he was out of sight. She couldn't decide how to react to his second kiss. It was only on her cheek, after all. Probably innocent. Maybe not. If she continued to ignore his subtle advances, would she bruise his ego? Would she lose his friendship because she wasn't ready for romance?

However, there was a bigger question. Would Gwen ever find the courage to file away her memories of life with Parker and make new memories with another man?

The house phone rang, pulling Gwen from her ponderings. She dashed inside to grab it.

"Good evening. I'm calling from the CVS pharmacy. May I speak to Henrietta Wickham?"

Gwen did a double-take. "She's not here at the moment. Can I help you?"

"I don't think so," the young man said. "Earlier today, Ms. Wickham dropped off a prescription to be refilled and was adamant that she'd pick it up this afternoon. I stayed after hours thinking she'd show up."

"I'm sorry. I don't know where she is, and I don't have her cell phone number."

"Well, all right. When you see her, please let her know her prescription is ready. She can pick it up tomorrow. On Sundays, the pharmacy doesn't open until nine."

"I'll tell her." Gwen said and eased the receiver into its cradle.

Damn it all, where was Henrietta?

Chapter Eighteen

On Sunday morning, dawn's pale light inched its way into
Gwen's gable bedroom. She bolted upright. During the night,
she hadn't heard the click of the front door latch. Had Henrietta
not returned? Tossing back her covers, Gwen sprang to her feet
and flung her robe over her pajamas.

At the guestroom door, she knocked and called Henrietta's
name. The unlatched door swung inward. Amber raised sleepy
eyes, yawning from the corner of the un-rumpled comforter.
Everything appeared the same as it had the other times Gwen
had peeked in here. The clothes remained untouched, the shoes
waited on the floor, the jewelry lay on the side table.

Gwen walked to the front window and looked toward the
cobblestones in front of Mrs. Martin's house. Henrietta's black
sedan sat in the same spot. Was Liz right? Had Henrietta
decided against switching outfits? Had she gone to Boston with
someone else? Perhaps her cousin had invited her to stay
overnight. But if that's what happened, why did Henrietta
bother to drive her car back here first? And why hadn't she
picked up her prescription from the pharmacy?

If Henrietta had found Gwen during the garden party and
let her know of the change in plans, Gwen would have been
less worried. Or at least Henrietta could have left a note.
Though courtesy was not in Henrietta's repertoire. At least not
where Gwen was concerned.

Wait a minute. Henrietta had stored some of her things in
the wardrobe at the top of the stairs for safekeeping from the
'riff-raff' during the house tour. Maybe there was a clue about
where she might have gone. Backtracking along the balcony,
Gwen stretched high to the top of the wardrobe and wiggled
her fingers until they touched on the key. She unlocked the
door and whipped it open. Three pairs of slacks and several

colorful silk blouses hung from the wooden bar. The floor was nearly obliterated by at least a half dozen pairs of designer shoes and a leather briefcase. Next to them sat the huge black purse, a cell phone peeking out from a side pocket, car keys dropped carelessly on the floor.

A chill went up Gwen's spine. Where would any woman go without her purse *and* cell phone? Gwen's mystery-loving brain began to create a timeline. After Henrietta parked her car, she came upstairs and locked these items in the wardrobe. But she hadn't changed her clothes. So where had she gone?

Gwen's hands trembled as she closed the wardrobe door, turned the key, and slid it into the pocket of her robe.

Tossing good manners aside, she stomped to the guest room and rummaged through the bedside table and the dresser, looking for something, anything, to explain where Henrietta could be. The only items of interest were a pair of red satin thongs and matching lace nightie. If Henrietta had planned to seduce Parker, the news of his death had rendered this lingerie useless. Gwen tossed the garments in the drawer and slammed it shut with a bang.

Her stomach clenched. How could she be so infuriated by Henrietta's intentions where Parker was concerned, and at the same time unsettled by the mystery of the woman's whereabouts?

Threads of rising panic tickled the back of Gwen's neck.

***

"Harbor Falls Police Station. Sergeant McNair. How can I help you?"

During all her years of living in Harbor Falls, this was the first time Gwen had called the police station. She rubbed a sweaty palm down her pajama-clad leg and took a deep breath.

"My name is Gwen Andrews. May I speak to Chief Upton, please?"

Chief Charles Upton was the only law enforcement officer

Gwen knew, and only because they'd shared a few lively conversations at Baylies-sponsored events over the years. Gwen considered the chief intelligent, quick-witted, and well informed.

"I'm sorry, ma'am," Officer McNair said. "The chief doesn't work on Sundays. If you'll tell me the reason you're calling, maybe someone else can help you."

"I, uh…" She'd only wanted to ask Charles if she should file a missing person report. Without his advice, she was on her own. "My name is Gwen Andrews. I live on the northwest corner of the village green." She swallowed. "I…I think my house guest is missing. I haven't seen her since yesterday morning."

"Calm down, Mrs. Andrews. I'll put out a call for the closest patrol car to come over and fill out a report." He confirmed her address and hung up.

A patrol car? I didn't expect that. Too late to back away now. The police are on their way.

She hurried upstairs, washed her face, brushed her teeth, and changed out of her pajamas. Halfway down the stairs, she realized she'd forgotten the wardrobe key, so she hurried back to her bedroom, fumbled through her robe, came up with the key, and transferred it to her jeans pocket.

Out front, she stood on the top granite step and waited until a police cruiser pulled to the curb. A young officer with a crew cut and a muscled physique emerged and headed her way.

"Mrs. Andrews? You need to submit a missing person report?"

She nodded and waved him inside, settling across from him at the dining room table.

His clipboard held a blank report. His fingers gripped a pencil. "What's your guest's name?"

She recited Henrietta's name, then spelled it for him.

"Home address and phone number?"

"I'm sorry, I don't have either. She lives in Vermont somewhere."

He looked at her, one eyebrow cocked. "In that case, why don't you explain why you think she's gone missing?"

Gwen told him about Henrietta's intention to change clothes and drive to Boston, then her later sighting of Henrietta's car parked in front of the neighbor's house.

The young officer was writing furiously when the front door bell rang. When she opened the door, a middle-aged man turned around and gave her the once-over. With his hat in his hand, his drastic buzz cut revealed a perfectly shaped skull. She looked over his shoulder to see a tan unmarked sedan parked behind the patrol car.

"Detective Mike Brown, ma'am. I heard the dispatcher mention a missing person. I was in the neighborhood and thought I'd stop in and see if I could be of help."

When he pushed his bomber jacket aside, Gwen spotted his gun and nearly jumped out of her skin. Guns had always made her nervous.

He unclipped a badge from his belt and held it close to her face as though she were extremely near-sighted. Even so, she didn't relax.

A detective? The only reason she'd called the police station was to ask the chief what she should do. *What have I gotten myself into?*

"Please come in, Detective. The patrol officer is in my dining room. We were filling out the form." She stood aside to let him pass. The leather of his jacket squeaked and he wasn't much taller than Gwen's five-foot-three.

He gazed around, nodding his approval. "I've been curious about this old library since I joined the force last year." Tilting his head toward the balcony, he said, "Impressive."

"Thank you," Gwen murmured, not sure if he was being genuine or just cordial.

He waved for the young officer to follow him. "Excuse us, Mrs. Andrews." They walked out the front door, closing it behind them. A few minutes later, the detective returned alone.

"I've told the patrol officer to wait outside. Why don't you and I have a chat?" He withdrew a wire-bound notebook and stubby pencil from his inside jacket pocket.

This was Gwen's first encounter with a real detective. For decades, she'd satisfied her love of a good mystery by reading a novel or following along with her favorite TV detectives while they wrapped up a case within an hour. This real detective unsettled her.

He licked the pencil tip and held it above the lined paper.

"My officer tells me you know your guest's name, but not her address or phone number."

"That's true. Henrietta lives somewhere in Vermont. If you need that information for your report, you can ask Jack Miller at the music shop or Dean Daniel Chartley at Baylies College. They were both involved in bringing Henrietta back to Harbor Falls."

Detective Brown lifted his head, his penetrating stare worrisome. "When did she arrive?"

"Thursday."

"And how long did you expect her to be here?"

"Until next Saturday."

He lowered his notebook. "I'm sorry to be asking all these questions, Mrs. Andrews. But the more I know, the more likely that we'll find her. Can you explain why she's staying here?"

There was no need to complicate matters. Gwen knew she should simply explain the circumstances surrounding Henrietta's return. The fact that Henrietta was a bully and a past romantic rival was irrelevant to her missing status.

"I was doing a favor for Jack."

He gave her a quizzical look. "What was the favor?"

Gwen inhaled and blew out the air before answering.

"Baylies College hired Henrietta as a replacement judge for the music competition next weekend. When Jack searched for housing, he discovered all the B&B's, hotels, and motels were full. That's why he asked if she could sleep in my guestroom."

The detective touched the tip of his pencil to paper. "And why did Mr. Miller think you'd agree?"

Revealing Jack's threat against Jenna might get him in trouble. He might get mad enough to enforce the registration rules and remove Jenna from the competitor's list. Not to mention that telling the detective would expose Gwen's anger not only at Jack, but at Henrietta as well. The detective might assume Gwen was involved in Henrietta's disappearance. If it was, in fact, a disappearance. Why couldn't Henrietta walk in this instant and toss a barbed insult?

A phrase from a mystery novel came to mind... *There's more than one way to tell the truth.* Gwen only needed to share the pertinent facts.

She turned to Detective Brown. "One of my private music students is performing in the competition. Jack knew I have a vested interest in making sure the event goes off without a hitch, so he thought I'd want to help." A true statement, as far as it went.

The detective's gaze did not leave her face.

"I know you started filling out the report with the officer, but why don't you just tell me why you think she's missing?"

"Well," Gwen began, "when Henrietta left yesterday morning, she said she'd be back before my garden tour began to switch outfits and drive to Boston. Around seven last evening, I spotted her car parked in front of my neighbor's house. It struck me as odd."

"So she *did* come back. Did you see her?"

"No, I didn't."

"What makes you think she didn't catch a ride with someone?"

119

"Because her evening outfit, her shoes, and her jewelry are untouched."

The detective shook his head. "She could have changed her mind about changing."

Gwen was losing her patience at the detective's lack of concern. She repeated what she'd told Hal, Liz, and Tony. "Henrietta isn't the kind of woman to plan an outfit and not wear it."

"What time did she park her car up the street?"

"I have no idea, Detective. My garden tour started around four, followed by the house tour, and then the garden club party in my backyard."

Detective Brown peered out the French door. "I have to say, your gardens are impressive."

"Thank you. It took years for me and my husband to create them."

His eyes darted back to her. "Where's your husband?"

Gwen felt her face warm. "Parker died more than two years ago."

The detective's face reddened. "Sorry, Mrs. Andrews. Like I said, I've only been on the force for a year. I didn't know you're a widow." He flipped to the next page in his notebook. "Uh, let's get back to Ms. Wickham. What did you do after you noticed her car and her clothing?"

"My friend Hal looked underneath the sedan and noticed dry spots on the cobblestones. We decided Henrietta parked there before the storm hit."

Detective Brown nodded as he made a note. "And who is Hal?"

"Hal Jenkins. He's the grandfather of my student who's in the competition. He stayed for a while after the garden party was rained-out. Along with my friends, Liz and Tony Phillips."

Detective Brown jotted the additional names. "Is there anything else that makes you think she's missing?"

Gwen paused. "Yes. The pharmacist phoned last night to let Henrietta know her prescription was ready. She told him she'd pick it up by the end of the day, but she didn't."

"Any idea what the prescription is for?" The detective's pencil was poised to write.

Not wanting to speculate that it was allergies, Gwen shook her head. "No idea."

"That's okay. If it becomes important, we can get a court order." *Scribble, scribble.* He again flipped the page. "Anything else?"

"My friend Liz helped me search inside, but Henrietta wasn't here. And then Hal and I checked the grounds and the woods."

"And did you two find anything?"

Gwen hesitated. Dangling footbridge railings. But Hal was right. There was nothing to connect the damaged lumber to Henrietta. Nothing to indicate Henrietta had been out there in the first place. Gwen adjusted her answer to Detective Brown.

"We didn't find Henrietta, if that's what you're asking."

He stopped writing. "Don't take this the wrong way, Mrs. Andrews, but if you were so concerned about her, why didn't you call the station last night?"

She stared at him. Had she been wrong to follow Hal's advice? "Because a person has to be missing twenty-four hours before the police will do anything. Isn't that right?"

Detective Brown shook his head. "That's a common misconception. Is that why you called this morning? Because the twenty-four hours had passed?"

"Not entirely. I remembered Henrietta stored some of her things in a wardrobe for safekeeping, and I thought maybe I'd find a clue in there about where she'd gone."

"And did you find any? Clues, that is?"

Gwen stared at the detective's impassive face, struggling to keep her voice level. "I don't know about the women in your life, Detective, but I wouldn't leave home without my purse, my cell phone, and my keys."

Chapter Nineteen

Detective Brown tucked his notebook in his jacket pocket.

"Show me, Mrs. Andrews."

Gwen led him up the stairs, unlocked the wardrobe door, and moved aside.

The detective snapped on a pair of thin plastic gloves before pushing Henrietta's slacks and blouses to one side. He ignored the designer shoes, but he reached into the huge black purse and pulled out an oversized red leather wallet, a matching wire-bound address book, a round vintage mirror, a sterling lipstick case, and a natural horn comb.

After flipping through the address book, he plucked the cell phone from the outer pouch. He punched a few buttons and scrolled before snapping it shut and slipping it into his outside pocket. "Where's your guestroom?"

The detective glanced at the outfit, the strappy shoes, and the jewelry. He stepped to the front window. "Where'd you see her car?"

Gwen moved to stand beside him and pointed toward Mrs. Martin's house next door. "That black sedan. It has Vermont plates and I recognized the stuffed animal in the back window."

He turned and fixed his gaze on Gwen. "I think you're right to be worried about your guest, Mrs. Andrews. Do you mind if I request a few more officers to search your property?"

A search of my property? "You think Hal and I could have missed her last night?"

"Hard to say. It was dark, wasn't it? Lots of things can be missed when it's dark."

He unclipped a two-way radio from his belt and rushed from the guestroom. Gwen tried to keep up as he flew down the staircase, straining to catch snatches of his conversation. He mumbled into his shoulder mic, so she didn't understand one word.

When they reached the foyer, he said, "I'll wait out front. When the two other officers arrive, we'll meet you on your back deck. Shouldn't be more than a few minutes."

Gwen stared at the front door as it closed behind the detective. Was he expecting to find Henrietta out there in the woods?

***

Gwen paced on the rear deck until Detective Brown came around the corner with the first patrol officer plus two new men, both in uniform. Their chiseled faces matched their somber expressions.

When one of them asked Gwen for a description of Henrietta, she mumbled, "Uh, she's tall." Gwen held her hand about six inches above her own head. "I'd guess around five eight or nine. Long black hair with gray streaks." She hesitated. "Yesterday morning she was wearing a sunflower yellow blouse and black slacks."

The three officers spread out and searched the yard, the gardens, the fish pond, and the potting shed. The same places she and Hal had looked. When they returned to Detective Brown, they spoke in low tones. One of them pointed to the woods. Gwen shivered as the three officers circumvented the huge boulder and entered the tree line.

They would surely notice that broken railing. Should she have mentioned it to the detective?

On the deck, Detective Brown paced back and forth, talking into his shoulder mic every now and then. Gwen assumed he was staying in touch with the three officers.

Unable to bear the tension, she retreated inside, circled and re-circled her first floor. She paused to inspect her Pothos plant and removed a dried leaf. She fluffed the couch pillows. And then re-fluffed them. After what seemed an eternity, she heard the intrusive squawk of the detective's radio. At the open French door she caught his final word, "...damn." When he turned, his expression implied the news wasn't good.

He cupped Gwen's elbow and guided her back inside. "Mrs. Andrews, my men have found a woman's body."

Gwen's heart lurched. A lump formed in her throat. She forced herself to pay attention as he kept talking.

"They think she was your guest."

Gwen slid bonelessly to the floor.

Chapter Twenty

When Gwen opened her eyes, she stiffened. The unsmiling face of Detective Brown loomed above her. Deep wrinkles distorted his forehead.

"Mrs. Andrews?"

Her fingertips recognized the tapestry of a wing chair. "How did I get here?"

"You fainted. I carried you."

Behind his gruff voice, she detected a hint of concern.

He glanced at his watch. "You haven't been out long."

"Why did I faint?" She struggled to a sitting position and gazed around the music studio.

"Uh, sorry I was so abrupt," he stumbled. "You collapsed when I told you my men found your guest's body."

His reminder hit Gwen like a tumbler of ice water. She sucked in her breath. No matter how much she'd resented Henrietta's intrusion, she never wished her old nemesis dead.

A distant siren pierced the quiet Sunday morning.

Detective Brown stepped away. "You stay right there. I need to call the chief." By the time he closed the French door behind him, the detective was speaking into his cell phone.

Gwen shivered and reached above her head to grab the throw from the back of the chair. She tucked the woolen softness around her body, got to her feet, and drifted toward a mullioned window to stare into the woods. Exactly where had the officers found Henrietta? She and Hal had searched with flashlights and hadn't spotted her. The gloomy shadows provided no answer.

Dropping her forehead to the cool glass, Gwen strained to summon one nice thing about Henrietta. To pay her respects.

How sad that nothing came to mind.

The door opened, and her head whirled in that direction.

126

The detective's gaze traveled to the empty wing chair. He turned his head, spotted her at the window, and covered the distance in a few short strides. "You look pale, Mrs. Andrews. Why don't you sit down?"

Chilly fingers of morning air had snuck in behind him and found their way to her. "Don't worry about me, Detective. I'll be fine." Not quite sure her statement was accurate, she lowered herself into the wing chair.

"Just so you know, Mrs. Andrews, I've opened an official investigation into Ms. Wickham's death."

Gwen took in a sharp breath.

"Don't let that disturb you. It's standard procedure when we find a body without a doctor present. Most times, there's a legitimate explanation and the case is closed pretty quickly."

"How did she die, Detective?"

"Too soon to know." His forehead creased in concentration. "The Medical Examiner will determine the cause of death."

"Where did your officers find her?"

He shook his head. "I haven't been to the scene yet."

Over the years, Gwen had watched repeat episodes of *Law and Order, The Closer,* and even *Columbo.* Enough to recognize the detective's stalling tactic. What harm could it do for her to know where they found Henrietta's body?

"Mrs. Andrews?...Mrs. Andrews?" his voice repeated, this time louder.

Gwen only half heard her name being spoken. When someone touched her arm, she jumped and looked up to see Detective Brown.

"Are you sure you're all right?"

"Uh, yes, I'm sure. This is very upsetting."

"Understandable. Can you give me a few more details before I go?"

Gwen nodded, easing her body backwards until the wing chair surrounded her.

127

"Do you know who Ms. Wickham has spoken to or visited since her arrival?"

Gwen hesitated, her mind whirling. "She mentioned her uncle on Friday. Yesterday, her cousin Mary. I don't know their full names or addresses." Gwen felt foolish for having so little information to provide.

The detective's faded blue eyes drilled into hers. "That's okay. We'll find them. Can you think of anything else?"

Gwen glanced around, looking for a clue to spark her memory. When her eyes landed on the wall phone in the kitchen, another detail surfaced. "Henrietta received a phone call yesterday that irritated her. I don't know who the caller was."

He reached into his pocket and pulled out Henrietta's cell phone, placed there after his search of the upstairs wardrobe. "Let's have a look."

Detective Brown held the phone at an angle as the first number scrolled into view: "The Olde Music Shop. What can you tell me about this one?"

Gwen didn't hesitate. "That could have been Jack Miller or his wife Emily. She owns the shop. Or their sales clerk Alex Fairfield. Probably to discuss details of the competition."

He scrolled to the previous call. The local pharmacy. They both knew it would have been about the prescription refill.

With each call, Gwen shared her best guess of Henrietta's connection:

Several boutiques on the harbor – Henrietta loved clothes.

A few more calls to and from the music shop: no further explanation needed.

Liz's *Fiction 'n Fables Bookstop* – people visit bookstores when they're away from home. Gwen didn't mention Henrietta's belittling of Liz's displays.

The dean's office at Baylies College: he'd suggested Henrietta for the judging seat.

Several local numbers came into view with no name.

"Henrietta's uncle or her cousin Mary?" Gwen suggested.

"I'll do reverse look-ups. Can you tell me anything else?"

"Henrietta mentioned a list of people she planned to see while she was here."

"A list? Did she show it to you?"

"No, she didn't." Gwen still suspected it had been in Henrietta's head, but she didn't think her speculation would carry any weight.

The detective flipped his notebook closed. "That's enough for now. I need to collect a few of Ms. Wickham's things. Please accompany me to your guestroom."

As they climbed the staircase, he again snapped on latex gloves. At the wardrobe, he removed Henrietta's purse with keys, plus the briefcase tucked at the back of the wardrobe. In the guest bathroom, he dumped the contents of the wastebasket into a zip-lock bag.

"Don't you want her clothes and shoes and other things?"

"No, ma'am. I've got everything we need."

With a start, Gwen realized she'd have to find the relatives herself and hope they'd take possession of Henrietta's belongings before Tess arrived on Thursday.

When Detective Brown approached the foyer entrance, he stopped and turned. "If we need any more details, I'll call you."

Gwen dismissed his statement as a standard line and didn't expect she'd ever hear from him again. "Let me get the door for you," she said, moving past him to reach for the knob.

"Thanks. The officers have all they need for the moment, and should be gone by now." The soles of the detective's hard shoes clicked on the solid tiles.

Outside, Gwen paused on her top step and watched the detective's movements. At his own car, Detective Brown withdrew the car keys from Henrietta's purse before tossing it and the briefcase into the back seat, along with the Ziploc bag, then walked to her black sedan. After a cursory examination of the interior and the trunk, he returned to his cruiser, saluted Gwen, and drove off.

She leaned against the wrought iron railing, trying to wrap her mind around the fact that Henrietta was dead. If only the woman had refused the invitation to judge the competition, and never stepped foot back in Harbor Falls, maybe she'd still be alive.

Another equally disturbing thought intruded. If Henrietta were still alive, she'd still be making Gwen's life miserable for as long as she stayed in town.

Disturbed by her own shallowness, Gwen shivered. Even the September sun, now drifting around to the front, was not strong enough to chase away her chill.

Detective Brown hadn't told her where they'd found Henrietta's body. Maybe Gwen should be grateful he hadn't connected Henrietta's death to that damn broken railing on the footbridge. At least he hadn't mentioned it.

And maybe there was no connection at all.

Chapter Twenty-One

Gwen heard a vague voice in the distance calling.

"Gwen!"

She looked up to see Hal hustling across the village green.

A frown distorted his rugged facial features. "I was pulling into the parking lot over at the Sugar 'n Spice and saw a police sedan leaving your place. What's going on?"

"Oh, Hal, it's horrible." Gwen began to shake.

They went inside together. Hal led her into the living room and eased her onto the leather sofa before sitting beside her.

"What's so horrible? Tell me."

"They found her body. She's dead, Hal. Henrietta's dead."

"What?" he shouted. His blue eyes searched her face. When he reached for her hand, she didn't pull away. "No wonder you're upset. You called the police?"

"Earlier this morning. She never came back last night. A patrolman came over to file a missing person report, and then a detective showed up. I explained about finding her car. And her change of clothes. He brought in three other officers to search..."

Hal interrupted. "Slow down. Why didn't we see any sign of her last night?"

"I don't know. The detective never said where they found her." A hiccup escaped and Gwen's hand flew to her mouth.

"What happens now?" Hal asked.

Hiccup. "I'm not sure. The detective opened an investigation. He said it's standard practice when there's no doctor present." *Hiccup.*

Hal stretched his arm around her shoulders and yanked her hard.

"Why'd you do that?"

"Did it work?" he asked, then waited.

It took Gwen a second to realize she'd stopped hiccupping.

"I guess it did. Thanks." She stared at him. He was morphing from her student's grandfather into a new role, but she had no idea how to label him. Concerned friend? Curious by-stander? Protective guardian?

"You're welcome." Hal let his arm drop away. "You were right to be worried last night."

"But I only wanted Henrietta gone. I never wanted her dead."

An awkward silence fell between them. Rising, she walked to the front windows and gazed into the village green where Sunday morning activity unfolded. A young couple strolled hand in hand. A trio of children ran the pathways, their parents chasing after them. A man threw a stick for his romping dog. She sensed Hal's nearness as he came up beside her.

"I wonder what Henrietta would have said to me tomorrow?" he murmured.

Gwen had nearly forgotten his Monday morning meeting with Henrietta. "Maybe Elizabeth confided something?" she ventured.

Hal's shoulders lifted in the barest shrug. "Guess I'll never know." He turned to her. "Is there anything you need?"

"Getting rid of my hiccups was plenty."

He grinned and waved off her thanks. "The least I could do. Do you want me to stay?"

"Thanks, but I'll be okay."

"All right, if you're sure. Jenna's planning to walk over from the high school after classes tomorrow. I'll pick her up around five."

***

"Did you call to brag, Gwen? About your garden and house tours? A raging success?"

Gwen sobered. The tours had taken place only yesterday,

yet it seemed like eons ago. "They were fine." Even over the phone, Gwen could sense Tess's antennae rising.

"What's wrong? What's Henrietta done now?"

"I *am* calling about Henrietta, but not because she's been up to her old tricks." Gwen wandered into the living room as she recounted Henrietta's failure to return, the police search, and their discovery of Henrietta's body.

Silent seconds passed.

Gwen bit her lip. "Tess, are you still there?"

"I'm here. Give me a minute." Tess didn't speak for a few more beats. "Okay, Gwen, here's the new plan." Tess had morphed into her big-sister take-charge mode. "I'm not waiting until Thursday to drive over. And when Nathan hears about this, I'm sure he'll want to come with me."

"Really, Tess, there's no need."

"I know you think you're invincible, little sister, but I'll feel better if you're not by yourself while the police sort this out. Besides, this will give me more time to rehearse with Jenna. I'll go find Nathan. We've both got doctor appointments tomorrow, so we'll drive over on Tuesday. Don't even try to change my mind."

A weak laugh bubbled up in Gwen's throat. "Me? I wouldn't dare."

Minutes later, the details finalized, Gwen closed her cell phone, relieved her sister was coming a couple of days earlier than planned. Could Tess convince Gwen to release the guilt of a guest dying while living under her roof? Not that Gwen felt any direct blame for Henrietta's death. Unless, of course, that loose railing had been involved. Then Gwen would have some major guilt weighing down on her.

A movement beyond the front window caught Gwen's attention. Liz's bright red jeep screeched to a halt at the front curb. She hopped out, her form-fitting jeans and bulky purple sweater a jarring switch from her usual bookstore attire of maxi skirt and flowing blouse. Liz's fiery auburn pixie cut blew sideways as she hurried up the sidewalk toward the granite steps. Gwen rushed over and opened the door before Liz's finger had a chance to press the button.

"Good morning." Liz swept past Gwen and headed for the kitchen, sniffing the air. "You haven't started the coffee? Did you forget about me?"

Gwen *had* forgotten. The two of them had shared every Sunday morning since Parker died.

Oblivious to Gwen's non-response, Liz scooped grounds into the filter, added cinnamon, and poured water into the reservoir. An instant later, the machine burped and wheezed. The captivating aroma of fresh-brewed coffee wafted to Gwen's nose.

Liz turned, her amber eyes bright with anticipation. "What's Henrietta's excuse for making you worry last night? Good God, I hope she's not here." Liz glanced up through the mezzanine, her expression darkening when she returned to the silent Gwen. "Something wrong?"

Gwen's chest tightened. She took a deep breath and collapsed onto a stool. "I don't know what happened. They found her this morning."

"What are you babbling about? Who did who find?"

With great effort, Gwen again explained Henrietta's failure to return, the police search, and the discovery of her body.

"Oh, my God!" Liz threw her arms around Gwen. "I don't usually speak ill of the dead, but you know there was no love lost between me and Henrietta." The buzzer on the coffee maker sounded and Liz released Gwen to fill two mugs. "Henrietta was a total bitch. Not to mention the way she bullied you." Liz scooped two teaspoons of sugar, clanging the spoon against the ceramic sides before taking a noisy sip.

"She didn't treat anyone else much better," Gwen said.

Liz snorted. "You should have heard her the other day.

Insulting my store displays, mocking my book offerings. She even ridiculed my view of the harbor."

"Sorry I didn't warn you in time," Gwen mumbled.

"That woman's sour personality is not your doing."

Gwen lowered her mug to the countertop and wrapped her hands around its warmth. "Well, maybe it was. Maybe she wouldn't have been so mean if I hadn't married Parker."

Liz slammed her palm on the granite. "I hope you don't believe what you just said. Parker never loved Henrietta. She was so jealous when he fell for you. Don't you dare take responsibility for that woman's arrogance."

"I suppose you're right." Gwen suddenly panicked. "Do you think her relatives will hold me responsible? After all, she was staying here when she died."

A stricken look transformed Liz's face. "Hard to know. Where'd they find her body?"

"No idea. Detective Brown didn't share the details. All I know is they started searching in my woods."

Again, Gwen kept the fact of her weak footbridge railing to herself. She hadn't told the detective, nor Hal, nor Tess, and now not even Liz. Gwen's shoulders slumped.

Liz noticed. "You look worn out, sweetie."

Gwen got up and lowered her half-empty mug into the sink.

"I haven't slept through the night since Henrietta showed up. Do you mind, Liz, if I cut our Sunday morning short? All I want to do is crawl into my bed and get some sleep."

Liz downed the remaining few sips of her own coffee. "Okay. I'll go down at the bookstore and take care of some paperwork. If you need me, call. I can be back in five minutes."

After Liz left, Gwen pulled herself up the staircase and glanced left toward the guestroom. Its door stood slightly ajar.

She hadn't fixed the latch Henrietta complained about.

Perhaps, Gwen decided, she'd been negligent in more ways than one.

Chapter Twenty-Two

The sound of raindrops thrumming against the window woke Gwen from a restless slumber. She glanced sideways at the digital clock: *8:00 p.m.* Above her, eerie shadows danced across the slanted ceiling, mimicking the wind-whipped trees outside her bedroom. She pulled the comforter up until only her eyes were exposed and listened to the creaks of the old library.

No footsteps. No rustle of clothing. No whispers. She slid one hand from beneath the covers and switched on the bedside lamp. No one there. Who did Gwen expect? Henrietta's ghost?

She released a breath she didn't realize she'd been holding.

A George Burns' line from the late '70s movie *Oh, God* popped into her head. *'Sometimes when you don't feel normal, doing a normal thing makes you feel normal.'*

Gwen threw back the covers, pulled her robe over her wrinkled clothing, and padded downstairs, flipping every light switch on her way to the kitchen. When the kettle started to whistle, heavy footfalls pounded across her rear deck. The glass of the French door rattled under insistent knuckles. Gwen's every nerve jumped to high alert.

A man yelled, "Gwen, open the door. I'm getting soaked."

When she recognized the voice, her jaw muscles tensed. Jack was the last person she wanted to see. He was the only reason Henrietta had taken up residence in the guestroom. Would things have turned out differently if he'd found lodging for the woman in someone else's home?

She turned off the burner beneath the shrieking kettle and flipped on the back floodlight, confirming Jack's cocky face before she whipped open the door. "You scared me half to death. What are you doing here?"

"Christ, Gwen. Let me in and I'll tell you." A sheet of rain whooshed inside.

"Hold on, Jack." She grabbed his jacket sleeve. "Leave your dirty shoes on the mat."

He pushed his dripping black hair from his face and looked down at his feet. "I walked through your woods from the new library. Didn't think about the mud."

"Well, that explains why you came to my back door." He slipped off his spattered loafers, his expression bleak. "The rescue team finally removed Henrietta's body. As soon as they left, I came over to see how you're doing."

She stared at him. "What about Henrietta's body?"

His face skewed in confusion. "They found her in the millpond near our waterwheel."

Gwen gasped. "I thought they found her in my woods."

He plopped down on an island stool. "Where'd you get that idea?"

"That's where they started their search this morning."

"Well, I guess you're half right. I overheard the cops telling the detective it looked like she fell from your footbridge and got washed downstream. Our willow tree slid into the mill pond during the storm and the branches caught her clothes as she floated by."

A chill ran its fingers up Gwen's spine. No one deserved such a wretched death. Not even wicked Henrietta. Gwen breathed deep and closed her eyes.

Jack was still talking. "...and Detective Brown kept asking questions Emily and I couldn't answer. I thought he'd never leave. By the way, I owe you an apology."

Her eyes flew open. "If you're referring to the underhanded way you forced me to host Henrietta, you're way too late."

He glanced at her, a child-like expression on his weary face. "I *am* sorry, Gwen."

"Easy to say now. If you hadn't brought Henrietta back to town, she'd be alive and bothering someone in Vermont. Not stretched out on a slab in the state morgue."

Jack reeled as though she'd slapped him. "Don't blame me for her death! I told you hiring Henrietta wasn't my idea. The dean suggested her. By the time I found out, she'd accepted the offer and the committee wouldn't let me cancel her contract. I sure as hell didn't want her here. "

"You said that the other day. Why is that, Jack? What happened between you two?"

"That's none of your damn business," he snapped. "My only part was to find lodging."

"Great solution, Jack. Forcing Henrietta into my home. You could have found another household if you'd tried harder."

Gwen stepped to the French door and yanked it open, gesturing for Jack to leave. "If you want someone to let you off the hook, go home to Emily."

Jack stomped over to the mat and shoved his bare feet into his muddy shoes. "Don't be so self-righteous, Gwen. I thought you'd appreciate me checking on you."

"Thanks, Jack, but I don't need any more of your favors." She slammed the French door behind him, finding satisfaction at the sound of his fading footfalls.

She stalked to the granite countertop and slammed her hand down on its surface, her aggravation boiling over. Why was she always the last one to know everything? She'd felt like an idiot finding out Henrietta's resting place from Jack. Damn Detective Brown for not telling her.

The millpond where they'd found Henrietta's body was the next stop for the creek water that coursed through Gwen's patch of woods. The creek where her footbridge crossed the gorge. She'd been right to speculate about that splintered railing. Would Gwen be held responsible for the woman's death because she neglected to hammer those loose struts back together?

Images of Henrietta's final moments flashed by in rapid succession. Crashing through the weak railing. Landing on the jagged rocks below. Flailing her arms in the raging torrent as she hurtled beneath the North Street Bridge. Clinging to the branches of the willow tree to avoid tumbling over the waterwheel. Gwen shuddered. Had Henrietta known her life was almost over?

The finality of death, even Henrietta's, squeezed Gwen's heart. Where did our spirit go when our body no longer lived in this earthly realm? Where was Parker? She went to the foyer table, then returned to the island stool, clutching his photograph tightly in both hands.

She stared at Parker's likeness for a long time. Without warning, her pent-up anger bubbled to the surface after being suppressed for more than two years. The story she'd told Hal the other day had not been strictly true. Actually, not true at all. She hadn't smiled and waved as Parker drove off to play his last round of golf.

Gwen had never considered herself psychic in any way, shape, or form, but on that particular day, her dread was palpable. At breakfast, she'd fought with Parker to stay home and help her transplant several heavy bushes, a lame excuse on her part. She hadn't been able to put her foreboding into words. At least not into words that convinced Parker not to drive to the club house. He said he'd help her when he got home. But he never *came* home.

"Damn you, Parker!" Gwen hurled his photograph across the kitchen. It bounced off the cabinet and crashed to the tiles, the glass shattering into a million pieces.

In a split second, she was on the floor, crying for Parker, crying for herself, even crying for Henrietta. Between sobs, she said, "I'm sorry. I'm sorry. I didn't mean to lose my temper. I'm so sorry, Parker." She started to collect the glass shards, cutting her fingers in the process. Her teardrops fell unchecked.

"Gwen?"

Her head whipped around, tears flinging off her cheeks.

Who called her name? She looked around the kitchen, over toward the dining room, behind her into the music studio. No one.

She heard it again.

"Gwen?" A soft whisper of her name.

Parker's voice. It seemed to be coming from the living room. Who was playing such a sick joke on her? Or was she hallucinating? She grasped the edge of the counter and got to her feet, leaving bloody fingerprints on the granite.

With all the stealth she could manage, she crept toward the row of weeping fig trees between the staircase and the chimney wall. Peeking through the branches, she focused on Parker's recliner.

And then she saw him.

For the second time in the same day, Gwen slid bonelessly to the floor.

Chapter Twenty-Three

Gwen drifted up into consciousness, sensing a hard surface beneath her body. She struggled to remember where she was. Then the memory rushed back. Parker's voice. The person sitting in his recliner. If she hadn't been already lying on the floor, she might have collapsed again.

Fearful of what she'd see, Gwen opened one eyelid at a time. She looked up, half expecting the fake Parker to be looming over her like Detective Brown had that morning. All she saw was the highest point of the library past the edge of the mezzanine railing above her.

And then her ears caught a sound she hadn't heard in years. Purring. Amber had only purred for Parker. Gwen moved her head left and then right. The cat was nowhere in sight. Finding a small patch of courage, she called out, "Parker?"

"Yes, Gwen. Are you all right, sweetheart?"

Her clenched fist covered her mouth. Whoever was mimicking Parker was damn good.

She lowered her hand, deciding to play along. "I'm fine," she lied. "Where are you?"

"Sitting in my recliner."

In the spirit of the game, Gwen scrambled to her feet, walked around the staircase, through the dining room, and past the foyer entrance for a full frontal view of the recliner.

The being sitting in Parker's chair looked like Parker, yet didn't look like him. Gwen could see right through the gossamer body to the upholstery fabric. His substance shimmered like a mirage on a stretch of hot summer highway.

His arm dangled beside the chair, his fingers stroking the top of Amber's head, who stretched up to meet his touch from her spot on the area rug at the fireplace hearth. Her eyes blinked in slow motion with catlike contentment, her throat bones rattling loud enough to echo.

"Parker?" she asked, her voice quaking.

"Yes, Gwen, it's me."

Though his pale lips barely moved, his words were perfectly formed and distinct.

She felt her way around the arm of the leather loveseat and eased into it without taking her eyes off the man. He wore a faded version of the red golf shirt and black slacks he'd been wearing on the day that turned out to be his last.

"But…" she began, realizing she had no idea what to say next. She and Parker had often discussed the likelihood of an afterlife, the existence of heaven and hell, the theory of reincarnation. Ghost stories had always fascinated them both, but was this really happening?

Nah. I must be dreaming. All I have to do is play along until I wake up.

She straightened her backbone. "Where have you been, Parker?"

The dream-man shifted his semi-transparent body, his lack of weight making no dent in the cushions. "Hard to explain. All rather hazy. Not intimidating. Not scary. Not uncomfortable. Quite pleasant, actually. How long have I been gone, Gwen?"

"Two years, four months, and twenty-five days."

His laughter did not reverberate. "You always were good with numbers."

She leaned her forearms on her knees, questions tumbling around in her head. "I don't understand. Why are you here?"

"You called me."

"I've called you lots of times since you died."

"You sounded different this time. More desperate."

She sat back, contemplating his statement. "I guess I am."

"Why don't you tell me what's going on?"

Accepting her freaky dream, Gwen spent the next half hour

explaining Henrietta's return, her machinations to stay in their home, her distress when she learned he'd died, the renewed harassment, her missing status Saturday night, and the discovery of her body Sunday morning.

"You said the detective didn't tell you where they found Henrietta?"

Newly irritated by the reminder, Gwen nodded. "He hasn't shared much beyond opening an investigation into her death. Something about a death without a doctor present. But I guess that's true of most accidents."

Parker's ethereal-double tilted his head. "Well, whatever happened to Henrietta, I'm sure it was her own fault. You can't possibly think you're responsible, Gwen."

Although soothed by his words, Gwen stared at him. Who was she kidding? This ghost wasn't Parker. He was a simply a figment of her active imagination, stimulated by her anxiety over events of the past few days. This faux Parker would say anything Gwen wanted to hear.

His transparent eyes met hers. "I don't know how long I can stay. No one gave me an owner's manual. I'm clueless." He chuckled at his macabre joke.

Gwen could not hold back a grin. Even if this see-through man was something her subconscious had created to deal with Henrietta's death, he was certainly entertaining.

"I'm wondering how it would feel to hug you, Gwen. Are you willing?"

"Oh, why not?" She rose from the loveseat and took a step toward him. If anyone peered through her living room windows, they'd see her talking to no one.

But who cared? What happens in a dream, stays in a dream.

Chapter Twenty-Four

Gwen's body jerked, waking her up. She was sitting on the kitchen floor, surrounded by broken glass. The framed photo of Parker was upside down in the middle of the disarray.

She forced herself to stand, noticing a cup of cold tea untouched on the countertop. The kitchen, bright in the morning sunshine, gave no indication of why she hadn't gone to bed.

Of course. Parker. At first, she'd thought him a real ghost. But no, he couldn't have been. She was sitting in her kitchen, not in the living room where she'd last seen him. That settled it. He'd been a dream. A thrilling dream.

This was the first time she'd recognized a dream as a dream *during* the dream. Usually, dream details poofed away like smoke up a chimney.

But this time Gwen could flash on every word, every laugh, every movement. Those moments with Parker were magical, no matter the why or the how of it. And when he suggested hugging her, she'd gotten all tingly. But the hug never happened. The dream ended before she reached him. Poof, just like that. How would his arms around her have felt?

Her pulse quickened. Would she be able to bring him back again?

A tiny nose touched Gwen's ankle and broke the spell. She bent down and lifted Amber, holding the cat suspended under her furry arms. They stared into each other's faces.

"Well, dearie, are you going to tell me if you purred for your master last night? Huh?"

Amber moved her feline focus from Gwen's right eye to her left and back again. Not a peep, not a purr, not a yip was offered.

Lowering the cat to the floor, Gwen trudged out to the front sidewalk and retrieved Monday's edition of the Harbor Falls Gazette, shaking her head. The paper girl never managed to toss it all the way to the top step.

Before heading inside, she snapped the paper open. The front page headline caught her attention:

BODY DISCOVERED NEAR HISTORIC WATERWHEEL

Late Sunday morning Harbor Falls police officers discovered a body in the millpond near The Olde Music Shop on North Street, ensnared by the branches of a willow tree that had fallen during the recent storm.

Detective Mike Brown stated that he suspects the flash flood caused by Saturday's downpour swept the body from an undisclosed location upstream. The combination of tumultuous water and the depth of the mill pond made it difficult for crews to retrieve the body.

The medical examiner's office has not yet determined the cause of death.

Emily Olde Miller, the current owner of the music shop, and her husband Jack Miller, claim no knowledge of the incident. Police Chief Charles Upton advises the circumstances of the death are being investigated and has no further comment at this time.

Identity is being withheld pending notification of next of kin.

Gwen had given no thought to Henrietta's death making the Monday edition. Luckily the article didn't disclose the entry point at Gwen's footbridge. The last thing she needed was curiosity seekers roaming about. Apparently Jack's overheard version of events was accurate.

The biggest question of all buzzed inside Gwen's head like a swarm of bees. Why had Henrietta – the least nature-loving person Gwen had ever known – walked out into those woods in the first place?

***

Gwen forced herself upstairs and entered the guest room. Before she could get it ready for Tess, and maybe Nathan, she had to remove Henrietta's belongings.

Reaching under the bedframe, she pulled out the black snakeskin luggage, tossed it onto the comforter, and unhitched the locks. The first things Gwen spotted when she opened the top dresser drawer were the red thong and lace shorty, along with assorted fancy bras and silk undies. Henrietta was taunting her even in death. It was all Gwen could do not to cut the lingerie into ribbons. But no, that would never do. What would Henrietta's relatives say if they came to collect her things and found them shredded? Still, Gwen didn't bother to fold anything before pitching the items into the gaping suitcase.

From the second drawer, she added bright sweaters and scarves. No surprise that there were no jeans or sweatshirts in sight. Gwen carried the matching tote bag into the guest bathroom. Makeup, powders, and perfumes costing probably hundreds of dollars tumbled inside.

Back-tracking to the wardrobe, she tossed in Henrietta's slacks, blouses, and fancy shoes. Gwen closed both pieces of luggage and stood on the upper landing, trying to figure out where she could store them.

Making a decision, she carried the luggage down the staircase to the mid-way split and up the other side into the sitting room. Above her craft area, Gwen pulled down the folding ladder and climbed into the small attic, plunking the luggage toward the front where it would be easy to retrieve if anyone was willing to take them.

Back in the guest room, Gwen cringed when she bundled up Henrietta's bed linens. Not that the sheets were contaminated, just creepy. Should she wash them or throw

146

them out in the trash? Gwen decided to decide later and carried them down to the basement laundry area.

As she remade the bed with clean sheets, Gwen considered those two local numbers from Henrietta's cell phone log with no name attached. Being good with numbers, she easily recalled them. She'd suggested to Detective Brown that they could belong to Henrietta's uncle and cousin. She wondered if she should call and offer her condolences.

After smoothing the comforter into place, she hurried to the kitchen, plucked her writing tablet and a pencil from a drawer, and wrote both numbers across the top of the page. From her great-grandma's hutch in the dining room, she retrieved her laptop and carried it to the island. After logging onto a reverse search site, she typed in the first number and it came up as John Wickham in Wareham, this side of the Cape Cod Canal.

John Wickham must have been the uncle Henrietta visited on Friday. Same last name. Gwen had never given any thought to Henrietta's unmarried status, but she was certain that the woman had dated after Parker's rejection. Her sexual conquests had been a favorite topic at the Baylies' water coolers. But Henrietta had never settled down with any one man. Now Gwen knew it was because Henrietta never gave up hope that one day she and Parker would marry. How ridiculous. How presumptuous! How sad.

"Stop that right now," Gwen scolded out loud. "Get back to those phone numbers."

She dialed the first one. It rang four times before bouncing to an answering machine. She hung up without leaving a message. Back at her laptop, she reverse-searched the second number. It was registered to Edward Evans in Sandwich, a beautiful little village located at the top of Cape Cod on the other side of the two bridges that were forever clogged with traffic during the tourist season. After all, that was the only way on or off the Cape.

Perhaps Edward was the husband of Mary?

Another answering machine. Again, Gwen disconnected and returned the receiver to its base, letting her hand linger.

Detective Brown had probably done this same reverse search and may have already contacted these relatives. What was their reaction to Henrietta's death? Would the uncle blame Gwen? Would Mary resent the loss of a rediscovered cousin?

The house phone shrilled beneath her hand. She lifted the receiver.

Before she could say hello, Detective Brown's voice barked into her ear. "Mrs. Andrews, can you come to the station? We have a few more questions."

The detective had said he'd let her know if he wanted to talk again. She hadn't expected him to call this soon, though, if at all.

"Good morning, Detective." She peeked at the kitchen clock. Nine-thirty. "When?"

"As soon as you can get here. Tell the officer at the front desk to take you to Interrogation Room Two." He disconnected the call.

Interrogation Room Two? Why so formal? She'd pictured them sitting in the detective's office, if he had one. He said he had a few more questions, right? Or was there more to it? He sounded different somehow, his voice curter. Was she misreading his attitude, or was it simply the result of a noisy police station? More worrisome, had he discovered her splintered railings? Was she walking into a trap? Would he arrest her for negligent homicide?

Or was she being paranoid? Should she call Ernie? Would he even take her call after she'd tossed him out the other day?

According to the TV detectives, showing up with a lawyer almost always meant a person was hiding something. The only thing Gwen was hiding was her knowledge of the aging lumber on her footbridge.

After a brief hesitation, she dialed Ernie's office. His legal assistant said Ernie was out of the office at a meeting. Gwen took a noisy breath. "Would you please let Attorney Maguire know I've been called to the police station about Henrietta Wickham? If he can possibly meet me there, I'd appreciate it."

Chapter Twenty-Five

Before driving across the North Street Bridge, Gwen pulled over and parked in an area designated for the scenic overlook. She again leaned over the stone parapet and peered into the millpond below. The willow, poised so gracefully just the other day, now stretched from one bank to the other. Its branches were spread like a spider web, still grasping woodland debris washed down by the storm. A cluster of boughs had been sawn off, creating an access path to the far bank. Gwen shivered at the sight of Henrietta's watery grave.

Returning to her car, Gwen drove past the new library, then the Baylies campus, its brick and stone buildings scattered throughout the picturesque grounds. Another mile up the road, she turned left into the parking lot of the police station.

Gripping her steering wheel, she considered waiting for Ernie. Had he gotten her message? How soon would he arrive? Would he even come?

Gwen dug deep to find a reserve of inner strength and got out of her car. She strolled through the glass door marked "Public Entrance," looking as nonchalant as she knew how. A bulletin board was plastered with wanted posters, a gun safety course, and public notices. Behind a glass panel, an officer watched her movements. She leaned over and spoke into the little box. "My name is Gwen Andrews. Detective Brown is expecting me." She didn't mention Interrogation Room Two.

He lifted the phone and punched a few buttons. After a brief conversation, he lumbered to his feet, made his way through the door behind him, and appeared in the hallway to her left. He opened the door, holding it until she passed through. His name badge read "Sergeant McNair." He was the officer she'd spoken to yesterday morning to report Henrietta missing.

As she followed him, it occurred to Gwen she'd never once been inside the police station. Garish florescent lights bounced off the green walls of the hallway, and it smelled like a high school gym locker. At the second metal door on the right, Sergeant McNair turned the handle and waved her inside. She fought the urge to turn and bolt, flinching when the latch clicked shut behind her.

Sitting behind a scratched metal table, Detective Brown didn't look up. He spoke in a toneless voice. "Have a seat, Mrs. Andrews. Chief Upton will join us in a minute." Flipping his fingers through his battered notebook, the detective leaned back on two chair legs.

Gwen sat down on the nearest metal chair, wriggling in search of an elusive comfortable spot. The minutes ticked by in silence. She gazed around the room, finding little distraction in the tired beige walls and sparse furniture.

When she was about at the end of her patience, the door opened and Chief Charles Upton strode into the room. An imposing man, his broad shoulders suggested physical strength, and the set of his wide jaw implied professional determination. His wavy brown hair was brushed back, exposing his high forehead.

He rested his massive hand on her shoulder. "Thanks for coming in, Gwen. I know this must be distressing for you. We need to ask you a few questions."

The chief dropped into the adjacent chair and opened his file folder. When Gwen leaned toward it, he shifted his forearm, hiding the documents. He turned toward her, his hazel eyes, the same color as Parker's, focusing on her with an intense stare. "Earlier this morning we interviewed several people about Ms. Wickham. We just need some clarification from you. Do you mind if we record your answers?"

Gwen nodded her permission and wondered who the others were.

Detective Brown picked up his pencil and poised it above a fresh page in his notebook.

The chief referred to his folder notes. "What time did you last see Ms. Wickham?"

Gwen sat up straight. "Saturday morning, just like I told Detective Brown yesterday."

Despite the recorder, and possibly video cameras whirring away behind the scenes, the detective bent to write her answer. The tip of his pencil broke. He mumbled a curse then yanked open a drawer, found another pencil, and slammed the drawer shut.

The chief's no-nonsense voice pulled her back from the detective's antics. "Did you see Ms. Wickham after she parked her car in front of your neighbor's house?"

"No," she answered. "Excuse me, Chief, but why are you asking me the same questions Detective Brown asked me yesterday?"

The chief angled his head. "I'm simply confirming his notes."

Gwen tried, without success, to relax. The chief continued with additional questions, most of them duplicates of the day before. Although the scratching of the detective's pencil grated on Gwen's nerves, she answered each question, figuring the quicker she gave her answers – repeats or not – the sooner she could escape this horrid room and go home.

At the end of the chief's questioning, Detective Brown leaned across the table. "Were you acquainted with Ms. Wickham before she came back to town?"

Gwen masked her surprise. The day before he hadn't asked, and she hadn't volunteered. She didn't want to appear uncooperative. After all, other than delaying the footbridge repair, she'd done nothing wrong.

Deciding to respond with the bare truth, she said, "We were both music professors at Baylies before she moved away."

Again, Detective Brown scribbled. "Did you consider her a friend?"

Gwen repositioned her body. "I wouldn't say we were friends. Just colleagues."

The detective raised his head, his eyes boring into hers. "Why didn't you mention this fact to me yesterday?"

Gwen hadn't expected this topic to come up. "For one thing, Detective, you didn't ask. And besides, what difference does it make if I knew her before?" She looked back and forth between the detective and the chief.

Detective Brown's eyes flashed, though his voice remained scarily calm. "It makes a big difference, Mrs. Andrews. It makes me think you're hiding something. What other details are you keeping to yourself?"

The chief interrupted. "I'll take it from here."

Detective Brown huffed, his breath riffling his pages. The chief again flipped through his own documents. "Like I said, we interviewed a few people this morning. We found out you and Ms. Wickham used to mix it up on a regular basis."

Gwen walked her fingers down her thighs and gripped her knees, hoping her hands would stop shaking. His statement waited for confirmation. Although it didn't matter who had revealed her checkered past with Henrietta, Chief Upton and Detective Brown needed to understand the true circumstances of their relationship.

Gwen sat tall. "Henrietta was always the aggressor. What does my past with her have to do with your investigation into her death?"

Chief Upton cleared his throat. "We've ruled her death suspicious, Gwen."

"You have?" Gwen asked, truly jolted. All this time, she'd assumed Henrietta's death was an accident. An accident that could most likely be blamed on Gwen's aged lumber.

"But why suspicious, Chief?"

"There's evidence of a struggle on your footbridge. The one closest to the North Street Bridge. Our techs found multiple scuffmarks."

Jack's eavesdropping had confirmed Henrietta fell through that damn railing. However, a struggle leaving scuffmarks, plus the police ruling of suspicious death, suggested an entirely different scenario. Not an accident at all.

"You're positive that's where it happened?" Gwen was stalling, not only to collect her thoughts but also to give Ernie time to get there.

"Quite sure. She either fell or was pushed from that platform. That's what we're trying to determine."

"By talking to me?" Gwen swiped sweaty palms on her jeans. This interview was heading in an unexpected direction, and she was apparently a suspect. She knew she hadn't been the one to struggle with Henrietta. But how could she prove it?

Gwen panicked. Had she made those scuffmarks herself? On Saturday night, when she and Hal searched the woods, she'd taken a tumble. But no, they'd been at the upper footbridge at the time, and she'd already stepped off the platform onto the slippery path. Relief flooded in.

Just as quickly, it faded. During her solitary walk the day before, when the weak railing hadn't supported her weight, she'd thrown her body backwards to avoid her own tumble into the gorge. Her gardening sneakers may have left a mark.

Gwen fought to remain calm. The scuffmarks had to be more than a single blemish. Right now, she had to convince these two men that she was the last person they should suspect.

"Charles," Gwen stated, unconcerned about using his first name in front of Detective Brown, "if you think I was involved with Henrietta's tumble, you are way off key. I'll give you a list of people who were in and out of my home all day Saturday. I'm sure every one of them will tell you I was *not* in my woods pushing my guest into the gorge."

Gwen raised her hands, preparing to tick off names on her fingers.

Chief Upton reached over and lowered her hands. "That won't be necessary just yet."

Her brain felt like it was playing a fast game of ping pong. The detective was definitely suspicious of her involvement in Henrietta's death. The chief appeared unconvinced. Gwen knew she was an innocent bystander but, at the same time, wondered who *had* been involved.

And then the detective reached down beside his chair, coming up with two bags. He set them both on the table directly in front of Gwen. "Do either of these belong to you?"

Gwen stared through the plastic sleeves at the contents. Unless she was mistaken, one held what appeared to be her clippers and the other a black trash bag.

But how did Detective Brown get them?

With a jolt, Gwen silently answered her own question. During her near-tumble on Friday, her clippers had plummeted into the gorge, nicking her calf on the way by. The empty trash bag had flown away. In her rush to check the second bridge, Gwen had forgotten all about them.

And now there they were, perched on the interrogation table. She lifted her eyes to see the detective's focus fixated on her. She tried to remain calm. She'd read hundreds of mysteries over the years. She could surely keep herself out of hot water by using her wits and a little common sense.

Chapter Twenty-Six

Staring down, Gwen kept her mouth closed and waited for
Ernie. He'd said to let him know if she needed his help. Had he
meant it? Was he on his way?

Not one second later the door behind her flew open and
Ernie burst into the interrogation room. He gave the group a
hard stare. "Chief Upton. Detective Brown."

The chief turned and nodded, but remained seated.

"Attorney Maguire."

Detective Brown looked down at his notes.

"Might you tell me why you're interrogatin' my client
without her attorney present?" Ernie demanded.

The chief's posture remained ramrod straight. "Mrs.
Andrews didn't request an attorney."

Ernie visually morphed into full lawyer mode. "She left a
message with my assistant to meet her here. In my book, that's
a request."

"But we're not interrogating Mrs. Andrews," the chief
continued, his tone even. "We're simply asking a few questions
about her house guest."

Ernie lifted his bushy eyebrows. "For what reason?"

The chief's forehead wrinkled. "Henrietta Wickham's body
was found in the millpond near the music shop yesterday
morning."

Ernie was quiet for a moment. "That article on the front
page...." He paused and looked down into Gwen's upturned
face. "That was Henrietta?"

"It was," the chief confirmed. "We've deemed Ms.
Wickham's death suspicious."

Moving behind Gwen, Ernie placed his hands on her
shoulders.

"And just why did you make that rulin', Chief Upton?"

"We found signs of a struggle on Mrs. Andrews' footbridge, plus broken railings."

"Is that why you're *not* interrogatin' my client?" Not waiting for the chief to respond, Ernie pointed at the two bags sitting in the center of the metal table. "What are those?"

Detective Brown snapped, "Like it says...evidence."

Ernie leaned over Gwen's shoulder until his face was even with hers. "Mrs. Andrews, were you asked about the contents of those two bags?"

"Yes," Gwen answered, her voice quavering.

Ernie tossed a business card onto the table. "If you need to speak with my client again, call my office." He cupped Gwen's elbow, eased her from the chair and out the door, then down the hallway until they exited into the parking lot.

"Sorry, Gwen, I came as soon as I could. Give me a dollar."

She jerked her head and stared at him. "Why on earth are you asking me for a dollar?"

Without speaking, he held out his hand, so Gwen rummaged in her wallet and plunked the bill in his palm. "There. Do you need something from the vending machine inside?"

He snorted and tucked the dollar in his briefcase. "Nope. This makes me officially your attorney. Anything you say to me from now on is privileged information."

"Oh," Gwen said, a bit chagrined she hadn't recognized the exchange. "But, Ernie, you were Parker's attorney for years."

"But not yours, Gwen darlin'. My assistant will register you as a new client. We need to talk."

Gwen glanced at the police station door, half expecting Detective Brown to rush out and haul her back inside. "Ernie, can we talk at my house?"

"Sure. Let me walk you to your car."

***

At Gwen's dining room table, Ernie asked questions and

157

she answered. He jotted notes on his legal pad, finally glancing up. "Did you recognize the contents of those evidence bags, Gwen?"

She got to her feet and began to pace near the staircase landing. "From what I could see through the plastic, they looked like the clippers and trash bag I took on my walk in the woods after you left on Friday. I nearly fell off the same footbridge where Henrietta apparently went in. The lumber is old and the nails were loose. I meant to go back out there with Parker's hammer to fix it until I could have the crossbeams replaced, but I kept getting sidetracked."

Ernie reached out and gently pulled on her sleeve. "You need to calm down. Sit."

She swallowed a sob and plopped back into the chair.

"What if it's my fault she died?"

"The police are basin' their rulin' of suspicious death on scuffmarks, not loose lumber. So there's no reason to blame yourself for her misfortune."

"Is there any chance they'll call it an accident?"

"Not likely. They seem sure of the struggle, which implies a second person. It's at least manslaughter, if not murder."

Gwen picked at her fingernails, avoiding his gaze. "In that case, there's one more thing."

"Tell me."

"When that railing wobbled, I threw my weight backwards and landed on my fanny. I might have left a scuffmark on the bridge boards."

His pen made several doodles next to his notes. "What shoes were you wearin', Gwen?"

She'd returned to her flower beds before taking that walk.

"My gardening sneakers."

"And what did you wear on Saturday for the tours?"

"My canvas shoes." Gwen's hand flew to her chest. "Ernie! If a mark was made by my sneakers on Friday, it wouldn't match the canvas shoes I was wearing on Saturday!" She paused and looked over at him. "Would it?"

"I'd guess different soles would leave different residue, but only a lab test could determine if they match the scuffmarks on the boards." Ernie jotted another note on his legal pad then ran his hand through his graying locks.

"Listen, I know this looks bad for you, but the police need something solid to make an arrest." He pulled his cell from his jacket pocket and got to his feet. "If you'll excuse me, Gwen, I'll make a few phone calls. See if I can stir the pot. Why don't you jot down what you can remember about Henrietta's movements since she arrived last week? And try to relax."

Relax? Gwen wouldn't relax until Detective Brown told her she was no longer a suspect.

Ernie scrolled through his cell directory, punched a number, then retreated to the rear deck. Gwen could hear the murmur of his conversation but couldn't make out his words.

She went to a kitchen drawer and pulled out her writing tablet, already noted with the two phone numbers of Henrietta's relatives. But before she could jot down a single word, the doorbell rang and she hurried to see who was visiting at midday on a Monday.

"Hi, Gwen." Hal's eyes searched her face. "I thought I'd stop by and see how you're holding up." He lifted a bag from *The Wharf Restaurant.* "I brought you an early lunch."

The scent of lasagna and garlic bread made Gwen's stomach rumble. Had she eaten breakfast? She couldn't remember.

"That was thoughtful of you, Hal. It smells great. Is there enough for three? My lawyer is here."

"Your lawyer?"

Until she spoke Ernie's title out loud, Gwen didn't grasp how ominous it sounded. She realized she was blocking the door, and threw it open. "Sorry, Hal. Come in."

When they reached the kitchen island, Ernie re-entered through the French door. His eyebrows lifted when he noticed Hal.

Gwen stepped forward. "Ernie, this is Hal Jenkins. He's the grandfather of Jenna Jenkins, my student who's competing this Saturday."

Ernie extended his hand. "Jenkins? You look familiar."

Hal accepted the handshake. "Jenkins Garden Center, south of town."

"Of course. I've been there with my Fiona many times. Sorry I didn't make the connection."

Hal lifted the restaurant bag. "I brought lunch for Gwen. There's plenty if you can join us."

Ernie sniffed the air. "Smells great. I will, thanks."

Gwen grabbed three plates and served the steaming lasagna. Both men wasted no time digging in.

"Ernie, did you learn anything new with your calls?" she asked, dividing the garlic bread.

When Ernie hesitated, she added, "You can talk in front of Hal. He's the one who helped me search the woods for Henrietta on Saturday."

Ernie nodded and put down his fork. "I spoke to someone on the inside who provided a few details. For one, the police have verified the presence of a second person. And, in addition to the scuffmarks, the techs found hair caught in the broken railin', and they don't think it's Henrietta's. They've requested DNA tests to see if there's a match in the system."

Gwen reached up and touched her ash-brown crop, hoping she hadn't left any hair behind during her near-disaster on Friday. "What color?"

"Dark, my informant said, but not as black as Henrietta's."

For the first time, Gwen was hearing some good news. But who in Harbor Falls had enticed Henrietta to a rendezvous on that footbridge?

Ernie reached over and laid his hand on Gwen's arm. "Now don't let this throw you, but Detective Brown is sayin' he's pretty sure you're the one who was out there with her. He just needs to find proof. He's convinced himself you wanted her out of your life for good, and my source doesn't think he's looking at anyone else."

"But why me, Ernie? Henrietta had loads of enemies! And what about that hair? That's clearly not mine!"

"This is just the way it works, Gwen. Detective Brown will focus on you until a better suspect comes along. If anything new comes to light, I'll be one of the first to know."

"Who's your contact, Ernie?" Hal asked.

"Sorry. I have to keep the identity to myself." Ernie lowered his voice. "Don't tell anyone I have an insider at the police department."

Gwen had no desire to cause problems for Ernie's informant. But what about reliability? What if Ernie's source provided inaccurate details? Gwen wasn't about to relax.

Then a disturbing thought pushed its way to the front. Would a small town detective – relatively new to the force – be eager to make an arrest regardless of the lack of evidence? Detective Brown might think a quick arrest would be a feather in his cap.

Ernie waved at Gwen's writing tablet, distracting her. "Did you write down anything?"

She glanced at the blankness below those two phone numbers and shook her head.

Hal grabbed a chunk of garlic bread. "Detective Brown called me into the police station early this morning."

"What did he ask you?" Ernie asked, his eyes gleaming.

"What time I arrived with the tour group, did I see Henrietta, how often did I see Gwen, where was I when Gwen says she spotted Henrietta's car down the street, how did we search the property..."

161

Gwen interrupted. "Did he ask about the railings?"

"He didn't mention them, but he did ask if you were out of my sight for more than a few minutes. I'm sorry, Gwen, I had to tell him."

Her fork clanged to her plate. "Tell him what?"

"That you disappeared for a while on Saturday night. Remember? I asked you where you'd been. You never said."

Gwen's mouth opened and closed like a goldfish. "Hang on a second, Hal. After Claudia and I cleaned up my kitchen, I walked her to her car behind the old schoolhouse. I was on my way back when I passed Henrietta's sedan in front of Mrs. Martin's house. When I climbed my deck steps, you and Liz and Tony didn't notice me, so I went inside and made hot chocolate."

Hal held up his hands in a defensive gesture. "I'm only saying I couldn't tell the detective where you were for that half hour."

Gwen snapped back, "Well, if I'd known my movements would be this important, I would've announced where I'd been."

She jumped to her feet then whirled around to face Hal. "You know what you've done? You've given Detective Brown the time frame he needed to back up his ridiculous theory that I slipped off into the woods to toss Henrietta into the creek."

Without stopping to take a breath, she turned to Ernie. "Isn't opportunity one of the things the detective has to prove?" Gwen felt an invisible net wrapping around her.

Ernie shook his head, his voice remained calm. "Hold on, Gwen. If you and Claudia cleaned up your kitchen and then walked to her car, she can confirm that timing to Detective Brown."

Gwen took in a lungful of air. "You're right, Ernie. Why didn't I think of that?" She glanced back at Hal. "I'm so sorry for yelling at you."

Hal waved away her apology. "You're under a lot of pressure."

"So what do we do now?" Gwen slumped onto her stool and stared at her half-eaten lasagna.

Ernie wiped his mouth with a napkin and pushed away his empty plate. "Seems to me we need to find someone else in Harbor Falls who has a stronger motive to get rid of Henrietta." He paused. "Maybe we should hire a private investigator to dig into her past and also find out who she's been seeing and where she's been going since she came back to town."

His suggestion threw Gwen for a loop. "I don't think most folks in Harbor Falls would speak to a private eye." Gwen gathered the dirty dishes and placed them in the sink before turning back to Ernie. "But they'd probably talk to me."

"You could be right, Gwen. But we need to discuss that idea before you do anything rash." Ernie glanced at his watch. "Sorry, but I've got to get back to the office and finish up some documents that need to be filed today; I can come back later. How's five o'clock?"

"That should work. Jenna's coming for her practice session at four. We should be finished by the time you get here, Ernie."

"Good. If you think of anything, write it down," he said, pointing at her tablet. He pulled out a business card and jotted a number on the back side before handing it to her. "That's my new cell number. Put it in your phone in case you need to call me."

He extended a hand to Hal. "Good to meet you."

Hal took a step sideways and blocked Ernie's path to the door. "Hold on a second. Like Gwen told you, I helped her search the woods for Henrietta on Saturday. If there's anything I can do, I'd like to help." He looked back and forth from Ernie to Gwen. "Can I sit in with the two of you later? I'll be back at five to pick up Jenna, and I can send her on an errand while we make plans."

Hal's offer was the last thing Gwen expected. She hadn't dreamed he would step up this way, but she could use all the help she could get. Besides, every amateur sleuth needed a sidekick. She glanced at Ernie to see him waiting for her response. "Sure, Hal. Thanks."

Ernie clapped Hal on the back. "If it's fine with Gwen, it's fine with me."

"Good." Hal turned to Gwen. "I've got work to do at the garden shop. See you at five."

***

After the door closed behind both men, Gwen sagged against it. Although she was grateful for Ernie's legal advice and Hal's willingness to lend a hand, she still worried about being arrested for a crime she hadn't committed.

Ernie said the police couldn't make an arrest without solid evidence. Gwen suspected Detective Brown was focusing on her because of her easy access to the footbridge and his assumption that she wanted Henrietta gone. She'd read about false arrests hinging on circumstantial evidence. Wrongly accused criminals sometimes spent years in jail until someone cleared them of wrong-doing.

And then there were her garden clippers. Gwen knew that if there was any blood on those blades, it was her own from her near-fall on Friday. But would the detective assume it was Henrietta's until DNA tests came back? In fact, Gwen had no idea if a tool had been involved in Henrietta's death. She should write that down for Ernie to check with his source.

She made her way to the tall studio windows and stared into the woods. In a perfect world, Detective Brown would uncover the truth surrounding Henrietta's death. But Ernie's source said the detective wasn't looking at any other persons of interest. How could a professional law enforcement officer ignore the dark hair, so obviously not Gwen's?

She thumped her fist against her thigh. She had to find a

more likely suspect. She could surely do what the heroines in all her mysteries did: follow the clues.

She walked over to her tablet and made a note about the possible blood on the clippers. When her gaze landed on her gardening sneakers near the French door, she grabbed them and marched upstairs. After a few minutes of rummaging around in her closet, she located her canvas shoes and flipped both pair upside down to study the soles.

They were not the same. Different material, different color, different pattern. Gwen had no way to determine if either pair would match the scuffmarks the techs found. She guessed it would depend on the shoes worn by both Henrietta and that second person. Frustrated, she tossed them onto the closet floor and headed back down the staircase.

At the halfway split, something niggled at the back of Gwen's mind. What was it? Then it struck her. Henrietta's excessive caution on these stairs and her avoidance of the balcony above. When Gwen had noticed Henrietta's behavior last Thursday, she'd blamed it on weak leg muscles. But maybe, just maybe, Henrietta had a fear of heights or a touch of vertigo.

If that was the case, why would the woman walk onto a platform spanning a deep gorge?

It made no sense. No sense at all.

Chapter Twenty-Seven

Gwen remained locked in her quandary until Amber cuffed her ankle. The cat turned her fluffy tail and strolled to her feeding station, her message abundantly clear. Gwen dutifully measured out dry cat food and re-filled the water bowl.

Seeing that Amber was happily munching, Gwen's thoughts returned to Henrietta's scuffle on the footbridge. Could her clash with that second person have been connected to the music competition? Jack was deeply involved in the organization of the competition. Maybe he'd overheard something.

Although Ernie had implied he wanted Gwen to stay home and write down anything Henrietta-related that had happened since the woman roared back into Harbor Falls, a little action might be more productive. Besides, she was way too restless to sit still and make a list.

Once more Gwen headed out her front door and down the granite steps, this time charging down the sidewalk that bordered her side yard, toward the majestic birch trees. By the time she crossed the North Street Bridge and pushed in the door of the music shop, her pledge to do whatever she had to do to prevent her arrest was firmly ensconced.

The shop was empty of customers. But then, with the college students and professors embroiled in classes, the quiet was no surprise. Alex stood behind his instrument counter, listening to Jack, who was leaning across the glass top. When Alex looked up and waved at Gwen, Jack turned his head, murmured something to Alex, and headed her way.

"I'm glad you stopped by, Gwen. We need to talk." Without waiting for her to react, he strode toward his office.

She raised a brow at Alex, telescoping her thought, *What now?* and followed Jack.

166

When Gwen entered Jack's office, he was pacing at the window that looked down on the waterwheel. The absence of its rumble was deafening. The water that usually sluiced down the mill race to drop onto the paddles must have been blocked during the removal of Henrietta's body and not yet released to flow its normal course.

"I'm sorry if I frightened you last night, Gwen."

Jack's voice made her jump. Was that an apology? How refreshing. "You did scare me, Jack. But I didn't come here about that. I need to ask you a question."

"Sure, sure. But first, there's something *I* need to ask *you*." He grinned and reached over to grab the competition folder sitting on the edge of his desk. "This may not have occurred to you, but with Henrietta gone, we're short one judge – again. Alex and I reviewed the judging protocol and found a little-used loophole that would allow you to replace Henrietta. If you're willing, that is." He tossed her a crooked smile.

Gwen couldn't believe his audacity. Could the man be any smarmier? Jack didn't seem to be the least bit upset that Henrietta was dead. His only concern was finding another replacement judge. But Gwen's curiosity got the best of her.

"What loophole is that?"

"Well, in similar competitions, judges who..." His voice fell off. "Well, let me read it to you." He slid a document from his file and read: "A jury of three distinguished musicians will serve as judges. The decision of the judges is final. If a contestant has studied with or otherwise had close professional or personal ties with a judge, that judge will be requested to disqualify himself / herself from judging of that contestant only. The scores from the other two judges will be averaged to provide a third score."

Jack lowered the sheet of paper and tapped his steepled fingers against his chin. "You'll simply sit out during Jenna's performance."

Gwen took a moment to consider his outrageous offer. "Why don't you step in, Jack?"

His smugness dropped away. "Even if I had a musical bone in my body – which I don't – I'm barred from being a judge because of my connection to the shop. Conflict of interest. The same applies to Emily and Alex." His smile returned. "I understand if you're not eager to do me another favor, Gwen. But the committee and our young musicians – *and Jenna* – would certainly appreciate your participation."

For the past twenty-four hours, Gwen had thought of little else besides Henrietta's ghastly death. Replacing the woman on the judging panel hadn't occurred to her. She stared out Jack's window at the silent wheel, weighing her options.

On the one hand, she could simply refuse, in order to punish Jack for strapping her with Henrietta. On the other hand, she'd endured the woman's intrusion to protect Jenna's chance at the scholarship. Gwen had no choice. She had to step in as the third judge.

Her decision made, she turned to see Jack watching her. "I don't see how I can refuse."

A low whistle escaped through his lips. "Good. Good. Of course Henrietta's judging fee will now go to you." He hurried to his doorway and shouted, "Alex, come here. Gwen's on board."

Within seconds, Alex entered the office, a folder under his arm.

Jack said, "Gwen's agreed to be our third judge."

"Thank you, Gwen." Alex released a heavy sigh. "You don't know how relieved I am."

He picked up a second manila folder from Jack's pile and handed it to her. "This is the judging packet. If you have any questions, any questions at all, just call me."

Gwen accepted the slim file. "Who are the other two judges this year?"

Jack stiffened and cleared his throat but didn't acknowledge Gwen's question.

Alex shot Jack a quizzical look, then answered, "Albert Hall, a music professor from Amherst, and Walter James, retired Baylies dean."

Gwen played with the edge of the judging folder, her days as a music professor flooding back. "I'm not acquainted with Mr. Hall. But it'll be good to see Dean James again." She recalled the old dean's inquisitive mind and his scary stare when dealing with difficult college students.

Placing her file on the edge of Jack's desk, Gwen opened it to the inside flap. "Would you give me their phone numbers, Alex?"

"Sure." He flipped open his own folder and copied the names and phone numbers.

Jack jumped to his feet. "There's no need to call them."

"Why not, Jack?"

His head wagged back and forth. "I'd prefer the judges don't fraternize before the competition. My own rule."

Gwen caught a vaguely hostile expression as it flashed across Jack's face. Where did that rule come from?

Jack fussed with his pile of papers but said nothing more.

Gwen and Alex turned to leave. Before they reached the door, she swiveled back. "Hold on, Jack. I came here to ask you a question."

His earlier cordiality vanished. "What is it?"

"Henrietta said she was second guessing her return to Harbor Falls. Do you know if anyone gave her a hard time about judging the competition?"

Jack shook his head. "Not that I'm aware of. Alex?"

Alex also shook his head, then blurted, "I've got to get back to my customer," and he left.

Gwen re-focused on Jack. "Did you hear any rumors? Overhear any comments? Innuendos?"

He narrowed his eyes. "Anything I might have heard – and I'm not saying I did – is academic now that Henrietta's dead, don't you think?"

"Actually, Jack, it's not academic. But I have another question."

"Now what?" he asked, his tone testy.

"I was called to the police station earlier and they have ruled Henrietta's death suspicious. Detective Brown seems to think I had something to do with it."

Jack sat still, his face a mask. "So what's your question?"

Gwen shouldn't have been surprised by his indifference to her plight, but she needed to rise above his snide attitude if she wanted to learn anything. "Did you tell the detective this morning about Henrietta's hateful insults whenever she bumped into me?"

A long moment passed until Jack shrugged. "I don't remember exactly. I may have."

She noted he didn't deny he'd been one of the people interviewed. "Come on, Jack, you're at least fifteen years younger than me. Too young to be forgetful."

He tossed his pen onto the blotter. "Fine. I'll tell you what I told him: that Henrietta was quite the bitch where you were concerned. It's nothing he won't find out from anyone who was on campus back then."

Gwen felt like Jack had whacked her upside the head with a brick. Unfortunately, he was right. As soon as Detective Brown spoke to Baylies office staff and tenured professors, he'd hear all about Henrietta's constant harassment. Would anyone say that Gwen never retaliated? Most likely not. It didn't sound like Jack had shared the complete scenario. Just the juicy part.

Defeated, Gwen waved the judging folder and turned to go. "I'll call if I have any questions."

When she exited Jack's office, Gwen recognized the trilling voice of Myrtle Mueller. The woman stood in front of Alex's

170

counter, shaking her finger in his face. Poor Alex was leaning backwards, his eyes blinking rapidly.

Gwen strode over, ready to rescue her friend and dueting partner.

Before Gwen could open her mouth, Myrtle whipped around. "I can't believe you're doing it."

Gwen wanted desperately to join Alex behind his counter. "Doing what, Myrtle?"

"You agreed to be a competition judge. I heard it all. I hope you're not planning to skew the scores in favor of your little flute student. My Herbert deserves a fair shot!"

On his grandmother's other side, Herbert hunched down, a flush coloring his cheeks.

Alex stepped up to his counter, keeping it between him and Myrtle. "Mrs. Mueller, you don't understand. The committee has a rule to cover this situation. Gwen will sit out during her student's performance. She won't be able to influence the vote."

"Humph, we'll have to wait and see, won't we?" Myrtle grabbed Herbert's sleeve and dragged him to the exit door, tossing one last withering glance in their direction.

Gwen turned back to Alex. "How did Myrtle find out I'm taking Henrietta's place?"

Alex took a deep breath and let it out in noisy exasperation.

"She brought her grandson in a little while ago to ask about professional tuba cleaners." Alex lowered his voice. "I have to tell you, I've heard the boy play, and he doesn't have a chance of winning."

Gwen raised both hands, palms forward. "Stop, Alex. Did you forget I'm the third judge?"

He rolled his eyes. "Sorry."

Gwen leaned on his counter and repeated her question. "So how did Myrtle find out?"

Alex shook his head. "I was flipping through my list of

contacts for her when Jack called me into his office. When I came back out, she was standing right there. Right outside his door. She must have listened to our conversation."

A young lady approached Alex's counter and he straightened up. "Gotta get back to work, Gwen. Thanks for rescuing me from Myrtle."

Gwen hugged the judging folder to her chest and headed toward the shop's exit, concerned that Myrtle might raise a stink on Saturday. Jack had been no help in uncovering a connection between Henrietta's demise and the competition itself, if there was a connection. At least Gwen had learned that Jack was the one who set Detective Brown on her tail. Not that knowing that fact made any difference to her situation.

Before Gwen reached the exit door, Emily emerged from the storeroom along the rear wall and rushed over. "Have you heard anything new about Henrietta?"

Gwen hadn't spoken with Emily since her weird phone call on Saturday. But, still, Emily's hunger for news about Henrietta's death was no surprise. After all, a body discovered near the antique waterwheel was hardly an everyday occurrence.

"Only what they told me at the police station this morning."

"What was that?"

"They've ruled her death suspicious."

Emily's eyes widened. "I thought she fell from your footbridge?"

For a second Emily's knowledge of that detail distracted Gwen. Then she decided Jack must have told his wife about the conversation he overheard as the rescue teams pulled Henrietta from the millpond, because the front page article in the that morning's edition of the Gazette had thankfully omitted the involvement of Gwen's property.

"That's what I thought, Emily. But the police found lots of scuffmarks on the bridge boards, so now they're calling her death suspicious." Not wanting to get Ernie in trouble, Gwen didn't reveal the dark hair caught in the splintered railing.

Emily slumped onto the bench beneath the north-facing window, biting her lip. "So the police think there was a struggle? Who do they think was out there with Henrietta?"

"To tell you the truth, Emily, Detective Brown thinks it was me."

Emily's breath hitched. "That's crazy. Who put that idea into the detective's head?"

"I'm not sure." Gwen didn't disclose that Jack had planted that seed.

Without saying goodbye, Emily left Gwen sitting on the bench and strode toward Jack's office at the other end. Gwen stood up and once again headed for the exit door. As she grasped the knob, Alex came up beside her.

"Can I speak to you, Gwen?" His voice was subdued. "Somewhere besides here?"

Gwen could not miss his troubled expression. "Of course, Alex. Where and when?"

"How about the *Sugar 'n Spice*? I take my lunch break in thirty minutes."

Chapter Twenty-Eight

A half hour later, Gwen approached the *Sugar & Spice Bakery and Café*, located on the southern edge of the village green. The mingled scents of homemade soups, baked bread, and sugary pastries filled the air. She spotted Alex hurrying along a pathway and waited for him at the entrance. His brow was furrowed, his mouth turned down.

"Thanks for meeting me, Gwen."

"No problem, Alex. Let's get you some lunch, and then you can tell me what's going on."

After Alex picked up his food tray, the two of them slid into a booth at the front window.

He shook out his napkin and placed it on his lap. "Gwen, I've got to get this off my chest or I'll bust. I was planning to tell you the first part after we dueted last Thursday afternoon, but then Henrietta interrupted us, so I didn't get a chance. And since she died, there's even more to tell."

Gwen recalled his cool reaction to Henrietta. Now she knew why. "What is it, Alex?"

He took a deep breath, letting it out with a whoosh. "Last Wednesday, our judge from Cape Cod suffered a heart attack, so Jack told me to contact the music professionals we'd hired as judges in the past, but none of them could step in on such short notice." Alex stirred his piping hot bisque. "That's when I called Dean Daniel Chartley to ask if he knew of anyone."

"That makes sense."

"I thought so." Alex's eyes darted around to the other tables, but no one seemed to be paying any attention to them. "When Daniel mentioned the names of some local musicians, I told him I'd already spoken to them with no success. That's when he suggested Henrietta Wickham."

Gwen sipped her hot mulled cider, the only thing she'd

ordered, since she'd eaten lasagna with Hal and Ernie not an hour earlier.

Alex continued his story. "I called her at home in Vermont. She haggled about the fee and insisted we pay her traveling expenses. When I told her I'd get back to her about lodging, she said she'd be driving down the next day and we should book a room at our expense for her entire stay. And…" his spoon clanged on the edge of the bowl, "she demanded meal vouchers. I think she sensed we were desperate."

"Sounds like the Henrietta I used to know." Gwen failed to keep the catty tone from her voice, but Alex was too involved in his narrative to notice.

"Jack was out of the shop, so I took it upon myself to call the hotels, motels and B&Bs in the area. None of them had a room available for her entire stay. When Jack waltzed in an hour later, I told him I'd located a replacement judge. He was pleased until I told him I couldn't find a room."

"Jack can't blame you for the overflow of visitors to Harbor Falls this time of year."

"To be honest, Gwen, I think he does. But wait, there's more. When I told him the judge's name, he stomped around his office like a bull with daggers dangling from his back. He chased me out, but he didn't fully close his office door, so I overheard him trying to convince the dean to let him cancel Henrietta's contract. He stormed out and yelled at me to contact the college committee members until I found one who would let Henrietta stay with them."

Gwen blew air out her nose. "That wasn't fair of Jack. He should have made those calls."

Alex pushed his half-empty bowl aside. "Well, he didn't. Each of them was willing to host our judge until I mentioned Henrietta's name. I never heard people invent lies so fast."

"Did any of them explain why?" Gwen tilted her head, interested in the answer.

"Oh, sure they did. When I reminded one professor he'd agreed to host our judge, he admitted Henrietta had been nasty to his wife, and he didn't want to expose her to more of Henrietta's snide remarks."

"And the other committee members?" Gwen's curiosity clicked to full throttle.

"Well, another professor *suddenly remembered* his mother-in-law was coming for a visit. Then he broke down and confessed Henrietta had gotten him into hot water with the old dean years ago. And a third professor, who *forgo*t her guest room floors were being refinished, disclosed that Henrietta had insulted her in front of students and laughed at her embarrassment."

Gwen cupped her mug and leaned across the table. "What did you do?"

Alex wrinkled his forehead. "Well, I went back to Jack and told him none of the committee members were willing to host Henrietta. When I suggested he and Emily let Henrietta stay with them in their private quarters above the shop, he said, and I quote, 'That will never happen'."

Alex ran his freckled hand through his thinning blonde hair streaked with pale gray. "Then Jack remembered Henrietta had relatives in the area and to tell her she should stay with them."

"How did Henrietta react to that?"

"When I called her back, she said no way in hell would she stay with any of them. And then she announced she had an idea of her own and hung up. The next morning, Jack called you into his office and, well, you know what happened then."

He let out a breath. "I'm sorry, Gwen. I've worked in the music shop since way before Emily took it over. Whenever Henrietta came into the shop at the same time as you, she insulted you non-stop. If I'd known Jack was going to force her into your home, I'd have worked harder to find another place. There must have been someone with an extra room."

"That's what I thought, too, Alex. I'd planned to start checking today." Gwen took one last sip, realizing she'd been cheated out of kicking Henrietta to the curb.

Alex drained his own cider and placed the empty mug and bowl on the tray.

"Let me tell you what happened *after* she arrived. When she walked in the shop last Thursday, Jack locked himself in his office and Emily left to run an errand, leaving me to deal with Henrietta."

"Did Henrietta notice their avoidance?"

"If she did, it didn't seem to faze her. She told me she was pleased to be visiting Harbor Falls after all these years. Which I don't understand, because just about everyone I knew used to resent her nasty disposition. You weren't the only one, Gwen."

He raised both hands. "In fact, when she walked in on our duet later that day, I was surprised how civil she was to you."

"She had plans of some kind, Alex. I just don't know what they were." Gwen paused. "You said there's more since she died?"

He reached for her empty mug and added it to his tray along with their used napkins. "Ever since the police fished her body from the mill pond, Jack couldn't be nicer to me."

"Why do you think that is?"

Alex drummed his fingers on the table. "I don't even want to guess." His head sagged. "Detective Brown wants to talk to me this afternoon. I don't know why. I'm only an employee at the shop. I can only tell him what I heard or saw. My personal opinions don't count."

Gwen considered confiding in Alex that she was the detective's primary suspect but didn't want him to feel obligated to defend her during his police interview. He might even make things worse since he was so aware of Henrietta's nasty tongue lashings.

Instead Gwen said, "Something's been bothering me. If

Henrietta had been sleeping under someone else's roof, do you think she'd still be alive?"

"There's no way to know, Gwen." Tapping his watch, Alex stood up. "I'd better get going. Thanks for listening, Gwen. Nothing has changed, but I don't feel so frustrated now." He hurried out and stepped into the village green.

The customers had thinned, so Gwen remained in the booth, digesting Alex's mistreatment by Jack. Alex's version of Henrietta's hiring differed from Jack's. He'd related the story as if he'd done all the legwork. Typical of Jack to take all the credit.

But what did any of that matter now?

Chapter Twenty-Nine

Back home, Gwen sat at the island, her mind filled with conflicting information. Jack had said it was none of her business why he didn't want Henrietta back in Harbor Falls. And he didn't seem all that upset that Henrietta had died. As ominous as that sounded, Gwen couldn't imagine Jack physically fighting with Henrietta out in the woods. The man was more coward than action figure. Most bullies were.

Could that theory have applied to Henrietta? If Gwen had stood up for herself even one time, would the woman have backed down and left Gwen alone? Another question that would never be answered.

The most Gwen could hope for was that Alex's statement would convince Detective Brown to consider other suspects.

She fingered the edge of the judging file, trying to analyze the strong responses to Henrietta's return: Jack's failed attempt to cancel her contract, Emily's refusal to provide lodging even if Jack had asked her, Claudia's unexplained fear, Ernie's anger that Henrietta had wormed her way under Gwen's roof, all the committee members who had found excuses not to offer their guest room to Henrietta. How many others had been unhappy that Henrietta was back in town?

Maybe the scuffmark person who left hair strands behind didn't even live in Harbor Falls. Maybe an out-of-towner followed Henrietta from Vermont.

Gwen paced the kitchen floor. Damn it! Someone had given Henrietta an irresistible reason to step foot in the woods, the last place she'd go if she had a choice. And then there was Gwen's notion of a link between Henrietta's death and the competition. Just because Jack and Alex hadn't heard anyone threaten the woman didn't mean it hadn't happened.

179

Gwen opened the judging folder and read the guidelines. Clear and straight-forward. Not one question. And nothing to imply trouble. She pushed it away.

Wait a minute. She pulled the folder back and flipped to the inside flap where Alex had written the names and phone numbers of the other two judges. Maybe Henrietta had contacted one or both of these men. Maybe she'd let something slip about her reception in Harbor Falls. It couldn't hurt to ask.

Regardless of Jack's ridiculous warning not to call the other judges, Gwen was now the third judge and perfectly justified to phone Albert Hall and Dean James. Common courtesy, right?

She pulled out her cell and dialed the first number.

A male voice answered. "Yes?"

Astonished she'd connected on her first try. Gwen said, "May I speak to Albert Hall?"

"Speaking." His tone was hesitant.

She squared her shoulders. "My name is Gwen Andrews. I understand we're sharing the judging panel for the music competition in Harbor Falls this Saturday."

A few seconds of silence passed. "I'm afraid you've caught me off guard, uh, Mrs. Andrews, is it? I thought my panel mates would be Henrietta Wickham and Walter James?"

Gwen swallowed. She'd wrongly assumed either Jack or Alex had contacted the other judges about Henrietta. Well, Gwen couldn't stop now. "Dean James is still on the panel. You may not have heard that Henrietta passed away on Saturday night. I've been asked to take her place."

His sharp intake of breath traveled from Amherst. "What happened to Ms. Wickham?"

Gwen was careful not to embellish the facts. "Her body was found in the millpond near the music shop. The medical examiner hasn't disclosed the cause of death."

For several beats Albert said nothing. "How tragic. So you phoned to let me know you'll be taking her place?"

"In part. I'm wondering if Henrietta spoke to you after she arrived last Thursday."

"I don't know why you're asking, but she didn't call me." An awkward silence filled the space. "Oh, all right, Mr. Hall. Nice to talk with you. I look forward to meeting you on Saturday."

After Albert disconnected, Gwen stared at her phone. Although she might be poking her nose into police business, she doubted Detective Brown – given his fixation on her unsubstantiated guilt – would think to call the competition judges to ask if they'd heard from Henrietta.

One down, one to go.

***

"Walter James speaking."

"Dean James, this is Gwen Andrews. I don't know if you remember me."

"Of course I remember you, Gwen! How are you?"

"I'm fine, sir. Do you have a minute?"

"Of course, of course. What can I do for you today?"

"Well…" She hesitated. She'd always had an amiable relationship with the old dean during her tenure at Baylies. But she might be pushing the bounds of their professional friendship with this phone call.

Nudging her concern aside, she proceeded to finish what she'd started. "I'm calling about a serious matter, sir."

"And what serious matter is that?"

She imagined the somber look on the old dean's face as she conveyed the information about Henrietta's passing, concluding with the police labeling her death suspicious.

"This is quite a shock." The old man paused. "Although you know better than most how difficult Henrietta could be, her dying like that is distressing." He paused again. "May I ask how this tragedy impacts the competition?"

"For one thing, Jack Miller offered me her judging chair."

181

"You'll be an excellent addition to the panel. Is there anything I can do to help?"

Gwen took a deep breath and let it out as softly as she could. Would the old dean change his mind after he found out she was a potential suspect? Maybe. But right now Gwen needed to know if Henrietta had contacted him. She gripped the receiver tight in her hand. "Well, actually there is something, sir. Did Henrietta call you since she returned to Harbor Falls last week?"

He didn't answer right away. "Actually, she did. Why do you ask?"

Biting her lower lip, Gwen tried to organize the words jumbling around in her head.

"Well, sir, I'm exploring a possible connection between her death and the competition."

"I have to say, Gwen, there seems to be more to your story." Again, he was silent, then cleared his throat. "I have an idea. I'm making a large pot of beef stew for lunch tomorrow. Why don't you join me? You can tell me what happened to Henrietta, then I'll tell you about her phone call last week."

Gwen sagged against the island. She hadn't expected his invitation. What was so important – or confidential – that the former dean didn't want to tell her over the phone? His conversation with Henrietta must have been quite interesting. If not that, perhaps the old man was simply lonely. Either way, Gwen didn't want to pass up this opportunity. She had to think fast. Tess wouldn't arrive until mid-afternoon, so lunch with Dean James would fit right in.

"I'd love to join you for lunch, sir. Thank you."

"Good, good," he muttered. "Since I retired and my sweet Sally died, I don't have much of a social life. Oh, sure, I'm still on a few boards, but that's all very stuffed-shirt. A visit from an old colleague such as yourself will make my day."

Feeling a bit like Annie Darling from Carolyn Hart's *Death on Demand* mystery series, Gwen jotted down the address. "See you at noon tomorrow, sir. And thanks."

As she hung up the phone, Gwen could barely contain her excitement. Henrietta *had* called the old dean last week. If she'd told him of a falling out with someone connected to the competition, it didn't mean that person had arranged the meeting out at the footbridge. But at least Gwen could pass along a name to Detective Brown.

Gwen tried to tamp down her overactive imagination, but she was chomping at the bit to tell Ernie and Hal about her progress.

Chapter Thirty

At four on Monday afternoon, Jenna arrived for the first of the week's daily practice sessions. Before Gwen could ask why Jenna was frowning, the girl said, "Granddad told me your house guest died over the weekend. Are you sure you want to work with me today?"

Gwen gazed at the teenager, touched by the empathy in one so young. "Of course I do. I've been looking forward to our session all day."

That wasn't quite true. Gwen had been so busy with her time at the police station, the meeting with Ernie afterwards, Hal's thoughtful lunch and his offer to help, plus Gwen's phone calls to the other two judges, that she'd barely given Jenna a second thought. But now that the girl was here, Gwen welcomed the musical distraction.

As they walked side by side toward the studio, Gwen said, "I have some news. My sister Tess is coming tomorrow instead of Thursday."

Jenna let a half-smile brighten her face. "That's great. I can't wait to meet her."

"She's looking forward to practicing with you to prepare for the competition. Now let's get to work. Which of your four pieces do you want to concentrate on today?"

After flipping through her folder, Jenna pulled the sheet music for Mozart's Concerto No. 2 in D major, and the practice began with Gwen's fingers softly tripping along the Steinway keys.

An hour later, Gwen lifted her hands and applauded. "That was beautiful."

Jenna beamed. "You always say that, Mrs. Andrews."

"Because it's always true." When Gwen tugged on Jenna's ponytail, the girl squealed.

Their bonding moment was interrupted by the chiming of the doorbell.

"That'll be Granddad. I'll get it." Jenna laid down her flute and raced for the front door.

Gwen made a notation in her lesson planner, then followed in Jenna's path.

Filling the doorframe was Ernie's tall, lanky frame. He grinned down at the surprised teenager. "Hello. My name is Ernie Maguire. You must be Jenna. Your grandfather was just tellin' me about your musical talent."

Jenna extended her hand. "So nice to meet you, Mr. Maguire." She backed inside and opened the door wide. Ernie headed for the dining room and placed his briefcase on the table.

Entering behind Ernie, Hal caught Gwen's eye and winked. Then he reached out and knuckled the top of Jenna's head. "I have a surprise for you."

"You do? What is it, granddad?"

"Do you remember a conversation we had at the beginning of the summer when you told me you wanted to enter the competition?"

Jenna's blonde head bobbed up and down. "You promised me a new dress to wear on Saturday if I took my lessons seriously. I wasn't sure you meant it."

"Of course I did. And if I know you as well as I think I do, you've been shopping all summer and have probably picked one out."

Jenna spun in a circle, clapping her hands. "You do. I have been. I did."

He reached into his pocket and pulled out his wallet. "Then, I think you should go buy it. How much is it going to cost me?"

A gleam came into the teenager's eyes. "I found a perfect dress in that new boutique at the bottom of Harbor Hill." She looked up hopefully. "It's less than fifty dollars."

185

"And this dress is appropriate for the competition?" Hal handed Jenna several twenties. "Can't be too flashy, you know. Don't want to give the judges the wrong impression."

Jenna tugged on the cash. "I'll have you know I have exquisite taste. When I get back, I'll model it for you and Mrs. Andrews." She shifted her gaze to Ernie. "And you, too, Mr. Maguire."

Hal pocketed his wallet. "Do you want me to drive you or would you rather walk?"

Jenna shook her head. "I'll walk. I won't be long." She kissed his cheek, tucked the cash into her tiny beaded purse, and rushed out.

Ernie cleared his throat. "Slick, old man. We can discuss Gwen's situation without bruisin' your granddaughter's sensibilities." He snapped open the latches of his briefcase, removed his legal pad, and sat down. "Give me a second to review my notes from this mornin'."

Hal took the chair to Ernie's left. Gwen sat across from the men and waited.

"Okay," Ernie said a minute later. "Gwen, have you remembered anything about Henrietta's visit that might help me divert the detective's suspicions?"

She felt the spotlight as both men waited for her answer.

"Sorry, Ernie, I've hardly been at home since you left, so I haven't written anything down, but I've been giving this a lot of thought. It occurred to me that her death might be somehow connected to the competition, so I went to see Jack at the music shop."

Ernie put down his pen. "Hold on a second, Gwen. You shouldn't be goin' anywhere by yourself until this is all sorted out."

Gwen felt her stomach drop. She'd thought he'd be impressed by her action. "But when you suggested this morning that we hire a private eye, I said I didn't think anyone

186

would talk to a stranger about Henrietta, but I thought they'd talk to me. You said I could be right."

"I also said we needed to discuss it. I'm not comfortable with you doing your own investigatin'."

"But, Ernie," Gwen said, "who will object to me asking a few little questions?"

"For one, Gwen, the person who tangled with Henrietta in your woods. If you start talkin' to everyone you know about the woman, and that other person hears about it, he'll get nervous that you'll expose him. And what's the first thing he'll want to do? Shut you up."

"Oh," Gwen said, staring into her lap. "I should have thought of that."

She felt like such an idiot. She wasn't wrapped up in one of her mysteries from the safety of her reading chair where the heroine always manages to pull through in the end. This was serious business.

"Well, since it's too late to stop you, let me ask you if you learned anything from Jack." Ernie's Waterman pen was poised to record her answer.

"Well, I need to tell you he asked me to take Henrietta's judging seat."

Hal tilted his head. "But Jenna…"

"That was my first thought, too, Hal. But Jack and Alex found a loophole that lets me sit out during her performance."

"Are you going to do it?" Hal asked.

"I was going to say no, then I realized they don't have enough time to locate another judge. If the committee cancels the competition, that'll rob Jenna of her chance to win that scholarship."

"In that case," Hal said, "I'm glad you stepped in. The competition is all that girl talks about."

Ernie sat forward. "Did Jack say anything to connect the competition to Henrietta's death?"

187

Gwen played with the wire binding of her writing tablet. "He claims he didn't hear anything."

Ernie seemed to relax. "Any other surprises while you were there?"

Gwen nodded. "Emily pulled me aside and wanted to know if I'd found out what happened to Henrietta. When I told her about the suspicious death ruling and the detective's theory that I was involved, she charged down to Jack's office."

Ernie nodded and made a note. "Anything else?"

"Alex asked me to meet him at Sugar 'n Spice." For the next few minutes, she repeated Alex's story about hiring Henrietta, the frustration of the lodging search, his regret that Jack had foisted Henrietta on Gwen, and Jack's odd behavior after Henrietta died.

"Does Alex think Jack was involved in Henrietta's death?" Ernie asked.

"No. I have to say I agree with him. Jack's a verbal bully, just like Henrietta was, but I can't imagine him in a physical fight. By the way, Alex was scheduled to give his statement to Detective Brown this afternoon."

"Well, at least the detective is makin' a show of investigatin'," Ernie quipped. "I'll ask my source if Alex's information had any impact on Detective Brown's assumption of your guilt."

Ernie made another note and looked up at Gwen. "You certainly had an interestin' afternoon."

"But I'm not finished, Ernie."

"There's more?"

Gwen nodded, finally proud of herself. "I thought maybe Henrietta contacted the other two judges, so I called them both."

"That was clever," Ernie said, one eyebrow lifting. "Did you actually talk to them?"

"I did. First off, neither man knew Henrietta had died, so I broke the news that I'm taking her place. Albert Hall said she didn't call him, so, assuming he's telling the truth, nothing there. But my conversation with the old dean was more fruitful." Gwen sat up straighter. "In fact, she did call him last week, but he didn't want to discuss it over the phone, so he invited me to his condo for lunch tomorrow." She glanced from Ernie to Hal, thinking they'd be impressed.

Hal stared at her, his look incredulous. "And you're going?"

"Of course I am. Why wouldn't I? Other than a brief conversation at Parker's funeral, I haven't seen Dean James since he retired."

Hal's head shook as he spoke. "Do you think he might have met Henrietta in your woods?" Gwen failed to stifle a snort. "That's very hard to imagine. Walter James was tough with the students, but he's one of the sweetest men I've ever known."

"You called him the 'old' dean," Ernie interjected. "Just how old is he?"

She paused to calculate. "He must be in his late seventies, maybe even eighty by now."

"Then he's probably a bad candidate to be tussling with Henrietta." Ernie shoved his chair back and folded his arms. "I'm thinking about his lunch invitation. Legally, Gwen, you won't be interferin' with the police investigation by visitin' an old friend. In fact, I doubt if Detective Brown would even think to talk to the other judges."

"That's what I thought!" Gwen exploded with enthusiasm.

"But," Ernie cautioned, wagging his finger, "like we discussed, you shouldn't be out and about by yourself. Whether Henrietta's fall was an accident or something more sinister, that second individual hasn't been identified. If you're right about a connection to the competition…"

Hal thumped the table. "I think you're onto something, Gwen. But you need to be careful, as you'll be sitting in

189

Henrietta's judging chair, and one of your private students is competing."

An image of Myrtle Mueller came to Gwen's mind, then she shook her head to dispel the woman's hateful expression at Alex's instrument counter a few hours ago. But Myrtle must realize that getting rid of any judge would jeopardize the competition and eliminate any chance for poor Herbert to compete. The same logic would apply to both Henrietta and Gwen herself. No, there was no way Myrtle was a threat. Besides, the woman never got her hands dirty.

Hal continued to speak. "Since we have no idea who this person is or why he was out in your woods with Henrietta, you need to be extra careful. Do you lock your doors and windows?"

The hairs on the back of Gwen's neck bristled. "I never lock up. This is Harbor Falls."

Ernie reached over and tapped the back of her hand. "Take Hal's advice, Gwen. At least until that second person is located and arrested."

"You think he's a threat to me?" Gwen asked, never thinking she'd find herself in a dangerous situation. Her life to this point had always been safe and secure.

"I do, and you should, too," Ernie said. "But let's not get ahead of ourselves. I've got an idea." Ernie addressed Hal. "If you're free tomorrow, why don't you drive Gwen to Walter James' for lunch?"

Gwen hadn't expected Ernie's suggestion, but it wasn't a bad one. She waited for Hal's reaction, thinking this would prove or disprove his earlier statement that he wanted to help.

Hal held up his index finger, got up from the table, and punched his cell as he walked into the living room. When he returned to his seat a minute later, he said, "All set. My foreman and garden shop manager said they could cover for me, so I'm in."

Gwen had to admit she'd feel a bit safer if she wasn't driving around by herself. "Thank you, Hal. I don't think the old dean will mind if you come with me. He said he'd welcome my company, so he'd probably appreciate another guest. I'll call him later and make sure."

Ernie reached for his briefcase. "You two work out the details, and let me know about his conversation with Henrietta when you get back. Between now and then, I'll find out if there's anything new brewin' at the police station."

Chapter Thirty-One

Half an hour later the front door slammed shut. Gwen flinched because she hadn't heard it open. Hal and Ernie's safety lecture popped into her head. Anyone could have walked in. Luckily, Jenna exited the foyer, her cheeks flushed.

The girl looked from her grandfather to Gwen to Ernie. "I'm back."

"Already?" Hal asked, getting to his feet.

"Doesn't take long when you know exactly what you're buying." Jenna nearly wiggled with excitement. "Wait until you see my outfit."

"I'm sorry, Jenna," Ernie said, heading for the door. "I'm sure your dress is stunnin', but I promised to take my wife to dinner tonight. If I don't see you beforehand, best of luck in the competition. "

"Thank you, Mr. Maguire. It was nice to meet you."

Gwen leaned over to peek into Jenna's shopping bags.

"No previews," Jenna scolded, grinning as she pulled the bag closed.

Amused, Gwen said, "Why don't you change in my bedroom? It's upstairs in the front gable. You can make a grand entrance down the staircase."

Jenna flew up the steps, her purchases flying behind her.

"Let's stay right here, Hal. Front row seats for Jenna's fashion show." They returned to their dining room chairs for an uninterrupted view of the lower staircase.

"I'm glad Ernie suggested I drive you to lunch tomorrow. I'd never forgive myself if you got into hot water and I wasn't there to rescue you."

Gwen glanced at Hal to see if he was teasing her. A quirky smile parted his lips and a twinkle wrinkled the skin around his dancing blue eyes.

"Never guessed you were a knight in shining armor, Mr. Jenkins."

Hearing a rustling along the second floor balcony, Gwen glanced up. Jenna soon came into view at the mid-way split. A solid black, knee-length sheath was topped by an ankle-length, black lace overlay. Three-quarter lace sleeves slid down Jenna's outstretched arms and a flattering scoop-neck, showing a bit of youthful cleavage, echoed the oval shape of Jenna's glowing face. High-topped black boots peeked out to complete the outfit.

"You look stunning!" Gwen shouted. "Stroll the rest of the way so I can see the dress move."

Jenna slinked down one tread at a time, then stopped and leaned against the banister. She extended one hand, her wrist bent at an artsy angle. "I'm ready for my close-up, Mr. DeMille."

Gwen laughed. "I'm surprised you know that old Gloria Swanson line."

"Granddad and I used to watch those old movies all the time. Norma Desmond was my favorite." Jenna glanced over Gwen's shoulder. Her smile faded.

Gwen turned around to see Hal standing ramrod straight, his face contorted with distaste. "Change out of that dress, Jenna. I'm taking you home."

The girl's shoulders sagged. She rushed up the stairs and disappeared beyond the balcony railing. Seconds later, Gwen's bedroom door slammed, the echo bouncing off the old walls.

Gwen spun to face Hal. "Why did you ruin her fashion show with that remark?"

"Don't you think that dress is too revealing? My God, I can see the tops of her breasts."

"Too revealing? Are you kidding me? Jenna's dress is quite demure compared to some I've seen at the competition. She's not a baby anymore, Hal."

He remained stony and waited in silence until Jenna came down, her head held high. "I'm sorry you don't approve of my dress, Granddad. But I'm wearing it on Saturday, and there's nothing you can do to stop me."

The teenager strutted out, the handles of her shopping bag clutched in her fingers.

Hal started to follow, then paused. His hand grasped the doorknob, his knuckles white. "Gwen, don't you think that dress is too mature for her?"

"Not at all. You're being overly protective."

Hal said nothing for a moment, and then looked down at Gwen, his expression icy. "Don't forget to lock your door."

Gwen made a face at his departing back, slammed the door shut, flipped the lock, then returned to the dining room and slumped into a chair. Jenna had clearly expected her grandfather to praise her competition dress. Instead, he'd not only rejected her choice, but her independence. She wondered if she should try to convince Hal to let his granddaughter grow up. Or should she stay out of it?

But would she even see Hal again? He might be so upset that she approved of Jenna's dress that he might not show up tomorrow to be her chauffer. No matter. Gwen could easily drive herself, despite Ernie's concern about her venturing out on her own. She'd rely on her common sense to avoid trouble, even if Hal didn't come with her.

And then a detail occurred to Gwen. Except for preparing Jenna for the competition and Kenneth's surprise lesson on Friday, her calendar was clear and would remain so until a new crop of private students signed up for fall lessons. She had the freedom to chase down the sordid details of Henrietta's past and the woman's activities since she came back to town.

***

"Tess, it's me again." Gwen paced the back deck, portable receiver in hand.

"Again, sis? This is getting to be a bad habit. Has something else happened?"

Gwen explained her time at the police station, the scuffmarks, the thought of suspicious death, Detective Brown's unfounded suspicion, plus her two meetings with Ernie.

"Oh, my God, Gwen; this is unbelievable. Do you want me to cancel my appointments tomorrow and drive over there tonight? I'm only a few hours away."

"No, Tess. I'm glad you're coming early, but tomorrow afternoon is soon enough. "Relax. I called to tell you I have a meeting with one of the competition judges tomorrow. I should be home before you get here. But, just in case I run late, let yourself in with the spare key. It's in the same place as always."

"Why are you meeting with a judge?"

Gwen smacked her forehead. "Oh, that's right, I didn't tell you. Jack asked me to take Henrietta's judging chair."

"And you accepted, I take it."

"I did. But listen, Tess. To answer your earlier question, I'm meeting Walter James because, when I contacted him, he told me Henrietta called him last week. He invited me to lunch so I can tell him about Henrietta's death and he will tell me about her phone call. I'm hoping she'll point the finger at the person who might have lured her onto my footbridge."

"Wait, wait, wait. You're confusing me. Why are you meeting with the judge?"

"Well, that's simple, Tess. Ernie's inside source confirmed Detective Brown is making a case against me and not looking at anyone else. If I can find someone with a stronger motive, the detective can chase that person instead."

There was another long silence on Tess's end. "I don't like the sound of this."

Gwen snorted into the phone. "You and Hal are such worry-warts."

"Who's Hal and what's he got to do with this?"

Gwen paused. Her conversations with Tess over the summer months had revolved around Jenna and the competition. There had been no reason to mention Hal.

Delaying an explanation of Hal's evolving role in her life, Gwen kept her answer simple. "He's Jenna's grandfather."

Chapter Thirty-Two

On Monday evening, loud bangs shook Gwen's front door.

She wasn't happy to find Detective Brown standing on her top step. He introduced three men stacked behind him on the lower steps: the uniformed patrol officer who'd responded to her missing person call on Sunday morning; a state police detective in plain clothes assigned to the district attorney's office; a lab tech carrying a satchel – the only man without a gun.

"Mrs. Andrews." The detective shoved a piece of paper at her. "This is a search warrant for the shoes and clothes you wore on Saturday, plus three hair samples."

Refusing to touch the document, Gwen pulled out her cell, scrolled through her directory and called Ernie, glad she'd registered his new number not five minutes earlier. "Ernie, this is Gwen. Detective Brown is here with a warrant. What should I do?"

"I'll be right there."

"Calling your attorney won't change anything, Mrs. Andrews."

She must have made a face because the detective added, "No need to be mad at me; I'm just doing my job."

"Well, your job, Detective Brown," she drew out each syllable of his titled name, "appears to be harassing innocent people. I'll expect an apology when you discover I did nothing wrong."

"If an apology is needed, I'll deliver mine personally." He tapped his head in mock salute.

The sound of a car squealing to a stop at the curb made all four men turn around. They watched Ernie slam his car door and lope up the sidewalk. "Let me see that, Detective."

197

Ernie took his time reading every word. "Sorry, Gwen. Give them the things listed here."

Reluctantly, Gwen backed into the foyer, forcing the detective to open the door himself. All five men followed her as she pulled herself up the staircase, echoing Henrietta's labored efforts.

In her bedroom, she opened the dirty clothes hamper and lifted out the beige khaki pants, eyeing the leaf-stains from her fall when she and Hal searched the woods Saturday night. Those stains could easily be misread as the result of a tussle with Henrietta. How would Ernie negate them as evidence?

The lab tech, his hands gloved, tucked them into an evidence bag.

The next garment was the pale green tee-shirt she'd worn during the garden tour.

His gloved hand pinched the shirt in two fingers and dropped it into a second bag.

From the closet, Gwen lifted her canvas shoes and held them out, hoping they didn't have the same soles as the shoes worn by the person who left those incriminating scuffmarks.

A third evidence bag snapped open, the shoes dropped inside.

Detective Brown waved at the closet floor. "How about those?"

His finger indicated her gardening sneakers, lying where she'd tossed them after her amateur and inconclusive comparison that morning.

Her heart raced. Those sneakers might have left a mark on the bridge boards when she saved herself on Friday. "I wear those when I'm working in my flower beds."

Ernie stepped forward to block the detective. "Your warrant doesn't include those."

Gwen seized the opportunity to strike back. "Honestly, Detective, do you think I'd wear those in public?"

The detective growled but didn't say anything.

Lastly, the tech came at Gwen with a pair of scissors. On instinct, she backed away, and glanced at Ernie.

"You have to let him, Gwen." To the tech, Ernie said, "You mind you don't clip more hair than necessary, and make sure you take your samples where it's not obvious."

The man glanced at Detective Brown and edged toward Gwen, asking her turn around. He lifted the hair at the nape of her neck.

She heard the snip of his blades, but the sensation was nothing like the gentle touch of her hair stylist.

He repeated his task on both sides and then the top of her head, placing each sample into its own evidence bag.

Gwen moved her hands around her head, fingering the various locations. Surprisingly, she could hardly feel the missing hair.

If Ernie's informant was right, Gwen's ash-brown strands would not match those left-behind. This was the only evidence Gwen was sure tilted in her favor.

***

That night Gwen tossed and turned, waking up nearly every hour and staring at her bedside clock. She must have fallen back to sleep once again because she sat bolt upright. A sound was bouncing off the gable rafters.

And then a male voice said, "Gwen?"

She stiffened, her eyes darting around the darkened room, lit only by the low light of the village green lampposts stippling through the window curtains behind her head.

"Who's there?" she murmured, her voice tremulous. She grabbed the covers and pulled them up to her chin.

Had Ernie been right about the threat from that second person? But how had this man gotten into her home? She distinctly remembered locking all the doors and windows. How could she defend herself? She was half-naked in her bed, for

God's sake. Nothing remotely considered a weapon was within her reach.

"It's me, Gwen," the voice said.

Recognition struck her. "Parker?"

"Yes, darling. You called my name."

"I did?"

"Yes," the voice answered.

"But I don't see you."

"Concentrate on our reading nook."

She shifted her gaze to the area between her bedroom door that exited onto the balcony and the other door leading into her bathroom.

When the touch lamp on the table suddenly lit up, she lifted her hand and shaded her eyes. Could Parker's ghost turn on a lamp? Of course he could. Especially in a dream.

As her eyes became accustomed to the light, she focused. Parker's shimmery bulk began to fill the upholstered chair on the left – his old seat. She laughed out loud.

"What's so funny, Gwen? A moment ago, you were screaming my name."

The banter with this dream man soothed her. "I was? I just may be losing my mind, Parker."

"Why do you say that?"

"Gosh, I don't know. Number one, you've appeared to me twice now."

He shook his head. "I told you last night. If I hear you call my name, I'll come if I can. I still don't know quite how this all works." His laugh tickled the air.

She smiled in the half-dark. "And number two, I seem to be Detective Brown's prime suspect for Henrietta's death."

"A suspect? I thought she died from an accident." After a brief hesitation, Gwen said, "So did I." Then she decided she may as well get her worries off her chest, even if she was talking in her sleep. She recounted the sequence of events in the past twenty-four hours, ending with Detective Brown's warrant.

Parker stroked his chin. "Okay, let's discuss the evidence one piece at a time. The police found scuffmarks on the bridge boards and have collected your canvas slip-ons for comparison. Think about it, Gwen. What are the chances you own the same brand the other person was wearing? My bet is the detective won't be able to prove anything based on your shoes."

"I can only hope you're right, Parker. How about the stains on my khakis?"

"That happened when you and this fellow Hal searched the woods. Won't he swear he was with you on the upper footbridge when you slipped on the wet leaves?"

Gwen nodded, presuming Hal would if necessary. "And my lock of hair?"

"Didn't Ernie's informant say the hair was dark? It can't possibly be a match to yours."

"That's the one fact I'm sure of," Gwen confirmed.

Parker's hand thumped the chair arm. "Damn, I miss Ernie. How's that old devil doing?"

"Just fine. Still happy with Fiona. Can't bring himself to retire."

"I guess telling him I said 'Hi' is out of the question?"

A snicker escaped Gwen. "Definitely not a good idea. He'd likely have me committed." Her fingers fiddled with the covers while her eyes explored Parker's pale face. "I feel so normal talking to you. I wish my dream would never end."

"Why do you keep insisting you're dreaming? I'm quite real, however corporeal I may appear. I guess I didn't explain my new reality very well last night."

She huffed. "But you're a figment, Parker. I can make you say or do whatever my imagination dictates."

His glowing self stood up and approached his side of the bed. "May I join you?"

Remembering her disappointment that they didn't hug the previous night, she anticipated that closing the distance might improve her chances and patted the comforter as an invitation.

When he lowered himself onto the mattress, she felt a slight motion. He leaned back into his pillow and sighed, crossing his hands behind his head in an old familiar pose. Amber hopped up on the bed, crawled across the covers, and settled against Parker as though he were a living, breathing person. His hand reached over and hovered above the cat's head.

"Why can't you believe I've come back to you, Gwen?" He shifted his gaze in her direction, the corner of his mouth lifting. "Oh, I see, my stubborn wife needs proof. What can I do to convince you I'm here?"

Gwen settled into the game. "Got any ideas?"

His focus moved around the bedroom, stopping briefly in each corner.

"Aha." He pointed to the left hand door. "Your bathroom."

She glanced back at him to find his pale hazel eyes less than a foot away, crinkled with amusement. "The bathroom, Parker? What do you have in mind?"

"You'll see. Follow me, wife." His see-through self pushed off the bed, causing another slight tremor in the mattress.

Amber yipped at the disturbance.

Gwen slipped out from under the covers and padded after him.

His transparent hand tried to move the shower door, only to pass through. "Gwen, honey, could you slide this open for me?"

After she obliged, he stepped inside the tub and turned to face her.

"What are you doing, Parker?"

"I thought I'd write you a note."

"Can you do that?"

His pale shoulders lifted and dropped. "I have no idea,

Gwen. I figured if I was able to turn on that touch-lamp, I might be able to do this."

Gwen tilted her head, folded her arms, and waited to see what would happen.

Parker lifted his left hand, swirled his index finger through the soap scum on the glass, then stepped back to admire his handiwork. His gaze switched to her and he grinned. "See? I'm a talented ghost."

It took Gwen a few seconds to read his message in reverse. *"It's me, Gwen. Love, Parker."*

She stared into the bathtub enclosure. Parker's spirit stuck out his tongue, crossed his eyes, and wiggled his fingers at her.

She started laughing and couldn't seem to stop.

Chapter Thirty-Three

The next morning Gwen awoke feeling more rested than she had for nearly a week. Had she actually summoned Parker a second time? She didn't remember crawling back into bed.

She slid out from beneath the covers and tip-toed into her bathroom, lowered the toilet seat, sat down, and studied the shower door. Had she written Parker's message? She didn't remember ever sleepwalking. Was it possible she had mimicked his left-handed scrawl?

Believing Parker had returned as a ghost was too unbelievable to believe. He'd been a dream. Of course he had. Both times. Two nights in a row was nothing more than a subconscious coincidence. Proof of Gwen's distress and her sadness that Parker was no longer in her life, not to mention her bone-deep loneliness. That's all it was. Period. She'd simply enjoy Parker while the phenomenon of his return lasted.

Unplugging her cell phone from the charger, Gwen snapped a picture of Parker's message, then stepped into the tub and took another from inside. Would anyone believe this? Maybe Liz, who hosted occult authors for bookstore signings. But did Liz actually believe in ghosts?

Or had Gwen gone over the edge? No one would blame her if she had. The combination of Henrietta's invasion, the woman's unexplained death, the detective's suspicions, and his warrant last evening would unbalance the most steadfast person.

Exiting her bathroom, Gwen walked the length of the sitting room and climbed to the storage loft at the far end. She retrieved a rectangular box embellished with bits of ribbon, buttons, and baubles. Lifting the lid, she looked inside to treasure the love letters and holiday cards from Parker, lovingly preserved. Swallowing hard, she lifted the top one, an anniversary card from three years prior. She opened the card and held her cell phone picture of the shower door message beside Parker's signature. The curlicues and spaces between letters appeared to be identical.

It would have been difficult for Gwen, a righty, to imitate Parker's leftie writing. Maybe she could find a hand-writing expert and have these samples compared and analyzed. She stared into the box, then began to laugh until tears streamed down her face. What was happening to her?

Gwen swiped at the wetness on her cheek and slid Parker's card into her jeans pocket, closed the lid and re-stashed the box, then headed down to the kitchen. After eating a quick breakfast, she donned a flannel jacket and stepped onto the rear deck, hugging herself against the morning chill of early September. She decided it was time for a distraction from her unhinged life. She'd check her gardens for damage from the storm.

"Yoo-hoo, Gwen, dear."

Turning toward the voice, Gwen waved at her neighbor Mrs. Martin, who was squeezing through the bamboo. Gwen hurried down the deck steps and stopped beside the little old lady.

"Your tour was a success, dear?"

Gwen grinned down at the delicate woman. "Yes, I think it was. At least until that storm hit. You should have come over and joined the group."

"I thought about it, but I confess I didn't buy a ticket."

"I wouldn't have turned you away. Walk with me now and I'll give you a private tour." Gwen cupped Mrs. Martin's elbow and guided her to the multiple flower beds in the back and side yards.

In spite of the heavy rain on Saturday, Gwen's perennials remained upright. The black-eyed Susans, deep red dahlias, purple asters, and Nippon daisies stood tall. Luckily, there had been no hail or her hostas would have suffered holes in their leaves. The more delicate annuals of impatiens and coleus were battered, but the geraniums, mums, and begonias were fine.

At the huge field boulder, Mrs. Martin stopped. "I don't want to be nosey, dear, but as Willard and I were leaving for church on Sunday we noticed a police car in front of your home. May I ask what happened?"

Gwen could think of no way to soften the news. "My house guest passed away."

The older woman stiffened. "Oh, my. You mean that woman with the black hair? You know, I saw her back here on Saturday afternoon."

Gwen leaned down until she was eye to eye with Mrs. Martin. "You did?"

"Why, yes. I confess I was spying on your tour." She clapped her small hands. "It was like watching one of those gardening shows on TV." The old lady stopped as suddenly as she'd started. "Oh, forgive me, dear. That was insensitive."

Gwen merely patted her on the shoulder. "That's okay. What did Henrietta do?"

"Well, she came out your French door and stared at your back for a second. You were talking with one of your guests. She seemed to be posing, though I didn't notice anyone taking pictures. And then she walked directly over there." She pointed to the path where it entered the woods.

Gwen's heart rate increased. "Was anyone with her?"

Mrs. Martin's eyes widened. "Not that I noticed. Why do you ask?"

"Just curious." Gwen could barely hide her disappointment that her tiny neighbor couldn't identify the mysterious second person. "Would you like to walk the woods with me?"

The octogenarian shook her head. "No, thank you, dear. I've got to get back to my oven. I'm baking a cake. Willard hates it when I burn his dessert."

Gwen brushed the wrinkled cheek. "A smudge of flour."

Mrs. Martin cackled. "No, dear, I used a mix. But don't tell Willard. He thinks I still make his cakes from scratch."

Gwen smothered a laugh. "Don't worry, it'll be our secret."

Mrs. Martin placed a spotted hand on Gwen's arm. "Thank you for showing me your gardens. I'm glad the storm didn't do too much damage." Turning, she toddled across the lawn.

Surely Mrs. Martin's observation would be helpful. Not only would it establish the time Henrietta entered the woods, but it would confirm that Gwen had not noticed her. She pulled out her cell and sent a text to Ernie.

When she was through, she lifted her head and stared into the woods. What *was* the condition of her footbridge? Neither the chief nor the detective had told her to stay out. With no hesitation, she scooted around the boulder and entered the tree line. The leaves rustled around her, and she couldn't miss the color creeping into the edges of the maple leaves. Within a few weeks, Harbor Falls would be overrun with leaf-peepers.

Gwen expected to see bright yellow crime scene tape surrounding the footbridge, but the area was not cordoned off. As she approached, she saw that the splintered railing was gone, as well as several planks from the bridge platform. She decided they'd likely been confiscated by the crime lab techs to compare those scuffmark forensics to her own canvas shoes. Gwen unconsciously crossed her fingers that the mystery person did not wear the same brand.

Avoiding the gaps in the decking, Gwen moved closer to the edge and looked down into the now-peaceful creek. Leaves, debris, and Hal's large branch covered the banks. What in the world had happened out here? Who had lured Henrietta to this spot on Saturday afternoon? And for what reason? And did that person intend to push Henrietta through the railing, or was it an accident?

Chapter Thirty-Four

As Gwen came through the French door, the front doorbell chimed.

Hal wasn't due for another hour – that is, if he came at all.

Was Detective Brown pressing the buzzer, coming to arrest her? She pulled her cell phone from her pocket, just in case she had to call Ernie again.

But it was not Detective Brown. Rather, a petite older lady stood there, nervously twisting the worn handles of her purse as she glanced up at the façade of the old village library.

Gwen gripped the door at the half-closed position. "Can I help you?"

The little woman brought her gaze down. Her owl-like eyes peered through oversized glasses. "Are you Gwen Andrews?"

"Yes, I am. And who are you?"

"My name is Mary Wickham Evans. I'm Henrietta's cousin. She and I were together on Saturday." Mary hesitated, seemingly unsure of what to say next. "Uh, we had breakfast in a café on your harbor. This is such a charming town." She tossed Gwen a quivering half grin.

Gwen was having a hard time believing her good fortune. Just yesterday afternoon, she'd dialed Edward Evans's phone number, one of the two unidentified calls on Henrietta's cell phone. And now here stood Cousin Mary, complete with gray streaks in her otherwise black hair. After a delay of several seconds, Gwen pushed the door wide. "Please come in."

Mary hesitated before stepping across the threshold. "Forgive me for stopping by uninvited."

"Not at all," Gwen murmured. *Too bad Henrietta hadn't had the same manners.* "May I ask the reason for your visit?"

"Of course." Mary pushed her glasses up. "I just drove down from the medical examiner's office in Boston. The

208

family asked me to identify Henrietta's body, and I'm still a bit shaky. When I realized I'd be driving through Harbor Falls on my way down to the Cape, I decided to stop by and meet you. I hope you don't mind."

Imagining the condition of Henrietta's battered body, Gwen's heart went out to Mary. "I don't mind at all, but unfortunately, I'm leaving in about an hour. You're welcome to visit until then. Would you like a cup of tea?"

"That would be very nice. Thank you."

In the kitchen, Mary hoisted her short, plump body onto an island stool while Gwen brewed a pot of Earl Grey. "May I ask, Mary, did Henrietta mention any problems since she arrived last Thursday? She told me she almost regretted her return to Harbor Falls."

Mary's voice quavered. "No, she didn't tell me anything like that. She did say she came back to clear her conscience and set a few things straight."

There was that damn phrase again. Gwen brooded. "Did she explain what she meant?"

"She didn't offer any details." Mary reached for the mug Gwen placed in front of her. "You need to understand; Henrietta and I were never close. I don't like to speak ill of the dead, but she wasn't all that nice when we were kids."

"How do you mean?"

Mary blew on the steaming liquid before answering.

"Henrietta was the youngest of us cousins. She was mean and whiny until she got her own way. Behind her back we used to call her the 'baby tyrant.'"

It didn't escape Gwen's notice that Henrietta's adult behavior was a carry-over from her childhood. No wonder she'd refused to give up on Parker. She must have thought that her visits to his office, combined with her belittling of Gwen, would eventually wear them both down and they'd divorce, leaving the path clear for Henrietta to move into Parker's life.

Mary's head jerked up, sending her glasses sliding down her tiny nose. "You wouldn't know this, but all the cousins were girls. Henrietta's father was always mad that the family name would be lost. What I mean is...," Mary once more pushed her spectacles into place, "that Henrietta wasn't a boy. After she was born, her mother had a hysterectomy, just like all the other aunts, so he had no hope of ever having a son. He used to call her Henry." Mary snickered. "She hated that name and used to throw temper tantrums when he left the room."

Gwen sat up. What an interesting bit of family history. Did the nickname explain Henrietta's combative behavior? Did she grow up acting like an aggressive boy to please her father?

Mary took a dainty sip. "Thank you for the tea, Mrs. Andrews."

"Please, call me Gwen."

Mary toyed with the mug handle. "Most of us avoided Henrietta. The summer after she graduated from Harbor Falls High, her parents found teaching jobs in Vermont and relocated. But instead of uprooting Henrietta, they enrolled her at Baylies College."

Gwen was fascinated by this glimpse into the family. "Did you find that strange?"

"Not really. Henrietta was headstrong. She didn't get along with her parents."

Gwen was beginning to understand Henrietta's personality a little better. Not that it excused the way she'd treated others. "How did she react to being left behind?"

Mary lifted her almost non-existent shoulders. "I only saw her at family dinners during her college years. Her parents rarely came down for a visit, and I don't recall that Henrietta ever talked about them."

"But why did Henrietta resign her professorship and relocate to Vermont if she didn't get along with her parents?"

"Oh, that's not how it happened. Her parents were long

deceased by the time she moved up there. She inherited their house, but it stood empty for years."

Gwen felt her eyebrows lift. Then why did Henrietta tell Hal she'd moved to Vermont years ago to take care of her parents? Why had she lied?

Emboldened by Mary's willingness to share the Wickham family history, Gwen reached for Mary's mug and refilled it.

"I've always wondered why she left town."

Mary's eyes darted around the kitchen before settling back on Gwen. "Well, like I told you, Henrietta and I weren't close, so she never confided in me. Family rumor says she'd been caught in a compromising position. None of us were brave enough to ask her for details."

Gwen's shoulders slumped.

"I have to confess, I had another reason for coming to see you today."

Gwen's hand knocked against her mug, but she managed to catch it before the tea sloshed over the side. "What's that?"

"You may not know but my family shares an odd link with you."

"I have no idea what you're talking about, Mary."

Mary's gaze traveled around the first floor. "When you and your husband purchased this place from Baylies, our Uncle John was on the Planning Committee."

"He was?" Gwen tried to recall the committee members of ten years ago. She wasn't sure she and Parker had known their names. The college lawyers had signed the real estate documents.

Mary kept talking. "Uncle John was upset when rumors started flying that the college was thinking of knocking down this old library. And then they decided to seek a buyer instead. Uncle John wasn't allowed to put in a bid. Conflict of interest, you know. When you and your husband bought it and then converted it into your home, my uncle was extremely jealous."

"I had no idea," Gwen murmured.

"Mrs. Andrews – Gwen – there's something else you should know."

"What's that?"

"First of all, Uncle John would *not* be happy if he knew I was telling you this, but you seem like a nice lady, and I'd feel awful if I didn't warn you."

Gwen sat up straight. "Warn me about what?"

Mary's eyes glistened. "After Uncle John learned Henrietta had died, and then found out she'd been staying here with you, he acted all giddy. He told the family that if she fell on your property, he's going to sue you in civil court for wrongful death. He's no expert, but he thinks you might even have to do time, and he's hoping you'll have to sell your home to pay for damages. That's when he'll scoop up this old library."

Chapter Thirty-Five

After Mary left, Gwen banged her fist on the granite
countertop. She would not allow John Wickham to take
possession of her home. Her sanctuary. Her remaining
connection to Parker.

If Gwen harbored any hesitation before, she didn't now.
She needed to uncover someone in Harbor Falls with a reason
to do away with Henrietta. With or without Ernie's sanction,
with or without Hal's assistance, she vowed to talk to anyone
who might know anything about Henrietta's life before she left
Harbor Falls, or her activities since returning last Thursday.
Today's lunch with Walter James was only the beginning.

At the stroke of eleven-thirty, she heard the purr of a car
engine. She swung open the door to see Hal mounting the
granite steps two at a time. A half-grin touched his lips. "Good
morning, Gwen. Ready?" Her face must have shown her
surprise. "Why are you looking at me that way?"

"I wasn't sure you'd show up."

"Why'd you think that?"

"Because you were so upset yesterday that I approved of
Jenna's dress."

"Oh, that." He waved his hand in dismissal. "Jenna lectured
me last night. I can't say I'm totally convinced her dress is
appropriate, but I've decided to let it go."

"You have to admit she looked lovely."

"If I weren't her grandfather, I might." His slight smile held
a hint of mischievousness. "If there's one thing you should
know about me, Gwen, it's that I keep my promises."

She twitched an eyebrow in his direction, saying, "I'll
remember that," then looked at her watch. "We'd better hit the
road. Give me a sec to grab my things."

With the judging folder in hand and her purse slung over her shoulder, Gwen locked the front door and brandished her key, eliciting an approving nod from Hal.

As soon as she'd settled into the soft leather of his passenger seat and buckled her seatbelt, Hal cast a sidelong glance in her direction. "Do you think the old dean will tell you something that will convince Detective Brown you're not the person he should be chasing?"

She lifted her shoulders. "I have no idea, Hal. All I know is Henrietta called him last week, and he's willing to tell me what she said."

Hal slid the gear shift into drive. "Where are we going?"

She removed the driving directions from her folder. "Oak Leaf Terrace, north of town. Do you know it?"

"Nope." Following her instructions, Hal circled the village green and turned north. "I was surprised Ernie let you keep this lunch date."

"Why? The dean's age makes him a very unlikely suspect. And you signed on as my chauffer, so I'm as safe as safe can be."

"What worries me is you intruding on the official police investigation. The last thing you need is another reason for Detective Brown to come after you."

"But Ernie agreed with me that the detective probably wouldn't think to call the judges. So having lunch with an old colleague from Baylies College is not interfering with anything."

"Fine, but what if Henrietta's phone conversation with the dean doesn't provide a connection to that second person?"

"If this is a dead end, another clue is bound to pop up."

"Don't forget," Hal cautioned. "The person who was on your bridge with Henrietta might be walking around Harbor Falls. You could be talking to him – or her – and not even know it."

Hal's tendency to lecture was beginning to get on Gwen's nerves, but since he'd agreed to drive her to the dean's condo, she let it slide. "Let's not worry about that until we get through today's lunch. Do you want to hear what happened since you met with me and Ernie yesterday?"

He nodded but kept his eyes on the road.

"Okay. Tell me if you're getting bored, and I'll stop."

Hal threw her a quick glance. "I don't think you could ever bore me, Gwen."

She lowered her head and smiled into her lap, pretending to be busy with her folder. "Well, the first thing. Last evening, Detective Brown showed up with a warrant for Saturday's clothing, shoes, and several locks of my hair." Hal slapped the wheel. "That man is like a dog with a bone. He won't find any evidence to prove you were out in your woods with Henrietta."

Pleased with his reaction, Gwen continued. She shared her concerns about the leaf-stained pants and her shoes matching the scuffmarks. Hal promised to provide a sworn statement that he was with her when she slipped on Saturday night, and he echoed Parker's words that a shoe match was slim. Thanks to Ernie's secret informant, they both knew Gwen's ash-brown hair was not the color of the strands collected from the splintered railing.

"So, what else happened?"

Gwen recounted Mrs. Martin's sighting of Henrietta during the garden party.

"Well, that's interesting. Too bad she didn't see a second person."

"I was disappointed, too. But she can at least confirm that I didn't see Henrietta walk into the woods, and I didn't follow her."

Before Gwen had a chance to tell him about Mary's visit and Uncle John's plan to sue, she spotted the sign for Oak Leaf Terrace and resumed her navigation duties. "Turn left, then a quick right onto Cranberry Lane." They drove through a complex of traditional colonial homes, then Victorian-style condominiums. A miniature village green offered pedestrian-friendly sidewalks.

Gwen pointed out Dean James' unit and Hal pulled to a stop. They headed up the sidewalk and the front door opened before her finger had a chance to touch the buzzer. "Dean James, you startled me!"

"Well, well, Gwen Andrews, you're a pleasant sight for these old eyes." Dressed in black slacks and a pale blue button down shirt, the elderly man grinned from ear to ear. Other than thinning hair and a slight hunch, he looked much as she remembered him.

She felt her lips widen in a smile. "You look wonderful, sir."

The dean chuckled. "You're being kind. And my dear, we're no longer dean and professor. You must call me Walter." He reached out and grasped her hand. "I haven't seen you since your husband's funeral. How are you holding up?"

Her face warmed. What would he think if he knew she was bringing Parker back in her dreams? "One day at a time, sir."

"Yes, yes. I know what you mean. That's what I'm doing."

His gaze shifted to Hal. "Who's your friend?"

"Sorry. This is Hal Jenkins. I meant to call and ask if you minded another guest for lunch."

"Not at all. The more the merrier. Come on in."

As she stepped inside, Gwen added, "Hal's granddaughter Jenna is one of my private students. She will be performing in the competition on Saturday."

Dean James cocked his head. "Does that create a problem for you as a judge?"

Gwen had a ready answer. "I asked Jack that same question. He found a little-used rule that allows me to sit out during Jenna's performance. Your score will be averaged with

Albert's to create a third score to replace mine."

"Well, that's a convenient loophole. They're lucky to have you, Gwen. You've always had a keen musical mind, and I'm quite sure you'll be fair in your judging. Let's go back to my kitchen and talk while I finish preparing lunch."

Dean James made a roux of butter, flour and beef broth to thicken the juices. "You're the first company I've had since I moved here." He stirred vigorously. "I don't eat breakfast, so I'm approaching starvation." With his free hand, he patted his round little belly for effect.

As the dean cooked, Gwen told him about her retirement in May and her new venture of private lessons. She threw in a few anecdotes about the characters at the garden and house tour.

After they carried their bowls of beef stew to the dining room table, Hal joined the conversation, explaining the trials and tribulations of owning a garden center and nursery. The three of them chatted non-stop throughout lunch, then finally laid down their spoons, their hunger satiated. Walter leaned back in his chair and focused on Gwen. "Now that we've gotten the social niceties out of the way, tell me what happened to Henrietta."

"Of course, sir – uh, Walter." Again, Gwen's cheeks warmed. "Well, you know she was hired as a judge, but you wouldn't know she that was staying with me."

He gasped. "I can't imagine how you allowed that to happen, Gwen." He waved his hand in the air. "Don't bother explaining. But tell me, had her attitude toward you changed?"

Gwen shook her head. "Not one bit. After all these decades, she still resented me for marrying Parker. But she didn't know he'd died." Gwen swallowed. Even with Parker's recent appearances, she still had trouble saying those words.

"Oh, my, that must have been quite a shock to her." His fingers moved back and forth across the tablecloth.

"Actually, I was surprised how quickly she got over the

news, given her obsession with him."

"Hard to explain what makes people hang on," Walter commented. "You mentioned a possible connection between her death and the competition. What made you think that?"

Gwen squirmed in her seat. "A few days ago she said she was second-guessing her decision to return to Harbor Falls. I thought maybe someone was giving her a hard time about judging the competition. I could be way off base, but that's why I asked both you and Albert Hall if she called, thinking she might have let something slip that would help explain."

"Did Albert hear from her?"

"No. That's why I got excited when you said she called you last week."

"Before we discuss her phone call, why don't you explain how she died? Apparently, it wasn't from natural causes."

Gwen glanced at Hal, who was resting his forearms on the table. He hadn't interrupted and seemed content to sit and listen.

"Based on a splintered railing and scuffmarks and some hair, the police are assuming a struggle before she fell into the gorge. Saturday's rainstorm had turned the creek into a small river. Her body was washed downstream and under the North Street Bridge, then caught in downed willow tree branches before she reached the mill race. That's the only thing that kept her from plunging over the old waterwheel and out into the bay."

"Oh, my. What a horrible way to die."

Gwen fought to keep the mental pictures at bay. "The police ruled her death suspicious."

"Understandable." Walter reached over and covered Gwen's hand. "Do they suspect you?"

She shouldn't have been surprised by his directness. He had scared many wayward Baylies students with his daunting stare and bold questions. With her other hand, Gwen rotated her water glass. "The police implied they consider me a suspect."

The old man's eyes softened. "You're searching for the truth, then?"

The tension eased from her shoulders. "That's exactly what I'm hoping to find."

Walter sat quietly for a moment then spoke in a slow, methodical voice. "Henrietta called me either Thursday or Friday. I don't recall which. She wanted to discuss the finer aspects of judging young musicians and how strictly she should adhere to the point system."

"Did she say anyone was giving her a hard time about being a judge?" Gwen asked.

"Not that I recall." Walter turned to Hal. "Did you know Henrietta, son?"

Hal shook his head. "When I bumped into her at Gwen's, Henrietta reminded me that we'd met years ago after a college concert when my daughter Elizabeth performed."

Walter's eyes lit up. "Elizabeth Jenkins? Of course, of course. I should have made the connection. Your Elizabeth was indeed a fine musician."

Hal shifted in his chair. Gwen sensed the reminders of Elizabeth stirred the ache of her loss.

Walter took a swig of water. "Let me tell you my history with Henrietta. When I was the dean of the music department at Baylies, she was one of several professors on my teaching staff. She was quite popular with her students, although many of us couldn't understand exactly why."

"Why do you say that?" Hal asked.

"Well..." Walter glanced at Gwen. "Henrietta offended the other professors and office staff on a regular basis." Walter swirled his half-melted ice cubes. "I was also the director of the college orchestra. When I announced my retirement, Henrietta asked if I'd put in a good word for her promotion to my position. But she wasn't interested in the directing duties, so the hiring committee selected Daniel Chartley instead."

This bit of news rattled Gwen. If Henrietta's bid for the Dean's position had been successful, the woman would have been the boss in the years before she moved to Vermont. Gwen shivered. She couldn't imagine a ghastlier plight than having to report to Henrietta.

That aside, the potential connection to Henrietta's demise was intriguing. If Henrietta resented being passed over for the dean's position, would she still harbor her bitterness a dozen years later? Had the hiring committee been on Henrietta's mysterious list to clear her conscience and set a few things straight? But even if she wanted revenge, which member would she have singled out? No, that didn't make sense. Someone went after Henrietta, not the other way around.

Walter kept talking. "I'd always wanted to know if she resigned because she wasn't chosen to replace me, and her phone call last week gave me the perfect opportunity to ask. Henrietta insisted there was no connection. When I pressed her to tell me why she left in such a hurry, she would only say that her reason for resigning was also the reason she came back."

Gwen sat quietly, absorbing his words. Her original thought that Henrietta's demise was connected to the competition appeared to be off track. Neither Jack, nor Alex, nor Walter had heard anything to indicate Henrietta was badgered about being a judge. But now it appeared there might be a link to her resignation.

Gwen didn't want to be cocky about it, but if she hadn't agreed to have lunch with the dean, she wouldn't have learned about this possible connection. The person who knew the secret behind Henrietta's resignation would be a definite candidate for Detective Brown's attentions. She wondered if she'd be able to unearth someone who had been privy to the details.

"I suppose I could have pushed harder," Walter continued, interrupting Gwen's thoughts. "Perhaps Henrietta would have confided in me. But I was no longer in any position to pull rank. I figured if she wanted me to know, she'd tell me. I didn't give it much thought at the time, but now that we're talking about this in a different light, I think she ended the call because she'd revealed more than she intended."

Gwen leaned back, her mind spinning. "Henrietta obviously returned to clear up some unfinished business in Harbor Falls. She had a list of people she wanted to see while she was here. I think someone on that list knows not only why she resigned, but why she died. The question is, who's on that list?"

Chapter Thirty-Six

Gwen glanced at Walter's dining room clock. "I'm sorry, but we need to head back. My sister's arriving this afternoon, and Jenna's coming at four. Thanks for that delicious beef stew and for sharing your history with Henrietta."

"My pleasure, my dear." He patted her on the hand. "We'll have to do this again sometime."

At his front door, Walter lifted a carved cane and walked them to Hal's Volvo. "I wish you luck in your quest to clear your name, Gwen. If I think of anything else, I'll let you know. See you on Saturday. Nice to meet you, Hal." Walter started up his walkway toward his front door.

Hal pulled away from the curb, sparing a quick glance in Gwen's direction. "I have to say, I didn't expect you to learn anything today."

"Well, I wasn't so sure myself." Gwen could barely contain her excitement. "Can you believe Henrietta's return to Harbor Falls was connected to her resignation? The dean's words were, *the reason she moved away was the reason she came back to town.* Our next step is a no-brainer. Uncover the reason she resigned."

Without skipping a beat, Hal said, "You should let Ernie's private detective check into that."

Gwen glared at him. "I don't understand, Hal. Yesterday, you offered to help."

Hal focused on the myriad of streets as he maneuvered through the complex. "I drove you to lunch today, didn't I?"

Gwen stiffened and opened the folder in her lap, pretending to check on some detail. Yesterday she'd slotted Hal into the position of sidekick. And now he was backing out after only one venture. "That's it, Hal?" she asked, daring to look over at him. "One day as chauffer and you're done?"

He pulled his Volvo into a parking lot at the edge of the dean's complex, put the gearshift into park, and turned to face her. "We're both rank amateurs, Gwen. I don't think you realize what a dangerous game you're playing."

"This is not a game," she shot back. "My freedom and my home are at stake. I'll do anything to keep from being arrested. With or without your help."

"Don't get mad at me, Gwen." Hal shot her a puppy dog look. "I worry about you. Let's ask Ernie what he thinks about Henrietta's resignation before you do any more snooping."

Hal pulled onto the road. For the rest of the ride, his attention was glued to the traffic and he didn't seem to notice Gwen was quiet. Inside she was boiling like a pot of water shrieking on the stove. Snooping? That's what Hal thought she was doing?

When he parked on Library Lane, Gwen busied herself gathering her belongings.

"You haven't told me when you'll be meeting with Ernie. I'd like to join you again."

"No need, Hal. You've done your good deed for the day. Thanks for driving me. I'll see you later when you come to pick up Jenna." She struggled from his passenger seat and resisted the urge to slam his car door. She rounded the car and marched toward the entrance.

Hal rolled down his window and shouted, "Gwen, wait!"

At the same time the double doors of the old library flew open and Gwen looked up to see Tess come over the threshold her arms spread wide. "I thought you'd never come home!"

Gwen's spirits soared as she clambered up the granite steps and into her sister's embrace. After a final squeeze, she pushed Tess to arm's length and inspected her older sibling. A few more wrinkles around her eyes, a few more gray hairs sprinkled into her pale brown bob. Although they saw each other several times each year, Gwen rarely took the time to take a good look

223

at her sister. But now, Gwen was so glad Tess had arrived, she couldn't stop staring. "What time did you get here, Sis?"

Nathan, dressed in khaki slacks and white button-down shirt, slid past his wife and extended his arms for a hug. "About an hour ago."

"Oh, Nathan, you came, too." Gwen squeezed him tight, letting go only when she noticed Hal coming up the steps. She tamped down her exasperation and introduced him, explaining that he'd driven her to a meeting with the competition judge.

Nathan extended his hand. "Nice of you to drive Gwen, Hal."

"I was glad to do it." Hal accepted the handshake. "Ernie didn't think she should be visiting anyone by herself until some headway is made regarding Henrietta's death."

Tess nodded. "I couldn't agree more. That's why Nathan and I came over a few days early. By the way, I can't wait to hear your granddaughter play."

"Jenna's excited about rehearsing with you, too."

Gwen moved between Tess and Nathan, linked arms, and turned them toward the front door. "Let's go inside and catch up." She'd hoped Hal would take the hint, return to his car and go home, but Hal followed them inside.

In the kitchen, ever mindful of good manners, Gwen pulled four glasses from the cabinet, poured iced tea, and handed it around.

Tess took a sip before speaking. "So tell me, Gwen, what did the judge have to say?"

Gwen turned her back on Hal and faced Tess. "First, I need to tell you what happened last night." She repeated the details of Detective Brown's warrant.

When she finished, Tess said, "This is not good. Did he explain his reason?"

"The detective doesn't explain anything. I think he's hoping the crime lab techs will compare my shoes to the scuffmarks on the bridge boards and report they're a match. No idea what my clothes can tell him, but my khakis were dirty from falling when Hal and I searched for Henrietta on Saturday night."

"You fell?" Nathan looked over at Hal.

"An unfortunate slip on wet leaves," Hal offered, his nostrils flaring as he backed up and leaned against the kitchen sink, crossing his arms.

Tess looked at Hal, then back at Gwen. "Sis, would you care to explain what's going on between you two? I hate to use a tired cliché, but I could cut the air with a knife."

Gwen spoke as though Hal was not there. "Yesterday, Hal said he wanted to help me and Ernie convince Detective Brown he was chasing the wrong suspect. When I told Ernie I'd made a lunch date with the old dean, he said he didn't want me out by myself, and suggested Hal drive, which he did. I thought Hal was planning to stick with me to chase down clues."

"And?" Tess asked.

"Well, on the way back from lunch," Gwen paused, still not looking at Hal, "Hal called me an amateur and said I should stop my snooping."

Hal stepped between Tess and Gwen. "That's not quite accurate. Ernie suggested we hire a private detective. I was trying to convince Gwen it was a good idea."

"There you go again with the *we*, Hal," Gwen said, her quiet voice ominous. "There is no *we*. You made that perfectly clear this afternoon."

The tone in Gwen's voice echoed in her ears and she noticed three pairs of widened eyes. What was she doing? She should be thankful Hal drove her today and not insult him because he wasn't sticking around to be her sidekick.

After all, Hal was not Parker.

She turned to Hal. "I'm so sorry. That wasn't fair. Please forgive me."

"Like I said yesterday, Gwen, you're under a lot of pressure." Hal retreated to the sink.

She noticed he didn't say he'd forgiven her outburst.

Tess shifted her gaze to Gwen and cleared her throat. "What I'd like to hear about is your meeting with the other judge."

Gwen did not dare look at Hal but settled onto the island stool next to Tess. "Henrietta called the old dean last week and let it slip that she returned to Harbor Falls, in her words, 'for the same reason she left.'"

"I thought she came back to judge the competition?"

Gwen shrugged her shoulders. "I guess the invitation was a convenient excuse."

"So what was her reason for leaving?"

"That's what I need to find out. Walter thought she resigned because she was passed over for his position after he retired, but she denied it on the phone."

"How will you find out if she meant it?"

"I thought the new dean at Baylies might remember the details surrounding Henrietta's resignation." Gwen glanced at her watch. "Too late today."

"Okay," Tess said. "Give me a second to follow your logic. The reason Henrietta resigned is the reason she returned to Harbor Falls. If you can discover who was involved with her decision to resign, you are thinking that that person might know – or be – the person who invited her to your footbridge."

"Exactly." Gwen was pleased with her sister's insight.

"But isn't it dangerous for you to search for this person by yourself?"

Nathan, who had remained quiet during most of this exchange, spoke up. "I have to agree with Tess. Whoever lured Henrietta into your woods won't like you nosing around."

Incredulous, Gwen glared first at Nathan, then at Hal and Tess. "Weren't any of you listening when I told you Detective

Brown confiscated my clothes and shoes last night? Oh, and let's not forget locks of my hair. It's obvious – to me, at least – that the detective isn't investigating anyone but me. He wants nothing more than to prove I left those scuffmarks so he can arrest me for doing away with good old Henrietta. I have no choice. I have to save myself."

Tess, Nathan, and Hal started talking over each other. Gwen caught the words *safety* and *dangerous* and *risky*.

"Stop!" Gwen shouted. "If any of you were suspected of killing your houseguest, you wouldn't be so quick to find fault with my methods."

When they started up again, Gwen covered her ears and roared, "Enough!"

The chatter came to a standstill. Gwen lowered her hands and focused on her sister. "I expected you to be on my side, Tess."

"I am, I am," Tess soothed. "I'm only watching out for you, little sis."

The front bell chimed and Gwen veered toward the door as though it were a life preserver.

Chapter Thirty-Seven

"You're right on time, Jenna." Despite her angst, Gwen managed a calm voice.

Jenna took in the group standing around the kitchen island.

"Hi, Granddad. I thought you weren't coming until five?"

"Uh...," Hal stumbled. "I drove Mrs. Andrews to a lunch meeting."

Gwen tossed him a sideways glance then turned to her student. "Jenna, meet the Walkers, Tess and Nathan."

"Nice to meet you, Mrs. Walker."

"Call me Tess, honey."

Jenna beamed. "I hear you competed when you were in high school."

Tess's chuckle echoed around the first floor. "More times than I care to remember. The prize money helped pay my college tuition. And you're competing for a scholarship to Baylies?"

Jenna's blonde ponytail bounced when she nodded.

Tess grabbed Jenna's hand and pulled her toward the music studio. "Well, then, my sister and I will do our best to improve your chances."

Nathan clapped his hand on Hal's shoulder. "Wanna walk to the harbor with me? I'm sure you've been there a million times, but I like to check out the shoreline when we visit Gwen."

"Sure," Hal stammered, looking surprised.

"Let me grab my binoculars from the car. I want to search for hooded mergansers flying through."

"So you're a birder, Nathan?" Hal asked.

Gwen relaxed, relieved that Nathan had the foresight to remove Hal, preventing another disagreement. Besides, she didn't want Jenna to sense they'd been arguing.

Nathan wiggled his fingers to draw Gwen's attention.

"Should I pick up dinner? Or have you got that covered?"

Inwardly, Gwen cringed. With all the uproar of the past few days, she hadn't had time to plan meals, let alone do any food shopping. Thank heavens for her brother-in-law. "That would be great, Nathan. Thanks."

"Any preferences?"

Hal spoke up. "*The Wharf* serves excellent Italian food."

Gwen flinched. Not only had Hal brought lasagna from *The Wharf* just yesterday, but if he helped provide tonight's dinner, she'd have to suggest he and Jenna join them, regardless of the potential fireworks. She dared to look at Hal as she extended the invitation. "You're both welcome to stay."

Hal's expression of relief was unmistakable. "Thank you, Gwen. We accept."

She swung her gaze to Nathan. "Whatever you choose is fine."

Nathan signed okay with his thumb and first finger, then pulled the door closed behind them.

Gwen knew her irritation with Hal was unreasonable, but she couldn't seem to let it go. But now was not the time to worry about the future of their friendship. Gwen strode to the music studio and guided Jenna through J.S. Bach's baroque piece Sonata in E minor. Tess stood at the mullioned windows, her eyes closed, and her head swaying as she listened.

When Jenna lowered her flute, Tess murmured, "Nice. Ready to try it with me?"

At Jenna's enthusiastic nod, Tess seated herself on Gwen's padded piano bench, played the first few chords, then nodded for Jenna to begin.

At the end of the first page, Jenna leaned over the sheet music and pointed a dainty finger at a specific passage, and they began again.

Easing into a wing chair, Gwen let her eyelids drift shut,

229

losing herself in the dance of the music. Tess softly layered her piano chords below the flute notes, letting Jenna's musicality shine. Pride in them both filled Gwen's heart to nearly bursting.

Her eyes flew open when a door slammed and a booming voice cracked the air. "Hope we're not back too early."

She jumped to her feet and skirted the staircase. "Not at all, Nathan. The musicians need a break. Set the bags on the island. I'll grab some plates."

Tess and Jenna strolled into the kitchen.

Nathan removed a large container and popped the lid. The scent of garlic permeated the old library. "I hope you're all hungry."

"I'm starving," Jenna said. "How can I help?" Tess cocked her head at Jenna. "You know what, Jenna? You're as sweet as my sister's been saying all summer long."

When Jenna blushed, Tess laughed. "Pink becomes you. Come on. You lay out the placemats and napkins. I'll add knives and forks and fill the water glasses."

The five of them loaded their plates with garden salad, spaghetti and meatballs, chicken parmesan, and garlic bread, and settled around the dining room table, Gwen at one end, Hal at the other. The animated chatter initiated by Jenna, Tess, and Nathan saved her from interacting with Hal, which was a good thing, because she didn't know what she'd say. Every once in a while she caught him glancing her way, but his face gave no clue as to what he was thinking.

After everyone had laid down their forks, Gwen finally spoke. "The best thing about Italian food," Gwen paused and looked toward Nathan and Tess, "is that it tastes even better the next day." She walked to the island, re-attached lids to the leftovers, and placed the containers in the fridge. When Tess and Jenna carried dirty dishes to the sink, Gwen shooed them to the music studio and proceeded to load the dishwasher.

She heard Hal get up from the table with a grunt. "If I sit

here any longer, Nathan, I won't be able to move." He wandered to the kitchen sink, stopping beside Gwen.

Gwen concentrated on sliding a dirty plate into the lower rack. She built up her courage to speak. "Can you forgive my earlier tirade?"

"Already forgotten, Gwen. But I haven't changed my mind about Ernie hiring a private eye."

"And I still think a gumshoe won't get very far Harbor Falls." She ripped a paper towel from the dispenser and wiped her hands, failing to control the volume of her voice. "Listen, Hal, I get it. You're not interested in gallivanting around town with me. But you know as well as I do that Walter's conversation with Henrietta provided a clue, and I intend to find out if her resignation is somehow connected to her death."

A movement diverted Gwen's attention.

Tess strode over with a disapproving *big sister* look on her face. "I can hear you both, and so can Jenna."

Gwen glanced to the music studio to see Jenna's stricken expression and decided it was time to bring everything out in the open. Jenna was certainly old enough to be exposed to legal problems and adult disagreements.

Clapping her hands like she had during the garden tour, Gwen waited until all eyes turned her way. "I'd like you all to hear my take about my current situation." She paused for breath. "Maybe Henrietta was never a friend of mine, and maybe I resented her for barging back into my life, but now I have no choice but to involve myself in her affairs. If I don't figure out who was on my footbridge with her, I could be arrested. I can't sit by and let that happen!"

"We understand why you feel compelled to do something," Nathan offered. "We're just worried that someone will try to stop you."

She glared at her brother-in-law. "You think I'd purposely put myself in harm's way?"

231

Hal stepped closer, his posture rigid. "Actually, that's exactly what I think, but apparently my concern carries no weight."

Gwen began to tear her paper towel into tiny pieces. "I'll tell you what. I won't visit anyone to discuss Henrietta unless Tess goes with me. How's that?"

Tess gave Gwen a quizzical look, then said, "That's fine with me."

Gwen noticed that Nathan's eyes were focused out the bay window, where the waning light was removing color from the gardens. If he had an opinion about Tess running around with Gwen, he kept it to himself.

Jenna remained silent at the Steinway, her eyes wide.

Hal walked to the studio, put an arm around his granddaughter's shoulders, and herded a reluctant Jenna toward the front door. "We're going home. Thanks for dinner. And Gwen...don't forget to call Ernie. And lock your door."

Gwen's mouth dropped open. Despite the clashes they'd endured all day, he still had the nerve to tell her what to do?

Nathan made a beeline for the staircase. Tess rounded on Gwen. "You sure can clear a room, sister."

"Another of my unsung talents." When Tess didn't crack a smile, Gwen sagged. "I can't believe what's happening to me. And everyone around me is upset for one reason or another."

Tess squatted down to pick up the pieces of Gwen's shredded paper towel. She tossed them into the wastebasket before speaking. "What on earth is going on between you and Hal?"

"To be honest, Tess, I'm not sure. I feel like a yo-yo. I think he's heading one direction, then he does a one-eighty."

"From where I sit it looks like he's developed feelings for you and only wants to keep you safe." Tess tossed her sister a sly smile.

"Oh, please, Tess. We're both too old for romance."

"He drove you to your lunch meeting today."

Gwen rested her hands on the edge of the sink. "Ernie suggested that. I'm not even sure why Hal agreed."

"I don't know, Gwen. I noticed him gazing at you during dinner." Tess touched her sister's shoulder. "Listen, Parker was a terrific guy, but he's been gone more than two years now. He wouldn't want you to be alone the rest of your life."

Gwen stared at Tess and had to wonder what Parker would say about that. Maybe Gwen would ask him next time his dream-form visited. "Quite a speech, Sis."

Tess turned Gwen around. "I'm not saying get married. But if I'm right about Hal, I'm only suggesting you don't dismiss the man without giving him a chance."

Gwen sat up straight and glanced at her watch. "Oh, damn. I forgot to call Ernie. Too late now. Remind me to call him first thing tomorrow, will you, Tess?"

"Sure."

A sound on the staircase made them turn. There stood pajama-clad Nathan on the halfway landing, looking over the banister at them. He hopped down the remaining treads and headed their way. When he got closer, Gwen smelled the comforting scent of bay rum.

He sidled next to Tess and threw his arm around his wife's shoulders. "If you ladies don't mind, I'm going to hit the sack. Long day. Too much driving, too much walking, too much food." Nathan swiped a hand across his forehead in mock exhaustion. Gwen had always loved Nathan's knack for well-timed comic relief.

Tess pulled Nathan down for a goodnight kiss. "I'll be up in a little while."

A pang of envy stabbed Gwen's heart.

Chapter Thirty-Eight

At midnight, Gwen bolted upright, her legs twisting in the
sheets. A dream. No, a nightmare. She'd tripped and fallen.

Who was chasing her? Poof…gone.

She retrieved the comforter from the floor, smoothed it
around her tucked-up knees, and looked around for Amber. The
little fiend was nowhere in sight. No hug from her pet tonight.
"Humph." Amber had probably snuck into the guest room for
extra attention from Tess and Nathan, knowing she'd be
welcomed instead of kicked to the floor.

Gwen glanced around her bedroom, faintly lit by the village
green lights. She took an extra-deep breath and let it out in a
slow stream. "Parker?"

Nothing.

Would he come again? "Parker?"

Still nothing.

Would the third time be a charm? "Parker?" she called as
loud as she dared, not wanting to wake Tess and Nathan. Gwen
focused on the reading nook, willing Parker to appear.

"You rang, Gwen?"

She jumped at the sound of his voice. Parker, ever the
jokester, grinned at her from the pillow on his side of their bed,
his hands clasped behind his head as before. His ethereal self
appeared unchanged from the previous night. Same red shirt,
same black pants.

"Are you trying to give me a heart attack?" she scolded,
failing to stifle a grin.

"Sorry, darling. I couldn't resist."

Gwen couldn't move her eyes from his face. "I wasn't sure
you'd come."

"I think I'm getting the hang of this, Gwen. You call, I
come." He flashed his boyish grin that always melted her heart.

Gwen wanted to touch his likeness but feared he'd disappear.

"Do you have news about Henrietta?" he asked.

Before easing into pillow-talk, Gwen once again questioned her sanity. In what skewed universe would Parker be lying next to her in their king-sized bed? Of course, he wasn't the fleshed-out Parker. He was only a shadow of the man she'd married all those years ago. But she couldn't move her eyes from his.

Failing to suppress the grin that widened her cheeks, she proceeded to tell him about lunch with the dean, the connection between Henrietta's resignation and her return, Hal's discouragement of Gwen's snooping, their argument after dinner, and Tess's encouragement for Gwen to explore a relationship with Hal.

She waited to hear Parker's opinion of that lamebrain idea. Parker cocked his pale head in a familiar gesture. "Tess is right, honey. Of course, I'd prefer your companion to be me, but since I can't do much other than scare you when I show up, you need to find someone else to keep you company." He paused and pressed a finger to his lips. "I remember Hal from his garden shop. Nice fellow. Knows his plants. Sounds like he cares for you. But who wouldn't?" Parker tossed her a bratty smile. "So what if he doesn't approve of your sleuthing, Gwen? Give the guy a break. See what develops."

How surreal that Gwen's deceased husband was giving her permission to move on.

Parker pulled one hand from behind his head and stretched it toward her.

His touch felt like a butterfly wing grazing her skin. Gwen lay completely still, not wanting to jinx the sensation.

A toilet flushed. Gwen jumped. "That's either Tess or Nathan. What if they heard us talking?"

Parker shook his head. "I don't know why, but I think you're the only one who can see or hear me."

The echo of a knock bounced around the bedroom. "Are you all right, Gwen? I heard voices."

Easing out from under the covers, Gwen stepped to the door and opened it. Tess leaned in, her eyes flitting around the bedroom. She clearly couldn't see Parker as he watched her.

Gwen had to think fast. "Uh, you might have heard the radio. I listen to late night talk shows if I can't fall asleep." She hoped Tess wouldn't notice that the alarm clock was just an alarm clock.

"Didn't mean to disturb you."

"You didn't." Gwen reached out for a hug. "Go back to bed. I'll see you in the morning."

With one last survey, Tess turned and padded along the balcony to the guest room. Before going in, she glanced back at Gwen, her eyebrows knit with concern.

Closing her door, Gwen jumped onto her bed, making Parker's pale form bounce.

He grinned at her. "I told you no one else can see me."

She grinned back. Dream or ghost, she was giddy that Parker lounged beside her. Not that physical intimacy was even possible, but she so hoped he'd stay for the rest of the night.

"Now, where were we?" he asked, waving his see-through hand in the air. "Oh, right, you feel compelled to dig into Henrietta's past. Maybe find someone with a grudge. But I have to agree with Ernie, Hal, Tess, and Nathan. The real culprit won't like you snooping around."

Gwen was about to protest when Parker held up his palm, his abbreviated life line faint.

"Hold on. I wouldn't dream of trying to stop you. If Tess tags along on your excursions, you'll be safe enough. Your sister can be quite vicious if the need arises."

Gwen laughed at his reference to heated debates with Tess over the years, then clapped her hand over her mouth, worried her laughter would draw Tess's attention again.

"What do you hope to find, Gwen?"

"Oh, I don't know, Parker. I may not discover anything useful. I told Ernie people would talk to me about Henrietta, but I could be dead wrong about that. On the other hand, I'm not the only one in town who's always wanted to know why Henrietta left."

"Who do you think you are…Nancy Drew?"

Gwen snickered at his mention of her favorite childhood sleuth. The entire set of novels sat on the shelves in the music studio downstairs. Maybe she should reread them and get some pointers. "Hardly, Parker. I'm only trying to solve the riddles surrounding Henrietta's death."

He stretched to his full length and once again cupped his hands behind his head.

Gwen eased off the mattress and gazed out her front window. The old-fashioned gas lamps of the village green lit the pathways, creating circles of light within the surrounding darkness. She spoke over her shoulder. "There's something I need to know, Parker."

"Go ahead."

Gwen paused for a few seconds before finding the courage to ask her question. "The other day, Ernie let something slip about you and Henrietta."

She peeked sideways to see his reaction.

Parker was gone.

Chapter Thirty-Nine

The next morning, the hum of voices pulled Gwen from the fog of sleep. She glanced over at a concave impression on Parker's pillow. She could easily have done it herself. But had she?

The murmur grew louder until a familiar laugh erupted. Gwen hopped out of bed, got dressed in a flash, and tiptoed to the mid-way landing of the staircase. When she spotted Tess planting little kisses on Nathan's neck, Gwen called out, "Did you two sleep well?"

Her sister's face shot up over Nathan's shoulder, her face turning bright pink. "Uh, I can't speak for Nathan, but I only got up that one time. Sorry I barged in on you."

Goose bumps broke out on Gwen's arms. She'd convinced herself that Parker's appearance and Tess's pop-in were both dreams. Knowing it was his ghost who had visited was both thrilling and unsettling. She held onto the banister the rest of way down.

Finding her voice, Gwen said, "No need to apologize, Tess. I like you watching out for me."

"That, little sister, is what big sisters are supposed to do."

Gwen grabbed the kettle, filled it with water, and set it on the back burner to boil. She so wanted to confide in Tess and Nathan, to hear their slant on the ghostly phenomenon. Maybe the three of them could test Parker's claim that only Gwen could see and hear him. Assuming he'd appear again, that is.

But would Tess and Nathan believe Gwen's story, or would they think she'd lost her mind – that the stress of Henrietta's visit, her unexpected death, and Detective Brown's suspicions had pushed her over the edge? Better not risk it.

A thump interrupted them and Gwen headed for the front door. On her top step lay the Harbor Falls Gazette. The paper girl had finally made the long toss from the sidewalk.

238

Gwen grabbed the paper from the stoop and returned to the kitchen. Settling herself, she whipped through the pages looking for an update. Finding it on page three, she plunked the paper onto the island and read aloud while Tess and Nathan peered over her shoulder:

BODY IDENTIFIED AS FORMER BAYLIES PROFESSOR

Harbor Falls Police Chief Charles Upton released the identity of the body discovered this past Sunday near the historic waterwheel at The Olde Music Shop.

Henrietta Wickham, age 66, served as a Professor of Music Theory at Baylies College from1973 through 2002, at which time Ms. Wickham moved to Vermont. She was recently invited back to judge this weekend's Young Musicians' Competition.

Circumstances surrounding Ms. Wickham's death remain under investigation by the Harbor Falls Police Department and state police detectives assigned to the District Attorney's office.

Gwen slapped the paper. "Some investigation. The only person they're looking at is me."

"You can't be sure," Tess said. "The detective probably wouldn't tell you if he's looking at any other suspects."

"And he also wouldn't tell me if he's not."

"There's something I don't understand, Gwen," Nathan said. "We know Henrietta came back to change her clothes and drive to Boston, but instead she walked into your woods."

Gwen turned to answer Nathan. "Believe me, that's a huge part of the puzzle. Henrietta detested dirt and the outdoors. Someone must have given her a good reason for her to risk direct contact with nature. I assume it was one of the people on her list."

239

Nathan swished the last dregs of his coffee. "What list?"

Gwen tossed her teabag into the recycling container. "Henrietta took a phone call on Saturday from a person she labeled 'one of the more irritating people on my list'. When I asked her about the list, she said to mind my own business. I don't know if it was written somewhere or in her head. And I have no idea what she had planned for those people lucky enough to be on it."

Tess snorted. "I'll admit, it sounds like there was more to her coming back to Harbor Falls than judging the competition."

"You know, if Henrietta agreed to meet someone in my woods – and I have to believe that's the only reason she'd go out there – she must not have considered that person a threat."

"That makes sense," Nathan said. "So this other person either pushed Henrietta off your footbridge or she fell in on her own."

Tess added, "But if she fell in, don't you think he would have called 911?"

"Not necessarily." Nathan hunched his broad shoulders. "It depends on why the two of them were meeting and whether this person would have been willing to be public about their rendezvous. And, what makes you so sure it was a man?"

Tess shrugged. "Automatic assumption, I guess."

Gwen wrapped her fingers around her warm mug. "Do you suppose the forensics lab can determine if the railing gave way because Henrietta casually leaned on it? Or could the splinter pattern indicate she was shoved?"

"Good question," Nathan said. "That would at least verify a physical conflict. But from what you've told us, those scuffmarks haven't been directly linked to Henrietta's fall."

Tess sat up straight. "When will the detective let you know the test results?"

"I wouldn't be surprised if I don't hear from him at all. He's not trying to prove me innocent."

Nathan popped a tiny doughnut into his mouth, drawing

Gwen's attention to the box labeled *Sugar 'n Spice*. All thoughts of Henrietta dissipated. "Where did that come from?"

Tess waved her hand in a southerly direction. "We walked to that bakery on the other side of the green. All you've got in your fridge is Italian leftovers."

Gwen grabbed a sticky bun and took a huge bite. "I'm sorry, guys, but I haven't had a chance to stock up."

"Are you eating healthy, Sis?"

"Of course I am." Gwen licked the sugary goo from her fingers, not admitting she gave little thought to what she put in her mouth. She grabbed a magnetic shopping list from the fridge.

Nathan swallowed his last sip of coffee. "What are you two doing today?"

Tess looked at Gwen, her eyes wide. "Geez, Gwen, I was supposed to remind you to call Ernie this morning."

Gwen smacked her forehead. "I can't believe I forgot!"

"So, call him now."

"I will, but I forgot something else, too."

"What was that?" Tess asked, closing the pastry box.

"Just before the garden party was rained out, my friend Rachel pulled me aside and said she'd overheard Henrietta argue with someone the day before she left town. On Saturday, that was simply juicy gossip, but now I'm thinking Rachel might have heard something about Henrietta's resignation. I'll call her right now."

"You'd better call Ernie first," Nathan suggested.

"Right."

Gwen scrolled through her cell phone directory and touched his number.

"Ernie? It's Gwen. You wanted to know what happened with the judge yesterday." For the next few minutes, she brought him up to date about Henrietta's phone call to the dean, the fact that she'd been passed over to replace him after his

241

retirement, and her slip that she'd returned to Harbor Falls *"for the same reason she'd resigned."*

"Well, isn't that interesting?" Ernie said. "I almost hate to ask, but do you have anyone in mind who might shed some light on her resignation?"

"Funny you should ask, Ernie," Gwen said. "I'm planning to call a friend who says she overheard an argument the day before Henrietta left town."

"What are the chances your friend hooked up with Henrietta in your woods?"

"Slim to none, Ernie. Rachel barely knew Henrietta." He was silent for a moment. "Tell you what, Gwen. If this friend won't discuss the hearsay over the phone and suggests getting together, I don't want you going by yourself. Do you think Hal is willing to go with you?"

"To tell you the truth, Ernie, I'm not planning to bother Hal with this. But my sister Tess is here and she'll go with me."

"Good, good. Sounds like there's things you're not sayin' about Hal, but we'll leave that for another time. I'm meeting with my contact again this morning, and I'll let you know if there's any news on the Detective Brown front. Let's keep each other updated."

Gwen hung up and turned to Tess. "Time to call Rachel."

***

"Rachel? Hi, it's Gwen." She paused then replied, "Yes, it's true." Another pause. "I'd like to hear about that conversation you overheard." A third pause. "You are? Yes, lunch sounds wonderful. My sister Tess is visiting. Do you mind if she joins us?" Another minute of finalizing details. "Thanks, Rachel. We'll see you at noon."

As Gwen pressed the end button, she fashioned a thumbs-up in Tess's direction. "Done and done. Rachel has the day off. She's invited us for lunch."

Nathan snorted. "You're going, despite Hal's objections?"

242

Gwen picked up their three empty mugs and placed them in the sink. "I don't know what you two men discussed during your walk yesterday, but Hal has no say in what I do or don't do."

Nathan held up both hands. "Sorry I asked. Do you girls need a bodyguard today?"

Tess stole a quick glance at Gwen. "I don't think so."

"In that case, I'll take a hike up the coastline."

Tess smacked a kiss on his forehead. "See you later."

After Nathan left, Tess turned to Gwen. "Are you sure you want to go down this path? Tracking down a potential killer?"

Gwen stared at her sister. "I wouldn't have pursued it if I didn't. Where's your sense of adventure, Tess?"

"Oh, I've still got it. I just don't want you to be disappointed."

"I'll be more disappointed if I don't find out what Rachel knows."

Tess laid a hand on Gwen's arm. "Why don't you tell me what you hope to learn?"

Gwen cleared her throat. "First of all, the argument she overheard might explain why Henrietta resigned and left town. That's a secret I've always wanted to unearth." Despite the gravity of the situation, Gwen trembled with anticipation. "But, more importantly, Tess, depending on what Henrietta and this other person were arguing about all those years ago, the other person might have panicked when Henrietta came back to town. That could be the person who met her on the footbridge."

"That's optimistic, but I can see where you're going with this, Gwen," Tess conceded. "Still, why do you have to be the one to track down these bits of information? Maybe Hal's right. Maybe you should let Ernie hire a private eye."

Gwen let her head droop. She'd been so sure Tess would replace Hal as the sidekick.

Tess waited a beat. "Well?"

"I guess I don't trust a stranger to look in the right places for answers. And there's something else I didn't mention last night, Tess."

Her sister waited.

"Yesterday morning, Henrietta's cousin Mary stopped by." Gwen shared the intriguing details of Henrietta's childhood, then recapped John Wickham's connection to the Baylies Planning Board ten years ago, his anger that he wasn't allowed to bid on the abandoned library, and his intention to sue Gwen if she was involved in his niece's death. "He thinks I'd have to sell to pay damages and, to be honest, that's not a completely outlandish assumption. That's when he'd buy." Gwen's voice trembled. "I can't let that happen, Tess. The thought of Henrietta's uncle living here makes my skin crawl."

Tess grabbed Gwen in a fierce hug. "I had no idea, Sis. I'll stick by your side like Juicy Fruit gum. I agree you have access to things a private detective would never think to chase down."

Gwen pulled herself from Tess's grasp. "Thanks, Tess. We've always made a great team."

"Is there anything I can do right now?"

"I don't think so." Gwen glanced at her watch. "I need to phone the current dean and find out if he can meet with us."

"You go ahead and make that call." Tess headed for the staircase. "I'll be upstairs."

Gwen dialed Daniel Chartley, only to find he was out of the office. She requested he call her when he had a free minute, hung up, and climbed the staircase.

At the guest room door, Gwen saw Tess sitting at the front window, staring out at the village green, an open book ignored in her lap.

Tess flinched when Gwen knocked on the doorframe, inserted a bookmark, and placed her paperback on the side table. "Any success with the dean?"

"He wasn't in. I left a message."

"Well, let's hope he'll remember something relevant." Tess stood up. "How soon do we need to leave for Rachel's?" Gwen glanced at her watch. "An hour or so. She lives down the coast, and I want to take the shore road instead of the highway. A slower drive but more scenic."

"In that case, I want you to treat me like a ticket holder and give me the guided tour of your gardens. Without the rainstorm, of course."

Gwen grinned, pleased to be asked. "Sure. How soon can you be ready?"

"Just let me find my shoes." Tess got down on her hands and knees, stretching her arm beneath the bed. She pulled out her sneakers, stuffed her feet in, and tied the laces. "Let's go."

Chapter Forty

An hour later, Gwen pulled to a stop at the traffic light where Library Lane met North Street. She glanced at Tess in the passenger seat and found her sister gazing through the windshield.

"What are you thinking about?"

Tess jerked as if startled by Gwen's voice. "Well, for one thing, this scenery is breathtaking. You're lucky to live near the shore."

Gwen followed Tess's line of vision. Above the tree tops of Harbor Hill a sail boat danced through the pass between the barrier islands and the rock jetty. Three lobster boats motored toward the docks with their morning catch.

"I guess 'lucky' is what you could call it, Tess. I was fortunate to land a teaching position at Baylies. Then I married Parker and it never occurred to us to move anywhere else." Gwen peered at the red light, her foot tapping the gas pedal. "And how about you, Sis, living in the Berkshires? The view of the mountains from your window wall is spectacular."

"I guess we have the best of both worlds," Tess said, pausing before she turned toward Gwen. "I don't know your friend Rachel, but could she be exaggerating Henrietta's argument?"

"I don't think so. But we can decide after she tells us what she overheard."

The light turned green, Gwen crossed the intersection, drove down Harbor Hill, and turned south on Coast Road. "Tell you what, Tess. I'd like to pretend, at least for a little while, that Henrietta never existed. Let's just enjoy our drive."

For the next twelve miles the sisters marveled at the majestic power of the ocean crashing onto the sandy beaches, the solace of a lighthouse perched atop granite, and the frolicking of harbor seals. Gwen was relieved to see no sign of great whites cruising along the coastline – they'd been spotted several times in recent weeks. A few years before, she and Parker had been walking the beach when a great white attacked some hapless seals within sight of the shoreline. When the red foamy seawater reduced Gwen to tears, Parker had put his arm around her shoulders and turned them both away from the bloody sight. Gwen didn't care to witness that carnage ever again.

A right turn onto a country lane took them inland. After another mile, Gwen pulled in front of a multi-colored cottage sitting fifty feet back from the road.

"Here we are," Gwen announced, double-checking the number on the mailbox.

The robin's egg blue of the house contrasted with the grass green porch walls, the soft pink of the shutters, and the sunny yellow front gable. A gingerbread house somewhat out of place in staid New England, but charming nevertheless.

Gwen and Tess got out and stepped onto the sidewalk.

Rachel waved as she scurried down her walkway. Her long beige skirt billowed around her husky frame. Her unruly hair flew in all directions.

"I've been watching for you!" Rachel huffed when she reached them, breathless from her sprint. "I'm glad you called on my day off. I had time to make my favorite soup."

Rachel reached down and squeezed Gwen, a repeat of her tour-day bear hug. "Baylies isn't the same without you, girl. Why'd you have to go and retire?"

Gwen hugged back with equal fondness. "It was time, Rachel. After Parker died, I lost the energy for a classroom of students. Private lessons in my home studio are enough now."

Rachel turned to Tess. "You must be Gwen's sister."

"That's me. Tess Walker. Thanks for letting me crash your lunch."

Rachel ignored Tess's extended hand and pulled her into a less aggressive embrace.

"Glad to have you." Arm in arm, Rachel led them toward the house, past beds of deep pink New Guinea impatiens lining the walkway. "My gardening efforts can't compare with yours, Gwen, but I do what I can as a working girl. Come in and let me show you my home."

After circling through a nautically-themed living room, a blue and white bedroom with matching bathroom, and a compact kitchen, they arrived in a pristine dining room.

Gwen touched the lace tablecloth and a rose-patterned china bowl. "Your table looks lovely, Rachel, but you didn't have to go to all this trouble."

"The least I could do, Gwen. I can't believe I've never invited you before now. Excuse me, ladies. I'll be right back."

Seconds later Rachel re-emerged through the swinging door, placed a steaming tureen at the head of the table, and ladled Italian wedding soup into their bowls.

Gwen savored her first spoonful. "Ummm. Delicious."

"Thanks. I pride myself on being a good cook. Maybe it shows." Rachel chuckled, patting her ample hips before taking her seat. She lifted the bread basket and passed it around.

"These tiny meatballs are perfectly spiced," Tess commented. "Care to share your recipe?"

"Sure thing. Give me your email address and I'll send it along."

"Hang on a sec," Tess said, reaching for her purse beside her chair. "I've got a personal card in here someplace."

As Tess searched, Rachel turned her attention to Gwen.

"You sure you want to hear about Henrietta's argument?"

Gwen swallowed her mouthful of soup and put down her spoon. "I'm sure. I was surprised when you mentioned it last Saturday. Why didn't you tell before?"

Rachel turned a lovely shade of pink. "Well, you and I

hadn't met yet, and Henrietta did leave Harbor Falls the next
day. Everyone in the office kinda had a 'good riddance'
attitude. What I mean is no one seemed to care why Henrietta
moved away. And, like I said, I was the newest hire, so I didn't
think anyone would believe me, or maybe they'd label me a
rumormonger. "

For a moment, Gwen's spirit soared. After all these years of
wondering, she finally knew why Henrietta resigned and left
town, although the details behind her exodus were still
unexplained. "So why bring it up now, Rachel?"

"Well, when I found out she was back in town and staying
with you, what I'd overheard launched from my memory like a
moth toward a light. I'd heard all about her nastiness toward
you back then, so with her living under your roof, I thought you
should know."

Gwen brought her temporary elation under control, waiting
for Rachel to go on.

Instead of talking, Rachel went quiet. "And then Henrietta
died. Seems like idle gossip now that she's gone." After of few
beats of silence, Rachel squinted at Gwen. "Don't take this the
wrong way, but why are you so keen to hear the details?"

Gwen fidgeted with her napkin. "I'm researching the details
of Henrietta's life before she left Harbor Falls."

"What on earth for?"

Tess pulled out her personal card and distracted Rachel for
a moment, giving Gwen a chance to consider her answer.

"There's something I haven't told you, Rachel." Gwen
gripped the edge of the table. "The police are calling
Henrietta's death suspicious, and the detective seems to think I
was involved. I'm trying to figure out who else might have
wanted her gone, which is why your overheard conversation is
so important."

Gwen waited, wondering if Rachel would talk to a 'person
of interest'.

Rachel slapped the table, making the utensils jingle. "Well, why didn't you say so?" She reached over and touched Gwen's arm. "I don't think I ever told you this, but I have recall like data on a hard drive. I can repeat Henrietta's argument like I heard it yesterday."

"Handy," Tess commented.

Gwen did a double-take. "No wonder you were promoted to manager of the Baylies business office in record time."

Rachel laughed. "Comes in useful every once in a while. Like now." Her fingers drummed on the lace tablecloth. "Okay. Let me tell you how it all started. As the newest member of the office staff, I was assigned to handle the filing on the far side of our building. That afternoon I stayed late. All that extra paperwork from the end of the school year, you know." She leaned her pudgy arms on the table, losing herself in the telling. "I'd been working for about an hour when I heard a female down the hall shout, 'Oh my God.' A young man's voice yelled, 'Stop.' Then I heard feet running. I wasn't concerned because students can be noisy, especially so close to graduation. At the same time there was another conversation further down the hallway, but I couldn't hear words. A few minutes later, an exit door rattled. I looked out and noticed a woman hurrying from the building. The window was open, and I could hear her crying – she was bawling, actually. Based on her Cleopatra hairstyle, I thought it was Claudia Moss, but I couldn't be sure."

Tess interrupted. "Who's Claudia Moss?"

"Her name is Claudia Smith now," Gwen explained. "Back then, she was the secretary to the old dean, Walter James. He's the judge I met with yesterday. Claudia married Pete Smith, the college sports coach. Their son Kenneth is my Friday afternoon student."

Tess nodded and Gwen turned back to Rachel. "Did anyone follow that crying woman?"

Rachel shook her head as she buttered a slice of Italian bread. "I don't think so, but I was distracted because a few seconds later I heard two other voices talking out in the hallway. They couldn't have known I was inside the room because the filing cabinets stood between me and the open doorway."

Gwen sat forward, her curiosity on high alert.

"Well, I did recognize the woman's voice. It was definitely Henrietta's. She had that haughty way of talking, you know. She said something like: 'How dare you threaten me. Whatever you think you found is totally irrelevant.' And then the man said, 'I don't think so, Henrietta. My research was quite thorough.' Then she said, 'Well, if you dare to even hint about this to the dean, I'll make sure your wife hears about your little love affair.'

"He got angry, Gwen. I thought he might slap her, but he didn't. He kept his voice real low. Real ominous-like, you know? He said, 'Don't you dare or you'll be sorry. I also witnessed that little tryst in your office a few minutes ago.'"

Gwen interrupted. "Do you know who he was?"

Rachel shook her capacious head. "Sorry, no. Henrietta never called him by name."

"Could he have been another professor? An office staffer? Someone from administration? "

"Sorry, I just don't know," Rachel replied. "His voice didn't sound familiar."

Tess held up a hand. "Sis, what makes you think he was from Baylies? Maybe he wasn't connected to the college at all. Maybe he wasn't even from Harbor Falls."

"You're right, Tess. No need to limit our thinking. I wonder what the man found that Henrietta wanted so desperately to keep from the dean. And what about that tryst in her office?"

"He never mentioned specifics," Rachel clarified, her eyes darting from Gwen to Tess and back again. "There's more. But first, let's have our dessert." Rachel disappeared into the kitchen.

Brought up short by the interruption of the story, Gwen nearly jumped out of her chair to follow Rachel and speed things along. Instead, she bit her lip and stayed put, her foot tapping with impatience as she tossed Tess a look of incredulity.

Seconds later, Rachel returned with three dessert cups on a metal tray, a sly smile brightening her face. "Crème brûlée. Another of my many favorites."

Between spoonfuls of the sweet pudding, Rachel continued her story. "Where was I? Oh, yeah. Henrietta said, 'You ruin my career, and I'll ruin your marriage.' Then the man said, 'You've got a lot more to lose than I do, bitch. First thing tomorrow morning, I'm going to have a little chat with the dean about your credentials. And, oh yeah, I might mention I saw you fraternizing with a student.' Then Henrietta said, 'No, you can't do that'."

Rachel's eyes widened. "I swear, Gwen, I think I heard her sob, if you can believe she was capable. She said, 'Okay. Okay. What if I promise never to mention to your wife what I just witnessed? Will you keep your research and that student to yourself?'

"Her attitude changed in an instant, Gwen." Rachel snapped her fingers, the sharp snick echoing off the ceiling. "She was pleading with him. Can you imagine?"

Gwen shook her head. "That is hard to believe of Henrietta."

"Well, let me go on. He said, 'But I don't trust you, Henrietta.'

"And she said, 'I beg you not to tell the dean. My career will be ruined. Not only here at Baylies, but at any college."

"So the guy said, 'Here's my best offer. Pack up and leave, and I won't expose your fraud to the dean.'"

Rachel sat back in her chair, breathing heavily and pushing at her fly-away locks in a futile effort for control.

"What did Henrietta say to that?" Gwen asked.

"She spoke so low, I couldn't hear her words. Then they both stomped off. From inside my room, it sounded like they went in opposite directions. I hurried into the hallway and saw a woman down at the end, but she wasn't Henrietta. The man was gone."

Gwen released her breath in a loud whoosh. "Wow, Rachel, I can't believe you remembered all that. Now I know why Henrietta resigned."

Tess tapped Gwen's hand. "Didn't she tell Walter James last week that her reason for resigning was the reason she returned?"

Gwen nodded. "She did. More importantly, is that man still in town? And, if he is, did he think Henrietta might reveal his affair? Did he lure her onto my footbridge?"

"But why bother after all these years?" Rachel asked. "And for what purpose?"

"Good questions," Gwen agreed. "There's a lot we still don't know."

Noticing the time on the wall clock, Gwen slid her chair back. "I'm sorry, Rachel, but Tess and I have to get back. We have an errand to run, and I have a student later this afternoon."

Rachel's hands flew to her face. "Oh, my gosh, I didn't realize how long I've been talking."

"No need to apologize. I'm glad you mentioned that argument."

"Do you think it will help you figure out what happened to Henrietta?" Rachel asked.

Gwen rose from her chair and placed her napkin on the table. "Too soon to tell. Thanks for lunch. It was delicious."

Rachel walked them out to the curb. "Good luck in your search, Gwen. Let me know what you find out."

"I will." Gwen kissed Rachel's chubby cheek, then slipped into her little red sedan.

Tess glanced over from the passenger seat. "What do you think that man found that scared Henrietta enough that she resigned?"

"Oh, any number of things, Tess. A detail of her education that didn't match her credentials. Maybe details of a criminal background that she failed to report. And then there was that fraternization with a student. Moral turpitude is frowned upon in all colleges."

Gwen started the engine. "But this is just like the meeting I had with Walter James yesterday. The more answers I find, the more questions I have."

Chapter Forty-One

Gwen and Tess trudged up the driveway steps and along the deck, carrying fabric sacks loaded with groceries. When Nathan stood up from a deck chair at the far end, he startled them both and they nearly dropped the bags.

"Sorry. I must have dozed off." He snagged both bags.

The house phone rang and Gwen rushed inside to pick it up. "Hello."

"Please hold for the dean," said a disembodied voice.

Within seconds, a man's deep voice came on the line. "Gwen, sorry I missed your call this morning. I've been meaning to touch base with you about Henrietta. I can't believe she died. How're you holding up?"

His concern touched her. "I'm doing okay, Daniel. Actually, Henrietta is the reason I'm calling. Can you fit me into your schedule for a personal chat?"

"Hang on, Gwen." Moments passed in a haze of soft classical music before he came back on the line. "How's eleven tomorrow morning?"

Grateful that her calendar was mostly empty, she said, "Perfect. See you then. And thanks."

She strode to the island to help stash the groceries and noticed Tess sniffing the air.

"You ate the leftover spaghetti and meatballs, Nathan?"

He tucked a carton of milk in the fridge. "Can't get anything past that nose of yours, wife. I also finished up the lasagna. Gwen's right. Italian food tastes better the next day."

They were still chuckling when the doorbell chimed. Gwen glanced at her watch and murmured, "Jenna's right on time."

As Jenna stepped across the threshold, Gwen caught a glimpse of Hal's Volvo driving off.

"You didn't walk from the high school?" Gwen asked.

"No. Granddad picked me up." Jenna took on a miserable expression. "He'll be back at five."

Since he'd bothered to drive into town and chauffer Jenna, Gwen expected him to hang around for the hour of practice. Obviously, he was still upset. But she wasn't about to change her plans to please Hal.

Despite Tess's encouragement and the approval of Parker's ghost – Gwen had to smile at that absurd memory – a relationship with Hal might not work with both of them so set in their ways.

She pasted a smile on her face and ushered Jenna to the music studio where Tess waited at the Steinway. Jenna's playing was not up to her usual proficiency.

With no improvement by the end of the hour, Gwen asked in her gentlest voice, "Is something bothering you today, Jenna?"

Jenna lowered her flute and turned red eyes toward her coach. "I'm sorry, Mrs. Andrews."

Before the girl had a chance to explain, a car horn beeped out front.

Jenna reached for her black case. "That'll be Granddad. I'd better go." Tears balanced precariously as she packed her instrument.

Gwen pushed a few stray hairs from the sullen young face. "Don't apologize. Everyone has a bad day once in a while."

Leaving Tess at the Steinway, Gwen walked Jenna to the front door. The girl's lethargic progress down the seven steps and her silence as she slid into Hal's passenger seat was cause for concern. Jenna turned and waved, her forlorn expression nearly breaking Gwen's heart.

Hal didn't even glance Gwen's way, which bothered her in a different way. Before Henrietta showed up, Gwen had enjoyed his company during Jenna's lessons. Over the summer, they'd developed an easy comradery, sparked by their shared admiration of Jenna's musicality. With everything that had happened since Henrietta arrived, would her friendship with him survive?

As Hal's tail lights disappeared, Gwen had to ask herself if she wanted to remain his friend. Lately she'd felt like a yo-yo at the end of his string, anticipating one reaction and getting another. Suspecting Jenna's rough practice session was the result of Gwen's head-bumping with Hal the previous evening, she felt awful that their disagreement had affected the girl. But, she decided, there was nothing more for her to do but cross her fingers that Jenna could push the bickering aside.

If Gwen's relationship with Hal rebounded, so be it. If not, she'd be down one new-found friend and sadder for it.

As far as Henrietta was concerned, Gwen had no choice but to untangle herself from the web of the woman's death so she could move along whatever remained of life's path.

She stayed on the top step and dialed Ernie's cell phone to fill him in on Rachel's story about Henrietta's argument and her thoughts about what the "mystery man" may have found out. "Very interestin', Gwen," Ernie commented. "We can't assume there's a connection between that man and Henrietta's walk into your woods, but it's not impossible. I hate to ask, but what are you plannin' to do next?"

She told him about her appointment with Dean Daniel Chartley the following morning.

"Well, talkin' to him is worth a try, but I don't think Henrietta would have shared any details about her departure. It's not as if she would have brought up the topic of being black-mailed about credential fraud to the man in charge."

"You're probably right, Ernie. I'll let you know if anything comes of my meeting."

* * *

That evening, Nathan cooked burgers on Gwen's outdoor

257

grill. Tess and Gwen prepared a garden salad, added a bag of low-salt chips, dill pickles, iced tea, and a bottle of raspberry Zinfandel wine. The three of them settled at a patio table near the fish pond.

"Hello," a voice called from the driveway.

They looked over to see Liz waving as she made her way across the lawn. She hesitated when she spotted Tess and Nathan. "I thought you guys were coming on Thursday?"

Tess held up a finger and swallowed a mouthful of burger. "When we heard about Henrietta, we decided Gwen shouldn't be living here by herself."

"Can't say I blame you. Wish I had a sister like you, Tess." When Tess waved off the compliment, Liz focused on Gwen. "I hope you don't mind me dropping by unannounced. I brought the book you ordered."

Gwen reached out to accept the debut novel of a new author. "Thanks, but you didn't need to make a special trip." She placed it on the table. "Where's Tony?"

"Oh, he's playing golf with his Wednesday night league. I won't see him for a few hours."

"Have you had supper?"

When Liz shook her head, Gwen said, "Nathan, did you cook any extra burgers?"

"There's one left." He headed for the grill.

Liz slid into the chair next to Gwen. "Any news about Henrietta?"

Gwen gave her a nod. "A lot has happened since you stopped by on Sunday morning."

Nathan handed a plate holding the burger to Liz and sat down next to Tess. The two of them continued their meal in silence. Liz munched while Gwen ticked off the events of the past few days, finally ending with Rachel's re-telling of Henrietta's argument.

"Damn that Henrietta. She's dead and still harassing you,"

Liz said, popping a potato chip into her mouth. "Are you sure Detective Brown thinks you're to blame?"

"Why else would he take my shoes and clothes for testing? Oh, yeah, and my hair."

"Well, there is that." Liz downed the rest of her iced tea. "You seem to be looking in all the right places for answers."

"So far, Liz, I've been following whatever clues crop up."

"You be careful, and let me know if there's anything I can do to help." Liz pulled her chair closer. "But delivering your book wasn't my only reason for stopping by."

Gwen eyed her best friend with more than a little wariness. "What are you up to, Liz?"

"Well, way before this Henrietta business, I was worried about you, Gwen. All you do is work in your gardens and tutor your private music students. You have virtually no social life."

"That's not true," Gwen objected. "I've gone out to lunch twice this week."

Liz let out an exasperated sigh. "That's not what I mean, and you know it. If it wasn't for Henrietta dying, those lunches wouldn't have happened. I'm talking about romance."

Getting to her feet and moving to the edge of the deck, Gwen expected the lazy swimming of the five koi in her small fish pond to distract her from Liz's matchmaking schemes. But when Liz moved to Gwen's side, the spell was broken.

Gwen looked into the face of her best friend. "I know you mean well, Liz, but I'm not ready to let go of Parker just yet." Could she risk telling Liz about Parker's return? Whether ghost or dream, talking to him had seemed so very real. Liz, with her exposure to occult authors, was probably the one person who might believe Gwen's nighttime rendezvous with Parker.

Gwen glanced back to make sure Tess and Nathan were out of earshot. At the patio table, their heads nearly touching, their whispers were indistinct. Were they discussing Liz's speech about romance or was their low chatter unrelated?

When she switched back to Liz, Gwen instantly changed her mind. Something about the eager look in Liz's eyes made Gwen think twice about confiding. Knowing Liz, she might try to schedule Gwen into the bookstore to give a ghost talk. No, no, no. That would never do. Disclosure wasn't worth the risk of exposure. Parker's appearances – in whatever form – had to remain Gwen's secret.

Liz went on. "Your Parker was a wonderful man. But I want to see you enjoying life again."

Gwen turned from the pond and reached for Liz's hand.

"Let me move on at my own pace. Please, Liz."

"All I'm asking is that you keep your options open." Liz squeezed Gwen's fingers and didn't let go. "Hal Jenkins seems nice."

Remembering how Liz had hung with Hal during the garden and house tour, Gwen pulled from Liz's grasp. "Hal Jenkins *is* a nice man, but our only link is Jenna. If he hadn't hired me to prepare her for the competition, he wouldn't be part of my life."

"Don't you think Jenna is old enough to bring herself to your studio? Yet Hal drove her over here every Saturday all summer long. I tell you, Gwen, he has feelings for you. He stayed after the garden party was rained out. He helped you search the woods for Henrietta. He was here on Sunday after the police found her body. He drove you to your lunch meeting yesterday. If the man didn't care for you, he wouldn't have done any of those things."

"Oh, don't be silly, Liz." Gwen wasn't going to encourage Liz's crusade of romance by revealing that Hal had invited her to join him and Jenna for dinner last week, or by mentioning his brief kisses on her cheek. If his cold shoulder that afternoon was any clue, she suspected he would make no more advances.

"Liz, even if I was ready to get involved with another man, I've got to get myself out of this Henrietta mess first."

"Good point."

Hoping to quell the subject, Gwen grabbed Liz's hand and pulled her back to the patio table. As they approached, Nathan repositioned his chair, but Tess cocked one eyebrow. Gwen knew her sister well enough to understand she'd overheard Liz's assessment of Hal's romantic potential. After all, she'd offered the same advice the previous evening. Luckily, Tess was subtle enough not to belabor the point in front of Liz.

"When will you hear the results of that lab work?" Liz asked as she sat down.

Liz's suspension of her match-making efforts released Gwen from the tension of resisting. "I doubt if Detective Brown would tell me, especially if the tests prove my shoes did *not* leave those scuffmarks. And Chief Upton seems to be giving the detective freedom to do what he wants. Ernie's contact is likely to know the results before we do."

For another two hours, the four of them reviewed all they knew about Henrietta, coming up empty on answers. The landscape lights blinked on and Liz said her goodbyes.

Inside, Tess and Nathan headed upstairs, leaving Gwen alone in the kitchen, staring out the bay window. Behind her, the old library was quiet. Should she summon Parker? Would he hear her again? How many more times could he come back? What were the rules? If Parker was truly a ghost, he didn't seem to know much about where he'd been since he passed away.

Gwen's skepticism reared its atheistic head. Could there possibly be a grand creator who knows what everyone on this one tiny planet is doing and thinking at all times? Is there a heaven? Is there a hell? Who's in charge, if anyone? That had always been the ultimate unanswered question in Gwen's mind.

She whispered Parker's name.

"Good evening, Gwen." Parker's melodious voice spoke behind her.

She whirled and watched his form take shape on the other side of the island. He grinned at her, his translucent hazel eyes again sparkling with mischief.

"Parker, I wasn't sure you'd come back again."

"Well, until something changes, if I hear you call my name, I'll come."

Gwen's quandary still lingered. During the past two and a half years since he passed, she had called his name many times, but had she only *thought* his name and not actually said it? Was it her anxiety over Henrietta's death that caused her to call his name aloud for the first time? Gwen didn't know for sure.

Forgetting she'd been miffed at Parker's sudden disappearance the night before, Gwen hurried around the island. She held out her arms, craving whatever sensation awaited her. Unlike the butterfly kisses when he touched her hand as he had lain beside her in their bed, his arms around her now felt more like a gentle squeeze: satisfying and frustrating at the same time.

When he released her, she backed away and looked into his pale but still-handsome face.

"Sorry, Gwen, that's the best I can do." The corners of his mouth dipped in apology.

She glanced up through the mezzanine opening to the second level balcony. "Let's go outside. I don't want to wake Tess or Nathan."

She was talking to Parker's ghost as if he were someone who'd stopped by for a chat. Actually, that's exactly who he was. He floated behind her through the French door and she eased it closed without making a sound before settling into an Adirondack chair.

Parker hovered at the deck railing. "What's on your mind tonight, Gwen?"

For a second she was flustered, not remembering why she'd been so desperate to see him.

Uninformed about how long Parker would stick around, she figured she may as well ask her most pressing question first.

"I started to ask you something last night, but you disappeared."

"Sorry about that." One eyebrow lifted at a cocky angle. "What do you want to know?"

She forged ahead, hoping he wouldn't abandon her again, because she needed to hear his answer. She cleared her throat.

"Ernie mentioned that Henrietta used to come to your office."

If a ghost could turn scarlet, Parker had, at least if the stricken look on his face was any indication.

"Damn it. I hoped you'd never hear about that." He began to stomp around the upper deck, but with his lack of bulk he didn't make the boards squeak.

"But why didn't you tell me, Parker? I thought we shared everything?"

He stopped pacing and kneeled before her. "Gwen, believe me that nothing was going on between that woman and me." When he rested his hands on her knees, she barely felt the weight. "If she said anything different, she was lying."

He got to his feet and began pacing, one hand gripping his chin. After a moment, he dropped his arm, seeming to have made a decision. "For the first few months of our marriage, you came home every day and told me how she lashed out at you. When she started showing up at my office, you stopped complaining, and I thought, honestly, that because she was constantly harassing me, she had stopped harassing you."

Until this second, Gwen had foolishly harbored doubts about Parker's loyalty. Now that she knew Parker's reason for keeping Henrietta's visits a secret, Gwen's skepticism dropped away. No longer caring that his wrongly-conceived strategy to protect her from Henrietta had not stopped the woman's barbed insults, Gwen wanted to stroke his gossamer hair and kiss his sallow lips. But knowing it was pointless, she folded her hands in her lap. "I believe you, Parker. I love you."

She tapped the arm of the next chair, inviting him to sit down. When he did, a feeling of tranquility settled over her like a blanket. She stretched her hand to cover his, not upset when they merged together. "Want to hear what Tess and I did today?"

His ashen head nodded and Gwen repeated Rachel's story about Henrietta's last day in Harbor Falls. When she finished, she posed a question. "Parker, did you have anything to do with Henrietta leaving town?"

"Me?" He shook his head. "I wish I could take credit. Why in the world would you ask?"

She reached out, frustrated when her hand passed through his arm. "The man who argued with Henrietta – I thought he might have been you."

Again, he shook his head. "Wasn't me."

Before she'd even asked, Gwen knew that including Parker on her mental list of men who might have confronted Henrietta was ludicrous, especially if that man was connected to the footbridge incident. Obviously Parker couldn't have tossed Henrietta into the gorge. After all, he wasn't able to slide open the shower door.

"What's your next move, my love?"

"Well, I've got a meeting with the new dean tomorrow morning. I'm hoping he'll know the reason for Henrietta's resignation."

Parker swayed, a look of panic contorting his face. "Gwen, darling, I think I'm about to go away. Remember…I've loved you since the moment you spilled tomato sauce on my jacket."

And he was gone.

Gwen couldn't help but laugh at his parting remark. Who would think that her clumsiness would lead to their decades-long love affair? A love affair not only during their earthbound life, but one apparently able to bridge into the next. Was it possible that Parker was truly a ghost and not a dream at all?

Gwen still couldn't be sure.

She glanced to the sitting room windows on the second floor, just in case Tess had woken and was looking down. No silhouette shadowed the glass. Gwen headed inside, warmed by Parker's love and loyalty.

She paused at the island to rehash her plans to identify Rachel's mystery man. Besides the dean tomorrow, there was one more person to talk to: Claudia Moss Smith. If she had been the crying woman who ran from the building, as Rachel had speculated, maybe she had witnessed whatever had happened before Henrietta's confrontation. Maybe she'd seen that man. Maybe she even knew who he was.

Chapter Forty-Two

Gwen stood at the island on Thursday morning, dunking her teabag, replaying last night's conversation with Parker, and watching Tess fry bacon in a cast iron pan.

When the front door opened, Gwen turned to see Nathan back from his morning walk. Close behind him was Hal.

"Good morning, Gwen. I hope you don't mind me stopping by uninvited."

She wrapped her hands around her cup and stared into it.

"You're welcome anytime, Hal," she said without looking at him. "But I'd prefer not to argue again if you don't mind."

Nathan joined Tess at the stove while Hal stayed on the opposite side of the island.

"That's why I'm here, Gwen. Jenna was upset about her practice session yesterday. And she told me in no uncertain terms it was my fault for quarreling with you the other night." He leaned on the countertop. "I explained that you and I were having a difference of opinion, but Jenna didn't buy it. When I dropped her off at school this morning, she made me promise to drive over here and tell you I'm sorry, which I am. Will you accept my apology?"

Gwen was impressed he had the guts to apologize but eyed him with suspicion.

He glanced over her shoulder at Tess and Nathan, who were absorbed in their own conversation, then leaned far over the island and said in a hushed voice, "I don't want our friendship to fall apart because we don't agree about everything, Gwen. I don't know what the future holds. Maybe we can be more than friends. I just know I can't tamp down my urge to protect you."

She studied Hal's rugged face. "Maybe you should rethink your methods."

266

"I'm open to anything you toss on the table." He swiped the granite with his hand.

"For one, you've got to stop telling me what to do." He gripped the edge of the island. "I never meant to be a bully, Gwen, but I'll try my best. Anything else?"

"Yes. Help me prove to Detective Brown that someone else did away with Henrietta."

"Done and done," Hal answered, echoing a line from a Scrooge movie released in the '80s. Was it possible that Hal *knew* that this movie – this line – was a favorite of Gwen's?

She could feel her lips forming a grin. "In that case, apology accepted."

When his chuckle released the tension between them, he stretched one hand across the counter and rested it on top of hers. Not a butterfly wing touch like Parker's, but a flesh and blood man. Gwen lowered her gaze to his gesture, still unsure if they would ever be more than friends.

Nevertheless, he was willing to help her search for Henrietta's attacker, and that was all Gwen cared about at the moment. With reluctance, she pulled her hand free to retrieve her writing tablet and pencil from the island drawer, then she motioned Hal to the dining room table and shared Rachel's telling of Henrietta's argument.

A few minutes later Tess and Nathan delivered four plates of bacon and eggs, complemented by toast and jam, and sat down on either side of Gwen and Hal.

Tess glanced at Gwen's blank page. "What are you two planning?"

Gwen grinned at her sister. "Hal's agreed to be my partner in crime."

Nathan leaned over and clapped him on the back. "Smart move."

"You know what they say." Hal smirked. "If you can't beat 'em, join 'em."

"So you're taking my place during Gwen's escapades, Hal?" Tess asked.

Gwen's mouth dropped. Was Tess upset about being usurped?

A half-smile appeared on Tess's face. "I'm only teasing, Hal. It's better than you fighting with my sister."

Relieved, Gwen tapped her pencil. "I just told Hal about Henrietta's argument."

Tess picked up her fork. "What's your take on it, Hal?" He chewed on a piece of toast and swallowed. "Well, there's at least one person – that unidentified man – who wouldn't want Henrietta back in Harbor Falls. But we don't know who he was – or is. For all we know, he might have moved away."

Gwen wrote *mystery man* at the top of her page with a double-line beneath. "What do you think of this idea, Hal? You come with me to the police station this morning and request an update from Chief Upton. Maybe you can learn things he won't tell me. Then we'll stop at the music shop and see what we can drag out of Jack. By then, it'll be time to meet with Daniel Chartley. After that, I want to drop in on Claudia. I think Rachel is right that Claudia was the crying woman. Her Cleopatra hairstyle is very distinctive. I want to ask if she heard or saw anything on the day of Henrietta's argument."

Tess eyes grew large. "That's an ambitious list."

"Probably sounds worse than it will be," Gwen said with all the gumption she could muster. For one second she considered calling Ernie. He knew about her meeting with the new dean but not about her impromptu visits to Chief Upton or Claudia.

Nah, she decided she'd wait until later, when she had more to tell.

Nathan collected the empty plates. "Anything Tess and I can do?"

"You're both free as birds. Why don't you go sight-seeing?"

Tess turned to Nathan, her voice belying her excitement.

"Let's drive up to Boston and walk the Rose Kennedy Greenway."

Gwen did a double-take. "I'm sorry, Tess. I should have taken you guys up there years ago, after the Big Dig was completed." Gwen glanced at the clock. "If you leave now, you'll be back in time for your practice session with Jenna. If I wasn't trying to keep myself out of jail, I'd come with you."

Tess and Nathan walked out, chattering like school children about to go on a field trip. Gwen noticed Hal watching her.

"What?"

"I was just thinking that hanging around with you has added some spice to my life."

Although she'd been butting heads with him since Sunday, Gwen had to admit she liked Hal. But unlike him, she wasn't ready to let their friendship bloom into something deeper. At least, not while she was sharing her nights with Parker. On the other hand, she felt more energized about searching for Henrietta's history with Hal by her side.

***

Ten minutes later, Gwen and Hal strode through the visitor's entrance to find Chief Upton crossing the reception area with a steaming mug. His eyes flicked back and forth between them. "Good morning, Gwen." He transferred the hot drink to his left hand and extended his right to Hal. "Mr. Jenkins."

Hal shook it. "Chief Upton."

Gwen took the lead, as they had planned. "Do you have a few minutes, Chief?"

"Of course." The chief led them down the hall to his office. Gwen had never been inside this inner sanctum before. She noted the polished wood moldings, a calming shade of taupe on the walls, and a massive oak desk which suited the chief's imposing size. He sat in his equally large swivel chair. "Does Attorney Maguire know you're here, Gwen?"

She shook her head. "I see no harm in a casual chat. We've been acquainted for a long time, Charles."

Her use of his first name in front of Hal made the chief sit up straight.

She forged ahead. "I noticed that several planks and the broken railings were removed from my footbridge."

"That's true. They're at the state forensics lab."

Hal sat back and rested one foot on his knee before speaking. "And the lab also has Gwen's shoes and clothing from last Saturday, plus a lock of her hair?"

"True again, Mr. Jenkins." The chief toggled his gaze from Hal to Gwen.

"You have no proof that Gwen's shoes left the scuffmarks?"

"You're moving into topics I cannot discuss. I'd like nothing more than to exonerate her."

She sat forward. "Are you investigating anyone else?"

The chief squinted. "I'm not at liberty to discuss other persons of interest. Detective Brown is doing his job by following the clues."

Hmmm, just like I'm doing, but I bet the detective is going in the opposite direction. Gwen did notice the chief's use of the plural and relaxed just a bit. "There's something you may not know about Henrietta, Chief."

"And what's that?"

"Henrietta hated getting dirty or communing with nature. For her to walk into my woods last Saturday afternoon, someone must have made her an offer she couldn't refuse, to use a well-worn line from *The Godfather.* I assure you it wasn't me, Chief, and I can prove it." She was thinking of all the people on her garden tour who could provide an alibi, plus Claudia's confirmation of the time they spent together afterwards, then her time with Liz, Tony, and Hal as they searched for Henrietta's whereabouts.

The chief stiffened. "What makes you think it was the afternoon and not later in the day?"

"Because my neighbor saw Henrietta come out my French door and walk into the woods during the garden party."

"Hold on there, Gwen. You told us the last time you saw her was Saturday morning."

"And that's still true. Mrs. Martin said my back was turned. I didn't see Henrietta."

The chief picked up a pencil and made a notation. "We'll take a statement from your neighbor to verify this."

"That won't be a problem. She'll tell you exactly what I just told you."

He turned his full gaze on her. "Are you running your own investigation, Gwen?"

She cocked her head. "Who, me? What do I know about investigating?"

He gave her a look that implied he doubted her words but let it ride. "Well, if there's nothing else…" He got to his feet. "I'll walk you out."

Gwen had hoped the chief would let some details slip out, but instead she'd been the one providing new information.

***

Out in the station's parking lot, Hal started the Volvo's engine. "You'd think Chief Upton would be calling in favors with the forensics techs to move those tests along."

Gwen was thrown by his words. "What are you getting at?"

Hal pulled into traffic. "The chief is covering for you."

"Charles thinks I pushed Henrietta to her death?" She was stunned at the possibility.

Hal spared her a glance. "That's not what I meant. I think he believes you're innocent and is giving you a chance to smoke out that second person."

Chapter Forty-Three

Hal pulled into the parking lot of The Olde Music Shop and shut off the engine. Sliding a look over at Gwen, he said, "There's something I've been meaning to ask you."

Gwen's hand stopped in mid-air as she reached for the door handle. "What is it?"

"Why did you agree to let Henrietta stay with you? From the little I've heard over the past few days, you two were never friends."

"We don't have time for that particular history lesson right now. I *will* tell you how I was roped into hosting her, because none of it matters now. Don't get upset, but Jack told me Jenna registered late for the competition, and if I didn't let Henrietta sleep in my guest room, he'd remove Jenna from the competitor's list. I wasn't about to let him bar her from competing."

Hal's face reddened and he smacked the steering wheel. "All this time, you were protecting Jenna?" He threw open his car door, slammed it shut, and stormed toward the shop's entrance.

Gwen hopped out and raced after him, grabbed his sleeve as he reached the door and whirled him around to face her. "Wait, Hal, wait. If you attack Jack, he won't tell us anything."

Hal inhaled a noisy breath and pulled his sleeve from her grasp. "You're assuming he has something he *can* tell us, Gwen."

She stood between Hal and the door. "If I've learned anything in the past few days, it's this: You never know what someone is going to tell you until they do." Then calmly, she pushed in the door and stepped inside.

In the middle of the shop Emily was speaking with a middle-aged couple and a be-speckled young lady. Alex stood behind his counter, his attention focused on a young man, an oboe sitting on the glass top between them. At the music rack, Jack was conversing with several older men. One of the men headed toward the exit. As he walked past, Gwen recognized him as the band teacher from Kenneth's school. She touched his sleeve. "Bill, do you have a minute?"

After a few seconds, recognition lit his face. "Gwen Andrews, haven't seen you for a while. What can I do for you?" He cupped her elbow and turned her toward the front window.

Glancing over her shoulder at Hal, she held up one finger to signal she needed a minute, then returned her attention to the band teacher.

"Well, here's the thing, Bill. One of my flute students wants to switch to cymbals. I promised his mother I'd ask you about it. Any chance you have room for another cymbal smacker?"

Bill hesitated. "Cymbals, huh? We've already got two, but I guess a third wouldn't hurt." He reached into his pocket and handed her a business card. "Send me an email with your student's name and I'll let you know what we need to do."

Thanking Bill, Gwen moved to join Hal. At the same instant, Jack approached. "Good morning, Gwen."

She tipped her head. "Same to you, Jack." She then turned to Hal. "I'm not sure if you know Hal Jenkins. He's Jenna's grandfather." When Jack stiffened, Gwen tamped down a smirk. He must be wondering if Hal knew about his underhanded use of Jenna's late registration to force Henrietta into Gwen's guest room.

"How are you today, Mr. Jenkins?"

When Hal only nodded, Jack extended his hand. "You must be proud that your granddaughter is participating in the competition on Saturday." Jack's solicitous manner nearly made Gwen choke.

Hal tucked his hands in his pants pockets. "I certainly am. Jenna's a fine musician."

How deep was Hal digging to find the strength not to throttle Jack?

A false smile broadened Jack's lips. "What can I do for the two of you this morning?"

Gwen stepped in front of Hal. "Do you have a minute to talk?"

Jack's eyes darted around the busy shop. "Yes, of course. Come with me."

Leading them down the ancient floorboards, he snapped his fingers in Alex's direction and pointed toward his office. Alex nodded and turned back to the potential oboe buyer.

In the office, Hal leaned against the windowsill, his arms folded. Gwen took the guest chair.

Jack settled behind his desk. "I haven't got much time. What do you want to discuss?"

"Henrietta."

Jack stiffened, his eyes narrowing. "Why can't you let her rest in peace?" He picked up a bottle of water and took a long slug. "Honestly, Gwen, I don't know why you care. You said yourself you hated the woman."

"No, Jack, you've got it backwards. I said *Henrietta* hated *me*. But she was a guest in my home when she died, whether I wanted her there or not." She paused to let Jack feel the weight of his involvement in that little arrangement. "I need to find out what happened to her." Gwen had no intention of telling Jack she was Detective Brown's prime suspect.

Jack stared out his side window, silent.

Gwen kept talking. "It's understandable you'd forget details in the uproar of Henrietta's retrieval. I know she phoned several times and came into the shop since she arrived last Thursday. Did you notice someone giving her a hard time?"

"I told you the other day, Gwen, I have nothing to tell you."

Jack slammed the bottle on his desk. Water jumped out the opening and drenched his papers.

"Now see what you've made me do." He grabbed a roll of paper towels from the shelf behind him and sopped up the water with exaggerated gestures.

Hal pushed himself off the window sill and moved to Gwen's side. "No need to be upset about a little spilled water."

Jack scowled and ripped off another towel.

Hal reached for Gwen's hand and pulled her toward the door. When she opened her mouth to protest, Hal squeezed. Hard. He turned back to Jack. "Let us know if you remember anything."

Busy drying his documents, Jack only grumbled.

After they left Jack's office, Gwen whirled on Hal. "What'd you do that for?"

"The man was about to explode."

Before Gwen could comment, Emily appeared beside them, her eyes wide and bright.

Reaching out, Gwen touched Emily's cheek. "You look flushed. Do you feel all right?"

Emily pulled back until she was out of Gwen's reach. "I'm fine." Then, as if she hadn't reacted, Emily casually tucked her arm through Gwen's and walked her the length of the shop, leaving Hal to trail behind them. "Is there any more news about the person on your bridge with Henrietta? There hasn't been much in the Gazette."

Glancing back at Hal, Gwen shrugged her shoulders. "We've made a little progress since Monday, but nothing that points the finger at anyone in particular."

When they reached the northern end of the shop, Emily slowed her pace and pulled Gwen down onto the window seat.

"Who have you talked to?"

Hal feigned interest in the music books on the rack near the exit, close enough to eavesdrop on their conversation.

Seeing no harm in satisfying Emily's curiosity, Gwen listed her recent activities. "Hal and I visited the old dean, Walter James, on Tuesday. Henrietta had called him last week and let it slip that the reason she returned to Harbor Falls was the same as the reason she left."

"And you think there's a connection to her death?"

"I have no idea, Emily. On Wednesday, my sister and I had lunch with my friend Rachel, who told us about an argument she overheard between an unidentified man and Henrietta the day before she left town."

"She didn't know who he was?"

"Didn't recognize his voice. I don't know if I'll ever find out who he was or if there's any connection to her death."

Emily tilted her head. "So why are you going to all this trouble?"

"Because, Emily, the only way Detective Brown will move his spotlight off me is if I provide him with another suspect or two. When we leave here, Hal and I are meeting with the new dean, Daniel Chartley, at Baylies. He might know some details about Henrietta's resignation."

"I thought Walter James was the dean when Henrietta resigned."

"I had the timing mixed up. Walter had retired by then."

"Anyone else on your list?"

"Only one other person at the moment. Claudia Smith. Rachel thinks she was at the Baylies offices the day before Henrietta left town. Maybe Claudia saw or heard something useful."

Before Emily had a chance to ask yet another question, Jack's voice boomed through the shop. "Emily!" They turned to see him standing at his office doorway, motioning to his wife. "Excuse me, Gwen. We'll talk again soon." Emily hurried away and disappeared into Jack's office. The door slammed shut.

Chapter Forty-Four

As they crossed the music shop's parking lot, Hal said, "That was strange."

"It was. Jack refuses to discuss Henrietta, but Emily wants to know everything."

Hal waited until Gwen fastened her seatbelt before pulling onto North Street. "They both make me nervous. You should stay clear."

For a split second, Gwen rebelled inside against Hal telling her what to do again. Then she breathed deeply and let it slide off like water from a merganser's back. "Why do you say that?"

"Based on what you've told me about Henrietta's quirks, it makes sense she wouldn't have walked into your woods unless someone lured her there. Since we don't know who that might be, we need to be suspicious of everyone – including Jack and Emily."

Gwen reached over and turned up the car heater to chase away a sudden chill. "I suppose you're right. If I wasn't afraid of being arrested, I'd drop all this spy business."

Hal reached for her hand. "We can't stop now. I've signed on as your Watson. Where to next, Sherlock?"

***

At precisely eleven o'clock, Gwen and Hal entered the dean's office. Daniel Chartley came around his huge walnut desk and reached out to shake Hal's hand, then kissed Gwen's cheek. She noted his tailored suit, his perfect haircut, the enticing musk of his aftershave.

"Good to see you, Gwen." She introduced Hal. "How's retirement?"

"I'm much busier than I thought I'd be."

"I hope you haven't given up music," Daniel commented, giving her a stern look.

His expression reminded her of Walter James. "I've opened my home studio for private lessons. In fact, one of my students is performing in the competition on Saturday."

A broad smile brightened his face. "Oh, that's right. I believe that detail came up when we were making arrangements for Henrietta to stay with you."

His demeanor told her he wasn't aware of her history with her uninvited guest nor had he been party to Jack's manipulation. "Henrietta is the reason I want to talk to you."

He gestured toward a pair of chairs facing his desk and returned to his own, lacing his fingers on the blotter. "Such a tragedy she died in that rainstorm."

"I'm trying to find out what happened to her."

Daniel's brow furrowed. "I assumed it was an accident."

"The police are calling it a suspicious death."

"That's disturbing. But isn't Chief Upton investigating?"

"The chief has assigned Detective Brown to the case."

Daniel studied her with obvious curiosity. "So why are you the one asking questions?"

Gwen smiled and determined that the new dean was not one to waste words. "I don't think the detective is looking in the right places for answers." She leaned her forearms on the front of his desk. "I should tell you that Detective Brown seems to think I was involved."

"That's preposterous!" Daniel leaned across the wide expanse. "Tell me how I can help."

Gwen met his gaze. "Do you remember anything about Henrietta's resignation?"

"It was a short meeting. I don't know how useful a recap will be."

"Did she happen to tell you *why* she resigned?"

Daniel sat back, staring past her shoulder into the distant

past. "Henrietta and I had a strained relationship after I bested her for the dean's position. She stopped in unannounced that day and gave me a hand-written resignation letter and advised me she'd be leaving Harbor Falls that evening. I remember that she didn't even sit down. I asked her if she was resigning because I was chosen for the dean's position, but she denied any connection."

That matched what Henrietta had told Walter James on the phone last week.

Daniel picked up his Mont Blanc pen and began doodling on a notepad. "I was never quite sure I believed her. To tell you the truth, Gwen, I hated to see her go. She was popular with her students, even though she was gruff with the other professors and staff."

Gwen made no comment about Henrietta's "gruffness." Why insert her own personal trouble into Daniel's memory of an effective professor?

He kept talking. "I'm not sure why I suggested her to Alex Fairfield when he asked me to recommend a replacement judge. I guess I'd always thought she didn't want to leave and assumed she'd appreciate the opportunity to return to Harbor Falls. As it turns out, I didn't do her any favors, did I?"

"No one could have predicted what would happen to her, Daniel. You can't blame yourself any more than I can."

Gwen stood and extended one hand. "Thanks for meeting with me."

Daniel enclosed her hand between both of his. "I wish I had more to tell you, Gwen." He turned to Hal. "Nice to meet you, Mr. Jenkins."

As she and Hal walked out, Gwen glanced back to see the dean staring out his window.

***

In the car, Hal said, "Dean Chartley wasn't very helpful." He waited for several cars to pass before merging into traffic.

279

"Do you think your friend saw anything the day before?"

Gwen settled into the passenger seat and closed her eyes. "All I know is Claudia was probably the crying woman Rachel saw running from the building. Hopefully she noticed the man with Henrietta and can identify him for us."

Ten minutes later they pulled up in front of a Cape-style house outside of town, freshly painted in classic white with black shutters. Flower gardens dotted the landscape in every direction. Hal parked at the curb and they got out.

After pressing the doorbell several times, Gwen knocked. At the same instant Hal gestured toward the back yard, the hum of yard equipment reached her ears. They rounded the corner of the house and spotted Claudia, her back to them, a pair of huge headphones clamped to either side of her head. Her hair swung with each movement of a Weed-Wacker, decimating the grass sprouting up around the posts of a basket-weave fence.

Not wanting to startle her friend, Gwen led Hal to the end of the wooden fence, where they came into Claudia's line of sight.

Claudia jumped when she spotted them, switched off the tool, and removed her headphones. "Gwen, how long have you been standing there?"

"Two seconds," Gwen called out as she walked closer. "We rang and knocked, but then we heard the buzzing back here."

Claudia glanced at Hal, then back at Gwen. "You should have let me know you were stopping by. I don't usually ignore visitors."

Gwen shook her head. "It was a last minute idea," she lied. "Do you have time to talk?"

"Sure. These weeds aren't going anywhere." Claudia rested the unwieldy tool against the fence and removed her heavy black work gloves.

Gwen nodded toward Hal. "This is Hal Jenkins. His granddaughter Jenna is my student."

Claudia tipped her head at him then waved them toward a patio set. "Sit here. I'll be right back." She hurried through her back door, emerging a minute later with a tray laden with ice-filled glasses and cans of soda.

Settling on the opposite side of the glass table, Claudia focused on Gwen. "Actually, I'm glad you stopped by. I have some news to share with you."

"What's that?" Gwen popped the top and filled her glass with the fizzing liquid.

Claudia and Hal did the same.

"During the bus ride back to their cars at the schoolhouse, the ticket holders said this year's tour was the best one ever. They couldn't stop talking about the gorgeous gardens, a peek inside the old library, and the delicious party food. A few of them even joked about the storm."

"That's good to hear, Claudia. You did a great job organizing this year's event."

"Thanks." Claudia took a sip of soda, smothering a delicate burp. "But I interrupted you. Why did you stop by?"

"I don't know how much you've heard about Henrietta's accident." Gwen wiped at the condensation on her glass, surprised that she was still calling it an accident.

"Accident? I haven't heard anything."

"You haven't? The Gazette has printed several reports this week."

"Oh, I hardly ever read the newspaper. Nothing much happens in Harbor Falls." Claudia paused. "Not that I care all that much, but is Henrietta all right?"

"No, she's not." Gwen slumped in her chair. "She died." Claudia's hand flew to her mouth. "Is that why you stopped by? To tell me Henrietta's dead?"

"Not exactly," Gwen ventured, assuming Claudia was probably relieved, given her negative reaction whenever Henrietta's name had been mentioned during the past week.

281

"Here's the thing, Claudia. I'm trying to find out all I can about Henrietta's life the day before she left town."

"But that was when? Thirteen years ago? Why would that be relevant now, and why do you care? If anyone should be glad she's gone, it's you, Gwen. She was a pure bitch whenever she bumped into you. She wanted Parker, but he married you instead."

Gwen circled her glass in the puddle at its base. "I have a very good reason for caring, Claudia. The police detective thinks I'm the one responsible for her death."

"That's ridiculous," Claudia said, her forehead wrinkling. "After all the years you turned the other cheek, why would you turn violent now? But that's a rhetorical question, isn't it? Why do you think I can help you?"

Gwen charged ahead. "A friend of mine overheard an argument between a man and Henrietta the day before she left town and thinks she saw you exiting the building at the same time. I'm hoping you saw them and can tell me the name of that man."

Pulling half-full glasses from their hands, Claudia stood up and placed them on her tray along with the soda cans. "Like I said, Gwen, that was thirteen years ago. Why would I remember any details now? I don't know why your friend thought she saw me, but she's mistaken. And I don't wish to discuss Henrietta, dead or alive. Can you see yourselves out?"

Claudia marched into the house and let the door slam behind her.

Hal looked at Gwen. "Add Claudia to your list for Detective Brown. The person who left the scuffmarks could have been a female."

"Oh, I don't know, Hal. Claudia's too small to overpower Henrietta." Gwen gazed at the back of the well-maintained house. "But I've never known Claudia to be rude."

***

Hal walked Gwen up the granite steps to her front door. "We've run into nothing but brick walls today. The chief didn't tell us anything, the detective is still blaming you, Jack is closed-mouth, and Claudia won't discuss Henrietta. We're no closer to a breakthrough than we were this morning. What's next?"

Gwen wagged her head as if it were heavy. "I guess we have to widen the circle of people who may know something. Tomorrow, let's try those college committee members who refused to let Henrietta stay in their homes. Maybe we'll find a connection we haven't thought of."

Gwen pushed open the heavy oak door and did a quick sidestep to avoid an envelope lying on the foyer tiles. As she stooped to pick it up, Hal peeked around her. "What's that?"

"No idea." She flipped the manila envelope back and forth, then headed to the kitchen and dropped her purse onto an island stool.

"That's odd," she commented. "No return address. No stamps. No cancellation mark."

She undid the clasp, pulled out a piece of construction paper folded in half, and flattered it on the counter. The boldly scrawled black letters shouted up at her:

"THAT BITCH HENRIETTA WOULDN'T BACK DOWN AND GOT WHAT SHE DESERVED. STOP TRYING TO FIND ME OR YOU'LL BE NEXT."

Chapter Forty-Five

Gwen grasped the edge of the counter.

Hal read the message, his eyes widening. "Do you know what this means, Gwen?"

She could only shake her head.

He pointed at the heavy paper. "This proves someone else – not you – was on that footbridge with Henrietta. We've got to take this to Chief Upton right now."

Regaining her composure, Gwen reached into a cabinet drawer and withdrew two plastic bags. She opened the first one.

"Good idea, Gwen." Hal dropped the note inside.

They repeated the process with the envelope. "Won't the chief think I planted it, Hal?"

"I've been with you all day. I'll swear this note wasn't here when we left."

"Don't get me wrong, I'm thrilled this message gets me off the hook, but why would the killer write it? He can't be very smart. Not only is he providing proof that Henrietta's death wasn't an accident, but he's implying he argued with her on my footbridge. On top of that he's threatening me, which entangles him even further." Gwen reached into her purse and pulled out her cell. "I've got to call Ernie."

"Talk to him in my car. Let's go."

***

Gwen hung up as Hal pulled into the police station lot. "What did Ernie say?"

"He's a half hour away but agreed we should put that note in the chief's hands right now and avoid Detective Brown if we can."

They rushed inside and up to the reception window, hopping from foot to foot as the officer dialed the chief. After a series of whispered comments, the officer waved them to the side door then led them to Chief Upton's office. Gwen and Hal burst inside without knocking.

The chief raised his head. "Back so soon?"

Hal handed him the plastic bags. "We found this in Gwen's foyer a few minutes ago."

Placing the bags on his blotter, the chief opened his desk drawer and came out with white cotton gloves. He put on the gloves before removing both items and arranging them on his blotter.

Unfolding the note by its corners, he read the message then looked up at Gwen. "Did you handle either of these?"

Gwen caught his implication that her own prints would be there and nodded. "Yes, I did."

"Good thinking to put them in these plastic bags."

"You can thank Gwen for that, Chief." Hal glanced over at her, pride gleaming in his eyes.

Gwen was finally rewarded for watching all those re-runs of *Law and Order*.

"Let's hope the person who delivered this left some nice clear fingerprints," the chief said, sliding each item into a separate evidence envelope. "As soon as the lab boys identify these, we'll know who to bring in."

Gwen's knees began to buckle. She reached for his side chair and sank into it.

The chief hurried around his desk, squatting beside her.

"Gwen, are you all right?"

Hal poured a cup of water from the cooler, subtly pushing the chief aside.

Gwen took a sip. "I'm fine. Just a little light-headed."

"Can't blame you," the chief murmured. He reached behind him, picked up his desk phone and pushed a few buttons.

"Come to my office."

A minute later, Detective Brown poked his head around the

open door. The chief held out the two envelopes. "New evidence. A note and the envelope it came in."

The detective stepped forward and reached for them. "Where did this come from?"

Before Gwen or Hal could answer, the chief spoke. "Mrs. Andrews found it in her foyer a few minutes ago."

"And you consider this valid evidence?" The detective strained not to snort.

"I do."

"Let me guess. You want these checked for prints."

"No need to be snide, Detective. Drive those personally to the Sudbury lab." The chief waited for a beat, then said, "Ask them to put a rush on it."

The detective appeared sufficiently chastised not to offer another snide remark. With a sour look, he did an about-face and disappeared.

The chief turned to Gwen. "Until we arrest this person, I don't want you to be alone." Gwen's feeling of relief morphed into panic. "My sister and brother-in-law are visiting."

"Are they at your house right now?"

"Well, no, they went into Boston this afternoon, but I expect them back by four."

Hal made a motion with his hand. "I can stay with Gwen until they get back."

"Thank you, Mr. Jenkins. I'll alert all patrol cars to increase their surveillance around the village green. That should discourage any intruders."

Gwen's panic exploded. "Are you saying that whoever wrote that note might come after me?"

Lifting his phone, the chief began to dial. "I'm just practicing due diligence. Now, if you'll excuse me, Gwen, I need to call Sudbury and let them know what's coming their way."

***

At quarter to four, Tess and Nathan burst through the front door to find Gwen and Hal talking quietly in the living room.

"What a fantastic park!" Tess squealed. "The walkways wander through trees and statues, and there's a gorgeous spouting fountain. You'd never guess the highway's underground."

Before Gwen could comment, the doorbell rang, startling them all.

"Damn," Hal muttered and jumped up from the couch. "That's probably Jenna. I forgot all about picking her up at the high school."

The girl's voice carried from the foyer. "Hi, Granddad. I didn't see your car, so I walked."

"I'm sorry, Jenna. Mrs. Andrews and I had to run an errand, and I lost track of the time."

"It's okay. It's only a few blocks."

Gwen struggled from the couch and came up beside them.

"Jenna, I'd like to apologize for arguing with your grandfather the other night. I know it upset you and I take total responsibility for your errors at yesterday's session."

Jenna stomped her tiny foot. "You did upset me, both of you. But I've gotten over it, and I'm ready for a flawless practice with you and your sister." She shook a dainty finger at Gwen and Hal. "Don't you two argue ever again." And then she grinned.

Tess joined them. "Are you ready to rehearse, Jenna?"

"Sure am. No mistakes today."

The two of them headed toward the music studio.

Hal stepped forward. "If you don't mind, Gwen, I need to check in at my garden shop."

"You go ahead. I'm not alone. You were a great Watson today." She squeezed his shoulder. "Why don't you and Jenna stay for dinner tonight? Tess and I are planning to make pizzas."

From the music studio, Jenna squealed, "I'm hungry already."

"Sounds great, Gwen." Hal leaned down and kissed her cheek. "I'll be back in about an hour."

Nathan winked at Gwen and turned to follow Hal out. "I'm going for a walk. I'll bring back some beverages."

When Gwen leaned on the Steinway a minute later, Tess said, "I saw that."

"Saw what?" Gwen said, knowing full well she was referring to Hal's kiss. Gwen tilted her head toward Jenna and Tess didn't pursue it any further.

When the practice session ended an hour later, Gwen clapped. "Very nice, you two. And not one stumble, Jenna." Gwen glanced at her watch. "Let's get to work on those pizzas, ladies."

Gwen pulled pizza crusts from the freezer. While they thawed in the microwave, she chopped onions and sliced peppers for Jenna to sauté, then browned mushrooms in a separate skillet. Tess warmed her homemade sauce and doctored it with garlic salt and oregano. They created three distinct pies: veggie, bacon, and pepperoni, spooning ricotta in the empty spaces, and sprinkling mozzarella cheese atop everything.

Shoving the pizzas into the oven, they chatted about the competition and waited for the timer to ding. A knock on the French door made them all jump. In walked Liz and Tony, with Nathan coming up behind them carrying six-packs of beer, liters of wine, and bottles of soda.

Liz thumbed over her shoulder. "We bumped into this guy at the package store and he invited us to dinner. Hope you made enough."

The buzzer buzzed and Gwen donned her oven mitts.

"Three large pies. Plenty to feed us all."

She placed the steaming pizzas on an elongated wooden

slat that protected the maple dining room table from the heat. By the time they all sat down, Hal had still not returned.

"Where's granddad? He said he'd be back in an hour."

Gwen was equally concerned but understood that tending flowers could cause lost time.

As if he'd sensed their unease, Hal walked through the front door, a frown on his face.

"What's wrong?" Gwen called over.

"Your door isn't locked."

She swallowed and tried to remember who had come through last. "Well, I guess you can point the finger at yourself, because you were the last one out."

He blushed. "Sorry. Guess I assumed you'd lock the door behind me." He walked toward Jenna's chair. "How was your practice session?"

"Stellar." Jenna patted the next chair. "Sit by me, Granddad."

During the disappearance of the three pizzas, Gwen noticed Hal sneaking glances at her. What was he thinking about? Their recent adventures? His kiss on her cheek? Something else?

He wiped his fingers on a napkin without breaking his eye contact. "They need to know what happened today."

When Gwen nodded in Jenna's direction, the legs of the girl's chair scraped against the pine floor boards.

"May I say something?"

Liz, Tony, Nathan, Tess, Gwen, and Hal all focused on her.

Jenna stood erect and cleared her throat. "I know you've been shielding me from the death of Mrs. Andrew's guest, but Granddad," she placed her hand on Hal's shoulder, "I'd like to point out that I'm no longer a little girl. I'm aware of what can happen to a person."

Hal looked at her. "You're right, Jenna. I guess it's time to let you grow up."

Satisfied, Jenna smiled and sat back down.

Gwen looked at this young lady and, with no warning, thoughts of her miscarried girl-child decades before surged forward, and Gwen wondered if she and Parker would have been fortunate enough to create a sweet daughter like Jenna. Or would they have been saddled with a roaring brat? It was the chance parents took, with no way out.

Liz broke in. "Hold on a second, Hal. What are you talking about? What happened today?"

He gazed over at Gwen. "Do you want to tell them, or should I?"

Filling her lungs with air, Gwen answered by recounting their frustration with Chief Upton's failure to provide an update, Jack's minor explosion, a non-productive chat with the new dean, and lastly Claudia's abruptness at the mention of Henrietta's last day.

A perplexed look skewed Tess's expression. "That's interesting, Gwen, but we knew you were seeing those people before we drove to Boston this morning. Did something else happen?"

Gwen nodded. Tess's antennae were as sharp as ever.

"When Hal and I came through my front door, we found an envelope on the floor. The note inside read, 'That bitch Henrietta wouldn't back down and got what she deserved. Stop trying to find me or you'll be next.'"

A collective gasp replaced the momentary silence.

Hal added, "We drove to the station and gave it to Chief Upton."

All of the guests started talking at once.

Liz jumped up and shouted, "Hush, everyone! Gwen, what happens now?"

"The chief put a rush on identifying the fingerprints. Plus he ordered patrol cars to increase their cruising around the village green. And he told me not to be by myself." She gazed at the faces around the table. "I guess I've got that part covered for the moment."

Liz pivoted in her chair and scanned the multiple windows rimming Gwen's first floor. "Aren't you nervous that the note writer might be watching you?"

"I hadn't thought about that. I've never pulled down the shades. I'm not even sure they work."

Liz got to her feet. "Well, they're coming down now." She and Tony started in the dining room, Tess and Jenna headed for the music studio, and Hal and Nathan went to the living room.

Gwen glanced around the now-darkened space, feeling a bit claustrophobic. She supposed this was a small price to pay to avoid exposing herself to an unknown man – or woman – who might be skulking around outside the old library.

As everyone pitched in to clear the table and wash the dishes, they rehashed every event and reaction since Henrietta's arrival, still unable to point the finger at any one person.

An hour later, Hal stretched. "Well, Gwen, I have to admit, you managed to flush out the person who fought with Henrietta. I tip my hat to you. You're off the hook with the police, but you're not out of danger yet."

"Not yet," she repeated. "Not until the chief arrests the note writer. That's when I'll finally be vindicated."

"Do you want me to stay tonight?" Hal asked. "I can sleep on the sofa, and Jenna will fit in your loveseat."

She glanced at him, not quite sure if he was serious. Given the possibility of an appearance by Parker, Gwen didn't think it would be smart for Hal to sleep over.

"Thanks, but Tess and Nathan can be ferocious when cornered." She grinned at her sister and brother-in-law who smirked in return.

"All right, but if you change your mind, call me." He touched Jenna's shoulder. "Let's get you home, young lady. I'll have you back here by nine tomorrow for your all-day rehearsal. Did you give my note to your teachers so you won't get into trouble?" Jenna nodded and they left.

Liz reached for her sweater. "We're gonna head out, too. Thanks for the pizza." Liz gave Gwen a hug, calling over her shoulder as she left, "Let me know the second you hear anything."

Tess reached for Nathan's hand. "I think we'll head up."

"You must be tired after a full day of sightseeing. I'll see you both in the morning."

Feeling relatively safe inside her home with the shades pulled down, Gwen sat in Parker's recliner. She called his name three times. Nothing. She walked into the music studio and tried again. Still no Parker. The same in the kitchen, the dining room, and on the rear deck.

Had last night been his last visit? Had he used up all his return tickets? Would she ever see him again?

Or had he been a figment of her wishful imagination all along?

Chapter Forty-Six

The sensation of cat's paws pressing into her body woke Gwen. Amber jumped off the bed and ran through the open door. The old library was too quiet.

Gwen slid out of bed, grabbed a robe, and crept out to the balcony then down to the midway point of the staircase. Through the French door she spotted Tess and Nathan sitting on the rear deck. Bounding down the remaining steps, she flung the door open wide. "There you are!"

Tess's hand flew to her chest. "Oh, Gwen, you startled me."

"Sorry, couldn't resist. What are you two doing out here this early?"

Nathan snickered. "Well, for one thing, we wanted to enjoy this invigorating morning air. And, for another, it's not that early." He lifted his mug in salute. "You missed a glorious sunrise."

"Gwen, do you remember mom saying, 'Red sails at night, sailors delight. Red sails in the morning, sailors take warning'?"

Gwen leaned out from the railing to gaze across the side yard toward the east. "Sure do. The sky was red this morning?"

"Yep. With brilliant orange mixed in. I predict a storm by the end of the day."

"Thank you, Miss Weather Lady. What time is it, anyway?" Nathan glanced at his wristwatch. "Eight forty-five."

"You're kidding! I never sleep this late. Jenna will be here at nine."

"I'm not worried. Thought you needed the sleep. You go upstairs and get dressed." Tess got to her feet. "I'll make you some breakfast."

"Thanks, Sis."

Tess plucked two eggs from the fridge and hefted the cast iron skillet to the stovetop. Ten minutes later, Gwen swallowed the last bite. The doorbell chimed. She put down her fork and went to the foyer.

Jenna bounced inside. "Hi."

Hal remained on the top step. "Good morning, Gwen. Sorry, but I can't stay. I've got things to catch up on at the nursery. I'll be back later this afternoon."

Nathan slid past Gwen. "Hal, do you mind if I come with you? I've never seen the inner workings of a nursery. And I'll be glad to pitch in and help."

"Sure." Hal backed down the step to give Nathan room to come out.

When the door closed, Gwen turned to Jenna. "Tess is waiting for us in the music studio."

The morning hours flew by as Jenna, Tess, and Gwen concentrated on two of the four musical arrangements chosen for the competition. They played and replayed one passage after another, picking at Jenna's performance note by note, seeking perfection. After a quick lunch break, they focused on the other two scores. Jenna improved with each suggestion, playing with delicate skill. By the end she glowed with confidence. Just before five, she lowered her flute and grinned. "I have butterflies."

Tess reached over from the piano bench. "Butterflies are your best friends. When they tickle your belly tomorrow afternoon, it'll mean your adrenaline is pumping, and you'll be primed to compete."

It occurred to Gwen that all day long she'd had no thoughts of Henrietta, the footbridge, the millpond, or anything else connected to the woman's death. Music had filled her mind and heart to the exclusion of everything else. Even the image of Detective Brown's sour face didn't loom until the piano keys went silent.

At five, when Hal brought Nathan back from their afternoon at the nursery, he walked to Gwen in the music studio. "Jenna needs a full night's sleep before tomorrow's competition. We'll be here first thing tomorrow morning."

Gwen was surprised to find herself disappointed that she wouldn't be sharing another meal with Hal. After they'd ironed out their differences and started working as a team, she'd enjoyed his companionship and his can-do attitude.

Her appetite gone, Gwen turned to Tess and Nathan. "Why don't you two go out tonight? Dinner? Maybe a movie?"

Tess tucked her piano music into her briefcase. "No way. We can't leave you here alone."

Gwen waved her off. "Claudia and Kenneth will be here any second."

"Wait a minute. Isn't Claudia the woman who sent you and Hal packing yesterday?"

"Yes." Gwen said it slowly, waiting for Tess to make her point.

"What makes you think she's going to show up today?"

"Because she and I made plans to surprise Kenneth about him switching instruments, and I don't think she'd back out now no matter what happened between us yesterday."

Before Tess could pursue it further, the bell chimed. Tess grabbed Gwen's arm to keep her from answering the front door. "Are you sure about this, Sis? I'm perfectly fine with hanging around here tonight."

Gwen gently pried Tess's fingers from her sleeve. "I've known Claudia for a long time. She might have been upset this afternoon, but she's no more of a threat than her son."

Remembering Tess's prediction of rain, Gwen yanked a huge golf umbrella from a brass stand and placed it in Nathan's hand. "You two have a nice evening. I'll see you in a few hours."

The chime echoed again. With reluctance, Tess grabbed

Nathan's hand and they left by the French door as Gwen
hurried to answer the front.

Claudia pushed Kenneth into the foyer ahead of her. "You
go on back to the music studio, son. We'll be with you in a
second."

Glancing out at the darkening sky, Gwen sensed Tess's
prediction of a storm was accurate. In slow motion, Gwen
closed the door, waiting for Claudia to reveal her mood.

Claudia moved closer to stand beside Gwen. "I owe you an
apology for my behavior yesterday. Henrietta was no friend of
mine, but that was no excuse to be rude to you and Mr.
Jenkins."

Gwen relaxed. She'd been worried that today's session
would be awkward. "Apology accepted, though I have to admit
your reaction made me even more curious about your history
with Henrietta."

Claudia flinched. "Let's leave the past in the past, shall
we?"

Entering the music studio, Claudia moved toward Kenneth,
who was fumbling to assemble his flute. "Son, we need to have
a chat."

He glanced sideways at Gwen. "I promise I'll practice
more. Honest." A distant clap of thunder underscored his
pledge.

Claudia reached up to push a lock of black hair from her
son's eyes. "A little birdie told me you don't like playing the
flute."

Kenneth screwed up his face, sending a sideways look of
concern in Gwen's direction. "Aw, mom, don't be mad. I'll
keep trying if you want me to."

"Well, son," Claudia drew out the word. "Here's the deal."

She stretched her arm upward until she could rest her hand
on his shoulder. "You don't have to take flute lessons anymore.
But I insist you learn how to smack the cymbals."

She paused to let her message sink in.

Gwen could barely suppress her laughter at Kenneth's confusion. He stared at his mother with wide eyes, his mouth slack.

After several awkward seconds he threw his arms around her neck, making her gasp for air. "You mean it?" Then he let go and turned to Gwen. "Oh, Mrs. Andrews, isn't this the greatest news? I mean, I'm going to miss you and all, but I sure won't miss that darned flute!"

Gwen squeezed his arm. "I'll miss you, too. By the way, your mom has agreed to take over your flute lesson. You're welcome to come with her on Friday afternoons."

The grin never left Kenneth's face as Gwen explained the band leader's agreement to teach him the finer points of "smacking them together" at just the right time, to use his own words.

Claudia winked at her son. "Your dad is waiting for you out front."

Kenneth reached down to hug his mother once more then whooped out the door, oblivious to the raindrops pelting his head.

With a lightness she hadn't felt in a while, Gwen walked to the front door and twisted the lock. She had to grin. She was following Hal's instructions.

***

As the storm raged against the old library, Gwen demonstrated the flute to Claudia, showing her how to assemble the sections and angle her mouth to blow across the lip plate. Claudia's homework? Coax sound from the instrument before they met the following Friday.

After disassembling and blotting the collected condensation from the instrument, Claudia packed the flute in its case. "This is thrilling, Gwen. I'm glad you suggested my taking over Kenneth's time slot." Claudia's smile brought an angelic cast to her face. She glanced at her watch. "Pete's supposed to pick me up in a little while. May I use your powder room before he gets here?"

"Of course. It's right over there." Gwen pointed past the kitchen island to the bump-out next to the fridge that looked like a closet. "The light switch is on the outside."

Claudia reached sideways to retrieve her purse from the wing chair and disappeared as the door closed behind her.

When she felt Amber brush against her ankles, Gwen looked down into green cat eyes. She glanced at the empty bowls at the end of the island and retrieved the canister from beneath the sink. "Sorry, sweetie," Gwen said as she replenished the dry food, then the water.

As an afterthought, Gwen walked to the sink to fill the kettle. Nothing like a hot cup of tea on a stormy evening. She didn't even know if Claudia drank tea, but she'd make the offer anyway.

What sounded to Gwen like another clap of thunder was the French door slamming open.

Amber whipped her head around, turned tail, and dashed up the staircase.

Kettle in hand, Gwen swiveled to see a man advancing toward her while swiping at the rain dripping from his dark hair onto his reddened face.

Instinctively, Gwen stepped back. "Jack?"

Hadn't she locked that door? No, not that one. She was remembering the snap of the front door lock after Kenneth whooped out. Tess and Nathan had been the last ones out the French door nearly an hour earlier. Too late to lock it now.

Jack quickened his step until he stood within inches of Gwen.

She couldn't imagine why he'd barged into her home on yet another stormy night. Gwen squared her shoulders. "What are you doing here, Jack?"

"Why couldn't you leave it alone, Gwen?" He sneered down from his taller height, his voice low and ominous.

She took another step backward, increasing the distance between them. Jack kept pace with her, forcing Gwen to tilt her head back. "Leave what alone?"

"Henrietta!"

The name bounced off the walls and echoed back to Gwen's ears.

When her arm muscles began to ache, Gwen glanced down at the heavy kettle. She twisted sideways and set it down on the stove, keeping her fingers wrapped around the handle. Taking a deep breath, she set her face in as nonchalant an expression as she could manage.

"Relax, Jack, and tell me what's bothering you." Gwen kept her tone even in an effort to avoid riling him up even further.

"I heard you've been going around town asking all sorts of questions about Henrietta. Why are you stirring up old history?

"I told you the other day, Jack. I need to find out why she died. Henrietta said she almost regretted coming back as a judge. Sounded to me like a possible link between her judging chair and her death. Just because you weren't aware of any threats doesn't mean they didn't exist."

"But why do you care, Gwen? You of all people should be glad the woman is dead."

"That's cold, Jack." Gwen tried desperately to collect her thoughts. "No matter how nasty Henrietta could be, she didn't deserve to lose her life."

Gwen was surprised to find that she meant those words. She'd only wanted Henrietta to pack her bags and drive back to Vermont.

"Oh, I don't know about that, Gwen. Depends on who you ask, I guess." Jack fingered the granite countertop.

She stared at him. Cold fish was not a strong enough label.

Without warning, Jack whipped back in her direction, his

eyes flaring. "Why did you have lunch with Walter James after I told you not to contact the other judges?"

Despite Jack's obvious anger, Gwen didn't feel threatened and held her ground. All she had to do was answer his question in a calm manner, and then he'd leave.

She laughed in a feeble attempt to diffuse his agitation. "To be honest, Jack, I didn't think you meant it. When I spoke to Walter on the phone, he told me Henrietta called him last week, but he preferred to discuss their conversation in person, so he invited me to lunch at his condo. I gladly accepted because it sounded like Henrietta told him something relevant."

"And did she?"

"Sort of. But not about the competition. Her return to Harbor Falls, according to Walter's account, was connected to her resignation."

Jack threw his hands into the air. "And I suppose that's why you spoke with Daniel Chartley, the new dean? To ask if he knew why she resigned?"

"That's right, Jack. That's exactly why." His aggressive mood was beginning to rankle.

"And did he?"

"No. Daniel claims Henrietta wouldn't give him a solid reason for resigning."

Jack thumped his closed fist against his thigh. "You need to stop your snooping, Gwen. Anything you find out about that woman doesn't matter now that she'd dead."

"But it matters to me, Jack. And I'm going to tell you why." Gwen shifted her weight onto her other foot. "Detective Brown has made me his prime suspect. And that's your fault, Jack. You're the one who told him about my past with Henrietta. That's why he's convinced himself I wanted revenge for all those times she put me down. I have no choice, I've got to figure out who else wanted Henrietta dead, and I need to satisfy the detective that it wasn't me."

Jack's mouth fell open. "But...but... I thought her death was an accident. I overheard those officers say she fell from your bridge..."

His words stopped, but his lips moved like her koi fish at feeding time.

Gwen said, "The police are calling Henrietta's death suspicious. Didn't Emily tell you?"

"No, she didn't." He started pacing like a caged tiger, stopping inches from Gwen, his jaw muscles working.

"Detective Brown is collecting evidence and building his case against me." Maybe Jack would empathize with her plight. After all, the detective could just as easily have focused on Jack himself or Emily or even Alex since Henrietta's body was found near the music shop.

Jack's eyes widened. "What evidence?"

"Well," Gwen began, "they took the splintered rails and platform boards from my footbridge, plus my shoes and clothing and a lock of my hair."

"Why your shoes?"

"They're trying to match the scuffmarks."

"What scuffmarks?"

He'd moved close again. Gwen had to squint up at him.

Without thinking, she blurted, "Did you write that note, Jack?"

His head jerked and he stepped away. "What note?"

"The note someone slipped through my mail slot yesterday. Was that you, Jack?"

"I didn't write any damn note," he yelled, his hands fisting by his side.

Gwen couldn't dislodge the icicle forming in the pit of her stomach. Was Jack lying? It wouldn't be the first time. Maybe he did write that note. Maybe he'd been involved in Henrietta's death. Sensing wetness in her armpits, Gwen sniffed the scent of her fear.

Was Jack the threat she'd been trying to avoid? Had Gwen been foolish to discount him as the person who lured Henrietta into the woods? Jack might not be as cowardly as Gwen had always assumed. She might have pushed him too far. He'd been right. She was an idiot.

Trying not to attract Jack's attention, Gwen slid her hand into her jeans pocket. Damn it, where was her cell? Would she be able to dial 911 before he grabbed the phone?

Again, Jack stopped inches from her. "Why don't you just leave it alone, Gwen?" He lifted his fist as if to strike her.

The powder room door opened.

Claudia's voice shouted, "What's going on out here?"

Chapter Forty-Seven

At the sound of Claudia's voice, Jack's attention shifted and Gwen backed away, stopping when her heels bumped against the drip tray beneath the row of weeping fig trees.

Jack brought his arm down and bellowed, "What are you doing here, Claudia?"

"Not that it's any of your business," Claudia snapped as she strode to the island, "but I've taken over my son's flute lesson. What are *you* doing here, Jack?"

"You should leave." Jack glared at Claudia.

"Trying to get rid of me again? That worked years ago, Jack, but it won't work now."

Gwen's focus bounced between the two of them. What did Claudia mean by that?

Jack sneered. "This is your fault, you know."

Through the bay window behind him, a flash of lightning lit-up the sky as if in protest.

Claudia stomped around the island and planted herself in front of him. "This is so typical of you, Jack." Claudia seemed to enjoy repeating his name with an accusatory inflection. "You always blame someone else when anything bad happens, *Jack*."

He straightened to his full height. "That's not true."

Drawing herself up, Claudia brought her mouth even with his Adam's apple, her head tilted back so she could look him in the eye. "It *is* true, Jack.

"Did you know Gwen's been asking questions about Henrietta all over town?"

Gwen remained motionless beneath the staircase. Both Jack and Claudia seemed to have forgotten that she was there. Should she try to squeeze through the weeping figs and escape out the front door? Or could she sneak upstairs to call 911?

"Well, guess what?" Claudia placed her hands on her hips. "If you hadn't brought Henrietta back to town, we wouldn't have to worry about anyone asking questions."

"I tried to cancel the woman's contract. The committee wouldn't let me."

"But, Jack, you made her go away before. You could have convinced her to *stay* away this time if you'd tried harder." He shook his head. "No, I couldn't. I had no leverage. Henrietta's faked certificate lost its power when she retired from teaching last year."

Gwen flashed back to Rachel's story. The puzzle pieces began to tumble into place. The man who had argued with Henrietta. The man who forced Henrietta to leave town by threatening to tell the dean he'd found something that would ruin her career.

That man had been Jack.

He'd blackmailed Gwen last Thursday just like he'd apparently blackmailed Henrietta thirteen years ago.

Gwen tried to inch backwards, only to find herself still wedged against the drip tray of the weeping fig trees. She reached behind her and gripped one of the slim trunks to regain her balance, standing as still as a statue while Claudia and Jack raged against each other.

Claudia bombarded Jack. "If you'd shared the responsibility for our baby, none of this would have happened."

Gwen's hand flew to her mouth to stifle her gasp. Jack was Kenneth's father? Not Pete? The resemblance between biological father and son now seemed obvious. Unruly black hair. Tall, lanky build. Pronounced lack of musical talent.

"But…but, Claudia, I told you Emily would never give me a divorce."

Claudia sagged against the island. "That's what you said, Jack. Nothing about making an effort to get out of your marriage. Nothing about your commitment to me and our baby.

Nothing about loving me." She raised her big round eyes to his. "When I told you I was pregnant, and I refused to get an abortion, what was your solution? Marry Pete. That's what you said, Jack. Because Pete had been trying to date me for months. You broke my heart that day, Jack. I couldn't stand to be near you. I ran away. You didn't come after me."

So Rachel had guessed right. Claudia *had* been the crying woman.

Another memory popped into Gwen's mind. A dozen or so years ago, a few staffers in the Baylies' offices had said unkind things about Claudia's whirlwind romance with the college sports coach and their quick wedding. When their first child arrived seven months later, everyone knew that baby Kenneth was not premature.

Jack shuffled his feet. "But you're happy with Pete, aren't you?"

Claudia's voice softened. "Pete's a wonderful husband. And he's been a better father to Kenneth than you would've ever been."

Claudia made an abrupt about-face toward the dining room. She stopped when she noticed Gwen hunched beneath the staircase. "Damn it, Gwen, I forgot you were here. Don't repeat what you just heard, or I'll…"

A flash of lightening lit the library, followed by a sharp crack of thunder. Heavy rain pelted against the library windows. The lights flickered for a moment before burning steady again. Claudia appeared frozen in place, her sculpted features skewed with malice.

Before Gwen could react to Claudia's undefined threat, the French door flew open. A flash of lightning lit up the black sky. Thunder boomed overhead, the half-second interval announcing its ominous proximity. Rain blew in.

The new arrival grasped the door frame up high, arms stretched to their full length.

Dripping water created a huge puddle on Gwen's tile floor. Another flash dramatized Emily's arrival.

Chapter Forty-Eight

Moving inside, Emily's wild eyes lighted upon Jack where he stood at the kitchen island. The French door remained open, allowing rain to sweep in, along with the noise of the storm. Gwen wanted to close it, but she couldn't seem to move her feet.

"Don't bother explaining why you came over here in a rainstorm, dear husband." Emily's gaze swung to Claudia near the dining room table. "I've been watching you and your little slut through the window."

"But you, Gwen," Emily accused in an unrecognizable voice, "you stooped so low as to give them a place to rendezvous? I thought you and I were friends?"

Gone was the gentle Emily who Gwen had always known. In her place stood a woman filled with rage, a woman whose eyes flitted from one person to the next in a frenzied dance of bitterness.

"I didn't... I don't..." Gwen stammered. "I'm not even sure what's going on here."

"Oh, don't play *Miss Innocent* with me." Emily's voice shook with anger. "Coming to the shop to talk to Jack. Making plans at the garden club meeting with little Miss Claudia over there. You thought I wouldn't figure this out?"

"You've got it all wrong, Emily. There was no plan. I had no idea Jack was going to show up here tonight."

Gwen had no clue what to do. Stay put near the weeping figs? Make a dash for the French door? Was Emily quick enough to block Gwen's escape?

Before Gwen could decide, Jack took several steps toward his wife.

Emily's hand shot out, her long fingers making solid

contact with his cheek. Jack pitched sideways, his legs tangling with an island stool as he tried and failed to regain his balance. His forehead bounced off the granite countertop before his body plummeted to the tiles. His head smacked the unforgiving ceramic squares with a resounding crack. He groaned and struggled to stand, only to flop back onto the kitchen floor. Gwen wanted to check his condition but was afraid of Emily's reaction.

Emily stared at him. "Why wasn't I enough for you, Jack? Why did you need *her*?"

When Claudia took a step closer, Emily hissed, "Stay away from him, tramp."

"But he's hurt." Claudia's face contorted with concern.

"I said stay back." Emily pushed Claudia away, then stooped and brushed Jack's black hair from his face. She reached around to the back of his head then waved her fingers in Claudia's direction. "No blood. See? He's fine. I suppose I've ruined whatever plans you were making?"

"You've got it all wrong," Claudia wailed. "I never even speak to Jack. I brought my son to Gwen for his music lesson. I had no idea Jack was coming over."

"Ah, yes. Your son. Your...precious...Kenneth." Emily drew out the name as she looked toward the music studio. "But I don't see Jack's boy. How do you explain that?"

Claudia's mouth fell open. "You *knew* Kenneth was Jack's baby?"

Gwen's knees almost gave out, but she stayed on her feet by sheer force of will. All these years, Emily had known about Jack's love child with Claudia. Were any more secrets lurking?

Squatting near Jack, Emily pummeled his chest with her fists. "This is all your fault. Every disgusting, adulterous bit of it. You weren't satisfied with an affair, you had to go and get your trollop *pregnant!*" Emily spat the word.

Gwen's panic escalated. Although she knew her cell phone

wasn't in her jeans pocket, she again patted. Looking around, she spotted it near the potted mint on the bay window. There was no clear path to retrieve it without crossing in front of Emily.

Jack's eyelids fluttered. "I'm sorry, Emily. I...I never wanted you to find out."

"I've known since before the boy was even born."

Emily's demeanor changed as tears slipped down her cheeks. "We should have had a baby, Jack. You and me. Now there's no one to inherit anything. The Olde family name will disappear."

Gwen shrank further into the weeping fig trees. The irony of Emily's situation struck Gwen as lamentable. Henrietta had suffered under her father's disappointment that she wasn't the son who would carry on the Wickham family name. Now Emily shared a similar plight because Jack had fathered a child with another woman, leaving Emily without a descendant.

Emily swiped at her tears. "I was so happy when you agreed to resign your office position at the college and be my business manager at the music shop. I thought you'd give up your sordid little affairs. But no, you snuck out of the shop on the pretense of running errands to meet with your lover here."

Emily stomped back and forth near Jack's prone body. "You thought you were so clever, my darling. No clue that I followed you that day to the college campus." Emily's voice could have frozen the pelting rain into razor-sharp icicles.

Jack struggled up onto one elbow. "What day? What are you talking about?"

Emily grinned, her eyes bright. She squatted down beside Jack. "Oh, you know the day I'm talking about. Let me refresh your memory, because I saw and heard it all in that Baylies hallway. First, those kids who ran from Henrietta's office. You peeked in, but you didn't say anything just then."

Rising to her feet, Emily thumbed toward Claudia, who

seemed glued in place. "Then you met this one and pulled her into a corner. The two of you started whispering, but you know those old buildings. Everything echoes and I've got great hearing, Jack...you've always known that. I was the in the perfect spot to hear every word you two said."

Emily began to pace. "Your lover here told you she was pregnant. I have to say, Jack, if I hadn't been afraid of giving myself away, I would have laughed out loud when you told her I'd never give you a divorce. She had no idea you were stringing her along. You've always been much too greedy to ask for a divorce. All you ever wanted from our marriage was ownership in my family's music shop."

"That's not true, Emily. I loved you when we got married."

She released a raucous cackle. "And I believed you for a few months, Jack. But we both know your sentiment only lasted until I refused to add your name to the deed. Your only option was to endure our marriage and hope I'd die first so you'd inherit. You weren't about to give up your plans for the likes of Claudia here."

Even in his dazed condition, Jack's mouth dropped open.

When Claudia made a noise, Emily swirled on her. "Shocked that he lied to you, girlie? Wait until you hear what happened after you ran off, crying like a baby."

Gwen's head was spinning. Rachel must have been too far away to overhear the conversation about Claudia's pregnancy, but her identity of the crying woman had been accurate.

Emily's eerie laughter bounced around the old library. She turned crazed eyes toward Gwen as if playing to a theater audience, almost speaking in a stage whisper. "So here's what happened." Emily's eyes were mere slits, her body rigid. "Henrietta came out of her office and tapped Jack on the shoulder. She'd also heard his conversation with Claudia. They started threatening each other. What a hoot. Jack saying he'd witnessed Henrietta in a tryst with a student. Henrietta coming

310

back that she'd overheard Claudia was pregnant and wouldn't I like to know about that? Jack trumping her that he'd discovered something that would ruin her career as a professor and threatening to expose her to the dean unless she left town the next day."

Emily lowered her gaze to Jack, her features skewed with fury. "Oh, get that *poor me* look off your face, dear husband."

Jack pleaded, "Emily, I washed my hands of Claudia long ago. You have to believe me. She's been married to Pete for years."

"Nice try, Jack. If that's true, why are you two here at Gwen's? Huh, tell me that."

Jack labored with each word. "Pure coincidence. Can't you let this go? What's done is done."

In a flash, Emily squatted on the floor beside him. "What's done is done? Is that the best you can do, Jack? You have no idea how right you are. Hold on, let me tell you the rest."

Bobbing and weaving like a prize fighter, Emily forged ahead in her story-telling, her arms waving wildly as each detail emerged. "After Gwen told me that Henrietta was back in town and living in this old library, I walked over through the woods and hid in the trees. I was looking for a place to meet Henrietta in private and find out what mischief she had in mind while she was here. I saw Gwen looking out her upstairs window that night. She almost caught me." Emily tittered like a little girl.

So Emily had been the wanderer a few evenings ago? Not a lost visitor at all. Gwen watched in horror as Emily plummeted into seeming insanity.

"Last Saturday afternoon," Emily announced to no one in particular, "I waited in Gwen's woods during her hoity-toity garden tour until Henrietta drove up in her fancy black car. I hurried back to the music shop and called her cell using our business line."

Gwen did another double-take. Of course, of course. The most recent number on Henrietta's cell phone had been from the music shop. It hadn't dawned on Gwen – or Detective Brown – that the call would have been anything other than a follow-up about the competition.

"Anyway," Emily went on, "I told her I had some dirt about the other judges and the competitors. I knew she wouldn't be able to resist, control freak that she is. Uh, was."

Emily rolled her eyes, her grin of triumph more than scary. "But I told her we shouldn't be seen together. She'd have to meet me on Gwen's footbridge. When she got there, all she did was complain about getting her shoes dirty. What a piece of work."

Emily's pacing became more frantic. "I confronted her straight out. Asked if she was going to keep Jack's love child to herself. She bragged that everyone in town was going to hear about Kenneth before she went back to Vermont."

Emily stood above Jack. "She said you'd not only ruined her career at Baylies but her life in Harbor Falls, and she would damn sure return the favor. She called you a slime ball, Jack, a slime ball! Your affair was my concern, not hers. She had no right sticking her nose into our business. Do you know she was going to tell everyone you fathered a child with Claudia?"

"But Emily, darling," Jack cajoled, attempting a laugh. "If you knew about Kenneth all these years, what difference would Henrietta's announcement have made?"

"What difference?" Emily shouted down at him. "Even if I divorced you, the scandal would shame my family's good name for years – maybe decades – to come."

Emily again squatted next to Jack. "I begged the bitch not to say anything. But she refused to back down."

Emily placed her hands on either side of his face. "I had no choice, Jack. I had to stop her. I had to do it. Tell me I did the right thing."

Jack flinched and slurred his words. "What did you do, Emily?"

Instead of directing her answer to him, Emily flashed on Gwen. "I shoved Henrietta, and she shoved me. We went back and forth a few times until she lost her balance and crashed through the railing. I leaned over and watched her sail into the gorge, heard her head thunk on a rock. I couldn't stop myself. I laughed and called 'good riddance'. I don't think the bitch heard me. When I stood up, my hair caught in the splintered wood."

Emily reached up and smoothed her dark brunette mane. "I hate it when I lose hair."

Stunned not only by Emily's matter-of-fact confession, but by her remark about Henrietta losing her balance, Gwen's memory tumbled backwards. She recalled Henrietta's white-knuckled ascent of the staircase and her avoidance of the second floor balcony. Rather than weak muscles, as Gwen had thought at the time, maybe Henrietta had suffered a touch of vertigo.

Had the footbridge lumber been so compromised that it gave way with little resistance? After losing her balance, would Henrietta have crashed through the railing with or without Emily's shove? In either case, if Gwen had hammered those struts back together, would Henrietta have won the shoving match and still be alive?

Outside the wind howled like a banshee. A loud crack split the night, followed by the sound of breaking glass. Shards cascaded downward as a tree branch breached the balcony opening above. Standing directly beneath the barrage, Gwen raised her arms and bent her head, wincing as the pointed slivers pierced her forearms, the backs of her hands, the nape of her neck, the sides of her face. All analysis of Henrietta's tumble evaporated.

Emily glared at Gwen, oblivious to her injuries. "This

confrontation is your fault. Why'd you have to start asking questions? For years I've suffered the shame of Jack's affair and love child in private. You have no more right than Henrietta to reveal my private hell."

Before Gwen could defend her intentions, Emily whirled toward Jack. "We could have avoided this whole mess if you hadn't brought Henrietta back to Harbor Falls." Emily's voice softened. "Why'd you let that happen, Jack?"

"But it wasn't me, Emily, sweetheart," Jack pleaded. "The dean and Alex did it. I told you. I tried to convince the committee not to hire Henrietta, but they overruled me."

"You never take responsibility for anything, Jack," Emily hissed.

Claudia made a second move toward Jack. "That's exactly what I told him."

"Shut up, slut!" Emily shouted. "If you hadn't let him get you pregnant…"

"Now hold on a minute, Emily," Claudia interrupted, squaring her shoulders. "Don't you think Jack had something to do with making our baby?"

Emily's eyes flashed, her face warping with rage. "You'll be sorry you said that, girlie."

Jack reached out toward his wife. "Emily, honey, why did you come here tonight and confess everything? Now Gwen and Claudia know what you did."

Emily fluttered her hands in the air. "Oh, what I said doesn't matter. The police are never going to find out I'm the one who got rid of that bitch Henrietta."

"What do you mean, Emily?" Again, Jack extended his hand. "Help me up, sweetheart. I'm sure we can convince Claudia and Gwen to keep our secret." He lifted his eyebrows at Gwen and Claudia, nodding his head several times to imply they'd agree.

Still bumped up against the weeping fig trees, Gwen had no

idea what to do. Emily was clearly not in her right mind, but Gwen didn't think she had any chance of escaping without Emily blocking her way.

How much longer before Emily exploded like she had with Henrietta on the footbridge? And why did she think the police would never find out? Gwen surveyed the area. On the stove was the tea kettle, filled with water, and the cast iron skillet. On the island was the dull gleam of satin knife handles poking out from the wooden block.

Emily must have spotted them too. In one swift movement, she grabbed the largest knife, stepped over Jack's body, and lunged at Claudia. "Bitch!"

Claudia jumped back, narrowly avoiding the blade.

Emily shifted her weight and made another pass, her second thrust making contact.

Grasping her arm, Claudia screamed as blood seeped through her fingers.

Gwen lunged across the tile floor and gripped Emily's wrist, shoving it upwards. "Stop, Emily, you're in enough trouble." Time slowed as Gwen attempted to wrest the knife from Emily's grasp, but Emily took a step backwards, throwing Gwen off balance.

Gwen scrambled to stay on her feet, holding on tight with unexpected strength.

Emily growled and fought like a tigress protecting her cubs.

"Just let me kill Miss Claudia," Emily snarled. "And then I'll take care of you, Gwen."

With chilling certainly, Gwen knew Emily meant every word.

Emily twisted away and stretched for a second knife with her other hand.

Without giving her action much thought, Gwen released Emily's wrist and lunged toward the stove. She grabbed the cast iron skillet and whacked Emily on the back of the head.

Chapter Forty-Nine

As Gwen looked on, Emily crumpled into a heap and the knife clattered onto the tile floor, Claudia's blood spattering from the sharp blade.

Footsteps thundered across the rear deck. Detective Brown burst through the French door with his gun drawn. "Everybody freeze! Put down the frying pan, Mrs. Andrews."

Looking down, Gwen registered surprise to be clutching her cast iron skillet, grease from the morning eggs dripping from its edge. The pan slipped from her fingers and crashed to the floor, cracking several ceramic squares. She'd never struck anyone in her life.

The detective hurried to Emily's prone body and kicked the knife away before holstering his gun. He pressed his fingers against her neck and nodded. Emily was still alive. He lifted her limp arm and handcuffed her to the chrome towel bar above her head. Pulling a plastic bag from his jacket, he lowered it over the knife, zipped it closed, and slipped the weapon into his pocket.

Hearing a sound, Gwen turned to see another person entering her home – uninvited, but not unwelcome. Hal paused in the frame, his hand gripping the handle of the French door.

Behind him, the rain seemed to have slowed.

His gaze jumped left to the detective, then to Emily and Jack on the kitchen floor. Swinging back, he caught sight of Gwen, rushed to her side, and pulled her into a fierce embrace. For an intense moment he pushed her away, his eyes traveling around her face. "You're bleeding."

Detective Brown must have heard Hal's voice because he turned around. "Mr. Jenkins. Perfect timing. Please help the women with their wounds. I'm calling for an ambulance." The detective headed for the rear deck, punching buttons on his cell.

Gwen grasped Hal's forearms. "Emily stabbed Claudia. Go help her."

"Are you sure, Gwen?"

She nodded, not so concerned about herself. "My cuts are superficial. Go now."

"All right, if that's what you want." Hal waited for her to nod a second time before stepping over Jack and around Emily to rip paper towels from the roll hanging near the sink. He hurried to Claudia, who was simpering in a dining room chair, clutching her upper arm, staring at the growing red stain. Hal pried her fingers loose, pressed the paper towels against the deep wound, and repositioned her hand to maintain the pressure.

Gwen continued to pick at the glass shards embedded in her forearm when yet another movement at the French door caught her eye. The deck spotlight backlit Pete's stocky, muscular body as he came inside and went immediately to Gwen.

"What's going on here, Gwen? Your front door is locked. I guess you didn't hear me knock, so I came around back. I'm here to pick up Claudia."

Gwen pointed toward the dining room. "She's been hurt."

He hustled to Claudia's side and helped Hal staunch the still-oozing wound.

Now that Kenneth's paternity was no longer a secret, how would Claudia explain to Pete? And how would preteen Kenneth react to Jack being his real father? Would Claudia tell her son?

When Pete leaned over his wife, Claudia lifted her face.

"Oh, Pete, I am *so* sorry."

"Who did this to you?" Pete asked.

Claudia leaned around him and nodded toward the kitchen. "Emily."

Pete whirled, spotted Emily, and roared, "You stabbed my wife? Why?"

317

Emily had woken up from Gwen's smack on her head and sat cross-legged with one arm dangling from the tower bar. She stared back at Pete with unfocused eyes. Her head wagged from side to side, but she didn't answer his question.

Pete yelled louder. "Aren't you going to explain yourself?" When Emily said nothing, Pete turned back to Claudia.

"Don't worry. We're gonna be fine."

Gwen felt like a voyeur listening to their conversation, but their voices carried easily in the open floor plan now that the wind had died down.

"Where's Kenneth?" Claudia asked.

"I dropped him at Todd's for an overnighter."

Claudia searched his eyes. "Pete, there's something I need to tell you."

"Shhh," he murmured. "Whatever it is, we'll deal with it later."

"But...but...there's something you need to know."

Pete touched her cheek and kissed her forehead. "Given the collection of people in here, this must be about Kenneth." He reached for her free hand. "I've always known I'm not his father, sweetheart. But I love that boy like he's my own, and I love you, too, Claudia."

"Oh, Pete," Claudia moaned, dropping her head onto his shoulder, spilling her tears.

Hal rose to his feet and went back to Gwen. He found her standing beneath the staircase, absorbing the heart-breaking drama that had taken place during the past hour.

Hal threw his arm around her waist. "You need to sit down, but let's avoid the broken glass." He guided Gwen around the staircase, past Pete and Claudia and the foyer entrance, then lowered her onto the loveseat in the living room. He sat next to her and inspected her cuts. "Those glass shards need to come out. As soon as Detective Brown says we can leave, I'll drive you to the emergency room."

"That's kind of you. Thanks."

Hal's gentle probing sent a pleasant jolt through Gwen. "I didn't think I'd see you until tomorrow morning. Why did you come back tonight?"

He lifted one shoulder and let it drop, his expression sheepish. "Well, after I settled Jenna for the night, I couldn't stop thinking about you. Can't say if I was worried or if I just missed you."

It dawned on Gwen that she'd missed him, too, and she was glad to have him by her side now.

Hal reached over and cradled the palm-side of her right hand without disturbing the glass shards on the top. "I finally left a note on the kitchen table and drove here like a mad man. Are you ready to tell me what happened here tonight?"

She waved her hand in the general direction of Jack and Emily in the kitchen, then Pete and Claudia in the dining room. "So many secrets. Their lives will never be the same."

Before Gwen had a chance to go into detail, Emily clanged her cuff against the towel bar. Gwen swiveled sideways on the loveseat at the same moment as Hal and they peeked through the leaves of the weeping fig trees into the kitchen.

In a little girl's voice, Emily called, "Jack?" Tears streamed down her cheeks. "Jack, please come back to me."

Jack twisted toward his wife's voice. After a moment of seeming indecision, he struggled to his knees and crawled awkwardly toward Emily. He sat beside her with his back against the cabinet doors, wrapped one arm around her and pressed her head against his shoulder.

Detective Brown came in from the rear deck and clapped his hands. "Heads up, folks. The ambulance is on its way. Chief Upton is on his way. I'm going to need statements from everyone."

Gwen called out, "Detective? Can I see you in the living room?"

As he approached, his eyes moved around her face. "Those cuts need to be checked."

She ran her fingers along her cheek, wincing when she encountered more tiny glass shards. "How did you get here so fast? Did someone hear the yelling and call the station?"

Detective Brown shook his head. "No one called. I was shadowing Jack."

"But why?" Gwen asked.

"After you brought that note to the chief, he convinced me to rethink your involvement. About what happened to Ms. Wickham, I mean. And besides, the hair caught in your shattered railing was darker than yours."

Gwen reached up and touched her ash brown hair.

Hal placed his arm around her shoulder and focused on the detective. "But why did that make you suspicious of Jack?"

"The chief and I both thought it was Jack's hair. He seemed a little too anxious to push us in Mrs. Andrew's direction. We decided to keep an eye on him." Detective Brown sat on the opposite couch. "About an hour ago, Jack left the music shop. He headed for the new library. Ducked into your woods. Crossed the footbridge higher on the ridge because, as you know, we'd removed the planks from the lower one."

The detective leaned closer. "I kept my eye on him from a spot in your backyard. He spoke with you and then with Ms. Smith. Jack's wife showed up and stood outside your bay window for a few minutes before she went inside and began her rant. That's when I moved closer, but I couldn't get a good sightline. After she stabbed Claudia with that knife, I rushed in, but you had already, well, taken care of Emily." He cocked his thumb toward the rear gardens. "I might have damaged some of your flowers out there."

She waved her hand in a cavalier movement of dismissal.

"A few crushed flowers are the least of my worries, Detective. I'm just glad you were close by."

And then it hit Gwen. She was no longer a suspect. A great weight lifted. Her fear of being arrested no longer cast a shadow over her life. And she could release her worry that John Wickham would sue for possession of the old library.

The detective rubbed his face with one hand. "I never suspected Jack's wife. I don't think the chief did either."

Red and blue strobe lights flashed through the front windows, lighting up the old library in a kaleidoscope of color. When the front doorbell sounded, the detective hurried over, unlocked the door, and admitted Chief Upton and two EMTs. He directed one toward Claudia and Pete at the dining room table, the other to Emily and Jack sprawled on the floor near the kitchen sink.

The chief moved toward Gwen. "You're bleeding."

"Superficial cuts from a broken window. Hal's going to drive me to the hospital."

"Well, all right." The chief sat down and glared at her. "I should be angry with you."

"I'm sorry I interfered with your investigation, Chief, but I was terrified Detective Brown would arrest me. John Wickham was waiting to sue me for wrongful death and take possession of my home. I had to do something."

Chief Upton's eyebrow lifted. "Well, that explains your motives for going behind our backs."

Hal glanced over at the chief. "Can I ask you a question?"

"Of course. What is it, Mr. Jenkins?"

"When we visited your office the other day, I got the impression you were giving her a chance to smoke out the real culprit."

The chief straightened his posture. "What did I say or do to make you think that?"

"Well, like I told Gwen, you didn't seem all that anxious to get the forensic test results. I thought you were making sure she wasn't arrested so she could continue her research."

Chief Upton snickered. "Research? That's what you're calling Gwen's unauthorized investigation?" For a moment, silence hung in the air until the chief grinned. "Relax, you two. I'm only half-kidding. Seriously, there's nothing I can do to move our particular evidence higher in the queue at the state lab. Sorry I gave the wrong impression."

He nodded toward Detective Brown, who was transferring the handcuff from the towel bar to Emily's other wrist. "I will admit I didn't think Gwen was involved with Ms. Wickham's death, but I had to let my detective follow the clues. I had no intention of letting Gwen expose the perp and put herself in danger."

Gwen cleared her throat. "Excuse me, Charles. I'm not one to pat myself on the back, but if I hadn't started nosing around…" Gwen tossed Hal a sly grin, "I don't think Jack or Emily would have shown up here tonight. If they hadn't been worried I was getting too close to their separate secrets, you'd be no closer to discovering Emily pushed Henrietta to her death."

"That may be true, Gwen," the chief agreed, "but in the future, just let us do our jobs, please." He fixed a stern gaze on her, seeming to doubt she would heed his warning.

She flashed her most reassuring smile. "I hope that's not necessary, chief."

Hearing a commotion, the three of them turned. Claudia, her arm bandaged, walked out the front door with Pete. Behind them, Jack was carried on one stretcher, Emily on a second. Detective Brown entered the living room. "Mrs. Andrews, I called some guys I know to remove that tree branch upstairs and nail some plywood over the hole. The window techs will replace the glass tomorrow morning."

"Thank you, Detective."

Chief Upton's voice interrupted. "Fill me in, Detective."

"Yes, sir. Mr. Smith is driving his wife to the emergency

room to have her arm stitched. Jack and Emily Miller are being taken there by ambulance. I'll make sure Mrs. Miller is secured in the psych ward."

"Good work," the chief said. "You follow them and take statements."

Detective Brown nodded and left.

The chief turned to Gwen. "We'll need a statement from you as well. Do you want to give it now or wait until you have those cuts tended to?"

"I'd just as soon tell you now while events are fresh in my mind."

They moved to the now-deserted dining room table and for the next half hour Gwen reported everything that had happened. When she got to the part about Emily grabbing the knife, Gwen reached for Hal's hand and squeezed hard.

A few minutes later, the chief snapped off his recorder. "I'll let you know when this is typed and ready for you to sign." He stood up. "I'll be in touch." And he was gone.

Abruptly, the old library was quiet. The downpour had slowed to a mist, the wind to a gentle breeze. Only a faint whistling through the broken window upstairs and Hal's soft breathing disturbed the quiet night.

Gwen looked down. She was still gripping Hal's hand. When he pulled away, warmth made its way up her neck to her face.

"Don't be embarrassed, Gwen. I like that you reached for me."

Somewhat relieved, her voice caught in her throat. "You were right, Hal. I should've let the police handle this."

Grateful he didn't say *I told you so*, her words tumbled out. "I didn't recognize Emily tonight. I still can't believe she pushed Henrietta to her death. And she didn't show any remorse."

The front door flew open and Tess stormed in. She rushed

over to Gwen and gripped her with a fierce strength. "Oh, thank goodness it wasn't you in that ambulance." Tess pushed Gwen to arm's length. "But you're bleeding."

"Minor cuts, Tess. A tree branch crashed through a sitting room window upstairs. Be careful where you walk in the music studio...there's glass all over the floor."

"Don't worry about that. I'll clean it up later," Tess said. "Well? Are you going to tell us what happened here tonight?"

"Hal's taking me to the emergency room. Ride with us and listen in on my phone call to Ernie so I don't have to repeat myself." Gwen strode to the bay window and grabbed her wayward cell.

Halfway to the hospital, she ended her phone call. "Ernie says he's glad this is over and to give you a message, Hal."

"What's that?" Hal asked without taking his eyes from the road.

"He wants you to keep me out of trouble from here on out." Everyone in the car roared with laughter at the futility of Ernie's instruction.

Tess reached from the backseat and rested her hand on Gwen's shoulder. "Well, sis, at least you don't have to worry anymore. Not about Henrietta's death. Not about being arrested. Not about losing your home."

Gwen finally relaxed and closed her eyes.

Chapter Fifty

On Saturday morning Gwen stood on her rear deck and closed her cell phone. She inhaled the scent of clean leaves and quenched earth, all that remained of Friday night's tempest. Lifting her face to the sun's rays, she soaked up the warmth.

Tess cranked open the bay window. "Who was that?"

Gwen turned toward her sister. "Chief Upton. He's on his way over. Before he gets here, I've got to call Alex. He probably doesn't know Jack and Emily are at the hospital. And if I don't update Liz about what happened here last night, she'll never speak to me again."

"Good idea," Tess said and closed the window.

Pacing the deck boards, Gwen made the two calls. After Alex's momentary shock at the news, he said he'd put a sign on the door and attend the competition to represent the music shop. Liz was appropriately mortified about Emily's part in Henrietta's demise, and then – in true Liz style – she jokingly reminded Gwen to brew Sunday morning coffee the next day.

As Gwen closed her cell phone, car doors slammed in the driveway, and seconds later Jenna hopped up the deck steps, dressed in jeans and a bright yellow tee-shirt. She carried her flute case in one hand and her black ankle boots in the other. Behind her, Hal carried the contentious black dress, encased in a transparent dry cleaning bag.

"Good morning," he called. "Jenna couldn't sit still since she woke up." He stopped beside Gwen and leaned close to inspect her face. "How are those cuts?"

"A little itchy. I'll look like a freak at the judging table today."

"No you won't. Those flesh tone Band-Aids are barely visible."

Tess poked her head out the French door. "Good morning, you two. Jenna, let's go warm up. You'll need to change into that classy dress soon enough."

The chime of the front bell worked its way to the rear deck. Gwen hurried inside with Hal close behind then swung the door wide to find Chief Upton about to push the buzzer again.

"I hope you don't mind us stopping by this morning, Gwen. Good morning, Mr. Jenkins."

Detective Brown stood one step down.

Gwen stepped back to allow them entry. "Not at all. We don't leave for another hour or so."

"That's right. The music competition is today."

The tapping of workmen replacing the glass panes upstairs competed with the opening movement of Poulenc's Sonata for Flute and Piano.

The chief glanced around. "No offense, but I can't hear with all this noise. Let's walk over to the village green." He switched his focus to Hal. "I'd like you to join us, Mr. Jenkins."

Detective Brown cleared his throat. "Before we head out, I have something for you, Mrs. Andrews." From behind his back, he pulled a potted chrysanthemum.

She felt her skin warm. "What's this for, Detective?"

"Remember the night I took your shoes and clothes and a lock of your hair? You said when I found out you had nothing to do with Ms. Wickham's death, I'd owe you an apology." He placed the plant in her hands. "I hope this is sufficient."

"It's beautiful, Detective. And purple, my favorite color. Thank you." She swiveled the pot toward Hal so he could see the label displayed on the cellophane wrapping. "Look. From your garden shop."

Hal extended his hand to the detective. "Good choice."

"Hang on a sec," Gwen said. "I'll put your plant in the kitchen and tell Tess where I'm going."

A minute later, the four of them crossed Library Lane and stepped into the village green.

They walked along the main pathway toward the tall blue spruce in the center.

Chief Upton was the first to speak. "Detective Brown listened to the details you provided last night. We both decided you deserve an update on the case." He pulled a piece of paper from his pocket. "This is your statement. If you could read it over for accuracy and sign it, you won't need to come to the station."

Gwen accepted the typed document and the pen he offered. She dropped onto a park bench, read the statement, signed it, and handed it back. "Thanks for bringing that with you. No offense, but I'd rather not see the inside of your station anytime soon."

The chief tucked the statement away. "None taken."

Hal said, "Chief, isn't it unusual to update a potential witness? Won't Gwen have to testify at Emily's trial?"

"Normally, yes. But the DA says Emily is unlikely to face a criminal trial. He's ordered psychiatric tests before he makes his recommendation to the court."

"Oh, dear," Gwen murmured. Sadness cloaked her like a blanket. Emily might spend the rest of her life in a mental hospital. If that's what the court decided, Jack would finally gain control of The Olde Music Shop.

Chief Upton sat down beside Gwen. "We thought you'd like to know how everyone is doing. First, Mrs. Smith's knife wound required stitches, but her arm should heal with little scarring."

"That's a relief. How's Pete doing?"

Detective Brown answered, "I took his statement while the doctor stitched up his wife. He's worried *she's* mad at *him*. He never let on he knew she was pregnant when they got married."

"Well, I hope their marriage survives. I've always thought

they were a good match." Gwen paused. "Did Pete say if they'll tell Kenneth that Jack is his father?"

The detective shrugged. "Pete considers himself the boy's *real* father, so I don't know."

Chief Upton's voice recaptured their attention. "Let me tell you the rest so you can get ready for the competition. Jack was admitted overnight to determine if he has a concussion."

Gwen slid her hands between her knees. "I can't say I'm overly fond of Jack, but I wouldn't want him to suffer permanent damage from his run-in with my granite countertop."

The detective trained his faded blue eyes on Gwen. "I have to say, Mrs. Andrews, I never expected you to bring down Emily before she stabbed Claudia a second time."

His unexpected compliment made Gwen blush. But to be commended for slamming a cast iron skillet onto someone's head was hardly a source of pride.

"Emily is restricted to the psychiatric ward until the tests are completed," Chief Upton went on. "By the way, your pan didn't do any damage to her skull."

"That's good news. I didn't want to hurt her. I only wanted her to drop that knife."

Then the chief glanced at Hal. "This next part may disturb you, Mr. Jenkins. It concerns your daughter."

Hal stiffened. "Elizabeth?"

"Yes. Let me explain." The chief shifted his weight. "This detail came from Jack last night. Thirteen years ago, when he arrived at the Baylies offices after hours to meet Claudia, a female student ran screaming from Henrietta's office. Jack looked in and saw Henrietta buttoning her blouse. A male student grabbed his shirt and ran out after the girl."

Hal sat down on Gwen's other side. "But what does that have to do with my daughter?"

"I'm sorry, Mr. Jenkins. Jack recognized the female student

as your daughter Elizabeth. The young man was her fiancé Matthew."

Hal drew in a sharp breath.

The chief pulled an envelope from his shirt pocket and held it out. "This is an apology written by Henrietta. We found it in her briefcase."

Hal hesitated before reaching over to accept it. He opened the flap – already loosened – removed the note, and walked a few feet away before scanning the message.

To give Hal a modicum of privacy, Gwen turned to the chief. "I have a few questions."

"Go ahead."

"Did Emily write that threatening note?"

"Yes," he answered. "After you mentioned Henrietta's call to the old dean and that your friend Rachel had overheard Henrietta arguing with someone, she panicked. You told her you were off to talk to the new dean and Claudia, so she wrote that note, ran over here through your woods, and shoved it in your mail slot. She assumed her threat would put an end to your investigation. Now we know she wasn't thinking clearly."

Hal rejoined them, tucking Henrietta's note into his pants pocket before standing near Gwen's end of the bench without saying a word.

"Is that why she came over last night?" Gwen asked. "To find out if it worked?"

The chief nodded toward Detective Brown. "Since you took her statement at the hospital last night, why don't you answer that one?"

"Sure, chief," the detective said. "I think that was her intent. But when she found Claudia and Jack in your kitchen, she assumed you'd found out he was Kenneth's father, and you'd tell everyone."

Gwen's heart pounded. "So Emily was serious when she said she'd get rid of me after she took care of Claudia?"

"She didn't come right out and say those words, but that's my guess."

Gwen was grateful to be sitting down or she might have collapsed. How could she have known Emily all these years and not realized she had such a dark side?

"One last question. Was Henrietta alive when the willow branches caught her?"

The detective bent down, pulled up several blades of grass, and tossed them into the air where they floated for a second before landing a few feet away. "I spoke to the medical examiner this morning. He said both of Henrietta's wrists were broken. So she tried to break her fall. The shape of her skull injury matches a bloody boulder my men retrieved from the bottom of the gorge. There was no water in her lungs, so she didn't take a breath underwater. His report will state that the head injury was the cause of death."

Knowing Henrietta had been unaware of floating downstream toward the antique waterwheel provided Gwen with some small comfort.

The chief spoke up. "It's ironic that Emily was the one who revealed the secret she was trying so hard to keep hidden."

Silent seconds ticked until Gwen said, "I somehow feel responsible that Henrietta died while staying in my home."

Chief Upton took a stance in front of her and gazed down.

"Emily had spiraled out of control. Henrietta might have died in a different location, and by a different method, but would probably still be dead. Believe me, her death had nothing to do with where she was sleeping."

Gwen latched onto his rationale, her relief palpable.

Rising from the bench, she walked with the three men to her front steps.

Detective Brown held up his hand. "Hold on a second." He retrieved a paper bag from the squad car parked at the curb and handed it to Gwen.

She peered inside, allowing a chuckle to escape. "My clothes and shoes."

"Sorry I had to confiscate them, Mrs. Andrews."

Gwen waved her hand in a dismissive gesture. "I know, I know, Detective. You were just doing your job."

Chapter Fifty-One

After Chief Upton and Detective Brown drove away, Gwen and Hal entered the old library through the front door.

The workmen had apparently finished repairing the upstairs window. Tess and Jenna were upstairs getting dressed. Only the deep ticking of the floor clock in the foyer broke the silence.

"So," Hal said. "It's over."

Gwen had only enough energy to nod. She threaded her arm through his and led him out onto the rear deck. They sat side by side without speaking for some time. A flock of chickadees and nuthatches fluttered around a birdfeeder hanging from a nearby post, their chatter filling the air. The maple trees at the edge of the woods, their leaves newly-tinged with a hint of approaching autumn color, waved in the morning breeze. Gwen welcomed the serenity.

Hal reached into his pants pocket, pulled out the note, and stared at it for a moment. "Henrietta's apology must be why she wanted to meet with me last Monday."

"I suppose so," Gwen commented. "She said she wanted to provide you with some closure about Elizabeth's death. Did she?"

He reached for her hand, flipped it over, and pressed the note into her palm. "Here. Read it first, and then we'll talk."

Gwen walked to the railing as she unfolded the note. Cross-outs and rewrites littered Henrietta's over-sized cursive style. Had she been organizing her thoughts, never intending to give Hal the actual letter?

Gwen read aloud:

Mr. Jenkins,

As I said the day I bumped into you at Gwen's, I extend my deepest condolences for the death of your daughter Elizabeth. I meant every word when I said she was a fabulous musical talent. I've heard no one before or since play the flute with quite the same finesse as Elizabeth. I look forward to hearing Jenna play at the competition.

I have carried a burden of guilt since I moved from Harbor Falls. It is my sincerest hope that you'll forgive me for my part in Elizabeth's accident. I admit I have weaknesses – like every human being – and mine happen to revolve around handsome men, be they young or old. It's unfortunate that I became involved with Elizabeth's fiancé Matthew. Our dalliance had only just begun when she spotted us in my office that day. Matthew ran after her, and well, we both know what happened when he finally caught up with her.

Again, I implore you to accept my apology. I never intended any harm.

> *Sincerely,*
> *Henrietta Wickham*

The letter dropped from Gwen's fingers and fluttered for a second before landing in a blue ceramic pot overflowing with purple verbena.

When she lifted her gaze to Hal, she found him watching her.

"What's your reaction?"

"I'm more interested in yours," Gwen countered. "This is quite an admission."

He nodded and drummed his fingers on the arm of his Adirondack chair. "I've had some time to think about what she says there. The woman had a lot of guts."

Gwen retrieved the letter, refolded it, and put it in the envelope before extending it to Hal.

"You know," she said, taking her seat beside him, "I don't know if I mentioned this before, but the day Henrietta arrived, I asked her why she accepted the invitation to return to Harbor

Falls. She said she wanted to clear her conscience and set a few things straight. I think we know now that Jack was the person she wanted to set straight, so you must be the person to clear her conscience. I have to say, you seem very calm."

"After my initial shock, I realized she *had* provided me with closure. After all these years, I know why Elizabeth was so angry with Matthew the day of her accident."

Gwen shook her head. "But you don't seem upset about Henrietta's involvement."

Hal got to his feet and went to the railing, gazing out across Gwen's rear gardens. "Henrietta wasn't the only person involved. Don't forget Matthew was there, too."

He turned to face her. "Remember I told you that Elizabeth didn't want to marry him just because he'd fathered her child? Well, her gut instincts may have been more accurate than I thought at the time. There's no way to guess how their lives would have turned out if they'd married when she first discovered she was pregnant. Their marriage might have ended in a disaster of a different sort."

Gwen couldn't argue with his reasoning. "None of us knows how our lives would be altered if we'd made other decisions." She receded into the past, to that dinner dance all those years ago. If she'd been sufficiently intimidated by the daggers shooting from Henrietta's eyes and declined Parker's invitation to dance, what direction would Gwen's life have taken? Would she have married someone else or would she have been a spinster all this time?

Hal interrupted her musing. "Knowing the chain of events that day doesn't ease my ache over Elizabeth's death, or Matthew's either, but they've been gone for thirteen years. Last Saturday, Emily shoved Henrietta to her death. Debating whether that was justice won't change anything. I have to let this go, Gwen, or I'll lose my mind. I can't hang onto a past I can't change."

His philosophical comment struck Gwen with its poignancy. She'd been dealing with the same conflict surrounding not only Parker's death, but his recent return, real or imagined. She, too, carried the baggage of a past she couldn't change. Now what?

"So where do you go from here, Hal?"

He shifted his weight to the other foot. "I have an idea or two. But first, I'd like to say something to you, Gwen. Actually, several things."

She started to rise, but he waved for her to stay put. "When Jenna was five, she told me she wanted to play the flute like her Mommy. She gave me hope that some part of Elizabeth lived on, so I enrolled her in the kindergarten music class. Jenna was a natural and very dedicated as she moved through the school system. This past spring, she came home all excited about the music competition. I offered to find her a professional tutor and checked around. Your name came up more than once. I already knew you as one of the nicer customers at my garden shop." He tossed her an impish grin. "I always noticed you when you stopped by, with or without Parker."

Parker. Gwen had been so exhausted the previous night after her stint at the ER that she'd fallen asleep without attempting to summon him. Would she ever see Parker again?

Hal pushed off the railing with a quiet groan, stretched, and pulled a deck chair to sit across from Gwen, their knees almost touching. "You must have wondered why I brought Jenna here every Saturday. I guess you figured out I won't let her drive?"

"I never gave it much thought. Now I understand you were afraid of losing her to an accident."

"The first time I brought her for a lesson, I felt a spark I hadn't felt for nearly twenty years since my Claire passed away." He hesitated. "I've become rather fond of you, Gwen."

With everything the two of them had been through during the past few days, Hal's words of affection didn't scare her. As she opened her mouth to respond, he shook his head.

He reached over and enclosed her small hands. "Do I dare ask if you've developed feelings for me, too?" He released one of her hands and placed his index finger to her lips.

"Wait. Don't say anything yet. I know you adored your Parker as much as I loved my Claire. But they're both gone and we're still here. I'm not asking for a commitment, Gwen. I just want you to think of me as someone more than just Jenna's grandfather."

Needing to collect her thoughts, Gwen withdrew her other hand, got up, and stood at the rail. Liz and Tess – and even Parker – had encouraged Gwen to give Hal a chance. Should she?

A movement in the tree line caught Gwen's attention. Behind the huge field bolder, Parker's translucent form stood with one arm raised, his hand moving in a good-bye gesture. The fingers of his other hand came to his lips, and he blew a kiss at her, then turned and drifted into the shade beneath the sugar maples.

Gwen stared after Parker's fading form. Could she trust that she hadn't lost her mind? For nearly a week, since his first appearance, she'd debated whether she'd imagined their nightly conversations. He also could have been a very lifelike dream. Or the other-worldly option was that his essence had truly returned to her as a ghost. How would Gwen ever know?

Her chest tightened as memories of her years with Parker flew by in rapid succession, like a movie in fast forward. If Parker's goodbye wave had been meant to release her, was it also time for Gwen to release Parker and move on?

She turned to face Hal. "You're right. I adored Parker." Her breath hitched. "Living without him has been difficult. I've tried to hold onto the past, but it's time for me to start living again."

As she moved toward him, Hal grinned and flung his arms

wide. With no doubt or hesitation, Gwen stepped into his embrace.

The sound of clapping filled the air. Jenna, resplendent in her competition dress, stood in the doorway and exclaimed, "It's about time you two got together!"

Grinning at Gwen, Jenna waved her hand toward the trees. "I saw a man over there in your woods when I came out." She pointed at the spot where Parker had stood moments before.

That settled it. He hadn't been a figment of Gwen's imagination. The reality of Parker's ghostly existence was both sobering and thought-provoking.

Twisting her head this way and that, Gwen pretended to be searching. "I don't see anyone, Jenna." It wasn't a lie. Within those few seconds, Parker had completely disappeared. Gwen reached over and tucked an errant strand of silky blonde hair behind Jenna's ear. "Probably the shadows playing tricks."

Jenna shrugged her shoulders. "I guess so."

With a subtle motion, Gwen finger-waved toward the trees in a final farewell.

"Well, well, what do we have here?" Tess teased from the doorway, her fists on her hips, a smile on her lips.

Gwen turned to look at her sister. "Oh, I'm just taking your advice."

"And which advice is that?"

"Not to dismiss Hal without giving him a chance."

Nathan squeezed out past Tess and extended a hand to Hal. "Congratulations, old man."

"All right, all right," Tess chided. "That's enough warm and fuzzy." She held the French door open and waved them inside. "We've got a competition to win. Let's get moving!"

Bending down, Hal brushed Gwen's hair with his lips and whispered, "I've been meaning to say you always smell like fresh-baked cookies. I like it."

Hal's sentiment echoed Parker's words spoken into her ear

on that dance floor so many years ago. Gwen smiled at the cherished memory, then tucked it away for safe keeping.

"Are you ready, Mr. Jenkins?"

"Ready for what, Mrs. Andrews?"

Catching his half-smile, she winked at him. "For whatever lies ahead?"

He bent down and kissed her forehead. "Wouldn't miss it."

Reaching past her, he turned the knob of the French door and motioned for her to enter. "But first, let's go watch Jenna win the music competition."

Gwen walked into the old village library, unable to wipe the grin from her face.

THE END

Made in the USA
Lexington, KY
16 July 2017